"*Hard* makes political activism sexier than it's been in years. As hot as it is humorous, Hoffman's *Hard* is the hard-to-resist read of the summer."
—*Chicago Free Press*

HARD

"This is one debut novel that packs a no-holds-barred wallop."
—*Gay and Lesbian Times*

"A quick-paced debut that neatly straddles the fence between politics and porn. By turns erotic and vulnerable, playful and deadly serious, *Hard* is refreshingly easy to like."
—Aaron Hamburger, author of *Faith for Beginners*

"A knockout. Reading *Hard* reminds us that the important, strong and vital gay novel is still with us. It vividly and movingly captures what it means to be an urban gay man living in the last decade of the 20th century, when everything looked so bleak and yet so bright at the same time."
— *Guide* magazine

"Sexual politics—both public and private—play out against the cityscape of mid-1990s Manhattan in Hoffman's absorbing year-in-the-life of a group of gay men.... The larger issues of sexual rights and AIDS add depth to their voices, making this sexually explicit debut novel an intriguing exploration of politics and psyche."
—*Publishers Weekly*

HARD

a novel by

WAYNE HOFFMAN

BEAR BONES BOOKS

Published in 2015 by Bear Bones Books,
an imprint of Lethe Press, Inc.
118 Heritage Avenue • Maple Shade, NJ 08052-3018
www.lethepressbooks.com • lethepress@aol.com
www.BearBonesBooks.com • bearsoup@gmail.com

ISBN: 978-1-59021-290-5 / 1-59021-290-8
Cover image from Shutterstock.com
Book design by Peachboy Distillery & Designs

Previously published by Carroll & Graf, 2006.

Library of Congress Cataloging-in-Publication Data

Hoffman, Wayne (Wayne Adam)
Hard : a novel / by Wayne Hoffman.
     pages ; cm
  ISBN 978-1-59021-290-5
(pbk. : alk. paper)
  1. Gay men--Fiction. 2. New York (N.Y.)--Fiction. I.
Title.
  PS3608.O479H37 2015
  813'.6--dc23

                    2015010723

HARD

WINTER

one

Moe Pearlman was the greatest cocksucker in New York City.

He knew this was true. Hundreds of men had told him so. They had also told their friends, boyfriends, and lovers. Some went further and said he was the best in the whole world; Moe paid little heed to the world outside New York — an extremely competitive cocksucking market, it should be noted — and was thus content to hold the undisputed city title. He had a "reputation." And he was proud of it.

His skill wasn't something that could be taught: It wasn't any trick of the tongue or a double-jointed jaw that made him the champion. He was the greatest because he was devoted, passionate about his vocation with the precision of a scientist and the creativity of an artist.

He was also an expert because he practiced regularly. More often than most people brush their teeth.

But not tonight, Moe thought as he walked out of his apartment on Cornelia Street and turned north, knapsack over his shoulder. Tonight Moe was going to try and keep his mouth shut, at least for a few hours. It wouldn't be easy, but it was for a good cause.

□ □ □

"Balloons?"

Moe smiled a little at the question as he emptied the knapsack onto the concrete floor in a heap.

"Black balloons?" Aaron asked again. "The rest I understand: the lube, the pamphlets, the CDs. But balloons?"

"I'm putting the 'party' in 'sex party,'" Moe replied. "What's a party without balloons?"

Aaron looked skeptical. "Whatever you say. But if you've got paper hats in that bag, girl, I'm hitting the road."

"Just the balloons, I promise," Moe said. "Can you help me blow them up?"

"What's a sister for?"

Moe grabbed a balloon. "Guess this is the only thing I'm gonna blow tonight."

"Yes, life is a struggle, sweetie. But I'm sure you'll live to suck another day."

Once they'd finished inflating all the balloons, they grabbed some tape and started putting them on the walls. "These don't do much to liven the place up," said Aaron, looking around at the dingy cement floor, the bare yellow lightbulbs hanging from the ceiling, the windowless gloom of the basement club. "You should've gotten pink ones."

"Too queeny. Black is sexier."

"I've been saying that for years," said Aaron, tugging at his short, kinky braids.

Moe laughed, and they continued with the decorating. Within a few minutes, they managed to transform the cheerless space into a *slightly* less cheerless space.

"We need some music," said Aaron, plugging in his boom box.

"Your choice," said Moe, pointing to the stack of CDs he'd brought. "Now, if you'll excuse me, I need to go butch up."

The men's room was dark, lit by a single red bulb, and Moe couldn't see much in the chipped mirror as he stripped off his oxford and T-shirt in front of the sinks. Probably better not to be able to make out his reflection clearly, he thought. It had been almost six months since he'd worn his leather vest, and those months hadn't been kind. He'd quit the gym in an effort to trim his expenses — at least that's the excuse he told himself — and had put on twenty pounds. That excess weight rested entirely in his gut, which was now protruding from his open vest and hanging over the silver Colt Studios belt buckle that crowned his 501s. Hopeless, he thought, as he crammed his street clothes into his bag and returned to help Aaron with the decorating.

"Looking good, honey!" Aaron whistled. "You'll have those daddies hungry for a scoop of that hot stuff."

Moe just blushed. He was straining, with difficulty, to appear confident. Aaron, he thought, would never understand. With his lithe dancer's body, he was sinewy without benefit of personal training, lean without a regimented diet. For Aaron, getting ready for a sex party simply meant stripping down to as little as possible. Here he stood in scandalously short cutoff jeans and running shoes. And he looked perfect.

"You still haven't picked a CD?" Moe said. "We've only got half an hour."

□ □ □

More than fifty men came to the safe-sex party at The Backdoor. Not bad for a snowy night in February, Aaron thought. The other members of the Alliance to Save Sex — ASS, for short — had wanted to advertise the event as a fundraiser for their nascent organization, but Aaron and Moe had talked them out of it. "If you want to have a sex party, you've got to make it sexy," Moe had argued at the inaugural meeting three weeks earlier. He designed the poster, with the words SEX PARTY plastered across a black-and-white photograph of four bare-chested men. Underneath the picture was written, "Come one, come all. Play safe at The Backdoor on Friday, February 13. Doors open 8 to 9 p.m. $20 admission." At the very bottom of the poster, in small, neatly typed letters, it said, "All proceeds to benefit the Alliance to Save Sex." Moe and Aaron had spent the previous week posting the notices on newspaper boxes and lightposts across Lower Manhattan.

Aaron was in charge of the music: deep house, they had agreed, anything with a steady beat that didn't have vocals. Nothing kills a mood at a sex party, Aaron said, like some queen having a diva moment, singing along. He also minded the coatroom, which was soon crammed with snow-dampened jackets, sweatshirts, and gym bags. Sitting in a folding chair behind a card table, Moe worked the door, ushering people in out of the cold and taking their money. He handed each man a pamphlet with the phrase ARE YOU AN ASS MAN? emblazoned on the front. Most guys stuffed it in a coat pocket without taking even a cursory glance. A few refused to take it at all.

Moe took mental attendance: Of the twenty-two men who had come to the first Alliance meeting, only ten showed up at the party, not including Moe and Aaron, the "party committee." As men walked in, Moe and Aaron each noted the guys he wanted to track down later. Their lists were mutually exclusive, as usual.

Actually, Aaron's list only had one name on it: Kevin. That was the name the boy told him when he introduced himself over the counter at the coat check. Kevin was small, Filipino, Aaron guessed, and couldn't be more than twenty or twenty-one. He had stripped off his shirt and pants in front of the coat check without a hint of embarrassment, and stood there, already hard beneath his white 2(x)ist briefs, staring Aaron straight in the eye. Only one man in a hundred truly looks good in briefs, Aaron thought, and here he is — too bad he's got attitude for days. No glint of warmth, just a beautiful body ready to be admired.

"Nice outfit," Aaron said dryly as he checked Kevin's bag. "I've got the same underwear, but I forgot to wear any tonight."

Kevin let out a chortle despite himself, and in that instant, Aaron saw that he had misjudged him.

"My name's Aaron."

"I'm Kevin," he replied with sudden shyness, shifting his gaze to the floor.

"I'll see you out there in a bit," Aaron said. "Save some for me."

When they stopped letting people in at nine, Aaron left his post to search for Kevin. He didn't have to look far to find him. In the back of the main room — a cavernous and dark space with wooden walls painted black and ceilings crisscrossed with aluminum ducts — there was a circle of men, two deep in places, around him. Kevin was standing under a yellow light, eyes closed, stroking himself. His briefs were nowhere to be seen. One man stood behind him, running his hands over Kevin's chest and stomach, but whenever the man wandered too far south, Kevin would push his arm away. Another man stood in front of Kevin, kissing his neck, his ears, his hair, but Kevin turned his head whenever the man sought out his lips. Others in the circle reached out to rub Kevin's pert butt, or to squeeze the muscles that rounded his shoulders and arms. In the midst of the crowd, Kevin offered himself freely, to a point, but touched nobody except himself.

Aaron was not deterred. He strode to the center of the circle, past the others. A few hands stretched out to touch Aaron's back, or stroke the lean, powerful thighs that strained his cutoffs. He deflected every grope with gentle firmness; people took the hint quickly. He lowered his mouth to Kevin's ear and whispered his name. Kevin's eyes opened. "I'm free," Aaron said. "Can we go somewhere alone?"

Without speaking, Kevin followed Aaron back into the coatroom and closed the door behind them. He expected Aaron to come to him, grab him, but Aaron did not. Kevin stood still, unsure, wishing he hadn't let some guy take his briefs as a souvenir a few minutes earlier.

"Let's talk," Aaron said.

It was the one thing nobody ever said to Kevin. He paused, folded his arms over his chest, and said, "Okay. You start."

□ □ □

Moe was less focused than Aaron was, but no less determined. He had counted fourteen men with facial hair who walked in the door. One was Gabe, a guy from the Alliance whom Moe had cruised in vain after the last meeting, so he figured that was a lost cause. Three of them had readily apparent "fatal flaws": one had long hair that hung down past his shoulders ("too Three Dog Night," Moe thought), one was younger than he was (Moe was partial to the over-forty set), and one had been smoking. That left ten possibilities. Some were higher on the list than others, of course. He gave extra points for balding men, extra points for men who smiled, and in what seemed like a paradox to everyone but himself, extra points for both muscles and beer bellies. There were other attributes that might get a man immediately scratched off Moe's list altogether, but he needed closer investigation to find out if someone possessed irredeemable qualities like chest stubble or a penchant for poppers. Moe always made such lists in his head, and men — in a bar, on the subway, in a barbershop — were always unknowingly moving up and down the rankings.

As he looked around the main room, he started crossing off prospects right away. One guy with a gray goatee was puffing on a fat cigar and was deemed unkissable. Another man whose bushy red beard seemed to promise a hirsute body was in fact, now that Moe could see him shirtless, entirely smooth — a disappointment. Then, in the maze of hallways behind the main room, he caught the eye of a man who was hovering around number three on the list, and unlike the top two candidates — who, predictably, were playing with each other — he was alone. He looked to be around forty, and was wearing black jeans, black motorcycle boots, and a black leather band on each arm. His bare torso was stocky, more solid than buff, and densely hairy. He sported a wide broom of a moustache over a broad grin, and he beckoned Moe to the alcove where he stood.

There were no introductions; plenty of time for chat afterward, Moe always said. Moe pulled the man toward him and kissed him, while the man opened Moe's vest and pulled on his nipples. The man brushed his moustache against Moe's neck while Moe began unbuttoning the man's jeans. "No fucking, no sucking," Moe reminded himself as he fought the urge to kneel; this was strictly a jack-off party. But he was having trouble keeping his mouth shut completely. In a moment, Moe had his tongue in the man's ripe armpit while he stroked the man's cock. The man grabbed Moe by the hair and held him in place as he came in an arc, spraying Moe's jeans in the process. Moe thought: One down.

The man growled his approval, and introduced himself as Bud. "I noticed you when I first got here," Bud said. "I was hoping you'd come find me."

Moe tugged Bud's chest hair without speaking, as he glanced around looking for the next candidate.

"I'm really into big guys," Bud said. "With your big hairy belly, I could hardly control myself."

Moe's heart sank, and his hard-on evaporated. He liked paunches on other men, but he'd been fighting his own for years, albeit with only intermittent success. And now he was "big." The worst. He was trying to muster a response when Aaron tapped him on the shoulder. "Sorry to interrupt, honey, but we've got a problem."

□ □ □

More than fifty men filed out of The Backdoor and into the snow. The police had cleared out the basement club in a matter of minutes. They didn't have to rush people too much; most men had headed for the door the second they saw uniforms. The cops let everyone retrieve their bags from the coat check, but didn't give anyone — except guys who were totally nude — time to put their clothes on before ushering them up the metal staircase to the sidewalk.

They didn't make any arrests — "It's a simple disturbing-the-peace complaint from a neighbor," the officer told Moe and Aaron, "so we just need everyone to leave the premises" — but they kept a row of police cars idling outside the club, red lights flashing on the shivering, half-naked partygoers. Two officers made sure everyone had left the club. On their way out, they held in their rubber-gloved hands an Alliance pamphlet, a packet of lubricant, and a pair of 2(x)ist briefs they had found on the floor. The balloons apparently struck them as unexceptional, so they didn't bother taking any.

"This is fucking unbelievable," Moe said to nobody in particular. He scanned the block and found no lights on in any nearby building, in fact no building at all where any noise-sensitive neighbor might live on this rundown block in Manhattan's Meatpacking District. Positano's Pork Wholesalers and Big Apple Beef were closed, with metal grates locked over their doors. A couple of storefronts were vacant, their broken windows visible under dim streetlights. The only people within earshot were a pair of transsexual hookers braving the weather in miniskirts and stiletto boots, navigating the narrow cobblestone streets in search of customers; surely they hadn't called the cops.

The party wasn't a complete bust, Moe realized — he had over a thousand dollars in admission fees in the strongbox in his knapsack — but it had lasted barely over an hour, and nobody would be talking the next day about how hot the orgy had been. The only thing anyone would remember would be the police.

And I didn't even get off, Moe thought, slipping his bomber jacket on over his leather vest.

Frank DeSoto tapped Moe on the shoulder. "Hello, Mr. Pearlman. I understand you were one of the organizers of tonight's soiree?"

Moe's shoulders tensed, and he turned to find Frank standing there, his notepad already open, his right glove removed so he could hold his pen. "Hi, Frank. Yes, I helped with the planning."

"The first public event for this new group, this Sex Alliance, right?"

"It's the Alliance to Save Sex, and yes, this was the first event," Moe said. "There will be more coming this spring, including a teach-in about how the new drug cocktails affect the risk of transmitting HIV, and a pamphlet we'll be putting together about negotiating safety with anonymous sex partners."

Moe noticed that Frank wasn't taking many notes. "Tell me, were there condoms provided at your party?"

"No, Frank, it was a jack-off party. There were no condoms."

"And how much did you raise tonight?"

"Over a thousand dollars."

"Some people would argue that encouraging anonymous sex — even in a so-called safe sex environment — is dangerous, that promiscuity is inherently unhealthy in the age of AIDS. What does the Sex Alliance say about that?"

"The Alliance to Save Sex," Moe said, putting on his public relations hat, "thinks that sex venues can be great places to promote safe sex, and that the more exciting safe sex is, the less people will be driven to have unsafe sex. HIV doesn't have to fundamentally change your sex life. Our desires don't have to go unsatisfied. Hot sex can endure both this epidemic and the mayor's ongoing campaign to close sex spaces."

This time, Frank was writing it all down. Moe realized that he should stop talking. He'd said too much already, and Frank DeSoto was sure to twist his words into something horrible in the next issue of *Outrageous*, the gay weekly he'd founded, published, and edited. "Sorry, Frank, I've got to get going."

"That's okay," Frank said. "I'm going to go talk to the cops about what happened. I'll call you if I have any other questions."

Frank walked toward The Backdoor against the tide of patrons, who had now put their clothes on and were walking around the corner to Hudson Street, past the phalanx of cop cars, to find cabs. Aaron was walking in the street, his hand on the shoulder of the short Asian man he'd been with inside. Aaron approached Moe and made introductions.

"Sorry the party got stopped short," Kevin said. "I guess holding it on Friday the thirteenth wasn't such a good idea."

Moe shrugged. That's exactly what several guys at the Alliance meeting had said. Maybe that's why so many of them hadn't shown up.

"I saw you talking with your reporter pal," said Aaron. "He got here awfully fast, if you know what I mean. What did he want to know?"

"He asked a few questions about the Alliance and the party. Nothing unusual."

"We'll see what he writes," Aaron said. "This could be big news. With all the cops out here, it looks like Stonewall."

"No, at Stonewall the queens fought back," Moe countered. "These queens are just going home."

Aaron hesitated for a moment, then looked at Kevin, shivering in the cold. "Myself included," he said, taking Kevin's hand. "I'm getting my ass into a warm taxi. I'll talk to you later, honey."

The snow had begun to collect in Moe's beard. The patrons were almost all gone by now, and even the police were starting to leave. Bud walked by and gave Moe a wink; Moe winked back. Then, realizing he couldn't start Stonewall Two alone, he turned and headed home.

□ □ □

"Make yourself comfortable," Aaron said as he and Kevin entered his walkup studio on Avenue C. There was no need to make excuses about the apartment being a mess, because unlike the building's stairway — littered with fast-food debris and reeking of cat urine and pot smoke — Aaron's studio was, as always, immaculate. Aaron's furniture consisted of a wood-frame futon sofa that folded out to become his bed, a small Formica table that served as both his dining surface and desk, two black kitchen chairs, and a pine wardrobe he'd found on the street and painted green. One wall was packed with shelves, which held a wide array of paperback books and CDs, as well as an incense burner. The opposite wall was covered with framed snapshots, arranged around a large poster.

Kevin put his wet jacket over a chair, left his snow-covered shoes by the door, and walked over to check out the photographs while Aaron went to the kitchen for drinks. He brought back two Diet Cokes. "It's all I've got. Sorry. I don't drink."

"That's okay, I don't either," Kevin replied. Aaron smiled, wondering if Kevin was even old enough to buy alcohol. "Some of your pictures are wonderful. The shadows in this shot are perfect."

"Nobody has ever commented on the shadows before," said Aaron. "And I guess I never paid much attention either."

"Well, I've been studying photography," said Kevin.

"That explains it."

"Wait a minute," said Kevin, "isn't that you in that poster?"

"Yeah, that was back before I grew out my braids," Aaron said. The poster was from two years ago during his fifth and final year with the Joshua Browne Dance Company, the season he danced lead in Joshua's latest suite, which he had choreographed just for Aaron, the season when a torn ligament in Aaron's knee forced him into retirement at age twenty-six. In the picture, he was in profile, one arm reaching up, one leg extended behind him, a yellow light reflecting on his dark brown scalp. "I'm a dancer. Or I *used* to be a dancer."

"That's funny, I'm a dancer myself," Kevin said, then looked down and added, "Well, sort of."

"Sort of?"

"I dance at Slick on Saturday nights."

"You're a go-go boy?"

"They call us 'featured dancers,'" Kevin said, taking a seat on the couch. "But I guess it's not exactly the same kind of thing you used to do."

Aaron thought, You're damn right — I spent fourteen years training to dance, worked my muscles till they ached, pushed my body until it couldn't take any more. I wasn't doing some robotic striptease on a box. But looking at the adorable boy, he softened; he sat down next to Kevin and said, "I suppose it's not so different."

"I'm only doing it for the money," Kevin said in his defense, explaining that he had to support himself while he was studying photography at the New York School of Art and Design.

If Aaron was upset to learn that Kevin was a go-go boy, his expression didn't betray him. He turned toward the wall and told Kevin about the other pictures. There were images from protests, with Aaron and a coterie of comrades holding signs urging divestiture in South Africa, a ban on animal testing, abortion on demand, and increased funding for AIDS drugs. The chronology of the pictures was clear from the varying length of Aaron's hair: In older photos he had dreadlocks that started short but eventually grew down to his shoulders before he shaved his head, and in more recent shots his hair had grown from fuzz through an awkward phase (hidden under do-rags) to its current shape, with short braids framing his forehead.

There was also one snapshot from Aaron's dancing days where he stood with his arms around Joshua.

"Was Joshua your boyfriend?" Kevin inquired.

"Yes, but that was a long time ago. I haven't seen him since I left the company. Once I stopped dancing for him, he didn't know what to do with me. And I haven't dated anyone seriously since." Aaron stopped and looked at Kevin. Christ, he thought, this kid probably hasn't ever dated anyone seriously — what on earth am I thinking? So he asked, "How about you? Do you date much?"

"Not really," Kevin said. "Usually, if I meet a guy I like, we'll go out on a date, and if it goes well, we end up fucking. But then I never hear from them again. I guess I must be a lousy lay." He chuckled.

"I think it says more about them," Aaron said, not laughing.

Kevin spotted one picture, evidently not from too long ago, of Aaron in a tight silver tube top and a spandex miniskirt, wearing red high heels and matching bangle bracelets. "Is that you?" Kevin asked.

"Let's save that story for another day."

"Another day?"

"Yes. Now help me unfold this futon."

□ □ □

Frank DeSoto got home around ten, his pad full of notes and his head full of ideas. He hung his coat in the hallway and walked into his bedroom to change into dry clothes. Then, lacking any other plans for a Friday night, he went into his second bedroom — the one that served as the offices of his newspaper, *Outrageous* — and turned on his computer. He sat without any lights on, taking in the views of Manhattan in a snowstorm. From the corner window in his sixteenth-floor apartment in the Chelsea Park Plaza — a building with enduring cachet despite lacking both a park and a plaza — he could see clear across town to the Empire State Building, glowing red through the snowflakes.

He had been expecting tonight's news story about the Backroom party, and had saved the entire front page for his exclusive coverage. He turned on a lamp and donned his glasses to read his notes, pulling down the blinds to keep the view from distracting him, and began to type.

□ □ □

As Moe walked through the West Village, the neighborhood's streets were filling with people just heading out. Friday night in the Village meant different things to different people: Straight kids from the outer boroughs crowded into West Fourth

Street's rowdy theme restaurants, eager to pay six dollars for a "yard of ale" in a souvenir mug. Older tourists headed to the tacky Italian trattorias on Bleecker Street, where second-rate pianists played "authentic Italian music" to distract them from their plates of store-bought linguine in watery marinara. Gay folks headed to the same bars they had always patronized on Christopher Street; by this point in the late '90s, these dank and smoky dens were no longer trendy, but neither were their middle-aged customers, who didn't care if Chelsea had long since stolen the neighborhood's thunder as the most fabulous place in town.

Moe wasn't in the mood for mingling, so he avoided Christopher Street and veered off Seventh Avenue by the Stonewall monument. As he turned the corner, he looked into the window of the Sheridan Square Diner out of habit. And sure enough, there he was. Him.

Moe saw him at least three nights a week, sitting on the same orange vinyl seat in the same window booth at the diner. He was always alone under the faux-Tiffany lamp, always working intently, looking utterly serious. A few times Moe had gone into the diner in an effort to catch his eye, but it never worked. He was always reading a manuscript, shaking his head, making notes in the margins. Moe decided he must be some sort of editor or playwright or author. This might have given Moe — who was also a writer, an avid reader, and as a freelance theater critic knew a few things about plays — a good excuse to start a conversation. But Moe didn't like to make the first move.

This guy was the stuff of Moe's fantasies. He was somewhere in his forties, with dark brown hair and a goatee. He clearly spent most of his free time working out, and the rest of his time showing off the results. Every time Moe saw him, he was wearing the same clothes: tight Levi's and a skin-tight ribbed tank top — not some trendy Raymond Dragon tank top, but the kind that straight men wear as undershirts. Even in winter.

He just threw a leather jacket on over it; the tank top was cut low enough to show off his chest hair and a thin gold chain.

Moe wasn't the type who jerked off thinking about guys he'd seen on the street, any more than he'd conjure up images of movie stars to get turned on. But this man had visited Moe in his imagination dozens of times since he had moved to the West Village two years earlier. He paused outside the diner in the snow, as he had done so often, debating whether to go inside and try to get the guy's attention. But then he remembered Bud's comment about his belly, and figured he'd better just head home.

After walking the last three blocks thinking about his mystery man, Moe was horny. Pulling his black swivel chair up to his black pressboard desk, he switched on his computer and dialed Men Online. This won't take long, Moe thought, when he noticed that twelve of the 146 men on his "buddies" list were logged on. He was rarely the one to make the first move, no matter how horny he was; "I'm a spider, not a fly," he was fond of saying. So he just sat back and waited for someone to request his services.

Within one minute, three men had sent messages. "First come, first served," Moe thought, choosing the buddy who was quickest to chat him. He'd be over in ten minutes. The scene was usually the same. Moe would be in the rocking chair under a reading lamp in the corner, a buddy would walk into the studio and he'd come over and sit on the dingy brown couch in front of the TV, where a porno movie would already be playing. Without a word, Moe would unzip the man's pants, blow him, and then wait for him to zip up and leave. Sometimes it took five minutes, sometimes forty-five. Either way, the scene was reliably good, efficient, and left everyone happy. After all, 146 regulars kept coming back for more.

Moe never asked for reciprocation. Partly, it was a question of numbers; Moe could take care of several men in one evening if he didn't ever finish himself off. Also, it was a question of control; he could set the scene and be sure that nobody would try to change it unexpectedly. And, truth be told, it was a question of practicality. With Moe doing the sucking, it was nearly guaranteed that every experience was satisfying. Moe felt an almost religious attachment to sucking dick, and loved almost every cock he had ever laid his lips on, and men typically left with smiles on their faces. When it came to getting his dick sucked, though, Moe often thought it was more trouble than it was worth. Few guys had Moe's talents; most were second-rate, or grew tired too quickly. Moe was usually happier to take care of himself after his buddies left.

After landing his catch online, Moe gave his other admirers rain checks (for later that weekend, or perhaps later that night) and logged off. He checked his notes — he kept a detailed database of his online tricks' names, outstanding attributes, and notable quirks — to make sure he would remember exactly how to turn this man on, which places to touch and which to avoid, what to lick gently and what to bite hard. Dan was the man's name — or that's what he had told Moe at any rate. Likes rough ball play, the notes recorded, and having his feet licked. Good thing I checked, Moe thought, or I would have forgotten about the feet.

The phone rang. It was Gene, calling from Washington. They had spoken only a few hours earlier — they spoke pretty much every day — but Gene wanted to find out how the sex party had gone.

"I didn't expect you to be home so early," Gene said. "What happened — you had sex with everyone there in under an hour? That's a record even for you."

"Things didn't turn out exactly as planned," Moe said, stretching out on his stained green bedspread. He explained about the police raid and the noise complaint.

"Yeah, the complaint sounds bogus to me," Gene agreed. "At least nobody was arrested."

Moe hadn't even thought about that. "And that schmuck from *Outrageous* was there, too, taking notes. I can hardly wait to see what he has to say about all this."

"You shouldn't have even talked to him," Gene said. "You know you won't like how he makes you come across."

The downstairs buzzer rang. Moe got up and walked to the door with his cordless phone. He hit the "listen" button on the intercom. "It's Dan," the voice said. Moe buzzed him up.

"Sorry, I've got to run," Moe told Gene with a businesslike tone. "Got a customer for drive-thru service."

"The usual order? A Happy Meal with a Slurpee?"

"Big Mac," said Moe. "Can't resist that special sauce."

"Disgusting," said Gene. "Talk to you tomorrow."

Moe knew Gene hated it when he cut the conversations short like this, but he made it a policy never to keep a hard man waiting. He hung up the phone, turned off the overhead light, and unlocked the front door. With the remote control, he turned on the television and the VCR, and started to play the video. Then he sat in his rocking chair, waiting for the fly to stumble into his web.

two

"Get a load of this headline: 'AIDS Den Shut Down,'" Moe said. "Can you fucking believe it? Clear across the front page."

"Can't say it's unexpected," Gene replied.

"Wait, the subhead is even better: 'Promoter Of Condom-Free Orgy Promises "More To Come."' At least I'm not identified by name until the third paragraph, where he calls me 'Moe Pearlman, party organizer and spokesman for a new group of reckless sex reactionaries with the cheeky acronym ASS: the Alliance to Save Sex.' I guess I should be thankful he got the name of the group right."

"Or maybe not," Gene countered. "What are the guys in the Alliance going to say at your next meeting?"

"I don't know. I guess it'll be a test of their mettle. Then again, the fact that I'm bringing a thousand bucks to the meeting might soothe some nerves." Moe sat up on the edge of his bed, waiting for a response. As he picked at his winter blanket, which had begun to pill, he heard the faint sound of Gene's computer keyboard at the other end of the line.

"Are you still there?"

"Listen, I'm sorry. I've got to run."

"But I haven't even read you the worst of it yet."

"Some of us have jobs, and I've got to get back to mine. Give me a call tonight. Remember, I'm coming up this weekend, so we'll have plenty of time to pick the article apart line by line, and plot a thousand acts of revenge."

"Still no hint about why you're coming up?"

"Nope. I'll tell you when I get there. Just wash your sheets. I never know who's been in your bed."

"Well, Saturday it'll just be you and me. Seems like old times, huh?"

Gene snorted and hung up, and Moe lay back in bed to read the rest of the article. Most of the facts were correct — the police raid, the number of attendees, the location — but somehow the article had a sinister tone. It didn't help, of course, that the photo Frank used was of half-naked men being led out of the club, shielding their eyes in shame. Nor did it help that Moe had said so many stupid things to Frank, like "HIV doesn't have to fundamentally change your sex life," or "Our desires don't have to go unsatisfied." Big mistake.

It was a lot to handle for a Monday morning. The only saving grace is that nobody reads this damn rag except me, Moe thought, as he took the newspaper into the bathroom, where he felt it most properly deserved to be read.

□ □ □

"Quite a scoop today. Mazel tov," said Emmett Kane, calling from his office on Monday morning. Emmett was not Jewish, but he believed that as a lifelong New Yorker he was entitled to borrow a bit of lingo. "I just picked up today's issue. Once again, you have beaten the *New York Times* to the punch."

"Thanks, as always," Frank replied. "I guess they don't think this news is fit to print."

"I'm just glad somebody does," Emmett continued. "This kind of crap is infuriating. People having orgies to celebrate unsafe sex — what are they calling it now? Barebacking? Just another name for suicide, if you ask me. Fifty strangers fucking without condoms. And paying someone for the privilege!"

Frank paused.

"I mean, that's what I'm getting out of your story," Emmett said. "It's accurate, isn't it?"

Frank responded: "Well, let's just say that it is *true*."

Now it was Emmett who paused.

"I think I understand you," Emmett said. "Then congratulations all the more. Truth is even harder to report."

□ □ ▷

Frank hung up the phone and went to the kitchen to pour himself a cup of coffee. He put his feet up on his couch and took a few minutes to read over the latest issue in his living room, which caught the morning sun.

With hardwood floors and ten-foot ceilings, it was an unusually luxurious apartment for someone with no real income to speak of. But as most gay New Yorkers of a certain age remembered, Frank had made his money when he was young. His father, a successful trial attorney in Westchester County, had died when Frank was twenty-four, leaving Frank a sizable nest egg. Frank, who had inherited his father's quick thinking and persuasive air but lacked his professional ambition, had quickly dropped out of law school, where he had been languishing for two years. At the suggestion of his then-lover Scott, Frank had invested in a business venture, a Midtown club called Snow. The year was 1975, and as any number of tell-all books and celebrity magazine profiles have recounted, Snow was to become the number one hot spot in Manhattan, where the fabulous and the nearly fabulous came to mix. Gay and straight, men and women, uptown and downtown came together under the disco ball and in the back rooms, where cocaine flowed freely and sex soon followed.

Frank and Scott had enjoyed their wild ride, snorting their fair share of coke and having at least their fair share of sex, in their own club, on the docks after they closed, or in the bathhouses. Scott, who had always been the one with business savvy, saw disco's demise coming, and wisely invested in this two-bedroom co-op and a small gay bar called The Cellar, which helped open up Chelsea as the next hot neighborhood as Greenwich Village got increasingly expensive.

When Scott died of AIDS in 1987, Frank was lost. He had no passion left for his business, no interest left in sex, and dreaded the memories that haunted his sixteenth-floor two-bedroom spread. Then, one night a few months after Scott died, Frank heard a speech at the Triangle Gay Community Center, a speech by Emmett, a Stonewall veteran who had earned a reputation as a gadfly or hero or general pain in the ass, depending on your perspective. Emmett was angry that night, in rare form, ranting about how the city was neglecting AIDS, how the Catholic Church's homophobia was killing people, how thousands of gay men continued to drink and drug and fuck like rabbits while their brothers lay dying. "This epidemic isn't sad, it's not tragic, and it's not inevitable. It's outrageous!"

Frank, who appreciated a good summation, was hooked. Emmett had unlocked something inside him, a rage he hadn't been able to tap into during the last months of Scott's life, or the first few months of his life alone. He was outraged, all right, outraged that his mother hadn't attended his lover's funeral, outraged that his neighbors hadn't even offered to walk his goddamn dog when he was spending long nights in the hospital with Scott, outraged that every day when he walked down Eighth Avenue, he saw hundreds of gay men going about their daily routines at the Chelsea Gym and the Muffin Man bakery and the D'Agostino's supermarket as if nothing had changed. As if the world wasn't splitting open and swallowing them whole, dozens at a time.

He sold the bar at a tidy profit and used the money to start a new gay newspaper, one that would tell the truth. One that wouldn't focus on glamorous parties and gossipy tidbits and the new hot number in town. One that would scream about the horrors and fight to change the way things were, one that would fight back and demand attention. One that would be *Outrageous*.

The paper had been Frank's personal project, and ten years later, he was still essentially a one-man operation, running

the newspaper out of his spare bedroom, writing the news
himself, editing the handful of freelance columns and arts
stories, selling the few classified and display ads that remained,
and laying out the paper every week on his Mac. There wasn't
much money in it, but Frank got other intangible rewards, like
an occasional call from Emmett Kane congratulating him on
a job well done.

□ □ □

Emmett saw his own adamant passions reflected in Frank.
He recalled the town meeting at the Triangle Center a year
earlier, in response to the city's closure of the last remaining
bathhouses on public health grounds. Lots of young radicals
— including some tattooed dykes, whatever the hell they had
to do with this he didn't know — had shouted about civil
liberties and freedom of association, about homophobia in the
police department and the mayor's administration, about how
outdated sex laws and health codes were being revived to bash
the queers once again. But in the midst of it all, Frank DeSoto
had the balls to tell it like it was. Reporter's notebook still in
hand, in the middle of someone else's ranting, he shouted
across the auditorium: "Why can't you keep your fucking
zippers closed for five minutes?!" He was booed and hissed,
of course, but Emmett himself had been treated similarly for
years at such community forums, only to be vindicated — if
never formally apologized to — much later. Here, he thought,
is a man who really gets it.

Emmett had long understood the selfishness, the laziness,
the lack of self-criticism that the gay movement seemed to
breed. Only a few years after Stonewall, living in Greenwich
Village as a well-educated but underemployed and increasingly
long-in-the-tooth thirtysomething waiter, he had rejected
the narrow political perspective and claustrophobic social
life of the gay ghetto, choosing instead to go back to school,
train as a psychologist and move to the East Side. In his

practice, he saw a number of gay clients, and he'd witnessed the mental gymnastics they went through to rationalize their sexual dysfunction, their emotional shallowness, their financial irresponsibility. He was one of the first to see what was happening with AIDS in the early '80s, because he saw a pattern developing among a few of his patients and the friends they discussed, a pattern that clearly linked what he deemed a promiscuous lifestyle with disease.

It was AIDS — or "gay cancer," as it was still known — that led Emmett back to the gay community. Using his clout as a Stonewall veteran, he was able to gather a small group of old time activists in his East Side home and launch MIGHT, Men in Good Health Together, which became New York's first and largest AIDS organization. This new association gave Emmett even greater credibility, and soon he was penning articles for psychology journals, gay magazines, and the *New York Times* about gay men's sex habits. His temper and penchant for hyperbole inevitably led to clashes with the other board members of MIGHT — he did have trouble with collaborative efforts, Emmett had to admit — and he soon left the organization. In fact, these days, he was one of its toughest critics.

But if he had thought he was alone in the fight to tell the truth, no matter how ugly, in the face of this epidemic, Emmett knew he had an ally in Frank DeSoto. Several years earlier, when he had met Frank in person for the first time, Emmett learned that the newspaper's name had been inspired by one of Emmett's early speeches about AIDS. He had told Frank at the time: "I'm glad to inspire you. Now let's see if you can inspire me." And, increasingly, he did.

□ □ □

By the time he met Carolyn Guttmacher in Midtown for lunch at half past noon, Moe had been stewing for hours. He looked forward to these occasional lunches with Carolyn — especially at places like this chic bistro, with linen napkins and Chilean wine and waiters in bowties — but he wasn't sure he could fully concentrate on what she wanted to talk about: theater. As editor of *Footlights* magazine, she had been throwing freelance reviews Moe's way for the past year, and had enlisted him as an assistant editor for the previous summer's special Tony Awards issue and December's year-end edition. He was indebted to her for the assignments — partly for the small paychecks and partly for the exposure, but mostly for the theater tickets that he could never otherwise afford. Plus, she took him out to fancy restaurants about once a month, and put the bill on her expense account; that's something you can do when your father owns the company.

He knew Carolyn considered herself "hip" on gay issues, but he wasn't sure she was hip enough to hear about a sex party without freaking out. What would shock her more: the trumped-up story in *Outrageous*, or the real story of the event that he had organized? Could she grasp the concept of a safe-sex orgy? Straight people, even gay-friendly straight people, had their limits.

So for a while, they chatted about the spring season of off-Broadway plays. A musical adaptation of *Charlotte's Web* (groans all around), a revival of a Joe Orton play (so rarely done well, Moe noted), a British import that should have reached Broadway but would have to settle for the Minetta Lane Theatre in the Village. But she could see he was preoccupied, and before the dessert tray rolled around, she had gotten the story out of him. Or at least the *Outrageous* outline.

"Sounds simple enough to fix, Moe. Just write a letter to the editor and tell your side of the story."

"That's not a solution, though. It's a systematic problem with that newspaper," Moe tried to explain. "It's not a forum for the exchange of ideas, or even a paper of record for factual information. It's just one angry queen's vanity vehicle to publicize his latest crazy campaigns. One month he's screaming to close a bar, and the next month the city has

closed it. He even got the city to close down The Cellar last
fall — and that's a bar he used to own! Then once the mayor
has done his bidding, Frank DeSoto moves on to another bar,
or a disco, or a bathhouse —"

"Bathhouse? My God, I thought those were all gone,"
Carolyn interjected. "I mean, with AIDS and all, who on earth
would go?"

There's the limit, Moe said to himself. Can't push any
further on that front.

"Well, there were a few left, but now they're closed," Moe
continued. "But the point is that his paper is a tremendously
damaging force in the gay community, and you can't write
a letter to the editor to complain, because it won't change
anything. Frank DeSoto owns the means of production. Not
to wave the red banner, but it's true."

"Can't you write a letter to another gay paper?"

"That's just the thing. There is no other gay paper. New York
City is home to what, a million gay people? And all we have
is one crummy newspaper with a circulation I could count on
two hands and still have enough fingers left over to pick my
nose."

"That's a colorful expression," she said with a grimace. "Be
sure to put that in one of your reviews."

Her grimace turned to a smile.

"Seriously, I don't know what to tell you then," she continued.
"You say you're part of this new group, this Alliance. Maybe
you should talk to them about how to respond. I mean, I'm
sure they're going to *want* to respond, if the article is as bad
as you make it sound."

"Yeah, you're right. I'm sure we'll figure out something. It'd
just be nice if we had a few better options," Moe said, suddenly
eager to get out of this discussion, which he was regretting
starting. "Anyway, sorry to bring all that up. Tell me more
about this *Charlotte's Web* musical. I can see it now: Act Two
opens with the curtain rising on a huge production number
called 'Some Pig' — and Charlotte herself appears doing an

eight-legged tap dance dressed as some sort of Bob Fosse spider in a black slinky dress, trailing a web behind her."

"I want to see if they change the story so it has a happy ending," Carolyn said. "Like maybe Charlotte doesn't have to die after all!"

"Don't knock the idea," Moe insisted. "It worked for *Rent*."

□ □ □

Water trickled from a small fountain. The scent of jasmine and sandalwood drifted from the potpourri warmer. New Age music by Kitaro floated gently from the bookshelf speakers.

Glancing at the clock on his shelf, Aaron knew it was time to wrap up. He leaned over and whispered softly into the man's ear, so as not to startle, "James, the hour is over now. I want you to take a deep breath and slowly let it out. Then, whenever you're ready, you can sit up on the table. You can take your time. There's no hurry."

But James didn't take his time. He turned over on the table and shot a confused look in Aaron's direction. "That's it? It's over?"

Aaron answered calmly, "Yes, that was an hour. I know sometimes it's hard to keep track of time on the massage table. Sometimes it seems like it was only a few minutes, other times it feels like a whole day."

"That's not what I mean," James said sharply. "That's the whole massage? Aren't you going to finish me off?"

Aaron froze a moment. He had joked about this possibility, but in a year of doing massage work, it hadn't ever happened.

"Finish you off?"

"You know, don't I get release?"

"I think you have me confused with a different kind of masseur."

The man was getting visibly upset. Aaron was wishing he would leave but he showed no signs of getting off the table. "What the hell did I just give you seventy-five bucks for?"

"You gave me seventy-five bucks for an hour of professional massage, and that's what you got."

"That's not what I thought I was getting."

"I'm sorry if you were confused, but I don't know why you were under the impression that this was a sexual service."

James — or whatever his name actually was — hopped off the table and reached for his underwear.

"The ad in the paper said this was a gay massage."

"That's true," Aaron said as James got quickly dressed. "I'm a gay man who believes in the power of healing touch. That doesn't mean I'm some kind of quote-unquote masseur."

James was tying his shoes. "That's fucked up, man. What the hell do you expect people to think 'gay massage' means, besides sex?"

"Actually, I think it's fucked up to think that 'gay' always means sex," Aaron replied, realizing now his wisdom in having clients pay cash before the massage.

"I get it, you're one of those uptight gay men who thinks sex is dirty, that I must be some sort of lowlife to want to get sexual satisfaction for my money."

Actually, what Aaron was thinking was that James was a decent looking guy, in pretty good shape for his fifties, and he couldn't see why he would have to pay to get laid. But he kept his mouth shut, opened the door for him, and handed him his coat. "I don't think you're some sort of lowlife. But you should've read my ad more carefully. The kind of massage you're looking for doesn't require a license, doesn't last a full hour, and I guarantee it'll cost more than seventy-five bucks."

He was out the door. Aaron stopped to catch his breath, and then jotted a few notes on the index card he had created for this latest client. Not that he'll be coming back, Aaron thought. But look on the bright side, he told himself: One incident in more than a year's worth of clients isn't so bad. This gig is still paying the rent and helping put me through grad school. And it comes with definite perks, like setting my own hours, being my own boss, and getting to rub oil into some pretty fine gentlemen's bodies.

Sometimes, he had to admit, he *had* been tempted to finish them off.

□ □ □

Aaron's braids still smelled faintly of jasmine when he arrived — five minutes late, as always — at Melody Penn's Queer Theory class. The first time such a course had been taught at Empire University, Professor Penn — newly tenured — always noted with pride.

He stomped the snow off his shoes at the door, mouthed a quick apology to Professor Penn — Mel, he called her, although she had never said she approved of such informality — and took a seat in the chair that Moe had saved for him, expecting his tardiness.

"Now where was I?" Professor Penn said, trying to recapture her train of thought. She was drawing diagrams on the board, illustrating schools of thought about identity politics and how they overlap, intersect, draw on one another. Moe and Aaron scribbled quick notes to each other every time she turned her back.

See the paper?
Don't get me started.
How's Kevin?
Coffee after?
Deal.

Aaron was having trouble concentrating. He was still preoccupied with that afternoon's fiasco. And he was trying to think of what to make for dinner when Kevin came over later. Something that said "homemade" but didn't seem like he was trying too hard to impress.

Moe was focusing better, but he wasn't happy. Professor Penn was explaining how identity politics — labels like "gay" and "lesbian" — had some strategic value once upon a time, in terms of helping others understand sexual difference and helping to create a minority model for civil rights advancement. But now, she continued, identity politics had outlived their usefulness, and truly progressive people were shedding these limiting, restrictive labels in favor of "queer," which was simultaneously more inclusive, less tied to specific acts or genders, and more challenging to the social, sexual, and political order. Moe had heard this many times before, and sometimes identified as queer himself just to raise a few hackles. But he wasn't done with "gay" yet — not after he'd spent so many years dealing with being "gay." And if anything, he wanted a term that was *more* specifically tied to sexual acts, not less. Something that forced people to remember that this was all about sex. He liked "cocksucker."

Yeah, she'll love that suggestion, Moe told himself. Best to keep quiet. Professor Penn already thinks you're some sort of frivolous throwback who's not ready for the queer revolution. (She'd given him a "C" on his paper about gay themes in Norman Lear's 1970s sitcoms, and she had laughed out loud when he'd suggested writing a paper about the radical political implications of disco.)

So Moe kept his mouth shut, and Aaron tried to look as though he was paying attention, and they both counted on other people in the class to volunteer to answer any questions Professor Penn might ask. This was a reliable strategy, since half of the dozen grad students in the seminar were major ass-kissers who loved to hear themselves pontificate, especially when they said exactly what the teacher wanted to hear.

Sure enough, five-thirty rolled around and neither of them had said a word. They filed past their classmates and out into the slushy downtown streets. They walked past two Starbucks — they both claimed to have "principles" about avoiding chain stores, even though each one bought the occasional espresso

HARD

there when the other wasn't around — and ducked into The Magic Bean, a locally owned place with mismatched vinyl chairs and a loud jukebox filled with old David Bowie and Jimi Hendrix records (also vinyl).

While they waited for their drinks, Aaron told Moe about his massage ordeal. Moe listened, laughed when he was supposed to, looked sufficiently shocked when Aaron expected it. Moe was thinking: What's the big deal? You should have offered to jerk him off for an extra twenty. It wouldn't have taken you more than a minute. That's what I would have done.

But Moe did not say this. He said, "That sounds awful. Are you okay?" He rubbed Aaron's shoulder. Their drinks came.

Moe started in about the *Outrageous* story. Aaron had seen it too, but had mostly laughed it off. Moe was not laughing. He was in a lather, talking about strangling Frank DeSoto, about the shit that would hit the fan at the next night's Alliance meeting. Aaron was thinking: What's the big deal? You never should have talked to that asshole in the first place, but what's done is done. And if the Alliance folks give you any crap, walk out and move on. You can't let these people aggravate you.

But Aaron did not say this. He said, "I know, it's unbelievable the stuff he can print in that rag. But I'm sure at the meeting, we'll all figure out how to respond. Don't lose any sleep over it." He rubbed Moe's shoulder. Moe felt a little better.

Friendship.

"So tell me about this new boy," Moe said. "How was it? Are you going to see him again?"

"I'm making him dinner tonight."

"I guess that means Friday night was good."

"Honey, it was the bomb. I can't remember the last time I connected with someone like this. I was freaked out at first because he's only twenty. He's eight years younger than I am. But we're on the same wavelength a lot of the time. He's smart and sweet and independent. He likes good music, he doesn't ask stupid questions, and he doesn't snore."

39

Moe waited. "And the sex?"

"Let me just say that this boy knows a great deal for someone so young. He can twist that body into any number of interesting positions. And speaking of that body, can we *talk* about that body?"

Kevin was not Moe's type, and they both knew that. But Moe didn't have to fib this time: "He's got an incredible body."

"You can say that again! I was pinching myself watching him sleep. Perfection! Those arms. That back. That ass!"

"But if you're cooking him dinner, this was more than sex."

"Could be, though of course it's too early to say. Maybe I'll know better after tonight. But it would be a great story to tell our grandkids, about how we met at a sex party."

Moe smiled. "So what did you do the next day?"

"We stayed in bed until noon, ordered out for bagels, and then went back to bed all afternoon."

"Impressive stamina. I guess that's the advantage of younger men."

"Actually we spent most of the day in bed talking. Not all of it, naturally, but most. He would have stayed over another night, but he had to go to work."

"On a Saturday night? I thought he was a student."

"He is a student," Aaron replied. "But he's also a go-go boy. At Slick."

Moe mulled this for a moment, eyes to the ceiling. "Yeah, I can see that."

"Anyway, the whole day seemed so perfect. I can't remember the last time I had such a romantic Valentine's Day."

Valentine's Day, Moe thought. I completely forgot.

□ □ □

It was obvious from the moment Moe entered the Mint Theater that something was wrong. The screen was showing the same tired old porno flicks as always, but the lights were up. Most of the seats were empty, and the few patrons present were seated singly instead of in pairs or groups. A man in a yellow T-shirt strode up and down the center aisle. His shirt said "Health Monitor." Moe knew exactly what that meant.

The bathhouses had been the first to go, over a year ago. Then the mayor's so-called public health campaign had targeted one type of sex establishment after another, first requiring that they pay "monitors" from the health department to patrol the premises to make sure nothing illegal — that is, any kind of sex — was taking place. What happened next was one of two things: Either the patrons got scared off and the business went under within a matter of weeks, once the word got around. Or the monitors wrote up a record of violations they witnessed on premises: "two acts of fellatio, one act of masturbation" or "one act of anal intercourse, three acts of masturbation." There was never any evidence, or any names, or any specifics in these records — not that Moe doubted that they were often accurate — but that was enough to get the health department to close these places down. This was all being done in the name of HIV prevention, but the health code didn't stipulate anything about safe sex or condoms, so everyplace that hosted any kind of sexual activity was subject to raids by the sex police. The dirty bookstores with their glory-hole cubicles near Times Square had fallen like dominoes. The male strip joints near the Hudson took even less time. Topless bars for straight men were still operating, but several backroom bars for gay men had been shuttered in the autumn, including The Cellar. The Backdoor was surely on the city's short list after Friday's party. And now, apparently, it was time for the movie houses.

The monitor stopped to look Moe in the eye, and Moe turned and walked back to the front desk. "What the hell is going on?"

The clerk, an Indian man in his twenties, didn't know Moe by name, but he recognized his face from the visits he sometimes made on the way home from class in the evening. He knew that Moe was a friendly guy, unafraid to make eye contact, quick with a smile and a 'hello,' and that he was fairly popular with the other customers. "Health department came in over the weekend," he told Moe. That explained everything.

"But all this is kind of hopeless, don't you think? Nobody's going to shell out eight dollars to watch a crummy porno movie in a brightly lit theater, alone, while some guy checks to make sure he's not playing with himself."

"I don't see as we have much of a choice," the clerk answered. "What can we do?"

Moe wasn't sure, but he certainly wasn't going to stand by and watch the demise of the Mint — "where you can always find something tasty to suck," he used to say. This East Village den had been around for nearly thirty years. Longer than he'd been alive. It was a community institution.

Moe knew he had other outlets. He knew he could always go home and find someone to play with on Men Online. That wasn't the point. The point was that he wanted options. More options. Endless options.

He flung his knapsack over his shoulder and walked back out into the cold, fuming. This crackdown outraged him politically and baffled him as an AIDS activist. But most of all, it was fucking with his sex life. That's where it hit him, deep down, on a gut level.

Protests and safe sex parties and letters to the editor couldn't do anything to appease this kind of anger, this kind of personal affront. Moe would have to take control of his sex life in spite of the closures. He'd have to go to the one place where monitors in yellow T-shirts could never reach him: his home.

As he walked west, Moe decided he'd get online with a vengeance, fighting for casual sex in the face of a governmental onslaught. He'd take a stand on his knees, blowing the huddled masses yearning to get off. If this was a war for his sex life, Moe was going to go down fighting.

A mathematical person since childhood — he'd amazed the parents at his seventh birthday party by figuring square roots in his head — Moe had long calculated the value of his sexual encounters using a cost-load analysis. A visit to the Mint cost eight dollars, so if he made four guys shoot, he had paid two bucks for each load. A visit to the baths, before they'd closed, cost twenty-two dollars once the subway was factored in; even if he got lucky with seven guys (which was rare, but not unheard of in a four-hour span), he'd still have paid over three dollars per load. As someone with limited cash and unlimited desire, Moe tended to favor sexual outlets with minimum cost and maximum load potential. This explained why he had never hired a hustler (about $150 per load), and why online sex (with a Men Online membership fee of $19.99 per month for unlimited use) was so appealing.

Usually, he was happy if he could get down to about two dollars per load. But tonight he'd paid eight bucks for nothing at the Mint, and he was pissed. Eight divided by zero isn't even a real number.

As his personal form of civil disobedience, he decided he'd stay online until he'd had eight men over to his apartment and gotten them all off. The specifics didn't much matter — it could be eight guys alone, four guys two at a time, one big orgy, or any combination. It could last eight minutes or eight hours. But he was going to get his money's worth. A buck a load.

Walking past the diner, he spotted his mystery man poring over some manuscript. Alone, as usual. Looking as good as ever. Moe stopped for a second to take a mental snapshot, then continued on his way with single-minded determination.

Eight. Tonight's magic number is eight, he thought, stopping for a slice of mushroom pizza on the corner near his apartment. He figured he'd eat it at the computer.

□ □ □

Aaron was cooking dinner when the phone rang.

"Hey, sweetie. Are you on your way over? It's a long ride from Washington Heights. You're gonna be late, and my tuna casserole is gonna burn."

There was no answer from Kevin's end for a moment. Aaron thought, This can't be good.

"Look, Aaron, I'm sorry, but can we get together another night instead?"

Oh, shit, Aaron thought. I didn't think this would start so soon. The bullshit excuses, dates getting canceled at the last minute. Kevin was supposed to be here at eight, and he first thinks to call to blow me off at seven forty-five?

"Why, what's up?"

"Well, I know it's last minute, but I just got a call from the photo lab at school and there's a slot open tonight. I've got a stack of negatives I need to develop, and I could use the extra time."

Aaron thought this sounded fishy, but what did he know about photo labs? "You're going to school now? How late is the lab open?"

"Till ten. If I hurry, I can get in a couple hours tonight and catch up on a few assignments. It'll really help me out."

Aaron wasn't sure what to believe. He was sure they'd had a great time all weekend. Or pretty sure. Was Kevin panicking because it had been too intense too fast? Was there someone else in the picture? No way to know for sure. He'd have to trust him this time and hope for the best. He told Kevin, "Okay, you run along to school, but I expect you here tomorrow night at the same time. No excuses."

"Promise," Kevin said. "And thanks for understanding."

□ □ □

Kevin hung up the phone and rushed to get ready. A quick shower, then into his tightest jeans and a hooded sweatshirt. White sneakers, very youthful. They always like that. He stuffed twenty dollars in his front pocket and left his wallet on the table; in his other pocket went a pack of Doublemint and his pepper spray. Then down to the street to catch a cab.

The ride was quick on the West Side Highway to Hell's Kitchen, to an old rowhouse on a dark street. He buzzed apartment #3, like the guy had told him, and waited for the man to open the door.

He wasn't bad looking. In pretty decent shape from what Kevin could tell. Not that it mattered much, but still, it helped. He asked, "James?"

"Yeah," came the reply, as the man stood in the doorway looking Kevin up and down. He smiled, seemingly satisfied. Kevin looked good, no two ways about it. "Truth in advertising. Just what I expected."

"Always the truth," Kevin said. "I'm Jason. It'll be $150, and I'll need the cash up front before I go inside."

three

Whenever Frank invited Donovan Cassidy — "D.C.," he called him — out for a drink, he always made sure to add, "I'll come downtown." He didn't expect D.C. to venture into Chelsea.

So Frank found himself waiting after work on Tuesday in a crowded bar called Boss Tweed, a spot near City Hall that had once housed an old-fashioned working man's pub but now catered to a more upscale white-collar crowd — Wall Street types enjoying the boom — with large-screen video monitors and six-dollar martinis. He was halfway through his seltzer water when D.C. walked in fifteen minutes late.

"Sorry to keep you waiting, Frankie," D.C. said. "Meeting with the mayor ran late."

"No problem at all," Frank replied. He knew that D.C. was possibly telling the truth, but he also knew that D.C. liked to create the impression that he was a Very Important Person. Chief of Staff for the mayor, you know. Very busy. He was more than a little arrogant — had been ever since they met in law school all those years ago — but he kept in touch with Frank through all his ups and downs, and always found time to meet him for a drink. Frank was grateful enough to look past his flaws.

"How's the paper?" D.C. asked, ordering a martini (Tanqueray, extra dry).

"Fine, fine," Frank replied, knowing there was no need for details. "How's your work?"

"Hectic. Gearing up for the re-election campaign. Nine months till Election Day. It's not such a long time. So I'm busy as hell."

"What does Katie think about that?"

"She's not thrilled, but she's got her own work. Most weekends she's in SoHo at the gallery. I'm not the only one with long hours."

"You know, if you two need to get away this summer, you're always welcome to come stay with me at the beach," Frank said. "Even just for a weekend. It's a great place to unplug." He had made this offer for years, and D.C. had always found an excuse not to come. Years ago, Scott had suggested that D.C. was too homophobic to handle Fire Island. Frank didn't share that view. D.C. was his *friend*.

"Thanks, Frankie," D.C. said. "We'll let you know."

Frank held out hope that this would be the year D.C. would show.

"But that's not why you wanted to talk, is it?" D.C. asked, running his fingers through his thinning, sand-colored hair. "What's up?"

"I've got the perfect spot to target next," Frank said. "It's big, high-profile, and right in Times Square. The mayor could show the family values types that he's hard on this kind of sleazy nightlife, while at the same time showing developers that he's concerned with cleaning up Times Square to make it more attractive to big business. Everyone wins."

"Another gay club?" D.C. asked.

"Well, yeah, a disco," Frank said. "But the point is that there's all sorts of stuff going on there — drug dealing and unsafe sex taking place right on the premises."

"Listen, the mayor's concerned about the gay vote heading into the next election," D.C. explained. "He starts off at a disadvantage as a Republican, and then he keeps closing all these bathhouses and sex clubs and porno theaters. Those places were safe enough to close — nobody is going to defend them publicly. But closing some huge disco is bound to piss people off and make him look antigay. Which he isn't, you know."

"That's just the thing," Frank interjected. "It's not a crackdown on gay places. It's a crackdown on places where HIV is being spread. That's *good* for gay people. They want these places gone. Trust me, I run the only gay newspaper in this city. I know what the gay community is thinking. They're *glad* the mayor is closing these places. They feel like the mayor is on *their* side in this fight against AIDS. Like he's closing these places for our own good."

D.C. had little choice but to trust Frank's judgment; Frank was his only gay friend. Plus, Frank had been giving him advice — mostly unsolicited — about places the mayor should target for over a year now, and there didn't seem to be any backlash from gay groups. "I suppose if we coupled it with a statement about AIDS prevention — something about funding for health programs in the schools — it might seem like part of a proactive health campaign."

"That's the idea!" Frank cheered. "You've got to believe me. Four years from now, at the end of the mayor's *second* term, New Yorkers are going to look back and thank him for cleaning up this city. We'll be fighting AIDS, saving lives, and making the city safer for everyone, gay and straight alike."

"Okay, Frankie," D.C. said, looking at his watch. "What's the name of this club?"

□ □ □

It doesn't take much to scare a bunch of queens, Moe thought as he counted the empty seats. The last Alliance meeting drew twenty-two people; this time, only twelve showed up at the Triangle Center.

Moe had arrived early to set up the gray metal folding chairs in a circle in the third-floor meeting room, a windowless space with drop ceilings, linoleum floors and buzzing fluorescent lights left over from the 1960s. He saved a seat for Aaron — he knew he'd be late as always. Gabe (one of the best reasons for coming to a meeting, Moe thought) showed up next, with a stack of *Outrageous* issues under his arm. He handed them out to people as they filed into the room. Only a handful had seen the article, although most of them had heard about the police raid.

"Did you have a good time? I didn't see much of you," Moe said to Gabe. "I was hoping to see more of you."

Gabe ignored the last part. "I had a pretty good time, at least until the police came."

"Yeah, cops are never as hot in real life as they are in the movies," Moe quipped. Gabe chuckled, then turned away and continued handing out newspapers.

Moe watched as people read the article, stopping to point out passages to their neighbors and occasionally looking up at him. He stared right back. It was so quiet, they could hear the lights buzzing and people's shoes squeaking on the linoleum.

Aaron walked in seven minutes late and sat next to Moe. Gabe — who was facilitating — began the meeting by going over the basic facts of what happened at the sex party, focusing on the point when the police arrived and everyone dispersed, before asking, "Does anyone else who was there have anything to add?"

Aside from Gabe, Aaron, and Moe, five other people in the room had been at the party, but none spoke up. Moe piped up with a bit of levity: "Well, it should be noted that other than the police raid, the party was a big success. Fifty guys showed up, we raised a thousand dollars, and got the group's name out there."

"I don't know if it's such a good thing that the whole city knows about the Alliance," said Ron, a somewhat nebbishy guy in his fifties who had not attended the party.

"I agree," said Theo, a thin, tattooed skinhead in his early twenties who had shown up on Friday. "We should be keeping a lower profile. I mean, I don't know what I'd have done if I'd been arrested."

"Nobody was going to get arrested," Moe protested. "The cops were just trying to scare you."

"Well, it worked," Theo said.

"If you're going to be an activist, you've got to be willing to stand up to the police, be public about what you believe in," Moe said.

"And what exactly do 'we' believe in?" Ron asked. "Who appointed you our spokesman? You talk to this newspaper on my behalf, and as a member of this group I'm suddenly implicated in taking a public stand in favor of unsafe sex?"

"Maybe if you'd been there, you could have spoken on your own behalf," Moe snapped, jumping to his feet.

Gabe intervened: "Everyone cool down for a minute. We all know how *Outrageous* twists the facts. I'm sure Moe didn't say all those things."

Moe sat back down. "Actually, I did say all those things. Not in that context, but I did say them."

Newspapers rustled as a few people shifted in their seats.

"I don't remember electing you our press representative," Ron said.

"I didn't say anything that we haven't all discussed at the last few meetings," Moe said.

He remembered the first Alliance meetings, full of anger and resolve only a month earlier. People had spoken eloquently about what sex meant to them, and why the mayor's crackdown pissed them off. They'd come up with creative ideas and eagerly volunteered time to plan events and draft pamphlets. They had productive discussions and heated arguments about things that really mattered — from HIV prevention to civil rights. One police raid, and this large group of committed activists had been whittled down to a small group of cowering losers.

"I don't want him speaking for us," Ron said loudly, talking about Moe in the third person as if he weren't in the room. Others vocally agreed.

Gabe turned to Moe: "You have not been authorized to speak on behalf of the group. Whatever happened last Friday is past, but you should not speak as a representative of the Alliance again."

Moe was pissed. Who else was going to speak to the press? Ron, who was still worried about being "too visible" as a gay man, afraid it might affect his relationship with his ex-wife and two college-age kids? Theo, who could barely get a sentence out without playing with the bar piercing his tongue? Gabe, who spoke vehemently about needing public places to get blown, but proved less emphatic about actually fighting to keep them open when it required any time or energy?

Moe looked at Aaron. No reaction, nothing to say, just a blank gaze at the floor. Moe had seen this before, watched Aaron become a silent spectator rather than get involved in a confrontation. He knew he'd support him privately later, but he couldn't count on him right now. He was on his own.

Fuck this, Moe thought. Fine, I won't speak for the group anymore. In a month, they'll be asking me to write a press release or talk to some reporter, and I'll refuse.

"I will not speak for this group ever again," Moe said curtly. "Now, can we move on? Like, can we discuss what we're going to do to respond?"

"Respond to what?" Gabe asked.

"The police raid, the crackdown in general, this article specifically."

Moe looked around the room. Silence. All eyes down, as if saying, "Teacher, please don't call on me, I don't know the answer."

"Well, if nobody else has any ideas," Moe started, "I'll throw out some options. We could write a letter to the editor at *Outrageous*, correcting his errors and explaining what this organization is truly about. We could write an op-ed piece for someone — I don't know, the *Village Voice*, the *New York Press*, the *Observer* — about the crackdown and how the Alliance is responding. We could organize a protest outside the Sixth Precinct against the cops' handling of the raid. We could stuff copies of Alliance pamphlets into every issue of *Outrageous* in the newspaper boxes. We could set up a second sex party, just to show everyone that we're not intimidated. There are a dozen things we could do."

Theo again, playing with his earring. "I think we need to keep a low profile until this blows over."

"This won't blow over until every sex space in New York is closed," Moe said. "And then it'll be too late."

The discussion continued for another half hour, but it soon became clear that the Alliance wasn't going to do anything. Some people who thought of themselves primarily as AIDS activists were already feeling that the group was moving in the wrong direction by focusing so much on this public sex crackdown and talk of "sexual freedom." Others, who saw themselves as real sex radicals — adamant barebackers, sexual outlaws, guys who were already positive and didn't much care about "prevention" — were turned off by other people's need to color inside the lines, always careful to do what was legal, respectable, and "safe." As these groups argued over what to do, they were both outvoted by the mushy middle, the people who wanted to do nothing at all and just hope for the best.

The hour was nearly over when he spoke up again: "We can't seem to agree on anything. But I feel like we absolutely need to respond in some way."

"We've already decided that you won't be the Alliance spokesperson," Gabe chided.

"Then I'll just do it myself, as Moe Pearlman. Anyone have any problem with me speaking for Moe Pearlman?"

Silence again. Then Aaron said something, for the first time in the evening, quietly: "You do whatever you need to do."

□ □ □

Moe felt like punching somebody, screaming till he was hoarse, smashing bottles against a brick wall.

And he felt like getting *his* dick sucked, for a change.

He slipped into this mode only rarely. Sometimes, if he was feeling on top of the world, he'd go to a sex club and let several suckers take a lick. He viewed this as spreading the joy; he knew how little it took to please a cocksucker — at least for a few minutes — and he knew he had both a nice enough package to please all but the most discriminating kneeler and enough stamina to outlast a half dozen takers.

Tonight, however, Moe was not on top of the world. This was one of those times when he felt angry and frustrated and needed to see someone on his knees in front of him, working hard to please him. He was a tough top on these occasions, talking nasty and holding guys by the ears and getting surprisingly forceful. When he was royally pissed off, Moe needed to get blown in order to relax.

The other ninety-nine percent of the time, when Moe was neither elated nor furious, he was content to do the sucking. But tonight he needed a mouth.

He headed from the Triangle Center to a dirty bookstore near Union Square — one of the only ones left in the city. Down the stairs to the dark corridor, into a cubicle, where he waited in the open doorway, lit only by the flickering images from the porno movie showing on the monitor. He was hard and impatient, feeling mean and extremely horny. This was evident from his expression, and it attracted the cocksuckers like moths to a flame. It didn't matter that he had a bit of a gut, or that he wasn't as handsome as some of the others. The look did it.

Moe gave the eye to a short Latin man with a moustache who appeared to be in his thirties. The man came into Moe's cubicle and shut the door. No words. Moe pushed him down and unbuttoned his fly, and the man went to work. Not too bad with his mouth — *although I could do better,* Moe thought, giving him a seven on a scale of one to ten. Seven was all he needed right now. A warm, wet seven on his dick. Moe leaned back against the wall and started to relax and enjoy it.

"Hey you in there! Open up! One guy per booth!" Someone was pounding on the door. "Open up right now!"

Moe tucked himself into his jeans hurriedly and his mustachioed buddy stood up and undid the latch.

"Get the hell out of that booth," scolded a man in a yellow T-shirt. "One person per booth. You want to get us shut down?"

The warm, wet seven ran out.

Moe was adamant. "I've been coming here for years and never had a problem before."

"That was then, this is now, buddy," the monitor told him, wagging a finger at a new poster: ONE PER BOOTH, NO EXCEPTIONS. "Now get out of here."

With no real choice, Moe walked out and started home. He walked by the Sheridan Square Diner. No mystery man tonight; maybe he was at home with his lover, or at the gym, or working on a big project. Moe sometimes tried to imagine who this man was and what his life might entail — jobs, apartments, family. The window booth looked empty without him.

When he got home at a quarter to eight, the first thing Moe did was call Gene and tell him all about the Alliance meeting. Gene let him rant for about ten minutes about how nobody's willing to fight and nobody understands how serious this is and everybody is too ashamed to speak up and admit what kind of sex they want to have.

"So I guess Aaron was the only one on your side?" Gene interjected.

"More or less."

"What does that mean?"

"More than anyone else, but less than I expected."

"What does *that* mean?"

"It means I'm going to do what I want to do as an individual. Aaron's not going to help me out this time. And the rest of the Alliance is just going to sit tight and take this abuse lying down."

Moe explained his plan: First, he'd write a letter to *Outrageous*, rebutting the article and explaining the truth about the Alliance and the sex party. Second, he'd write an op-ed piece for the *Village Voice* about the ongoing sex crackdown in New York City and the importance of maintaining sexual freedoms in the age of AIDS. He wouldn't mention the Alliance specifically, but would instead speak broadly about the city's gay community. If there was no alternative gay newspaper, he figured, at least he could find one outlet that pretty much all gay people read: the *Voice*.

"Sounds like a good plan," Gene said. "So does this mean you won't be free this weekend?"

"Oh no, I'll be free for your visit, don't worry. I'll have all this done before then. I want nothing to distract me when you reveal why you've made this surprise trip. It's not like you to keep secrets. At least not lately."

"Jews never do forgive and forget, do you?"

"No and no."

"I'll fill you in on Saturday. My train gets in around noon."

"I'll have bagels and lox waiting for you for Saturday brunch. And I've got press tickets to a show on Saturday night."

"Broadway?"

"Off-off Broadway. But they're free, so don't complain."

"Wouldn't dream of complaining."

Moe let the conversation drift onto other topics — the upcoming theater season, Gene's job at the travel agency, his latest boy-toy infatuation — until it naturally came to an end an hour later. Moe was feeling better, more mellow than before. Back to his old self.

He hung up the phone and dialed Men Online to see who was looking to hook up.

□ □ □

Aaron's tuna casserole (his grandmother's recipe) held up pretty well from the previous night. But, still stung from being blown off, he didn't even put it in the microwave to reheat until Kevin buzzed him from downstairs at eight o'clock sharp.

Kevin brought a bag of chocolate chip cookies as an apology. Homemade, not Chips Ahoy.

"That's sweet, but you didn't have to," Aaron said. How little it took to melt away his anger. "Chocolate chip, I love chocolate chip."

"I know, you mentioned it the other night," Kevin said, hanging his coat in the closet.

"Did I?" Aaron asked, making a mental note: This one pays attention.

Without asking, Kevin set the table while Aaron made a salad. Considerate, Aaron thought. Maybe he's just feeling guilty about last night, but considerate nonetheless.

Over dinner, Aaron told Kevin about his day. A few hours in the library doing research for a paper, an hour doing yoga at the school gym, one massage client (Perry, a regular), a class in Black Experience on Film. And the Alliance meeting.

"Sounds like Moe shouldn't have talked to that reporter in the first place," said Kevin, who had never read *Outrageous* and didn't know about the newspaper's slant.

"True, but you'd best keep that to yourself," Aaron said. "He takes all this very personally, like his own private battle, and he gets very defensive when other people offer advice."

Aaron outlined how the Alliance was split among different factions with different agendas. It wasn't easy to sort out for Kevin, who usually got his view of the gay world from the top of a go-go box. Everyone looked pretty much the same from up there.

Kevin listened as Aaron explained how one newspaper article could splinter a group like the Alliance: "Moe wants to tackle it head-on, explaining the group's real mission, exposing the 'public health' crackdown as a fraud and *Outrageous* as a collaborator in the whole debacle. A few people want to change the group's mission to a less radical one of HIV prevention. A few others want us to focus on sexual liberation and personal freedom and let people make up their own minds about safe sex. Most of the people in the group would rather keep doing pretty much what we're doing, but keeping a lower profile and avoiding spending our energy on this kind of public debate."

"And what do you think?" Kevin asked.

"Somewhere in between, I guess. I don't have a problem with Moe doing what he's got to do. But I'm not going to spend my time writing letters to some uptight asshole editor with a chip on his shoulder. It's a no-win battle and it's not worth the stress."

"So you're not willing to stand up for sexual liberation, huh?" Kevin asked — smirking.

"I'd rather lie down for sexual liberation, if you know what I mean," Aaron said, squeezing Kevin's hand and winking. "I like the Alliance, but if it vanished tomorrow, I'd just keep doing what I can do on my own. Sexual liberation isn't about one group or one sex club or one sexual act. It's about changing what's inside, about changing attitudes."

"Yeah, yeah, free your mind and the rest will follow," Kevin quipped.

"I know you're not dissing En Vogue," Aaron shot back with fake seriousness. "Those girls are *fierce*."

□ □ □

After they'd cleared the dishes, Aaron brought out the chocolate chip cookies on a plate, and while they sat close together on the futon, he asked Kevin about the previous night's work at the photo lab.

"What are you working on that's taking so much time?"

"Actually, I brought over my portfolio so you can see exactly what I've been doing," said Kevin, getting up to fetch the knapsack he'd left by the front door.

If the presentation was a bit low-budget — a cheap three-ring binder with plastic looseleaf sleeves inside — the photos were anything but amateurish.

There were studies of flowers in black-and-white. ("I was trying to find the beauty beyond color — since that's their most obvious appeal," Kevin explained.) There were posed portraits, all shot from behind. ("I wanted to see what you could understand without reading facial expressions," he said.) There were photos of garbage men, metermaids, newspaper boys. ("We know these people exist, but we almost never see them.")

Aaron was impressed with Kevin's work. It was technically excellent — good use of light, smart sense of composition — but also thoughtful and unusual. "I don't know a lot about photography," he said, "but I think your stuff looks great."

Kevin blushed. "It's just my homework, really. I don't normally show it to anyone else."

"Well I'm glad you did," said Aaron, munching on a cookie. "And now I know what you do in that darkroom."

"Yeah, well I'm sorry I had to cancel last night."

"Don't feel bad," said Aaron. "I know all about the demands of work. Did I tell you about my crazy massage client yesterday?"

Aaron proceeded to tell Kevin the story. Kevin — who had never had a "real" massage — had wondered if Aaron's massage business was strictly non-sexual when he'd heard about it Friday night, but he'd been afraid to ask, worried that it would make him look naive, no matter what Aaron's answer was. Now he knew.

The incident, which had seemed so intense a day earlier, took on the cadence of a joke in the retelling. Aaron stopped at the punch line and turned to Kevin: "I mean, do I *look* like a hustler?"

"How would I know?"

"It's a rhetorical question, sweetie. I mean, what was I supposed to do with him? Jerk him off just because that's what he was expecting?"

"Was he cute?"

"A bit, yes. But that's not the point. I trained a long time to do massage, and what I do is *legitimate* bodywork. It's insulting to be compared to some cheap hustler."

"Yeah," Kevin said, "I get it."

four

Moe was slicing bagels when Gene buzzed at a few minutes past noon on Saturday.

"Hey there, sugar bear," Gene said as he opened the door.

"Come in," Moe said, hugging him in the doorway.

"You look like crap," Gene said, throwing his jacket and bag onto the bed.

It was true enough. Moe hadn't slept well. He'd been worked up the night before over the call he'd gotten from the submissions editor at the *Voice*, rejecting the column he'd taken two solid days (and skipped a graduate seminar) to write. "We've already got a column on the crackdowns," the editor said. "By Emmett Kane. It's slated to run next week." Moe knew Emmett would come out in support of the closures as effective "AIDS prevention" and slam anyone who opposed the mayor's campaign as "irresponsible."

Moe told this to Gene, who tried to console him: "So you can write a letter to the editor next week about Emmett's column. You'll still get your opinion heard."

"Sure, all these letters to the editor, like I'm some old crank sitting by my typewriter with nothing better to do. I sent one letter to *Outrageous* this week, and we'll see if they bother to print that, and I'll send one to the *Voice* next week, and maybe I'll get a hundred words to rebut Emmett Kane's two thousand words. I'm sick of playing defense all the time. It's fucking frustrating. Last night, I was so pissed off, I wasn't even horny. It's like I was beyond sex. I couldn't even think about it. I spent hours scrubbing the shower and reorganizing my desk drawers. I cleaned my fucking oven."

"Do you even *use* your oven?"

"That's not the point."

"I know, you chose oven-cleaning over cocksucking. You *are* upset!" Gene teased.

Moe smiled. "No, I *was* upset. But I'm not going to think about that today. Today, all I want to think about is what this big secret is you've been keeping from me."

Gene sat down at the table and took a sesame seed bagel. He waited for Moe to sit down, too.

"I'm here to look for an apartment," Gene said. "I'm moving to New York."

Moe was stunned. He sat silent for a moment, scanning Gene's face to see if he was serious.

"Why?" Moe asked. "When? Where?"

Gene explained that Final Frontier Travel, the agency in Washington where he had been manager for the last six years, was opening an office in New York. The owner, Eleanor, had plans to turn Final Frontier into a nationwide gay and lesbian — or, as she said, lesbian and gay — travel agency. New York was just the first step. She would commute between the two cities, and Gene would be in charge of day-to-day operations in New York.

"I move up April first," said Gene. "I've got a tenant all lined up to take my place in Washington, but I need to find a place up here pretty quick."

It was happening too fast for Moe to take it all in. He didn't know if he was happy that Gene would be a local call away, or worried about how it would change the rest of his social life. They hadn't lived in the same city since Moe moved to New York to start graduate school two years earlier.

"Why didn't you tell me?" Moe asked. "I could've started looking for you."

"I just found out last week. And I know you're too busy to go house hunting for me, so I've already made an appointment with a real estate agent. I'm meeting him at two."

"This wouldn't happen to be the real estate agent you met at that New Year's Eve party, would it?"

Gene grinned. "His name is Dustin, and yes, it's him. I'm impressed that you remember."

"Sometimes I do listen when we talk on the phone."

"Well, don't be jealous. It's purely business."

"I'm not jealous. Not that I believe for a minute that it's purely business. After the way you went on and on about him after that dinner. So handsome, so sweet, such smoldering eyes."

"Yeah, that's him. I'm hoping he can get me into a studio in a decent neighborhood for less than a thousand a month."

"And you'll sleep with him if that'll help get you a lease."

"Hey, it's a tough market," Gene said. "I'll do what I gotta do."

□ □ □

It was getting dark when Dustin suggested stopping for a drink. He'd been showing Gene apartments all afternoon — six of them to be exact — and nothing seemed right. Gene was hard to please.

"This is more depressing than I thought," Gene said, sitting in the window at Boardwalk, a trendy Chelsea lounge best known for its views of the cruisy Eighth Avenue sidewalk that gave the place its name.

"What you're looking for isn't easy to find," Dustin said. Gene had rejected two apartments for having insufficient closet space, one for lacking a cross-breeze, one for being a sixth-floor walk-up, and two for being "funny-shaped."

"There's more to see tomorrow, right?"

"A few. But they're either out of your price range or a bit further uptown than the ones you saw today. You might have to settle for Hell's Kitchen."

Gene frowned.

"Or maybe I can find something that I overlooked today," Dustin added.

Gene smiled at this and touched Dustin's hand. Dustin blushed. Even though he was smitten, he barely knew this guy. They'd met just once, on New Year's Eve at a party of a mutual acquaintance in Washington. Dustin had been immediately captivated by Gene's striking looks — red hair, strong chin, broad shoulders — but had been too shy to approach. When Gene noticed the glances and came over to chat, Dustin had found himself at a loss for words. Mostly he'd nodded at everything Gene said, answered every question Gene asked, and laughed at Gene's quips. By the end of that night, after an hour of one-sided conversation, Dustin asked if they could go home together, but Gene instead took his number and gave him a kiss good night. He hadn't called.

Faced with a move to Manhattan, however, Gene remembered Dustin's business card and belatedly gave him a call, figuring he might be able to get a good deal on an apartment if he flirted a bit. But he hadn't remembered how sexy Dustin was until he saw him again in person, dressed up in shirt and tie and acting professional as he showed him properties, and now looking longingly in Gene's direction over a beer.

Was this business or pleasure? Gene wasn't sure anymore.

Dustin worked up the courage to ask Gene to dinner.

"I've got plans tonight, actually," Gene said. "I'm going to a show with my ex."

Dustin looked a bit deflated. "Well, I'll meet you tomorrow morning at ten, and we'll check out a few more apartments."

Gene felt bad about declining Dustin's invitation. And he also wanted to keep Dustin interested, in case it might help him find a place to live. He stood up, pulled on his jacket, and leaned down to kiss Dustin on the lips.

"Maybe, if we get done early enough, you can show me *your* apartment," Gene said softly, winking. "Just for the sake of comparison."

□ □ □

Moe was waiting outside the theater, chatting with the publicist, when Gene arrived.

"So how's Dustin?" Moe asked.

"Handsome as ever, thanks for asking. And no, we did not have sex — which I know is your next question."

"Actually, my next question was, Did you have any luck finding a place?"

"Nothing," Gene said. "But I'm meeting him tomorrow morning, and we'll give it another try."

"Maybe you need to adjust your expectations. New York isn't Washington. You're not going to find the perfect apartment in the perfect location for the perfect price. Something's gotta give."

Gene put his hand on Moe's shoulder. "I'm not worried. If I can't find anything, I'll just move in with you for a while."

Moe pushed Gene's hand away. "Actually, you can have the place to yourself, because I'd jump off the roof."

Both chuckled. They'd lived together for a few months before they broke up; Gene remembered it as a fine experiment, but Moe recalled it as a period of unrelenting tension and fighting. Moe's memory was always more accurate, but he often wondered if Gene's rosy hindsight wasn't easier to live with.

"Let's not get into this again. Tonight, let's just enjoy the show," Gene said.

"Maybe you can just enjoy it, but I'm working, remember? While you're making goo-goo eyes at your dreamboat tomorrow, I'll be writing a review of this show for Carolyn."

"Ah yes, work. You seem to have so much play time in New York, sometimes I forget that you do occasionally work."

Moe handed Gene his ticket. "I can hardly wait to have you living here full-time. Now let's go inside and find our seats."

□ □ □

When Aaron arrived at eleven, there wasn't even a line yet outside Slick. He paid his twenty dollars to get past the velvet ropes, another four dollars to check his coat, and another five dollars for a bottle of water. He made his way to the balcony, found a velvet couch in a dark corner with a good view of the main floor, and ensconced himself. Waiting.

The go-go boys climbed up on their boxes around eleven thirty, Kevin had told him. Aaron hadn't mentioned to Kevin that he was going to show up, and Kevin had no reason to think Aaron would ever come to Slick — it wasn't his scene. Thousands of shirtless muscle men, almost all white, most high on Ecstasy or crystal or Special K or all three, dancing to a throbbing, unchanging beat that was unbearably dull to anyone not in an altered state. Aaron loved to dance, but he preferred smaller places with more inventive DJs and lower cover charges.

Still, Aaron was curious. He wanted to see how Kevin — who, despite a bit of cockiness about his body, was basically a shy kid — transformed himself into the object of these men's erections. He wanted to watch Kevin perform. He wanted to see if he could *dance*. So that Kevin wouldn't feel nervous or uncomfortable, he decided to watch from a distance. At least for a while.

Half an hour later, a small crowd had begun to amass downstairs, but most people were standing in the bar area. So the dance floor was relatively clear when three dancers — Kevin, a short and stocky black guy built like a fireplug, and a lean white boy with perfect pecs and a glassy stare — strode out and hopped up on their platforms. An Asian guy, a black guy, and a white guy, Aaron thought — at least they've got diversity *somewhere* in here.

With the dancers in place, people slowly started drifting to the dance floor, if for no other reason than to get a closer look at the boys on the boxes. Despite their different body types and skin tones, all three had physical similarities: defined abs, rounded biceps, and a complete lack of body fat and body hair. Their brief outfits — workboots and short shorts — were variations on a single theme. Each one moved differently, however, as Aaron was quick to notice. The white dancer looked up toward the lights, gyrating slowly and raising his arms over his head. The black guy kept his eyes closed and moved very little, keeping low to the ground and marking the beat with small thrusts of his hips. Kevin was altogether different. He scanned the crowd, making eye contact, running his hands over his body, as if to say to every customer, "These could be *your* hands. Imagine this is *you* touching me."

The customers responded. From his vantage point in the balcony, Aaron could see that Kevin drew the largest group around his platform. Aaron was a bit proud.

Over the next hour, as Aaron watched Kevin from his hidden spot, the dance floor filled up and the music's tempo quickened. The balcony was getting noisy and smoky, and Aaron decided to take a walk around the club.

He surveyed the upstairs lounge, with its chill-out music and tropical-fish aquariums and entirely blue decor. (Too early for chilling out, he noted.) He took a peek in the legendary men's room to see if there really was a bar inside serving drinks (true) and a claw-footed bathtub urinal with access from both sides, so guys could watch the guy across from them piss (also true, simultaneously old-school hot and new-school trendy, but a non-starter for the pee-shy Aaron). He ducked into the Slip & Slide room, a pitch-black area behind the coatroom where guys pushed past the dark red curtain to do what came naturally (or whatever they could manage in their druggy haze).

Within fifteen minutes, after exploring the whole club, he was ready to hit the main dance floor. As one of perhaps five black people in the club, Aaron knew that Kevin would see him immediately. But he thought that Kevin looked confident enough in his performance that he wouldn't be easily flustered by a little surprise.

Kevin didn't miss a beat. He winked at Aaron, and a broad smile crept across his face. As he danced, he kept his eyes focused on Aaron, dancing for him, imagining it was Aaron's hands on his chest, his stomach, his ass. Aaron smiled back, pleased at this silently intimate communication. For a moment he felt bad about monopolizing Kevin's attention — but only for a moment.

Their eyes on each other, Aaron and Kevin danced, together but separately, on different levels. As Kevin caressed his chest, Aaron stripped off his shirt and did the same. For several minutes they danced in synch, the mass of bodies around them melting into the background.

Their wordless connection was only severed when, without warning, the music stopped, the overhead lights came on, and a voice came over the sound system: "This establishment has been closed by order of the mayor of the City of New York. You have fifteen minutes to vacate the premises."

People were utterly confused. Was it a joke? They shielded their eyes from the bright lights and asked their neighbors if this was for real.

Aaron knew it was no joke. He put his shirt back on and held up a hand to help Kevin down from his platform. "I've got to go get my stuff from the coat check, and you've got to get some clothes on. Meet me outside as soon as you can."

Kevin rushed to the back office behind the main bar, threw off his boots and peeled off his shorts, replacing them with his winter street clothes. The other dancers seemed confused; Kevin, by this point, had the most experience when it came to police raids. "Don't worry, it'll all be okay," he told them. "Just take your stuff and get out, and we'll figure out what happens next tomorrow."

"But if everything starts up again later on, we'll need to go back to work," said Antoine, the black dancer.

"I ain't leaving," said Austin, the white dancer. "The manager says we don't get paid unless we work until closing time."

"This *is* closing time, guys," Kevin said. "I'm sure we'll get paid. But tonight is over. Just go home."

While Kevin tried to convince his co-workers that it was okay to leave, Aaron wormed his way to the front of the coat check like a true New Yorker. While most guys were still fishing around for their check stubs, Aaron was already on the sidewalk outside, amid the blinking and buzzing lights of Times Square.

This is just like last weekend, he thought as he waited for Kevin to emerge. There's the line of police cars. There's the stream of guys putting their clothes on in the cold. And there's Frank DeSoto, first on the scene, snapping photos with his pocket camera.

□ □ □

It was after midnight when Gene and Moe got home. After the show, they'd stopped in a piano bar to have a couple of drinks. This was Gene's idea of a good time. Moe liked the music, but he wasn't so keen on the divas and the drunks. Nonetheless, they did this every time Gene came to visit. It was something of a tradition.

By midnight, Gene was ready to hit the sack. He'd had a long day and knew the next day would be just as tiring. More apartment hunting, another train ride. He needed his sleep. He climbed into Moe's bed.

"You're on my side," Moe said. "I always sleep on that side."

"Well, so do I," Gene replied.

"But it's my bed," Moe insisted.

"But I'm the one going to sleep now," Gene countered. "You're probably going to go trolling around for dick. Saturday night in the big city, right?"

"Trolling around for dick isn't something I do on Saturday nights," Moe said. "It's something I do *every* night!"

They laughed.

"Trouble is, I don't have many places to go anymore," Moe explained. "Most of the spots I used to go are closed."

"What about online? I thought that's where you met most of your buddies lately."

"Yeah, but they all come over here. That won't work tonight. I mean, we're close, but we're not that close."

"Not anymore," Gene said. "It's bad enough I have to hear about your escapades. I sure don't want to watch!"

More laughter.

"Maybe you could go online and try to find someone else looking for company," Gene suggested.

"I've never done that."

"First time for everything."

True enough, Moe thought. He left Gene to get comfortable in bed while he logged on to Men Online.

It was an unusual mission for Moe, better known in cyberspace as HotLipsNYC. His list of playmates now totaled 147 (he had added one daddy he met during his Monday night marathon). Only two were logged on — most of his buddies went out on Saturday nights, or stayed at home with their lovers. Both buddies sent him messages instantly, but he told them he wasn't free to host tonight. Then he started scanning profiles.

With a bit of careful searching, Moe found a few guys who wanted a blowjob who were looking for company. One of them seemed particularly promising: DownTheHatch was his screen name. His profile was quick and to the point: "Hairy, muscular, 48, goatee, hung 8 thick. Needs expert draining in the Village. You come here, blow me, and get the fuck out. No pic exchange

— I don't give a shit what you look like. No gaggers, party boys, or chatty queens."

Moe liked the direct approach. He sent him a message.

HotLipsNYC: Hot profile. Looking to service.
DownTheHatch: Cool. You good?
HotLipsNYC: Best in town.
DownTheHatch: We'll see. Come on over.
HotLipsNYC: Where are you?
DownTheHatch: 144 West 4th St. #22
HotLipsNYC: I'm Moe.
DownTheHatch: Max.
HotLipsNYC: See you in 5 minutes.

"Gotta run," Moe told Gene as he logged off the computer.

"That was quick. Took you about six minutes to find someone. What does he look like?"

"He didn't send a picture," Moe replied. "But his profile says he's forty-eight, hairy, and muscular. Sounds good to me."

"But you know that probably means he's fifty-eight, with ear hair and a beer gut."

"That's okay," Moe said. "I'd like that, too."

Moe grabbed his coat and opened the door. "I'll be back soon," he said. Gene rolled over in bed.

This isn't like me, Moe thought as he walked up the block; I'm sure it's not going to work out. He's going to be some horrible toad, or some psychotic ax murderer, or some dizzy queen with a lisp who thinks she's all butch.

Blocking out the voice inside that screamed, "This is a mistake," Moe turned the corner onto West Fourth Street and walked briskly toward Seventh Avenue looking for the exact address. He reached number 144 and buzzed apartment 22. He entered, walked up one flight of steps, and found the apartment door ajar. He walked in, and in the dim light of the cluttered apartment he saw a familiar figure wearing tight jeans and a ribbed tank top cut low enough to reveal a gold chain.

The mystery man. The man Moe had fantasized about, jerked off to for the past two years. Without saying a word that might betray him as a crazed stalker — or, worse yet, a chatty queen — Moe sank to his knees and unbuttoned the man's Levi's.

Max. Mystery solved.

five

This is what makes Moe hard: novelty.

Yes, of course, as hundreds or perhaps thousands of New Yorkers well know, there are certain physical attributes that make Moe hard. Thick forearms. Hairy thighs. Bushy eyebrows. And while his tastes are sometimes unusual, Moe is driven to lust like many other men by more pedestrian, perhaps even cliché, masculine features: broad shoulders, strong jaw lines, uncut penises.

There are certain acts, too, that make Moe hard, and these too are well catalogued in gay New York. By squeezing his nipples (not too hard), licking his ear (not too wet), or kissing the back of his neck, almost anyone — even a man with bony arms, stubbly thighs, and plucked eyebrows — can make Moe hard. It's not that difficult; he's twenty-six years old.

But looking beneath the external fetishes, the mechanical reflexes of sex, it's novelty that really turns Moe on. His sex life to date, which had spanned approximately nine years and three months by the time he met Max, could best be summed up as the constant search for "the new."

If he was still something of a johnny-one-note when it came to sex — as a cocksucker, he had singular interest and focus — it wasn't for lack of trying new things. He had undertaken any number of experiments to widen his sexual repertoire, but they rarely seemed to bear fruit.

He'd gone to his first — and last — piss party at The Backdoor the previous summer. Wearing only a jock strap — Moe's insecurity about his body proved less potent than his embarrassment at bringing urine-soaked clothes to the Laundromat — he had found several men a the club whom he deemed appealing. One of them, a bearish man in his fifties, smelled new meat and came over to play with Moe. Everything seemed to be progressing at an appropriate pace, when the man asked if Moe wanted to get pissed on. "Yeah, I do. That's why I'm here," Moe said. "Then get down on the floor," the piss daddy commanded. "On this floor? But it's filthy!" Moe replied.

"I'm gonna piss all over your face, and you're worried about the floor being dirty?"

"I'm sorry, man," Moe told him. "I've got limits."

Moe had tried bondage with an older man named Ronald who aspired to leather-daddyhood, whom he'd dated for a month when he first came to New York. But Moe could never figure out if he was supposed to lie there passive, immobilized, and accept whatever happened, or if he was supposed to struggle against the restraints, pretending to resist what they both knew he wanted anyway. "You're gonna suck my cock, boy," Ronald had told him sternly, straddling Moe's face as he lay strapped down to the bed. Moe opened his mouth, ready, even eager. "No, no, I'm going to make you do it," Ronald said. Moe broke character: "I'm sorry, Ronald. Can you just tell me how I'm supposed to react? Am I supposed to pretend like I don't want to suck your dick? Or am I supposed to pretend like I'm only doing it because you've got me tied up and I have no choice? Or am I supposed to beg for it while you tease me with it? I'll go along with whatever the scene is, but I need a bit of direction here." Ronald would never believe for one second that Moe didn't want to suck his cock. He was a rotten actor.

He was also unable to pretend that pain was anything more or less than what it was, so his two attempts at S/M — one involving a trick who used a paddle to spank Moe, and the other involving Ronald trying out a leather whip on his back — were both horrible failures. All Moe could say was, "Stop it, that fucking hurts!" And when the beating stopped, he was in no mood for sex.

*The fact that Moe had never gotten in touch with assholes —
his own, or other men's — also limited him when it came to sex.
He had tried most everything at least once. Eating butt turned
him off completely; even getting rimmed left him cold. A finger
up his ass was a sure way to get him to lose his erection — no
matter what the context, it always felt like a medical exam. It
wasn't a question of pain, but of confusion. "With enough K-Y,
you could probably slide your index finger all the way into my
ear canal — but why?" he told a former trick. Needless to say,
fucking was never an appealing idea to Moe, and fisting even
less so. But he tried both — fucking from both sides, fisting from
only one side — in a valiant effort to find something novel.*

Nothing.

*So with his sexual menu reduced to a few key items
— in addition to giving blowjobs as frequently as possible,
occasionally he'd be on the receiving end of one, or jerk off with
someone — Moe had to search for novelty in other ways. New
locations. New combinations. New partners. Lots and lots of
new partners.*

*In Washington, when he was still at George Washington
University, he had discovered the wonder of tearooms. There was
a place right on campus in the student center, third floor, where
he could meet dozens of new guys at any given time. Some were
students, others faculty, others simply visitors looking for a bit of
action with college kids. The primary activity was cocksucking.
There was no need for clever conversation or "compatibility." It
didn't require more than foot-tapping and a bit of patience to
get what you wanted. And it was within walking distance of his
dormitory. It proved a great way to meet men.*

*That's where he met Gene. They were together for nearly
three years, and they were monogamous for most of that time.
That, too, was novel, in a way. For a while. But it was only a
phase.*

*When he left Gene and moved to New York, Moe got back to
his old routine. He found other men's rooms — in department
stores, train stations, and on his new campus at Empire. None*

of them was as reliable as the one in Washington, but he still stopped by occasionally to check on the action.

If Moe developed a taste for glory holes in the tearooms, he found even better ones in the dirty bookstores near Times Square. Filled mostly with straight guys looking for a quick blowjob after work, these booth-shops were Moe's primary entertainment when he first came to the city. He soon broadened his scope to include the triple-X movie theaters, the strip joints, and, when he had cash in his pocket, the baths. All the places that had either closed in the past year or seemed destined to close in the next.

He never got too involved in the bar scene — he didn't like the smoke and didn't like hooking up with drunks — but he did visit a few favorites occasionally. Some of the discos had backrooms where Moe found satisfaction, but these were too expensive to become a regular habit. The remaining leather bars in New York didn't have backrooms, but he could always manage to find someone to sneak into a bathroom stall for a few minutes. If he had failed in his attempts at S/M, he still liked the leather itself. It gave a man a different look, a sexual air, a toughness that was obvious, even if it seemed forced much of the time. "I'm not into leather," Moe said. "I'm into guys who are into leather."

There wasn't much truly public sex left in New York by the time Moe arrived in the mid 1990s; the piers and the trucks were long gone. But Moe still managed to explore Central Park a few times, and played with late-night joggers once or twice, just to try something different. And he visited a handful of ongoing sex parties where the clientele was up his alley — Daddy's Boys, Hairy And Hung, Bare Bears; each had its own crowd of regulars, but also attracted a rotating crop of new guys every month.

Later, Moe got into online sex. Not cybersex, but real sex arranged over the Internet. The fact that he didn't have to leave the comfort of his own apartment was particularly appealing to

Moe, who said, "In New York, you can have everything delivered
— even cock."

Some people found online cruising too reductive, unable to
sum up their complex sexuality in a fifty-word profile. Not Moe.
After writing "best cocksucker in town," he still had forty-six
words to spare. And once guys found out that his description
was accurate, Moe became a very popular man in cyberspace.

For the first year or so, Moe was only on the lookout for
new guys to come to his house and experience his hot lips. But
lately, he'd been trying to find creative ways to interact with
his repeat customers. He'd get a few of them over at the same
time — without telling them, of course, so they'd be surprised
at the scene. He'd organize parties where he'd suck off four or
five or six men in a row. He'd blindfold himself or handcuff his
partner or take a guy onto his roof to breathe new excitement
into a regular visitor's latest session. He'd change the porno
tape, try a straight movie, for a change of pace. On the one
hand, everyone knew what they were going to get when they
visited Moe; the scene remained essentially the same. On the
other hand, there was always some new element, something to
keep it interesting.

With the buddies he liked the most, the ones where he could
sense an unspoken tenderness beneath the surface, he'd recently
begun to change the scene into one he had never discussed or
described in his online profile. Instead of sitting in the chair,
fully clothed, Moe would leave the door open and climb into
bed in his boxers. If the visitor was uncomfortable with the new
scenario when he arrived, he'd sit on the couch as usual and
Moe would get out of bed and revert to the standard script. But
nine times out of ten — Moe was an excellent judge of men —
the man would climb into bed with Moe.

The sex itself was largely the same either way. Whether on
a couch or under the covers, Moe serviced his buddies with
unparalleled selflessness, never asking for reciprocation. But if
sex itself was the same in bed, what followed was vastly different
from the couch scenario. Instead of sitting up and waiting for

the man to leave as soon as he came, Moe would pull up the covers, nestle into the man's arms, and rest his head on his chest. He'd close his eyes as he felt the man's arm around him, the man's hands drowsily rubbing Moe's shoulder and pulling him closer. Moe would imagine that this man was his lover — this man whose name he often did not know for certain, whose professional talents, musical tastes, and political leanings were unknown to him, who more often than not had a lover waiting for him at home. Sometimes, the man would kiss Moe, on the forehead or on the lips. Sometimes, the man would whisper in Moe's ear and tug on a nipple as Moe jerked himself off. Sometimes — this was Moe's deepest desire, his favorite outcome — the man would drift off to sleep. And sometimes, he would not wake up until morning.

Moe knew which guys would spend the night. He kept excellent notes.

When he was younger, he'd tried to keep track of how many men he'd had sex with. He'd gotten the idea from a television special about AIDS where several men talked about having thousands of sexual partners. "That's impossible!" said one of Moe's friends. But when he did the math, it seemed perfectly plausible to him. Even just two guys a week comes out to a hundred a year, he figured, and that comes to a thousand every decade.

For a time, Moe kept a log of his exploits, but he had lost count a few years back. It was hard to keep track in places like tearooms and movie theaters, and difficult to remember who was new and who had already been counted. So he gave up. But he knew that as he approached the end of his first decade as a sexually active man, even taking two years of monogamy into consideration, he'd been averaging more than two men a week.

And the novelty hadn't worn off yet.

SPRING

Moe's years as a journalist had come in handy as he launched his investigation into his fantasy man.

That first night he'd gone over to Max's apartment on West Fourth Street, Moe had been sure to note the name on the mailbox for apartment 22. Milano. Max Milano. He'd gone home after a memorable session and while Gene slept, he'd searched for information on Mr. Milano on the Internet. Turned out Moe's hunch had been correct. Max was involved in theater — as artistic director of the Rainbow Stage, a not-for-profit gay theatrical company in the Village. (Moe had seen one or two decent shows there when he moved to New York, but since *Footlights* focused its reviews on bigger productions, Moe hadn't frequented the Rainbow Stage since then.)

The following week, Moe stopped by the offices of *Footlights* to dig up information in the archives. Apparently Max had a moderately successful run as a director in the 1970s and '80s — mostly off-Broadway, but with two or three shows on the Great White Way — before moving to the low-profile, non-Equity Rainbow Stage. Why, Moe wondered, would anyone voluntarily leave Broadway?

He would have asked Max directly, but they didn't talk much. Moe wasn't even sure if he'd recognize Max's voice on the telephone. It was April already, and they'd been having sex three or four times a week for two months, but they hadn't exchanged more than a couple of sentences in all that time. Moe had never mentioned that he'd researched Max's identity, and Max had never given any indication that he knew so much as Moe's last name — nor that he cared to know. When Moe saw Max sitting in the diner now, he rarely got so much as a nod. If Moe was hoping Max might welcome him with a hug and say, "Why don't you sit down and join me for dinner?" — he'd be hoping a long, long time.

The sex was everything Moe dreamed it would be, so he didn't ask questions. But he was itching to know more, to find out everything about the man he'd watched for two years.

□ □ □

"I don't understand why you're so curious," Gene told him over lunch one Tuesday afternoon. "You sleep with plenty of guys who don't tell you their last names, or anything about themselves."

But somehow this one was different. Max was unlike anyone Moe had ever met over the Internet. Moe thought about him every day and logged on to Men Online every night hoping to find him there, eager to see more of him, taste him again, connect on a deeper level. Max must be satisfied, Moe realized, because he keeps coming back for more. But is he just looking for a great blowjob? Or something more?

Moe wasn't sure what *he* wanted either.

"I've never seen you so worked up over a trick," Gene said. "Usually, when they're out the door, they're off your mind."

This was an exaggeration, but not entirely untrue. "I'm trying to figure it out myself," Moe said. "I'll let you know what I come up with."

"I'm trying to figure out what's up with Dustin," Gene said, switching the subject back to himself. They'd been dating ever since Gene moved into the shoebox studio Dustin had found him in Little Italy a few weeks before. The fact that the place was noisy and cramped was mitigated by its $800 rent; besides, Gene spent most of his time after work hanging out at Moe's place (until Moe would send him home so he could look for Max online).

"You've gone out every weekend since you got here," Moe said. "That's something. You must be interested, right?"

"Well, going out with him is pretty easy. We don't have any arguments, because he goes along with whatever I want to do. I get to pick the movie and the restaurant, we stop at a piano bar afterward even though he doesn't know anything about show tunes, and then we go back to his place, where once again, he does whatever I want." Gene grinned. "Plus, I get to spend the night in his apartment, which is much nicer than mine, and he makes me breakfast. What's not to like?"

"Doesn't sound like much of a challenge," Moe said.

"I've done 'challenging' before," Gene said, looking Moe in the eye. "Maybe it'd be nice to have something a bit less stressful for a change. Don't I deserve a sexy, attentive lover who does whatever I tell him to do?"

"Don't we all?"

□ □ □

After lunch, Gene opened the door to Final Frontier's office, located just off the Eighth Avenue boardwalk in Chelsea, and greeted Ben and Jay, the two young travel agents who worked out front greeting customers and taking calls. Gene had made sure both of them sat by windows. Ben and Jay, he figured, might help bring in street business, since both of the twentysomethings were pretty much eye candy. WASPy Ben, with his blond curly hair and broad smile, sat at one desk, while the dark-haired, Puerto Rican Jay sat facing him, his narrow face accented by a pair of trendy eyeglasses. Gene thought of them as a single unit. Like Salt-N-Pepa.

"Eleanor's waiting for you," said Jay.

"She's in your office," said Ben.

"Thanks, boys," Gene replied. They were friendly, but Gene knew that as a man over thirty (even just barely), he was off their radar.

Gene walked back into his office — actually an area penned off by six-foot-tall partitions, without a real door — and found her sitting at his desk, flipping through his papers.

"Looking for something?" he asked.

Eleanor — whose own office was just a few feet away — turned around, pushed her wire-rimmed glasses up and brushed her limp, gray hair out of her eyes. "No, just checking to see what's been going on the last few days," she answered, turning back to continue her rifling.

"Well, I fixed the problem with our Internet server," Gene said, "and switched our phone service like you wanted, and hired a new cleaning crew, and ordered a new sign for the front door."

"All since we talked yesterday?"

"Yup."

"Well, it looks like you're getting things whipped into shape up here. Not that I had any doubts. How's life outside the office? You settling into New York yet?"

"That part's been pretty easy. I've got Moe here, and I've been dating this guy, and you know, it's New York. There's always plenty to do. You never get bored."

"That's what they say," said Eleanor. "Although I've personally never been a fan. It's too noisy here, too crowded. A few days a week is all I can handle. Give me Washington any day. Rock Creek Park, the monuments, the Smithsonian. What does New York have that can beat all that?"

Outside the doorway of his office, Gene glimpsed a customer talking to Ben and Jay. He was easily six feet tall, with black wavy hair, and muscle definition that was visible even under his V-neck sweater. As Gene's gaze roamed over the man's body, he turned, noticed Gene staring, and winked.

"Gene?" Eleanor asked, snapping her fingers.

"I'm sorry," said Gene. "What were you saying?"

□ □ □

"I don't have much time, Frankie," said D.C. as he walked into Boss Tweed. "Campaign's kicking into high gear. Not that I think there's any real threat, but you know, this is New York. Always an uphill battle for a Republican."

"I imagine that's true," said Frank. He'd voted against the mayor in the last election — he always voted Democratic — but he had to admit he was pretty happy with how things had run during his first term.

D.C. ordered his usual martini. "So tell me why you called, Frankie. And make it quick. I'm a busy guy." His tone was more brusque than usual. No small talk about the newspaper or Katie. Ten seconds and down to business.

Frank cleared his throat. "Well, now that it's spring, and the weather is getting warmer, everyone's spending more time outside," he began. "I don't know if you know this, but a lot of men cruise Central Park looking for sex."

"Who'd walk around Central Park at night?"

"Actually, since the mayor has been so successful at fighting crime, a lot of people aren't afraid of Central Park the way we were twenty years ago. Any warm night, you'll find dozens of guys cruising a part of the park called the Ramble."

"So it's a gay thing."

"Mostly it's closet cases who aren't out, or people too ashamed to deal with their sexuality openly," Frank said. He knew this wasn't entirely true; there were plenty of openly gay men who cruised there — he'd cruised there himself with Scott many years ago. But he thought it was best to keep the message simple.

"This is petty shit, Frankie, go talk to the cops," D.C. said with a dismissive wave of his hand.

Frank didn't want to go to the police. Arresting a handful of closet queens wouldn't kill the Ramble — they'd just come back the next night. He wanted to make it clear that the city wouldn't tolerate this kind of behavior, with a big public move that would clear the park for good. "It could be part of his plan to clean up New York. Part of a campaign to make

Central Park safe for all New Yorkers. And, at the same time, part of his AIDS awareness program, by eliminating this place where guys have sex without protection. It's a public health nightmare, and a big quality of life issue, and both of those have the mayor's name written all over them."

D.C. wasn't biting. "Look, Frankie, I've gone along with a lot of things you've suggested in the last year. But you've got to stop relying on the mayor to do your dirty work."

"What do you mean?"

"Remember that big raid on that disco in February? You were sure that nobody would complain. But it made pretty nasty headlines and turned a lot of people off. The *Voice* called him a Nightlife Nazi, and even the *Times* said that the crackdown had gone too far. You got what you wanted, but the mayor got burned."

Frank had read the headlines. He had cheered the move in *Outrageous*. But the alternative press, which had ignored the crackdown until that point, took offense, and reporters were watching the mayor more closely now. There hadn't been any more closures since that one two full months ago.

"That's all blown over by now," Frank offered. "And nobody's going to stand up and defend closet cases cruising Central Park."

"I don't know if all the bad press was a fluke, or if you snowed me into thinking it'd be a snap. But either way, my top priority is to protect the mayor. I can't risk getting him into hot water because of your personal crusade."

Frank had prepared more arguments for tackling the Ramble. But it was clear that D.C. wasn't open to hearing them, so Frank sat there in silence.

D.C. checked his watch. "I've got to get running, Frankie. I promised Katie I'd make it home for dinner once this week."

He put ten bucks on the bar and walked out without a handshake, before Frank could think of a single thing to say.

As he sat at the bar alone, sipping his ginger ale, Frank thought, If D.C. can't help me anymore, I'll have to find another approach.

□ □ □

Kevin was waiting in front of the Triangle Center when the Alliance meeting ended at seven. Aaron and Moe walked out first, rolling their eyes.

"What's wrong?" Kevin asked.

"It's impossible to get a room full of fags to agree on anything, that's what's wrong," said Moe.

"We were trying to plan this teach-in for later this month, the one about how protease inhibitors affect HIV transmission, whether guys with no viral load can still infect people," Aaron explained. "But all anyone wants to do is argue."

"About what?"

"We'll talk over dinner," Aaron said. "Is pizza okay?"

While Moe chattered for a few minutes about a big presentation he was working on for Melody Penn's class — he was nervous, because she hadn't like most of his previous proposals — the three of them walked toward Sixth Avenue to a new coal-oven pizzeria that was getting good word of mouth.

Inside, they sat in a booth, Moe on one side and Kevin on the other. Aaron scooted in next to Moe, so it'd be easier to look directly at Kevin.

Moe had never seen Aaron so hung up on anyone. From the handful of times they'd met, Moe already sensed that Kevin was a good sort who wasn't going to jerk anyone around. Mature for his age.

They ordered a pie, and Aaron explained what the arguments had been about at the Alliance meeting. A couple of the old-school AIDS activists — negative themselves — were worried that safe-sex messages needed to be reinforced rather than muddled, while a couple of positive guys countered that being able to fuck without infection was perhaps the greatest reason to take the new medications and lower their viral loads. There was a debate over whether to have a speaker specifically about barebacking; some members thought discussing it might make it seem like the group endorsed it, while others said that people were already doing it and it was the Alliance's responsibility to help them do it in an informed way. And, of course, there were the usual debates about the publicity materials, the time, and the refreshments.

"I'm just glad we're not on the planning committee again," Moe said.

"I don't think they'd let us on the planning committee if we wanted to be," said Aaron.

"Fine by me," said Moe. "I don't care a whole lot about this stuff. Not really up my alley. I wouldn't even go if Gene didn't want to check it out. He's been doing pretty well on his cocktail now that they've got the right combination for him, and he'd like to hear what other people have to say about safe sex for poz guys."

"I didn't know Gene was positive," Kevin said. He'd only met Gene once, when the four of them went out to dinner at the end of March. This was the closest he'd been to someone who was positive.

"He's never been seriously ill," Moe said. "He's been on meds for a few years. There were some problems at first — trouble sleeping, impotence, horrible dreams, numbness in his feet, those weird hollow cheeks. But all that's pretty much under control now thanks to those new protease inhibitors, and he's doing okay. His viral load's been way down lately. His doctor thinks he might even get an undetectable viral load if he can get his medications just right."

Kevin was silent.

Aaron sensed his discomfort and decided to change the subject. "I'm tired of talking about all that. Tell us what you did today, honey."

Kevin told them about the photography class he had that afternoon, the one his adviser taught. "I need to figure out my final project by next week. It's got to be something good, too, since this is my last semester. Something that stands out."

"Any ideas?" Moe asked.

"No. That's the problem."

"If I had a camera, I'd be taking pictures of naked guys," Moe said. "You'd have the perfect pickup line: 'Can I take your picture? It's for a class.' You could choose any guy on the street that you wanted to see naked and I bet you dollars to doughnuts you could get him to take his clothes off for you."

Kevin didn't generally have a hard time getting hot guys to take their clothes off for him *without* a camera, but he didn't mention that. "Interesting idea, but I don't think a porno shoot is exactly what my professor is looking for."

"Too uptight?" Moe asked.

"Actually that's not the problem. There's just not enough subtext there. It'd be fun to take the pictures, but I'm not sure she'd be impressed."

"That's a shame," Moe said. "I was going to volunteer to be the fluffer."

Aaron chimed in. "Girl, you've been a fluffer for years now, even without any photo shoot."

They all laughed. Then the ringing started.

"Shit, that's me," Kevin said, pulling his cell phone out of his jacket. "I thought I turned the ringer off. I'm sorry."

"That's okay, you can answer it, we don't mind," Moe said.

Kevin pushed out of the booth and headed toward the door. "I hate it when people do this, but I should see who it is. I'll be right back." And he was out the door, just as the waiter brought the pizza.

Aaron's good mood had evaporated; he sat squinty-eyed, watching Kevin through the window.

"What's wrong?" Moe asked. "It's just a phone call."

"I wonder if it's really just a phone call," Aaron said. "He got a call when he was at my house Sunday afternoon, and he stepped into the hall to take it. When he came back in, he said it was someone from school and he had to run to the photo lab. It sounded fishy to me. But he was gone before I could ask him any more questions."

"Did you ask him about it later?"

"Yeah I did, but he stuck to his story about needing to get to the lab in a hurry."

"Maybe he's telling the truth."

Aaron took a slice of pizza. "I don't think the photo lab is even open on Sundays."

"I see. So where do you think he went?"

"I don't know, but if he walks in here and says he's got to run again, I'll know something is going on."

Kevin opened the door and stuffed his cell phone into his pocket. "Pizza's getting cold, sweetie," Aaron said as he walked toward the booth.

"I'm sorry, but I'm gonna have to run. Last-minute opening at the photo lab again. I'll just grab a slice and go."

He took a piece of pizza on a napkin and leaned over to give a quick kiss to Moe and a longer one to Aaron. Aaron gave Kevin his cheek: "Call me later tonight, okay?"

"I'll try," he answered. "Sorry to run. I'll see you soon, Moe."

And he was off.

"You're right," Moe said to Aaron. "Something's going on."

"I don't know what it is, but I'm gonna get to the bottom of it, and quick."

□ □ □

Max's visits to Moe's house had developed into a familiar pattern, and this Tuesday night was no exception.

When he got home after the Alliance meeting, Moe logged onto Men Online and checked to see if Max was there. If Max wasn't around, Moe would play with his usual list of men, who were as anxious as ever for another shot at that incredible mouth.

But Max was indeed online. He sent Moe a message immediately.

DownTheHatch: You home?
HotLipsNYC: Yup.
DownTheHatch: 5 minutes?
HotLipsNYC: Yup.

Okay, so he wasn't much of a conversationalist. In fact, the only conversation they'd had that lasted more than fifteen seconds was when Moe convinced Max that his apartment on Cornelia Street would be more comfortable for hooking up. (Max, looking around his bedroom, cluttered with papers and books, had conceded without argument.)

Moe turned on the TV, rewound the porno tape in the VCR, dimmed the lights, and waited. When Max rang, Moe buzzed him up, opened the door, pressed the play button on the VCR, and went to wait in his chair.

And it was the same as usual with Max: sex in three rounds.

Round one took four minutes — Moe could tell by the timer on the VCR. Max came in, hung his leather jacket on the doorknob, and walked wordlessly to Moe. Without sitting down, he opened his fly and took out his uncut dick. Moe, still seated in the chair, blew him. For Max, this first time was just warming up.

For round two, Max peeled off all his clothes, revealing the body that Moe longed to worship. He sat on the couch, legs apart, and watched the movie silently while Moe knelt before him and started again. He took it slow this time, pulling out some of his patented tricks that he used to drive men crazy. It took Max seventeen minutes to climax.

But if Max seemed spent after shooting twice, the scene wasn't over yet. He moved to the bed for round three, lying on his back with his hands behind his head. Here, Max finally relaxed into the moment — the first two orgasms apparently lessened the edge a bit — and Moe could do almost anything he wanted. He spent half an hour nuzzling Max's balls, licking his armpits, chewing his nipples, and sucking his toes. Whatever it took to get Max hard yet again. Max just lay there, accepting the pleasure without comment. When he was ready, he flipped Moe over onto his back, straddled his face, and popped his cock into Moe's mouth. As Moe worked to get load number three out of Max, he looked up at him. Max rarely made eye contact in return, but that only gave Moe a greater opportunity to ogle him.

What turned Moe on the most, though, wasn't Max's rock-hard stomach, or his dense goatee, or the pelt of dark hair covering his chest. The thing that pushed Moe's buttons the most was the gold crucifix Max wore on a gold chain. He never took it off, and every time Moe looked up when he was blowing Max, he'd see the cross resting between Max's pecs.

He isn't just a goy, Moe thought, gazing up from between Max's thighs. He *advertises*. With that in his mind, Moe pushed Max's cock deeper into his throat, and sent Max right over the edge.

SEVEN

When Aaron opened his eyes on Monday morning, Kevin was already awake, sitting up.

"What time is it?" he asked, sure that he must have overslept.

"It's not even eight o'clock, don't worry. Your first massage isn't until ten. You're not late for anything."

"Then why are you awake? Are you okay?"

"Better than okay," Kevin said. "I just couldn't sleep. I was thinking."

"About what?"

"About Moe," said Kevin.

I must be sleepy, Aaron thought, because that doesn't make any sense. He sat up. "What about him?"

"I think he might be onto something with his idea about my final project. I didn't take him seriously last night, but now I think he's on the right track."

"The porno idea? Honey, he was only joking."

"No, no, not exactly his porn idea. But that got me thinking. I could do a photo project *about* porn, one that comments on the conventions of erotic photography, that isn't necessarily porn itself."

"You've lost me."

Kevin explained further, hurriedly, getting more excited as he talked it through. His idea was to do a mock porn shoot, one that was completely typical in most ways, with some of the most common poses and settings and angles, but featuring a model who challenged all of porn's underlying assumptions about physical beauty. It would simultaneously mimic pornography's conventions and undermine them, all the while highlighting the power of photography to define and redefine objects of people's erotic gaze. Or so Kevin hoped.

"Interesting," Aaron said. "Think your professor will go for it?"

"I think so. If I do it right."

"You've only got a few weeks to get it done, though. Where are you going to find a model?"

"Moe," said Kevin.

"Moe? Sweetie, have you seen the men Moe picks up? None of them is someone I'd want to see naked."

Kevin clarified: "I'm going to ask Moe to model."

"I'm not sure that's going to work."

"But he'd be perfect. He's completely nontraditional as a porn star. The fact that he's a guy is the first thing, but plenty of guys are still stereotypical sex objects in front of the camera. Moe's unusual because he's got a different body. He's hairy, he's not particularly muscular, he's got a belly..."

"I'm sure if you put it to him like that, he'll go along in a second."

"You know what I mean," Kevin continued. "He goes against type for the average model, but he's still got a serious sexual energy. Before I knew him, I never would have thought that a guy who looked like him would get much play, but he has sex all the time. That's because of his energy, and that's sure to come through in the photos."

Aaron was skeptical. "Even if you're right about him being a good choice, I don't think he'll go along with it. You think Moe has a great self-image, but he doesn't. He's very insecure about his body. Telling him that he's perfect for your project because he's so *unsexy* won't do wonders for his ego."

"There's one thing you're forgetting," Kevin said. "Above all else, Moe is a ham. I noticed it the first time I met him. He loves to be the guy speaking in front of a room, getting cruised in the middle of a meal, getting checked out on the streets.

He loves attention above all else, and I'll bet he jumps at the chance to take his clothes off for the camera. In fact, I think it'll boost his ego just to be asked."

He had a point. "Maybe you're right," said Aaron. "Just make sure it's clear that this was your idea, and leave me out of it."

"Deal," said Kevin. "Now are you getting up?"

Aaron pulled Kevin back onto the futon. "No, sweetie, all this talk about porn has made me horny."

Kevin reached down and felt Aaron's erection under the blanket. "Apparently so," he said. "What do you want me to do about it?"

There were multiple answers to that question, and Kevin obliged every one. He caressed Aaron's cock in his hands. He lay on top of Aaron and rubbed both their cocks against their flat, smooth stomachs. He put Aaron's cock in his mouth, putting his own in Aaron's mouth at the same time. Lastly, he slipped a condom over Aaron's cock, lubed it up, and sat himself down on it, using every bit of fine-tuned muscle control he had perfected to squeeze and tease Aaron's cock inside him, as Aaron looked up in delight at Kevin's taut body above him. Only when Aaron could truly take no more did Kevin increase the pressure and the speed, bringing Aaron to a climax inside him as he shot his own load across Aaron's chest, hitting him on the chin.

After they caught their breath and wiped up with a nearby washcloth, Aaron hopped out of bed and gave Kevin a kiss. "I'm going to shower."

"I'll make the bed," Kevin said.

Aaron didn't object. He'd been sore at Kevin for canceling their plans at the last minute on Saturday night — the lab again — but Kevin had made it up to him by coming over Sunday night with Mexican food and a video of *My Beautiful Laundrette*, a movie Aaron had raved about but Kevin had never heard of. Aaron had intended to confront Kevin about bagging out the night before, but he'd melted when faced with black-bean burritos and a heartfelt apology. This morning, with Kevin's devoted attention, Aaron thought perhaps he'd let Saturday night slide.

The hot water always took a minute or two to reach his fifth-floor walkup, so Aaron brushed his teeth while he waited. Standing naked in front of the mirror, he scanned his body as he brushed. His stomach was itchy, and he could see in the mirror that he had a rash around his waistline. He turned on the light under the medicine chest to get a closer look, and that's when he realized that he had visitors.

Tiny, creepy-crawly visitors.

He turned off the water, wrapped his towel around his waist, and strode out into the kitchen.

"Take off your underwear," he said to Kevin.

"Ooh, he's gotta have it!" Kevin replied with a smile.

"I'm serious, take them off," Aaron said, and when Kevin didn't move, Aaron reached over and pulled them down himself.

"We can go back to bed if you want."

"That's not what I'm doing," said Aaron. "Turn around so I can see you in the light better."

Aaron crouched down. Kevin still expected Aaron to take his penis in his hand or put it in his mouth, but Aaron simply moved his face closer to Kevin's crotch.

"You've got them too," he said brusquely.

"I've got what?"

"Crabs," said Aaron. "You've got crabs, and so do I."

"Oh, shit! Do you have any idea where you got them?"

"I've got a pretty good idea," said Aaron, looking Kevin in the eye. "I think you've got a pretty good idea too. And you're going to tell me all about it."

Kevin gulped and reached down to pull up his briefs.

"First, though, you're going to run downstairs to the Duane Reade and buy two bottles of Rid while I strip the bed. Then, after we've both shampooed, we're going to have a little talk."

□ □ □

"So who is he?" Aaron asked, sitting down on the futon, which he had folded back into a couch. Kevin, coming out of the bathroom in his towel, had just finished the first antilice shampoo of his life; he didn't respond.

Aaron continued: "I assume from these little critters that you've been seeing someone else — because I know I haven't. And I have the right to know who I'm competing against. So let's just get it all out in the open. Who is he?"

Kevin, standing in his towel, remained silent. He looked at the floor.

Aaron picked up again: "Am I going to have to put all the pieces together here? This is the same guy who's been calling you on your cell phone, making dates with you. The one you run off to see whenever you tell me you're working in the lab. The one you stood me up for on Saturday night. Am I right?"

Still nothing from Kevin.

"I don't know why I didn't figure it out before. Maybe I just didn't want to see it. Now that I think about it, I probably don't need to ask if it's serious, because I can think of three times in the last few weeks alone that you've ditched me to go be with him. So I suppose you've already made your choice, right?"

Kevin's lip started to quiver. And then he started to cry. "It's not like that."

"Oh, isn't it?" Aaron prodded.

"No, you've got it all wrong," Kevin sobbed. "You're the only guy I'm dating. I don't want to be with anyone else."

"Then what exactly is going on? And don't tell me you picked up crabs at the gym, because I'm not buying it."

"I've been hustling," Kevin said, and then waited a moment for Aaron to take in the words.

"You've been what? For how long?"

"Ever since I've been in school," Kevin said, sitting down on the futon next to Aaron but still avoiding eye contact. "That's where I've been going. And that must be where I got crabs. If I'd known I had them, I never would have come over."

"Well, in a way, maybe it's a good thing you did, or else I never would have found out the truth," said Aaron. "Why the hell didn't you tell me this? You've had two months to tell me."

"I didn't think you'd understand."

"Of course I understand why people hustle," Aaron said. "I'm not judgmental about that kind of thing."

Kevin looked him in the eye. "Actually, you are. I know you don't think you look down on guys for hustling or dancing in clubs, but you do, underneath all your politics and theorizing about 'the commodification of sex.' "

"Don't you blame this on me."

"I'm not blaming you, I'm just explaining why it was hard to talk about. I wanted to tell you when we first met, but I was afraid. In fact, I'm still afraid."

"Afraid of what?"

"Afraid that you'll leave," said Kevin. "I've never dated anyone for this long. I know two months seems like nothing, but it's the longest I've ever been with anyone. I really care about you, and I didn't want to blow it."

"You might have blown it anyway."

"See? That's what I was afraid of."

"No, you didn't blow it by hustling, or even by giving me crabs — even though that's not winning you any gold stars. You blew it by sneaking around behind my back, lying to me, and making me feel like I wasn't important to you."

"I promise I'll be completely up-front with you from now on," said Kevin, who was still sniffling. "No more secrets."

Aaron put a hand on his shoulder — the first time he'd touched him — and said, "It might be too late for that."

Kevin's eyes widened.

Aaron took his hand away: "It's been a pretty crazy morning. You should go home, and give me some time to think. I'll call you in a day or two."

Kevin got up without a word and put on the clean sweatpants and T-shirt that Aaron had laid out for him. He slung his bag over his shoulder and walked out without looking back.

□ □ □

Frank missed the closures. The blare of sirens, the slamming of doors, the sounds of shifty lowlifes scurrying away as the police turned on the lights. *That* was front-page news.

But there hadn't been a closure in weeks; the mayor was laying low on that front. So instead of ranting about the sex clubs again, the new issue of *Outrageous* lambasted MIGHT for its latest round of educational materials, which Frank deemed wishy-washy and complacent. "AIDS Group Fails To Sound Alarms On Drugs, Barebacking," read the front page headline.

He had already written the next issue's lead article, about the growth in online chat rooms devoted to barebacking. He'd spent two months lurking undercover in these chat rooms, learning about bug-chasers (negative men who intentionally try to get infected) and gift-givers (positive men who oblige). He'd done anonymous interviews, taken notes on what he'd witnessed, written down details taken from people's profiles. He'd already written the headline: "New Route Opens for HIV Transmission: The Internet."

Two weeks from now, he'd have extensive coverage of the Alliance's so-called "teach-in," where, he was certain, a bunch of positive men were going to rationalize their reasons for throwing caution to the wind. The event would take place Saturday, after his deadline, but he'd be sure to do some in-depth analysis the next week.

He called Emmett Kane to ask if he'd contribute an op-ed piece for that issue. As a therapist, Emmett was in a perfect position to speculate about why positive men seemed so driven toward irresponsibility. In the old days, of course, guys contracted HIV without knowing what hit them — just the way Scott did. But now, these positive guys were looking for any excuse to share their misery, and negative guys were just as happy to engage in unsafe behavior, no matter what the consequences. Had living with HIV become so normalized that people didn't see that their behavior was reckless? Or were the people who were seroconverting so reckless to begin with that they made a conscious decision to disregard what they knew about safety?

"The biggest part of it is generational," Emmett told Frank, sliding into therapist mode. "It's the younger generation trying to rebel against the older generation — people like you and me."

Frank, who was some fifteen years younger than Emmett, wasn't wild about being lumped together like this, but he didn't say anything.

Emmett continued: "These kids see safe sex as something older guys whipped up to prevent them from having the great time that we had in the '70s. To them, it looks like we had all the fun, and now we're telling them that they can't do the same in the '90s. What they're missing is that a lot of the guys who were having the fun in the '70s are dead."

Not all of them, Frank thought. But most. The ones who mattered. Scott.

"Another part is that we've made HIV seem like no big deal," Emmett continued. "You take a few pills, and you go on with life. Nothing to lose sleep over. Years ago, we knew how serious it was, because we saw people dying. Those of us with positive friends still know how serious it is, because we still see people dying. But these kids don't see what we've seen. They don't see where the path they're on is leading."

"Then we've got to show it to them," Frank said.

But how?

□ □ □

The afternoon seemed to be moving in slow motion. Would five-thirty never come?

Melody Penn's Queer Theory class had started in unremarkable fashion: her brief introduction to the subject at hand — "theorizing history," a few kiss-ass remarks from some of her pet students, Aaron walking in late. Nothing unusual so far.

Fifteen minutes into the class, it was time for Moe's presentation. This, too, should have been nothing but routine. Each week, a student gave a ten-minute presentation critiquing a book related to that session's theme. Moe had read *Greek to Me*, a book examining homosexuality in Ancient Greece.

The author's premise was that although homosexuality — male homosexuality, at any rate — was widespread in Ancient Greece, there was no "gay identity" that would be recognizable to people in modern-day America. Homosexuality was the norm in Greece, entirely one-sided in terms of activity (free men fucked young boys and slaves), and didn't preclude heterosexual marriage; today, of course, gayness was a minority identity, gay men were sexually flexible (at least potentially), and most gay men lived outside heterosexual marriage. So homosexuality in Ancient Greece was not identical to gayness today.

This was presented as a radical argument delivered against an overwhelming tide of dissenting public opinion. The way Moe figured it, though, nobody ever seriously thought that Ancient Greece and modern Greenwich Village were even remotely culturally similar, so the entire "radical argument" was being waged against a conventional wisdom that didn't exist. Had anyone actually made a case that modern gay life could be traced back two thousand years? Comparing gay life today to gay life *twenty* years ago seemed like a reach. The entire premise of the book was based on beating up a straw man.

The truly interesting part of the book, Moe told the class, was that in the midst of his insipid argument, the author acknowledged in passing that there was indeed a small minority of men in Ancient Greece who were sexually versatile, slept with each other rather than their slave boys, and avoided marriage and sex with women. These men had a completely separate identity and different set of sexual behaviors from the majority of Greek men, who considered themselves "normal," had families, and fucked boys on the side. But after mentioning these unusual men, the author dismissed them, because they basically disproved his central argument.

"*Greek to Me* ends up failing in two important ways," Moe said. "First, it spends too much time defending a position that has no opponents in the first place, and then, seemingly by accident, it stumbles across a case that undermines this entire argument — finding amazing parallels to modern gay life that haven't been widely discussed before — but the author decides to drop this interesting and unusual story to return to hammering home his seemingly obvious, albeit now much less clear-cut, conclusions."

With that, Moe took his seat again and waited for the discussion. This won't take long, he thought; I've done everything Professor Penn likes: I examined the book critically, supported my assertions, and explained how the scholarship might be improved.

But Professor Penn was not happy. Instead of letting the other students ask questions and make comments, she started herself: "Moe, I'm very disappointed in this presentation. It seems that after three months in this class, you're still heavily invested in the so-called 'gay community.' We've discussed at great length how this notion of gayness has been socially constructed, as well as the concept of community in general. These aren't naturally occurring categories — they're strategic, politically useful shorthand perhaps, but they're not real. The gay community has no history that predates the invention of the term itself; the words created an illusion, but they're only words. You stood here just now and made the argument that the gay community is over two thousand years old. That makes me think that you didn't learn anything from this book. And maybe that you haven't learned anything from this class."

Moe was dumbstruck. She had never reacted like this to a student presentation. He didn't know what to say. Nobody else spoke up.

She continued. "I want to know why you're so invested in finding historical precedents for your modern identity."

She waited for an answer.

What could he say? Moe didn't believe there was much history to the "gay community" as it currently existed. He didn't believe there were pride parades and rainbow flags and leather bars in Ancient Greece. But he didn't believe, either, that the notion of gay identity had materialized out of thin air. And if there was any sort of precursor in past cultures — bearing any similarity at all — wasn't that interesting enough to warrant attention?

He responded: "I'm not looking for precedents. I'm just trying to figure out why some theorists are so invested in *ignoring* whatever precedents may or may not exist."

"You're looking at ancient history through the eyes of a gay man in the late twentieth century," she said.

"Of course I am," he said.

"You're searching for things that aren't there," she said.

"No, I'm just opening my eyes to see things that *might* be there."

She wouldn't relent. She spent the next half hour in a one-on-one argument with Moe, berating him for being a political throwback, too '70s in his outlook, too hung up on his own personal identity.

It was Moe's nightmare. All he wanted was to move on to another subject, leave the class, never see Melody Penn again.

After half an hour, she opened the discussion to his classmates. Most of them quickly chimed in to agree with the professor — they knew by now what she wanted to hear and were only too willing to parrot it back.

Moe looked to Aaron to help him. But Aaron, once again, was silent. He didn't even seem to be paying attention.

103

When the class finally ended at five-thirty, Moe was on the verge of tears. Professor Penn could be tough, he knew, but he'd never seen her pillory a student like that in front of the class.

Moe walked out quickly, alone. Lisa, one of the ass-kissers, caught up with him on the stairs.

"That was ugly," she said. "I'm sorry you got put through that."

"Thanks," Moe said, wondering why she hadn't spoken up to defend him. She had remained quiet, which was better than some, but no help. "I've never seen her go off on someone like that before."

"Didn't you know you were crossing a line?" Lisa asked.

"What are you talking about?"

"The author of that book was Professor Penn's adviser at Yale. He's the one who got her through grad school and helped get her this position. She loves that guy."

"If I'd known that…" Moe began, but as he said it, he realized he wasn't sure if he would have changed his presentation even if he had possessed this bit of important information.

As Lisa walked away, Aaron came up next to Moe and put a hand on his shoulder.

"Are you okay, honey? That was pretty brutal."

"I can take it, as long as I know I've got people backing me up," Moe said sarcastically. "So thanks for your support in there."

"Look, I want to apologize," Aaron said. "It's been a horrible day for me, too. I've got a lot of things on my mind."

"Uh huh."

"You want to grab a coffee, sweetie?" Aaron asked. "I'll tell you about what happened this morning. It's the kind of story you'd appreciate."

Moe turned to Aaron. "Go fuck yourself," he said, "*sweetie.*"

He left Aaron standing in the stairwell as he stormed off. What he really wanted to do was take out his aggression on some willing cocksucker at the Mint Theater, but it had gone out of business. Ditto the last dirty bookstore near Union Square. So Moe suppressed his libido and swallowed his anger and walked home to change into nicer clothes and a sunnier mood.

□ □ □

With the help of a quick shot of vodka at his apartment, Moe had calmed down considerably by the time he reached the Guttmachers' "classic six" co-op on West Eighty-second Street.

Normally, Moe would have gone home for Passover, but this year he'd told his parents that he couldn't afford to miss class. After this afternoon's fiasco, he was wishing he'd made a different decision, but staying in New York for Passover had seemed like the best option at the time.

When he'd spoken to Carolyn the week before and mentioned that he didn't have plans for the holiday, she invited him to come with her to her parents' house. So here he was, just a couple of hours after his disastrous afternoon at the university, sporting his neatest clothes and his biggest smile, celebrating the first Seder at the Guttmachers'.

It was a small gathering — Carolyn, her parents, her brother and sister-in-law, and a college-age cousin who was attending Barnard. Moe had known Carolyn for two years, had met her father Abe twice in the office at *Footlights*. Everyone else was new to him, but like any good Jewish family, they welcomed with open arms any Jewish acquaintance who was "orphaned" for the holiday.

At Moe's parents' house outside Baltimore — although he was now a "secular" Jew, he'd been raised Conservative — the Seder was a much bigger affair, with two dozen relatives and friends of the family, lasting many hours and including a broad assortment of prayers, songs, and recitations in English, Hebrew, and Aramaic. The Guttmachers were Reform, and their Seder was a simpler affair. After a few quick readings in English, a handful of prayers in Hebrew (spelled out phonetically in their hagaddahs), they were ready for "the festive meal." Moe's family would have taken an hour and a half to get through the first half of the Seder; the Guttmachers took about twenty minutes. Not that Moe minded.

The meal itself was quite similar to the one Moe's mother made: matzo ball soup, turkey with stuffing made from matzo farfel, sweet potatoes, and white potatoes. Pretty heavy stuff, but delicious. Moe felt at home.

During the meal, the table split into two or three conversations. Moe was seated between Carolyn and her father, an old-school Upper West Side Jewish liberal who had worked in newspapers for thirty years. In addition to *Footlights*, he published the *West Side Citizen*, the *East Side Report* (which was mostly the same as the *Citizen*, with different ads and a different cover), and a dance-oriented magazine called *Step*.

With her shoulder-length, straight brown hair and angular face, Carolyn physically resembled her mother more than her father, with his wavy gray hair, chubby face, and teeth yellowed from smoking. In terms of attitude, however, she was clearly her father's daughter — both were driven and direct, unlikely to suffer fools but quick to support anyone they favored. She was clearly her father's daughter — which was why they worked together well, even if they bickered.

"We're glad you could join us, Moe," Abe said as he passed Moe the sweet potatoes.

"Yeah, my parents always wanted me to bring home a nice Jewish boy," Carolyn — over thirty and still single — said in Moe's other ear.

"Mine, too," said Moe.

She laughed.

"Carolyn tells me that you've been quite upset with the state of gay journalism in New York," Abe said. "Is it that bad?"

"You'd be surprised," said Moe. "We have a bar rag called *The A-List* — which is fine for what it is, but it's not a newspaper —

and then we have this one awful paper called *Outrageous*, run by an old-time activist who's so burned out, he thinks being radical means shouting the loudest. He's archconservative in many ways, and nobody reads his paper or advertises in it. But it's the only thing we've got right now."

Carolyn piped in. "Don't forget, Moe, that there are plenty of other publications with gay content, gay editors, and gay readers. Like the *Voice*."

Abe nodded: "That's true."

Moe had heard this before. "It's great that places like the *Voice* cover gay issues once in a while, but that's not the same thing as having a community newspaper," he said. He turned to Abe. "The *Times* does a lot of reporting on Jewish issues, and has dozens of Jewish writers and a ton of Jewish readers, but you wouldn't say that means a Jewish press is obsolete, would you?"

"Good point," said Abe, who read the Jewish press only occasionally, but subscribed to three or four Jewish publications nonetheless.

"Besides, sometimes those other papers are a bit hazy on where gay politics should be right now," Moe continued. "For instance, Emmett Kane wrote a piece in the *Voice* last month..."

"I read that," said Carolyn.

"Me, too," said Abe. "Was there a problem with that? I know Emmett Kane is a well-respected gay activist. I've read his stuff in the *Voice* before, and in the *Times*, too. If I remember, this piece was about fighting AIDS, right? What was the problem with that?"

Abe lit a cigarette, and Carolyn made coughing noises. Abe glowered for a moment, then shifted his cigarette to his other hand as Moe explained: Emmett Kane had a long history as an AIDS activist, and that was something that Moe couldn't assail — not entirely, anyway. He'd been one of the first to rail against the Catholic Church, the United Nations, and the U.S. government for their inaction in the early years of the epidemic. But lately, he'd been siding with Frank DeSoto and the mayor over the crackdowns, and when he wrote about AIDS now, he didn't find anyone to blame but gay men themselves. Blaming gay men for their own deaths, and siding with an anti-gay mayor who was closing down gay businesses by pretending it was in the name of public health was more than reprehensible, Moe argued — it was counterproductive from the perspective of AIDS prevention.

"AIDS activists are never going to succeed by forcing sex underground and shaming people into lying about their sexual behavior," Moe said as Carolyn and Abe ate, listening attentively. "And gay activists are never going to succeed if they abandon the fundamental idea that consenting adults should be able to control their own bodies."

Abe took a puff. "You should write all that down, Moe. You've got a very strong point of view."

"That's just it," he replied. "I did write it down. But there's nowhere to print it. The *Voice* rejected my column in favor of Emmett Kane's. *Outrageous* is run by one of the leading proponents of the mayor's crackdown — he wouldn't even run a letter to the editor that I wrote because he disagreed with me. And *The A-List* doesn't want to get into anything 'political.' This is why we need a real gay newspaper. Not just one man's rant sheet, but a real newspaper where these things can get aired."

Carolyn jumped in. "And then *they* can refuse to print articles by people *they* disagree with!"

"That's not what I'm saying," Moe said.

"I was only kidding, Moe."

"I'm sorry, Carolyn. You know I take this stuff seriously."

Abe raised a finger of caution. "It's not a sin to take things seriously. You're talking about important issues."

Carolyn's mother stood behind them: "My, my, quite the heavy discussion at this end of the table. If I can interrupt, I'll clear your plates and bring out dessert."

Moe turned to Carolyn: "When do we start the second half of the Seder?" The second half was Moe's favorite, with all the songs he learned as a child.

"We don't do a second half," she said. "We're Reform."

For a moment, Moe was disappointed. Then he realized he'd have more time to play with Max later, and he forgot about Emmett Kane, Frank DeSoto, and the Israelites wandering through the desert for forty long years.

□ □ □

Gene didn't want to spend the evening alone. So when Dustin called at work — as he did every day — Gene asked him to dinner. Dustin accepted without hesitation.

When Gene walked into Trattoria Due Amici — Gene's favorite place in Little Italy — at a few minutes past seven, Dustin was there waiting, moon-eyed as ever. He had already ordered a bottle of Chianti.

"To what do I owe the pleasure of your company on a weeknight?" Dustin asked. "Usually I don't get to see you until the weekend."

Gene poured a glass of wine. "I had a free night tonight. It just worked out this way." He tapped his glass against Dustin's in a silent toast.

"Where's Moe?"

"Why do you ask?"

"You usually have dinner with him during the week. Where is he?"

"It's the first night of Passover," Gene said. "He's at a Seder."

"I've never been to one of those. Have you?"

"Actually, I used to go to the Passover Seders at his family's house when we were together."

"You two seem like you're still close," Dustin said. "You see him all the time."

"Well, I still love him. We were soulmates, and that kind of thing doesn't just end when you stop calling each other 'lover.'

There's still a connection there, like we're family. You know what I mean, don't you?"

"Not really," Dustin said. "I don't keep in touch with my ex-boyfriends."

"Nasty breakups?"

"Some, yes, but even when they're not so nasty, I feel like it's just time to move on. Can't hold on to the past forever."

Gene pushed his glass away. "But Moe's not just a part of my past. He's part of my present, too."

Dustin topped off his own glass and asked, "And what about your future?"

eight

Moe didn't have much time. He had to be in Times Square for a two o'clock Wednesday matinee. When Aaron called in the morning and said he wanted to have lunch, Moe told him it wasn't a good day; he was still pissed about Monday's class, and wasn't about to let Aaron off the hook.

"I really need to talk to you," Aaron said, pleading. "It's about Kevin."

Moe agreed to meet him for a burger before the show. But he didn't promise to be pleasant.

Moe was halfway through his cheese fries when Aaron arrived late, apologizing profusely — for his tardiness.

"I'm used to it by now," Moe said flatly, without looking up.

"Ouch," said Aaron. "You still mad?"

"Mad? Why would I be mad? I have the most humiliating experience of my graduate school career and my best friend sits next to me completely silent. He doesn't defend me. He just lets me twist in the wind. Why would that make me mad?"

Aaron was taken aback. "What do you want me to do?"

"I want you to apologize. And next time something like that happens, I want you to speak up like a friend is supposed to."

Aaron was contrite. "I'm sorry I didn't intervene. I should have said something. I'll do better next time."

"If there is a next time," said Moe.

"Huh?"

"I've been thinking about grad school a lot lately, and Monday confirmed for me that the program might not be right for me. Or maybe I'm not right for the program. I'm not sure. But Professor Penn sure doesn't think I belong there."

"She's just one professor," Aaron said.

"But she's my adviser. She's the one who's supposed to be my role model and mentor, and she doesn't have any confidence that I deserve a degree from Empire."

Aaron leaned over the table. "You haven't made any rash decisions since Monday, have you?"

"No, nothing like that. Just thinking that grad school might not be the place for me. Of course, I don't have any other great options on the table, so for the time being I guess it's moot."

"Promise you'll discuss it with me before you make any moves?"

"Of course. That's what sisters are for, right?" Moe hadn't explicitly accepted Aaron's apology, but their fight was over. "But that's not why we're here. What's up with Kevin? Does this have anything to do with his mysterious cell phone call last week?"

While Moe ate his hamburger — leaving the bun aside in a token observance of Passover — Aaron recounted his weekend, from being stood up on Saturday to making up on Sunday to getting crabs and finding out the big secret on Monday. Moe suddenly understood why Aaron had been preoccupied, why he seemed so out of sorts in class.

"It could be worse," Moe offered. "This is better than him seeing someone else, don't you think?"

"Actually, this seems even worse," Aaron said. "I was thinking about it all day yesterday — I skipped a class and canceled my massages — because I didn't understand what was bothering me so much. But now I know. He's not just seeing another man, he's seeing *dozens* of other men. He's not having sex on the side, he's having sex *for a living* and seeing *me* on the side. I'm sitting at home waiting for him while he's out making sure his paying customers are satisfied. He'll come sleep with me, but only if he doesn't have a client — if there's a conflict, he'll drop me in a second. I'm his screw of last resort."

Moe couldn't quite relate. He didn't think Kevin's escorting was a particularly big deal, except for the occasional case of crabs. But he knew that Aaron saw things differently, viewed Kevin's work as a reflection on him, and felt possessive of Kevin's sexuality in a way that Moe didn't comprehend. Still, he thought, it's not *that* bad.

"I don't think you should feel threatened by him hustling," Moe told Aaron. "Hustling is his work, just like massage is your work."

Aaron furrowed his brow. "Don't you compare what I do with hustling. I'm a licensed massage therapist."

"God forbid I should compare you touching naked men for money to Kevin touching naked men for money."

"I trained for a solid year to get my license. How long did he train to hustle?"

"At least that long, I'm sure."

"I'm not liking this conversation, sweetie."

Moe didn't want to start a new fight so soon after they'd made up. "Tell you what: I'll admit that your work and Kevin's work aren't exactly the same, if you can admit that they're not entirely different."

Aaron paused. "Well, we both touch naked men for money, that's true I suppose. Although my men don't get to touch me back."

"And Kevin's men probably pay more," Moe added with a wink.

Aaron's brow unfurrowed.

"Anyway," Moe continued, "my point was that it's his job, and if money's tight, of course he'd change a date with you to earn a bit of cash. You'd probably do the same if you had a massage client who wanted to make an appointment that conflicted with plans you'd made with Kevin."

Aaron had, in fact, changed their plans once or twice to accommodate a massage client. Not that he'd ever lied about it.

"Besides, you have no reason to feel jealous of those other guys," Moe continued. "Those guys have to pay to spend time with Kevin. You're the one he wants to be with. He said so himself, right?"

That much was true, Aaron knew. But underneath the surface feelings of jealousy and judgment — the more he thought about it, the more Aaron realized that Kevin was right when he called him judgmental — there was something deeper.

"Even if I'm fine with him hustling, the way I didn't mind him being a go-go boy, there's still the question of deception," Aaron said. "He's been lying to me for months and sneaking around behind my back."

"That's something you'll have to work on together," Moe said. "That is, if you want to work through it."

Aaron sat for a moment, thinking.

Moe looked at his watch. Time to go.

"I've got to run if I'm going to catch this show," Moe said. "But I'll chat with Kevin myself to see what's going on in his head. He's coming over to my place after dinner."

"He is? Why?"

"He's going to take some photographs of me for his class project," said Moe. "Naked. He called me yesterday and told me he had this idea that involved me, and naturally I said yes. Can you believe it?"

So Kevin was right, Aaron thought. I've known Moe for two years, and I didn't think he'd agree to do this, but Kevin had a feeling after meeting him just a few times. He's a pretty good judge of character for someone so young.

"Of course I can believe it," Aaron said. "I'm the one who suggested he ask you in the first place."

□ □ □

Frank met Angie and Lou Zacarias outside the theater. He'd been looking forward to seeing them all day.

Even though they were Scott's parents, he thought of them more fondly than he did his own parents — his late father, always demanding, and his mother, doting but incompetent. Scott's parents, in contrast, were educated but down-to-earth, supportive but from a respectful distance. Since Scott died, he saw them only once or twice a year, on occasions like this one, where they stopped in New York for a day on their way from Louisville to a European vacation. But he always looked forward to seeing them, or opening their Christmas cards, or getting a phone call from them on his birthday. They never forgot.

This time, Frank had snagged three seats for a new play still in previews. He didn't know much about the show except that it was a drama and it had a good cast.

"You look marvelous!" Angie said, folding her arms around him as Lou took his hand in a firm shake.

After more than twenty years, Frank still didn't know what to call them — Angie and Lou, Mom and Dad, Mr. and Mrs. Zacarias — so he simply returned their greetings and said, "You look great, too. Both of you."

"Mighty nice of you to take time off from work to meet us," said Lou.

"One of the advantages of being your own boss," Frank replied. "Sometimes, it's the only advantage."

They laughed.

They made their way inside, through the Art Deco lobby and up the carpeted steps to their plush but cramped balcony seats, where they chatted briefly. Nothing too weighty — work, the weather, travel. But it was comfortable, never awkward.

During the first act, however, Frank started to think he'd made a mistake. The play was much heavier than he'd thought it would be. Lots of angst and tension, all the characters chafing at each other. Several scenes into the play, the source of the conflict was revealed: the death of a child many years earlier, an event none of the characters has truly dealt with.

Maybe this is hitting too close to home, Frank thought as the lights came up for intermission. He looked to see if Angie was crying; she was.

"We don't have to stay for the second act," Frank said. "I didn't realize it would be such a downer."

Angie patted her eyes with a tissue. "No, no, it's not a bad thing to cry. I was just thinking of Scotty, that's all."

"Me, too," said Frank. "But if it's too much to handle..."

"Don't you worry about me, sweetheart," she said. "It feels good to remember him."

Lou hugged her from behind, and she managed a weak smile.

Frank recalled how they'd helped him during Scott's illness. They had been reluctant to come to New York at first — they both felt a bit awkward staying in Frank and Scott's apartment. But even then, they were on the phone every day, talking to Scott to lift his spirits and then talking to Frank to find out what the doctors were saying. Toward the end, they got over their hesitance about staying in their son's home with his lover, and they spent a great deal of time in the second bedroom. It was during that time that Frank grew closer to them than he'd been in the previous ten years.

Just watching Angie was getting Frank choked up. He excused himself to use the men's room. And as he walked down the staircase, he found himself looking Moe Pearlman in the eye.

"Hello, Mister Pearlman," he said, not too friendly, but not unfriendly.

"Can I quote you on that?" Moe replied. Definitely unfriendly.

"Moe, you can't still be angry. I didn't put any words in your mouth at The Backdoor. And as for your letter, I already explained that I didn't think your letter warranted publication. But it's nothing personal."

"You can print whatever you want," Moe said. "I think your paper's a piece of fascist crap, I think you're collaborating with the Nightlife Nazi, and I think you're a pathetic toad who's angry that everyone else is still getting laid. But it's nothing personal."

And he was gone. Although Frank was a bit rattled — he'd heard similar epithets thrown around, but rarely to his face — he recovered quickly. After all, he thought, who the hell is Moe Pearlman anyway? Just one of those arrogant young guys who doesn't know anything about life or death. He'll find out soon enough. In the meantime, fuck him.

Frank regained his composure and was back in his seat when the blinking lights signaled the end of intermission. Angie had regained her composure, too, and she took her seat between the two men.

"You know, Frank, I only wish Scotty could be here today," she whispered in his ear, putting her hand on his. "He always said that Broadway was one of the reasons he moved to New York. He loved the theater."

"He did, didn't he?" Frank said as the lights went down. And the light bulb in his head went on.

□ □ □

Gene left a message for Moe around noon. Moe called him back at work just before five.

"And where were you all day?" Gene asked. "I know you don't have class on Wednesday."

"I was at the theater."

"Rough life! Some of us have to work."

"Hello? Theater is work for me, remember?"

"I keep forgetting. You've got to start getting tickets for evening and weekend performances so I can use your spare ticket — and by 'spare' I mean 'free.' "

"Suggestion noted."

"So did you see anything good?"

"It was okay. A bit of a downer," Moe said. "But the low point came during intermission. Frank DeSoto in the men's room."

"Good God! Did you realize it was him before you finished sucking him off?"

"Very funny. I did not have any contact with that man's penis, assuming he still has one. I saw him when I was *leaving* the men's room."

"So what did he say?"

"He said hello," said Moe. "Then I told him what I think of him."

"You didn't."

"I did. The short version anyway. Just came right out. I have a hard time keeping my mouth shut sometimes."

"That's what they say about you."

"You're in a sunny mood," Moe said. "What's up?"

"Just stupid stuff. Eleanor lectured Ben and Jay today about flirting with the customers."

"Did she want them to do it more or do it less?" Moe asked.

"Take a guess. The boys were kind of dumbfounded, because they didn't even think they'd been flirting. I mean, they were, a little, but nothing too risqué. Eleanor told them it was unprofessional."

"So what did you say?"

"To her, nothing. I went straight to the boys when she left for lunch and told them to ignore everything she said. I told them that if they had to use their masculine wiles to bring in the customers, I was all for it. They've got the goods, why not use them?"

"Amen to that."

Gene asked, "So what are you going to make me for dinner?"

"Tonight's no good, sorry."

"Got a better offer, huh? Who is it, your dream man, Max Headroom?"

"Actually I'm doing a porno shoot tonight."

"Yeah, *that* could happen."

"Laugh all you want, but it's true. Kevin's coming over to shoot naked pictures of me for his photography class."

"And you agreed to it?"

"Of course."

"Amazing," Gene said. "Is there anything you won't do?"

"Yes, dear," Moe said wryly. "You."

□ □ □

Perry had pulled his tie off on the stairway, and by the time he got through Aaron's door he was already untucking his shirt. "It's so good to see you," he said. "I need this bad."

Tax season had just ended, and Perry — an accountant — was so tight with stress that he could barely move. He'd been coming to Aaron every week for months, but he'd had to cancel the previous three sessions because work was too hectic; now he was desperate. He kicked off his shoes and started to unbutton his pants.

Aaron was usually happy to see Perry. He was a steady customer who always tipped. More than that, he had a body that was a pleasure to gaze upon. The kind of body that gave Aaron ideas. But not today. Aaron couldn't muster as much as a smile.

"What's wrong?" Perry asked, folding his slacks, standing in his boxer shorts. "You look like *you* could use a massage."

"I'm sorry, Perry, it's just boy trouble."

Perry looked at Aaron. "Do you want to talk about it?"

Aaron always had a feeling that Perry was different from his other clients — a genuinely decent guy trapped in a gym bunny's body and Cole Haan shoes.

"As a matter of fact, I do," said Aaron.

Perry lay down on the massage table, and as Aaron rubbed oil into his broad shoulders and worked the kinks out of his lower back, he told Perry about Kevin. Perry listened silently —

out of deference and politeness, Aaron figured, not indifference. For a solid hour, Aaron talked about how much he'd come to care for Kevin, how conflicted he felt about his hustling, how much he worried that he'd never be able to trust him.

When the hour was up, Perry sat up on the table. Aaron said, "You've listened to me all this time, and you haven't told me what you think. What would you do, Perry?"

"Honestly?" said Perry. "If I found out a guy I was dating was hustling on the side, I don't think I could handle it. But that's just me. The fact that you didn't simply end it means that you've got something invested in this guy, something serious."

Aaron looked over at Perry, his lightly hairy chest glistening with oil, his thighs parted slightly. Aaron had been touching this body, this beautiful body, for the last hour, and for the first time during one of his sessions with Perry, Aaron hadn't entertained any erotic fantasies about him. He'd been thinking only of Kevin. He realized then that what he felt for Kevin was stronger than jealousy, stronger than suspicion, stronger even than lust. Something serious indeed.

□ □ □

Kevin was still unpacking his photo equipment when Moe broached the subject: "I hear you've been practicing the world's oldest profession."

Subtlety was not Moe's forte.

"You've talked to Aaron?"

"This morning."

"That's more than I can say. We haven't spoken since Monday."

"Aaron just needs some time to think. He'll call you when he's ready."

"What do you think about it?"

"It sounds disgusting, depraved, and perverted. I love it."

"Seriously."

"Seriously? I think hustling sounds pretty interesting. I thought about hustling myself, but of course I don't have the kind of body that guys pay money to see."

"You're talking to a guy who came over to take nude photos of you, Moe."

"But you're not paying me," he said, grinning. "Or are you?"

"Um, no," said Kevin.

"Didn't think so. Look, you've got the kind of body that makes guys get out their checkbooks. I see no reason why you shouldn't follow through. I don't know if I could be a hustler — I'm pretty picky about who I sleep with, despite what you might have heard. But if you can do it, more power to you. Sounds like a good way to make money and meet people.

"But that's just how it looks from the outside," Moe continued. "You're the one with the inside scoop. Do you like doing it?"

"Sometimes I do," Kevin said. "I've got an exhibitionist streak. That's why I liked dancing at Slick. But this goes further than that. It's about being desired, about seeing a hunger in someone's eyes, and being able to satisfy that hunger just by being there.

"Besides," he added, "most of the guys are decent looking. You'd be surprised."

"Maybe you're right. But what I think about hustling isn't the point. What matters is what Aaron thinks about it, and how much that affects you."

"I know. But I don't know what Aaron thinks. He talks a good game about sexual liberation and all that, but I'm not sure he's so crazy about having to deal with it in his personal life."

"Aaron may not be the libertine that I am, but he's not as far off as you might believe. I have a feeling he'll come around."

"You do? Did he say something to you?"

"Not in so many words, no. But he's working through his feelings on that subject."

"That's good news."

"Now can we please make some porno here?" Moe said, gesturing at the camera. "This Viagra won't last all night!"

Kevin looked up. "You took a Viagra?"

"I'm kidding, Kevin. A joke. I'm twenty-six years old. I know that seems old to you, but believe me, I don't need a pill to get it up. I've got at least four more years before I turn into Bob Dole."

Kevin laughed. "You've got pretty impressive stamina for an old guy. You must think about sex twenty-four hours a day."

"Not really," said Moe. "Just the sixteen hours I'm awake. Plus one or two hours while I'm asleep."

□ □ □

After taking four rolls of film of Moe in very basic shots — splayed on the bed, getting out of the shower — Kevin left at three past ten. They made a date to shoot some outside pictures — in a hay loft, on a horse, in the backseat of a car — the next week on a friend's farm upstate in Sullivan County.

At six past ten, Moe logged onto Men Online and found Max waiting for him. Max made the first move:

DownTheHatch: Finally!
HotLipsNYC: Waiting for me?
DownTheHatch: All night. 5 minutes?
HotLipsNYC: See you then.

Moe logged off without even replying to two other guys who'd sent him messages. He didn't feel like talking to anyone else.

Having spent most of his time with Kevin in the nude, Moe had on only a pair of boxers. He opened his closet to get out his 501s and a T-shirt, then thought: How would Max react if I changed the scene?

Not that he didn't like the usual three-round session. On the contrary, he dreamed about it. It was perfect every time.

Max had never even hinted that he might be interested in anything else. He hadn't ever kissed Moe, held him, or stayed more than a few seconds after his third and final orgasm. He had been in Moe's bed, but he always remained above the covers.

It's bound to be a mistake to push anything with Max, he thought, looking at himself in the bathroom mirror as he brushed his teeth. He can't possibly be attracted to me — I mean, look at his body and then look at mine. He lifts weights every day, and I don't look like I've lifted anything besides a pint of Häagen-Dazs. He could have sex with anyone he wants; he just comes over here because it's convenient and reliable. He doesn't even look at me. He watches the porn on the TV.

Still, Moe thought, he does come back pretty often. He must find something appealing about me. Even if it's just my mouth, that's something, right? And I'm sure he'd enjoy a little more. He wouldn't even have to *do* anything.

Moe often imagined what it would be like to rest his head on Max's hairy chest, to take in his scent, to rub his stomach softly. Even more, he dreamed what it would be like to lie in Max's arms, his back to Max's chest, Max's arms wrapped around him, with Max tickling Moe's neck with his goatee and breathing warm sleepy air in his ear. In this fantasy, they talked while intertwined — about theater, politics, New York, their families — and Max realized with sudden tenderness that Moe was more than a hot mouth.

This fantasy alone was enough to make Moe want to push their sexual relationship to another level. But he knew there was a risk. If Max wasn't interested, he might well leave forever, figuring Moe was some starry-eyed kid who'd grown too attached. Moe might ruin what he had sought for two solid years — hot sex with his fantasy man. He'd gotten his wish at last, and so much more, too. He wasn't eager to fuck that up.

123

Max rang from downstairs. Moe buzzed him in, turned on the VCR, and opened the door. Only one minute to make a decision. Put on the jeans and get in the chair like he usually did, or leave the jeans off and climb into bed?

Figuring that his first dream had already come true, Moe decided to pursue the next one. He left the jeans on his desk chair and climbed into bed.

When Max walked in, he stopped to evaluate the situation. The TV was playing the usual porn, and the apartment was dark as usual, but Moe wasn't in his usual spot. He was in bed. Max seemed unsure what to do.

He approached the bed and stood beside Moe's head. He unbuttoned his jeans and pulled out his cock, already half-hard, and said simply, "Suck it."

Moe did. *He's not getting it,* Moe thought, *this is just the same thing in a different part of the room. He's just going to stand here while I blow him, same as always. Although he didn't tell me to get back in the chair. And he didn't turn around and leave. That's a step.*

Five minutes, about the same as usual, and Max came for the first time. As usual, he stripped off his clothes for round two. But this time instead of taking a seat on the couch, he pulled back the covers, motioned for Moe to scoot over, and got into bed beside him. This is it, Moe thought, the part where everything changes.

But Max didn't turn and take Moe in his arms, or kiss his forehead, or ask how his day was. He pushed Moe's head down under the covers to blow him. Moe obliged. And once again, Max was watching the video while Moe was doing the work. Moe was thinking that perhaps this was a mistake.

Nineteen minutes later, Max had shot a second load, and he let Moe up from beneath the blanket. Moe was ready to start working on the third when Max said, "Come here," and motioned to his chest. Moe looked up and met Max's eyes.

Max put his arm under Moe's neck, and rubbed his back with his hand. Moe rested his cheek on Max's hairy chest and reached out to take Max's crucifix in his fingers. Max bent down and kissed the top of Moe's head, and said, "This was a nice surprise."

Moe was speechless. What could he say? "Thank you"? "Any time"? "No problem"? He nodded into Max's chest hair.

"How do you turn this thing off?" Max asked, reaching for the remote control on the nightstand. Moe took the clicker and shut off the porn. They were together in the dark, without any distractions.

Moe was overcome by his good fortune. He thought, *Dare I push it even further?*

He rolled over onto his side, facing away from Max. It was a test. A test that Max passed.

Immediately after Moe rolled onto his side, Max rolled over too, enveloping him in his arms and spooning right behind him. Moe reached down and took Max's hands in his own, pulling his arms tighter around his waist. Within a few short minutes, and after only two orgasms, Max was asleep in Moe's bed. He stayed the whole night.

As for Moe, he didn't sleep much. He didn't want to miss a thing.

nine

"So are you going to tell me what this is all about?" Moe asked Carolyn, standing in front of her desk at *Footlights* on Friday morning. "First you wake me up at nine, and tell me to come in right away, and then you get all cryptic when I ask you what for. 'Something important.' I can't begin to imagine."

Carolyn was quiet, yet smiling.

"Something about a show? A problem with the last review?"

No answer.

"A Pulitzer Prize for criticism? A cute guy I've simply *got* to meet? What could be so important?"

Still nothing. Nothing but a grin.

"Well, I'm here," Moe continued. "Are you going to fill me in? It's nine forty-three in the morning, and I'm too tired to play guessing games."

Carolyn stood up. "Let's go into my dad's office."

Moe had never been in Abe Guttmacher's office before. But here he was, being led in by Carolyn, who was holding his hand. Moe took in the surroundings: crowded bookcases, walls cluttered with framed articles and photographs, stacks of newspapers piled on the floor next to the desk. And Mr. Guttmacher, sitting behind the mess in a high-back leather chair, a faint smell of cigarettes coming off his clothes, waiting expectantly. And, like Carolyn, smiling.

"Glad you could come in, Moe," he said. "I've got something I'd like to discuss with you."

Moe took a seat. Carolyn closed the door behind them and stood next to Moe.

"My daughter came to me about two months ago with an idea," Abe said. "A publishing niche that needed to be filled, a market that was underserved. I had my business manager look into it, and I believe she is right. I also believe that I have the resources to fix the situation, so I sat down with my accountant and crunched the numbers, to see if what I wanted was feasible. And it seems like it is."

Moe wondered what this had to do with him.

"Carolyn told me that her idea had come from you, so I wanted you to be here when I first announced the news," Abe said. "I will be launching a new gay newspaper in New York City this summer."

Moe was speechless, an unusual state for him.

Carolyn was about to burst. "Surprised?"

"Um, yeah!" was all Moe could manage. "How long have you been planning this?"

Carolyn said, "After we chatted about the lack of a decent gay paper in February, I had a talk with Daddy."

"I hadn't thought about it before," Abe picked up. "But she — that is, both of you are correct. The gay community here doesn't have a newspaper of record, the way that most cities do. I had heard of *Outrageous*, though I confess I had never found cause to read it. When Carolyn came to me, I checked it out and realized that it isn't the kind of newspaper you're talking about. I think New York deserves better, and I think we can deliver something better."

"That sounds great, Mr. Guttmacher," Moe said. "I'm sure you can do it." This was true. Moe had faith in Abe. *Footlights* was a well-run publication. Despite what appeared to be nepotism, his daughter was a great editor. And the other publications he oversaw were solid and respectable.

"The paper will be called *New York Gay News*. Just a simple title without any agenda behind it but delivering news," Abe said. "Our plan is to launch our first issue in time for Gay Pride, the last weekend in June."

Abe ran down the basic outline of what was coming. In the next ten weeks, he'd assemble a staff, solicit advertisers, buy some equipment, and set up an area in the office alongside his other publications. The paper would launch as a free weekly, with an initial circulation larger than *Outrageous*.

Moe was thrilled at the prospect, and told them so.

"But you haven't heard the best part," said Carolyn, by this point so excited she could hardly stand still.

Abe looked at him. "Moe, I'd like you to come aboard and be my editor."

□ □ □

"You're the first person I've told," Moe said to Aaron.

This wasn't quite true; he'd called Gene the minute he got home. But Gene didn't have much time to chat at work, so they'd made a plan to get together that night. Aaron was the second person he told. But that wasn't worth noting.

"Honey, that's great news!" Aaron said. "I mean, it's good news about the paper, but it's really, really great news about the job."

Aaron was exactly right. The mere launch of the paper was cause enough for celebration. But editing that new paper was something else altogether.

"So are you going to take it?" he asked Moe.

"You know what my mother would say? She'd say, 'Moshe, it's *beshert*.' That's Yiddish, sort of like kismet, or fate. The universe telling you that something's meant to be. The same week I start looking for a way out of grad school, this drops in my lap out of nowhere. That's *beshert*. And if it's meant to be, it's meant to be."

Aaron counseled caution. "Are you sure about this? Did you already tell that guy that you'd take the job? Have you talked to Mel yet?"

"No, I haven't made any definite decision yet," said Moe. "I'm going to think about it over the weekend. But I'm pretty sure I know what the answer is. I'm not cut out for graduate school — this week basically confirmed that. This paper is an amazing opportunity. It'd be interesting politically, it'd pay my bills, and it could open up a whole new career for me. I've got years of writing behind me, and a few short-term editing gigs, but this'll be my first chance to run a publication by myself, not counting my college paper. I'd be stupid to let this slip by."

Moe was probably right, Aaron thought. He hated the idea of Moe leaving grad school; who would he have coffee with after class, or pass notes to during seminars? But it was true that Moe wasn't cut out for grad school. He didn't care much about theory or research or academic journals. He wanted to get onto the streets and deal with real people living real lives and make a real difference.

□ □ □

Aaron had been thinking about what to do for four days, but he hadn't spoken to Kevin since Monday. Now he was ready. He picked up the phone and dialed Kevin's number. Voice mail. Just as well, since Aaron didn't want to have the conversation on the phone. He left Kevin a message — asking him to come over tonight at ten to "chat" — and then focused on the immediate task at hand: setting up the massage table, warming the potpourri, and finding the right CD for his next massage appointment.

□ □ □

Dustin was getting blown off.

"I'm busy tonight," Gene told him when he called at work. "Moe's got some big news, so I'm going over there tonight to celebrate."

Dustin didn't ask what the big news was. He didn't care, and Gene didn't volunteer.

130

"What about tomorrow?" Dustin asked.

The Alliance teach-in. Gene hadn't invited Dustin — he was going with Moe — and anyway, even though he was dating a positive guy, Dustin wasn't the type to sit through an "educational" session about safe sex on a Saturday. It was his day off. He wanted to play.

"How about Sunday?" he asked.

Gene had a matinee at an off-Broadway theater. With Moe. Of course.

It would be the first weekend since Gene moved to the city that he hadn't made time for Dustin. True, it had only been a couple of days since they'd had dinner in Little Italy. But still, Dustin thought. The weekend.

"Sounds like you'll be spending the whole weekend with Moe," he said, the hurt in his voice apparent.

"I guess it just worked out that way," Gene said. He hadn't planned it. He hadn't even thought about it. "Maybe we can have dinner Sunday night after the show," Gene offered after a moment.

Dustin took what he could get.

"Gene, can I ask you a question?"

"Sure. What is it?"

"You and Moe. Are you two sleeping together?"

"Me and Moe? Good Lord, no! We broke up years ago, remember? Besides, he's not my type, and I'm sure not his type. I can't even imagine it!"

"Well, you were sleeping together at some point in the past. Why would it be any different now?"

Dustin wasn't grasping it, wasn't understanding how ex-lovers could remain close without getting back together.

"Things were different then. Our tastes were different, we were different people. And we were in love. Sometimes, when you're in love, it changes how you look at someone."

That much Dustin understood quite well.

□ □ □

Moe had only intended to check his email and log off quickly, but as soon as he connected to Men Online, Max caught him.

> DownTheHatch: Free tonight?
> HotLipsNYC: Maybe later.
> DownTheHatch: Not now?
> HotLipsNYC: No, got a friend coming over.
> DownTheHatch: Online buddy?
> HotLipsNYC: No, my ex.
> DownTheHatch: You still blow him?
> HotLipsNYC: No. Never. No.
> DownTheHatch: What you gonna do with him?
> HotLipsNYC: Have dinner, talk, maybe catch a movie.
> DownTheHatch: I see.
> HotLipsNYC: But I should be free later, like 11 or 12.
> DownTheHatch: OK then I guess.
> HotLipsNYC: Something wrong?
> DownTheHatch: No. Later sounds fine.
> HotLipsNYC: You sure? What's up?
> DownTheHatch: Nothing. Dinner & movie sounds nice.
> HotLipsNYC: Should be.
> DownTheHatch: Maybe we could do that sometime.

What? Moe didn't respond right away. He scrolled back up in their chat box to see if he'd missed something.

First of all, it was the longest chat they'd ever had online. And second of all, Moe thought: Is he asking me on a date?

Moe had fantasies, true, of having Max as his lover. That they slept together every night, Max holding Moe. That they talked about their interests, their lives. That they looked into each other's eyes with love and warmth, and had lustful bouts of sex that never waned in frequency.

But if Moe's fantasy was to have Max as an attentive and romantic lover, and his reality — for two years his fantasy, but now his reality — was to have Max as a no-nonsense fuckbuddy who never said a word, he had never entertained the notion that to get from his reality to his fantasy, they'd have to take a long journey through dating, building something, getting to know each other. Out loud. With the lights on. With their *clothes* on.

Dinner and a movie? Could it be that Max — the man who'd turned heads on Christopher Street for more than twenty years, the man who could have anyone he wanted — was interested in getting to know Moe? Moe? Overweight, neurotic, opinionated, slutty Moe?

DownTheHatch: Still there?
HotLipsNYC: Yeah, I'm here.
DownTheHatch: Forget I mentioned it.
HotLipsNYC: No, no. I'd like to do that. With you.
DownTheHatch: I just thought after the other night...

Aha. Moe had been thrilled beyond words when Max spent the night on Wednesday. He had been hoping he could move one step beyond their purely sexual routine into something a bit more physically affectionate. He hadn't anticipated that Max would see the physical affection as a romantic overture. But perhaps it was. Subconsciously.

HotLipsNYC: Let's do it.
DownTheHatch: When?
HotLipsNYC: Let's talk about it tonight.
DownTheHatch: I'll look for you around 11.
HotLipsNYC: I'll be here.

□ □ □

"Two great bits of news in one day. Your stars must be in perfect alignment," Gene told Moe over carry-out Chinese food.

"I'm not sure which I'm more excited about, running the newspaper or going on a date with Max," Moe said. "They're both dreams I never quite knew I had. And they both fill me with terror."

"Terror?"

"The fear that they won't work out. The fear that these two opportunities are too good to be true. The fear that I'm not up to the challenges of a real job and a real relationship."

Gene smirked. "Ah yes, the inner workings of the Jewish mind. I'd almost forgotten that you're riddled with self-doubt. You cover it so well."

"Don't be fooled," Moe said. "Nobody else is."

"Moe, *everybody* else is fooled. But don't worry. Your secret's safe with me."

Over sweet and sour chicken (Moe's deep-fried weakness) and steamed pepper steak (Gene's low-fat choice), they talked about the day's big news. There wasn't much to tell about Max; Moe would see him later that night and figure out if they could make a "date" for the coming weekend. The newspaper, on the other hand, warranted a great deal of discussion.

Moe worried that he wasn't up to the task. Gene countered that he was perfectly ready.

"You were editing a newspaper when I first met you," Gene said. "You can do it again."

"The G.W. *Hatchet*? That was a college paper. This is different."

"It's not entirely different," said Gene. "It's bigger, but so are you, sugar bear."

"Thanks."

Moe worried that he was making a mistake by dropping out of grad school — even if he was ninety-nine percent sure that it was the right thing to do. Gene convinced him that instead of quitting, he could take a leave of absence for a year so that it wouldn't seem like he was closing the door on his Ph.D. forever.

Gene also pointed out the benefits of working that Moe hadn't fully considered. The ability to pay off his credit cards. The opportunity to have his voice heard, along with all the other voices that currently had no outlet. The chance, if everything went perfectly smoothly, to drive *Outrageous* out of business once and for all. This notion delighted Moe, schadenfreude be damned.

By the time dinner was finished, Moe was feeling at ease about his decision. He'd visit Melody Penn on Monday and tell her he was taking a leave of absence at the end of the semester; she wouldn't argue. Then he'd phone Abe Guttmacher and accept the job. Then he'd call his parents and listen to them *kvell* at his good fortune. (Yes, they'd be upset about him dropping out of school — "You never know when you'll need that degree," they'd say — but they'd be excited about the job nonetheless.)

Gene paid for dinner, since it was sort of a celebration for Moe. Then they walked over to the cineplex in Chelsea. Moe preferred the artsy theaters in the Village, where he could check out indie films and foreign movies, but Gene was a fan of big Hollywood blockbusters. Gene got grouchy whenever he had to sit through a movie that anyone else chose. Moe didn't think it was worth the trouble, so he agreed, as always, to go see whatever Gene wanted to see. In this case, a Julia Roberts romantic comedy. The film was dull and predictable and virtually indistinguishable from every other Julia Roberts movie. But he survived. Besides, Gene was happy. And that made the evening much more pleasant.

"Why aren't you seeing Dustin tonight?" Moe asked as they walked out of the theater. Partly, he was curious. And partly, he didn't want Gene to ask what he'd thought of the film, since it would only start the same old argument they'd had for years about Moe's elitist attitude toward pop culture.

"Long story, don't ask," Gene replied. "He was pretty ticked that I'm not going to see him much this weekend. Especially since I'm spending most of it with you."

"He's jealous?"

"And how. He thinks we're sleeping together."

"Gross me out!"

"I know! It's bad enough when I see you with your shirt off. Can you imagine being completely naked?"

"The mere thought is enough to turn me straight."

"Anyway, I tried to fill him in about our relationship, but I don't think he gets it."

"Nobody does. Do you?"

"Not particularly. You don't even like Julia Roberts."

"I didn't say that."

"Didn't have to."

Moe smiled.

Gene said, "Want to stop by the Monster and sing a few around the piano?"

"No, I've got to get home," Moe demurred. "I told Max I'd be there by eleven."

"Geez, he proposes one date and already he's your ball and chain! You won't come for one drink? Not even for a few minutes, just until they sing one Sondheim number?"

"Sorry, mister, I've got the hottest man in the Big Apple waiting for me, and I ain't gonna let him slip away," Moe said. "But I'll meet you tomorrow at the teach-in."

Even though Gene wasn't a member of the Alliance — he didn't want to tread on Moe's turf, and didn't like the groupthink that often dominated this kind of organization — he was excited about the event. His viral load had been dropping steadily for four months, and he was eager to find out if he could still put his partners at risk for HIV if he ever became "undetectable." He wasn't sure what he'd want to do with the information — stop using condoms, stop telling tricks he was positive, just stop worrying all the time — but he wanted to hear what everyone else had to say.

Moe was going because he wanted to show the Alliance folks that he was committed to the group, despite their previous fallout. And he was going because Gene was going. Personally, he didn't feel he had much at stake in discussions of HIV transmission. As a cocksucker, Moe knew that HIV wasn't as pressing a concern as it was for guys who liked to fuck. Moe had been sucking cocks — hundreds and hundreds of cocks — for a long time without any problems. And he didn't just suck. He swallowed.

Plenty of guys swallow, Moe knew quite well, but very few were upfront about doing it deliberately. Moe sought it out. It was the ultimate prize, the cherry on the sundae, the focus of his insatiable appetite for cock. Swallow: That's the word in his online profile that had guys knocking on his virtual door.

Every once in a while, someone would ask Moe if he was afraid of getting infected that way. His short answer was no. His long answer was that if eating loads were a good way to get sick, every gay man would be dead — one hundred percent of gay men would be positive, not two percent or twelve percent or forty-two percent. Based on the data Moe had read — in depth, of course, with endless analysis — it just didn't follow logic to think that eating cum was notably riskier than sharing Q-tips. Moe had been doing it for years and had never gotten so much as a sore throat.

"I'll see you at the Triangle Center, then," Gene said. "Good luck with your new lover."

"Very funny," said Moe, turning to walk home.

Gene walked to the Monster, stopping outside for a moment while he briefly considered phoning Dustin to come join him. Then he opened the door and entered alone.

□ □ □

At the end of Act I, everyone would be dead. Everyone except for one man.

That was the first thing Frank knew about the play he was going to write. The second thing he knew was the title: *Buried Alive.*

Frank had put the paper to bed early. It was a slow news week, and his mind was elsewhere, so he'd sent the pages off to the printer Friday morning. By Friday evening, he could turn his full attention to his new project.

The idea had come to him after seeing Scott's parents. They had reminded him that Scott had always loved the theater. He had even pushed Frank to write a play before, but Frank — who considered himself a journalist, unable to conquer fiction or narrative — never took it seriously. But now, he was looking for a way to reach people, a way to wake people up to what was happening with the epidemic, to the fact that AIDS wasn't over. He reached a lot of people through his newspaper, and he knew he'd made a real difference by working with the mayor's office to close places down. He had saved lives. He was sure of it.

But he needed to do more. Needed a new way to get people to pay attention. So he would belatedly take Scott's advice and try to write a play. As a tribute to Scott.

Sitting in his second bedroom — the *Outrageous* office — Frank stared out at the Empire State Building. He remembered how Scott had prized the view, how it was this perfect picture of the skyscraper in the distance that had sold Scott on the apartment all those years earlier. Many nights they had sat staring at the tower, silent in each other's arms, without a sound in the apartment. When Scott fell ill, he always liked to have the blinds pulled up so he could see the Empire State Building from his sickbed.

As he remembered Scott, he remembered the other friends he had lost to AIDS. People he knew from the club, guys who'd shared their house in the Fire Island Pines, men he'd had brief flings with before he met Scott (and a few he'd had flings with during his relationship, too). They'd all died, some early and some later, leaving Frank without the circle of friends he'd spent so much time cultivating. Nobody to invite over for a dinner party. Nobody to send Christmas cards to.

Sure, he had friends today, but everyone was on guard, afraid to get too close for fear of losing another loved one. Frank had changed too, and he knew it. He felt hard.

Act I of *Buried Alive* would follow a circle of friends not unlike Frank's old friends. It would take place in the early

1980s, and this group of a half dozen men would go dancing at the big discos and snort coke all night, troll the baths for new meat, count calories and work out at the gym, split off into nonmonogamous couples, and live like there was no tomorrow. Then, one by one, they would die, until only one was left standing. A man named Freddy. The sole survivor.

In Act II of *Buried Alive*, taking place today, in the late 1990s, Freddy would meet a young man who would become his new lover. A handsome guy, smart and sexy and confident, who would breathe new spirit into Freddy's life. But Freddy would soon realize that this young man had his own circle of friends, too young to remember the first wave of AIDS. These young men would fly around the country, dancing at circuit parties and snorting crystal meth, fucking strangers in backrooms, cheating on their supposedly faithful boyfriends, pumping up their muscles with protein supplements to keep themselves buff. Freddy would tell his story to this new lover, warning him not to repeat the mistakes of his generation. But one by one, the young men would fall, too.

This, Frank thought, was the truth. The essential truth of his own experience. No, he hadn't actually found a new boyfriend since Scott died. No, he didn't actually relate to guys in their twenties anymore. No, he hadn't actually been to a circuit party — or a gym, for that matter, for many years. But those details aside, the story was true.

At the end of the play, Frank thought, Freddy is left alone with his young lover, who has now endured the loss of all his friends. The dramatic cycle is complete, leaving the audience to wonder if anything has changed. Are we simply repeating the same destructive patterns as those who fell before us, this time with our eyes open and no excuses?

Frank worked clear through the night, sketching an outline, refining scenes and making sure key elements of Act I were mirrored in Act II. By the time he started getting tired, the basic pieces were there on the page.

But something was still amiss.

Yes, Frank thought, Freddy's young lover must die. At the end of Act II, Freddy would stand completely alone once again, just as he had at the end of Act I. Nobody from the younger generation would survive.

□ □ □

Kevin wasn't sure what to put in his knapsack. Cookies had warmed Aaron's heart before, and Mexican food had worked well a few days earlier, but he wasn't sure this was the kind of discussion to be had over food. He knew he should bring back the clothes he'd borrowed from Aaron, but wasn't sure if he should pack fresh clothes for himself. Would he be spending the night? Or would this be goodbye?

He threw a clean pair of briefs and a toothbrush in his bag just in case. Then he hailed a cab.

Aaron had incense burning. It helped calm him down, clear his thoughts. When Kevin arrived, Aaron left the door ajar so he could let himself in. As he removed his shoes, he caught the scent of sage.

The futon was empty. Aaron was sitting in a chair. He didn't offer Kevin a soda. Nor did he kiss him hello. This was not a good sign. Kevin was nervous. He sat in the other chair.

"This has been a hard week for me," Aaron started. "I've had a lot of thinking to do. Not just about you, but about me."

Kevin listened.

"First, I want to say that you were right," Aaron said. "I guess I don't honestly understand why people hustle. I do tend to intellectualize it, turn it into a political issue. Which it is. But there's more to it, I know. I was hoping you could tell me why you started doing it, so I could understand it better."

Kevin didn't speak up.

"I promise I'll just listen," Aaron said. "But you've got to do some talking."

Spotlight on Kevin. He took a breath and began.

"When I graduated high school in Rochester, my parents wanted me to major in business or prelaw at SUNY. So when I moved to the city two years ago to study photography, they were upset and stopped supporting me. I needed money. I had a couple of stupid jobs at first. I bused tables at a diner. I made copies at a Kinko's. I mean, that's the only kind of job I could get, just out of high school. And there was no way I was going to make rent as a busboy. Especially when I had to keep rearranging my hours to make time for classes.

"I was underage then — well, I guess I still am until this summer — but I got a fake ID so I could go to clubs. I started going out on Saturday nights, dancing and drinking and picking up guys. Nothing too serious. I used to lie about my age to the guys I met, too. They would've freaked out if they knew I was eighteen. Well, a few of them would have gotten off on that, I suppose, but I told them I was twenty-one anyway. This one guy I picked up, I don't remember his name but he must have been thirty-five. A lot older. He told me that I should find a sugar daddy, someone to pay my bills. Now that I look back on it, he was probably just joking, but at the time I didn't know that. He said lots of older guys pay young guys for dates at this bar on the East Side called Jackpot."

"I've never been there," Aaron interjected, "but I've heard of it."

"I went the next weekend to see what it was about, and sure enough, this guy in a fancy suit started buying me drinks and chatting me up. He was old, but pretty good looking, so I went along with it. Then he asked if I'd go home with him. I told him yes, right away. Then he said, 'How does a hundred sound?' I don't know what came over me, but as soon as I realized that I had the power to reject his offer, I said, 'A hundred fifty.' And he said that sounded fair, and we took off for his place.

"It wasn't bad. He was a nice guy, he treated me okay. Not much different from the other guys I'd been going home with. Except this time I got a hundred and fifty bucks when it was all over. That was more than I was bringing home in a week working part-time at Kinko's. So I went back to Jackpot the next weekend. And the next. And I kept making money.

"But Jackpot is a pretty creepy scene once you spend time there. The same guys every week, looking for a new boy to take home. Lots of drunks. And those hustlers are competitive, if they see you making a move on someone they've got their eyes on. I figured I needed a better place. So I placed an escort ad in *The A-List*. Focusing on what I knew would sell. Young, Asian, swimmer's build. Not that I swim — I mean, where is there a pool in Manhattan? — but it sounds good. And it worked. I was making more money in less time with less hassle. And I've been doing it ever since.

"It was always just a way to make some easy money and help pay my rent. I wasn't doing it that much. I even used to turn guys away sometimes if I had enough to pay the bills. And then I got that gig dancing at Slick, which I liked a lot, so I was seeing fewer people. But after Slick closed, I needed more money, and I started doing it more often, and telling my clients that they could see me more frequently. That's why I've been getting calls on my cell phone, and that's why I've backed out on a few dates with you. I didn't think I could tell you. I didn't think you'd understand."

"Why?"

"Remember when you had that massage client who thought you were doing erotic massage?"

"Yeah."

"When you told me about him, you made it sound like anyone who had sex for money was some sort of scumbag. I was going to tell you everything that night — honestly — but after you told me about that guy, I figured you'd think I was some sort of scumbag, too."

It came back to Aaron. He'd been joking when he told Kevin about that client. At least mostly joking. But now that he thought about it again, he could see why Kevin was put off.

"What I'd like to know is, do you enjoy it? Or is it something you feel like you have to do?"

Kevin took a breath and weighed his response.

"I enjoy it sometimes. Not all the time, but sometimes. I've met a lot of nice guys, had some hot sex, and stayed out of debt. I can't deny that. But yeah, I'd rather be doing work I care about. I'd rather be a photographer. That's why I'm in school. Once I have my degree this spring, I'll be looking for a job in photography."

"In addition to hustling? Or instead of hustling?"

"I guess that depends."

"On what?"

"On what you think."

So young, Aaron thought. But perhaps I can teach him something.

"When I first met Joshua, I was about your age," Aaron said. "I was in total awe of him as a dancer, and as a black gay man. He was out and successful, and didn't take crap from anyone. Total confidence. He knew what he wanted, and knew how to get it. One thing he wanted was me. And he got me.

"But the more time we spent together, the more Joshua found things he didn't like about me. He had a lot of issues. For example, he was totally comfortable being out as a gay man, but he wanted to make sure nobody ever thought he was a queen. Masculinity was a big deal to him. He didn't like the way I called people 'sweetie' and 'honey.' So I stopped. He didn't like my dreadlocks, he thought they were too femme. We argued about that for a good year, but in the end, I shaved my head.

"And," Aaron continued, "the thing he hated most was drag. He didn't like drag shows in bars, didn't think it was funny on any level. He didn't understand the politics behind drag, either. Now, I didn't know how he felt at first, and he didn't know I used to do drag with my friends — drag had never come up in conversation, and I wasn't doing it all the time anyway. Just for special occasions, you know? Anyway, one night shortly after we'd started dating, maybe a month or two after I'd started dancing in his company, he showed up at this club where my friends and I were hanging out. I didn't know he was going to be there, so I ran up and kissed him hello and yelled, 'Surprise!' Did I mention that I was wearing a blonde wig and makeup at the time? He was not amused.

"He walked out of that club and called me the next night to say we should stop seeing each other. I didn't know what to do. He told me he was into *men,* and he couldn't sleep with anyone who wasn't really a *man.* Bullshit, right? But what did I know? I told him I'd stop doing drag. And I did. I also stopped seeing those friends, and stopped going to that club. At the time, I thought it was worth it to hang onto Joshua. But you know what? If he truly cared about me, we could have worked through it.

"That's not to say that I might not have given up that whole scene anyway. But it would have been my decision. Today, Joshua is nowhere to be found, but I could still have those friends if I'd played my cards differently."

"Are you still doing drag? That picture on your wall seems pretty recent."

"Just once in a while. When I'm feeling in the mood. Just to prove that I can. But now it's different. I know what it means to be a proud gay man, and I know that putting on a wig doesn't change that."

"I don't mind drag a bit," Kevin offered.

"That's good to know," Aaron answered, and smiled. "What I'm trying to say here is that you shouldn't be making decisions based on what I think. You should be making decisions based on what *you* think."

"I hear you," Kevin said. "But you do have something to do with my decision."

"How so?"

"To be honest, since we've been dating, I haven't been as interested in having sex with other guys. I'd rather be spending my time with you."

Aaron felt warm. "That's sweet."

"It's true."

"So what does that mean about your career as a rent boy?"

"I guess it means that I'm looking for a new job," Kevin said. "I can't quit right away, because I've got to get through the rest of the semester. But as soon as I graduate, I'm going to look for a real job as a photographer, and as soon as I get one, I'm going to retire as a hustler."

"Probably a good idea," Aaron said. "You're getting a bit old for the job."

Kevin cracked a grin, relieved by the moment of levity at last.

"In the meantime, I'd like to set a couple of ground rules," Aaron said.

"Go ahead."

"First, I won't be stood up for some trick again. If you make a date with me, you keep it. I don't care if some old sap offers you a million dollars, you don't leave me in the lurch for a trick. I've got to come first."

"Deal."

"The second thing is even more important. You've got to be honest with me. Completely honest. That doesn't mean I want a thorough rundown of everything you've done with every client, but it does mean that I want to know what you're doing. Especially because what you do affects me. If you're keeping things from me, there's no way I can trust you. And if I can't trust you, there's no way that this is going to work out."

"I'm going to work on that," Kevin said. "But it's going to be hard, I have to say. I'm not used to sharing everything. I've always had a lot of things I keep to myself. I never had a real best friend growing up, the kind you tell everything. I was very close to my parents, but that all changed when I moved away to go to art school. Now I can hardly list the things I keep from them."

"Believe me, there's plenty I don't tell my parents," Aaron said. He thought of his mother — "a church-going lady," he called her — and his father, who always preferred being kept in the dark to dealing openly with uncomfortable subjects. His parents knew the basics of his life. They knew Joshua had been more than a mentor. They knew, in vague terms, his political views. But they didn't discuss the specifics of his queer studies classes, his massage business, the Alliance. They didn't want to know. Nor did Aaron want to tell them.

"So you know how I feel," Kevin said.

"Yes, I know how you feel. But honey, there's a difference. I am not your father. Or your mother. I understand withholding information from your parents. But keeping things from your boyfriend is something else."

Boyfriend. First time that word had been used. Kevin noticed immediately, and though he made no comment, inside he recognized that this single word meant that tonight was not the end.

"I've got a question for you," Kevin said.

"Shoot."

"Can I spend the night here with you?"

"Of course you can," Aaron said. "I want you to."

"Good," Kevin said. "I was worried that the other night might have been the last night we'd spend together. And that didn't exactly turn out the way I'd planned."

"We'll have plenty more nights together," Aaron said, getting up from his chair and moving behind Kevin. He put his arms over Kevin's shoulders. "We'll get through this. I love you."

It was the first time Aaron had said these words since Joshua.

Kevin's heart was beating hard. "I love you," he said. It was the first time he'd said these words. Ever.

ten

This is what makes Aaron hard: intimacy.

It is such a quaint romantic notion that he is too ashamed to share this fact even with his closest friends. But it's true. At heart, Aaron is a one-man man.

Now, politically, he understands the importance of sexual liberation, of having the freedom to determine the shape of your own sex life, and the right to express your own erotic desires in any way you see fit. He's willing to stand up and fight for legalized prostitution, abortion on demand, transgender rights, and sexual self-determination in any number of forms.

He goes to public sex spaces sometimes, to help support them during this time of closures. To show that he thinks these spaces need to exist, that they serve a valuable purpose. He wants to keep his options — everybody's options — open.

But when he's at these sex clubs, Aaron hovers around the periphery, watching other people play. He rarely gets involved himself, and when he does, it's always with one other person, usually in private.

Call him old-fashioned: What he really wants is a boyfriend. Someone to come home to every night. Someone to make love to every night. Over and over again. That turns him on.

Sure, Aaron has one-night stands just like anyone else. And yes, he enjoys them. But once he finds what he's looking for, he has no trouble remaining faithful.

After all, for Aaron, the sex just keeps getting better the longer he's with someone. So why would he risk a long-term relationship just to have a trick? It'd be like taking the crosstown bus when you've got a Ferrari sitting in the driveway.

He met his first boyfriend during his freshman year at Ohio State. He'd resigned himself to being unhappy — he had wanted to head east to a smaller college with a better dance program, but his parents outside Dayton insisted he stay in-state so he'd be closer to home, and, though they never said it, to save money. In his first semester, he hadn't made many friends at school; Ohio State was pretty much a party school for jocks, and he didn't fit in.

Even though he knew he was gay, Aaron wasn't ready to go public yet. He was afraid someone on campus would find out, and he'd lose the one protection he'd created against getting teased and beaten up: invisibility. So he avoided the gay discos and bars in Columbus. He didn't have any social life to speak of, or any sex life either.

During the spring semester, though, he'd started hanging around at Mean Mr. Mustard's, a straight but "alternative" club that drew a college crowd. It was here that he met Seth, a twenty-two-year-old kid with dyed black hair and pale white skin who listened to the Cure and wore a ring through his eyebrow and smoked clove cigarettes.

Aaron fell in love. Not head over heels — just in love. It wasn't the sort of soulful connection he'd hoped for, but Seth was his refuge, a true friend, someone who allowed Aaron to let his guard down. Aaron opened up to Seth about what he wanted from life — a career in dance, an escape from the Midwest, distance from his parents, an all-consuming romance — and Seth listened, even prodding Aaron to probe deeper inside himself. For the first time in his life, Aaron felt comfortable, not just with another man, but with himself.

As they grew closer, their sex life grew deeper, too. Aaron had a little experience before — one or two quick, groping evenings with a high school friend who liked to pretend nothing was happening the next day, and a handful of blowjobs in the university library men's room — but Seth showed him a lot *more. Seth was the first man he fucked, and the first man who fucked him. At first, Aaron thought getting fucked was physically uncomfortable, and he couldn't understand the pleasure of it until he understood the pleasure of fucking someone else; after that, once he knew exactly what Seth was feeling, he relished the times when Seth would fuck him.*

Seth found another boyfriend while Aaron was at home in Dayton that first summer, and although Aaron felt the loss, he realized that Seth hadn't been the man he'd been looking for anyway. During his remaining years at Ohio State, he worked up the courage to go to the gay discos, picking up a trick every once in a while, and befriending a group of young queens who taught him how to style a wig and dance in heels. He also had a series of minor boyfriends who lasted anywhere from several weeks to several months: Jerry, the Jewish bookstore clerk who introduced him to cultural studies; Todd, the blond clothing designer who bought him his first tab of Ecstasy; and Juan Carlos, the thirty-five-year-old Mexican papi *who taught him how to cook.*

Each was a good man, Aaron knew, in some way or another. But not the man he was looking for. And when it was time for him to graduate, he made up his mind to move to New York, and he never looked back.

He found a new crop of fierce friends in Manhattan's discos — ones who put Ohio's queens to shame. He found a new dance teacher who showed him what he'd never learned at Ohio State, and at the end of the summer, Aaron sailed through his audition for the Joshua Browne Dance Company.

He had escaped the Midwest, gained distance from his parents, and started a career in dance. By Christmas, he'd complete the equation when Joshua told him that he loved him. This one was going to be the endless romance Aaron had dreamed about. With a man Aaron admired and respected. A black man. If a few details were different, Aaron's parents would have been thrilled. But the details were all they cared about.

The relationship was difficult at times. Joshua didn't like Aaron's friends, lacked Aaron's passion for politics, was jealous whenever he spent time with someone else, hated the fey affectations he'd adopted from his clubby friends. Joshua was demanding and controlling; Aaron, being both several years younger and terrified of losing what he was sure was his one and only chance at true love, was afraid to disobey. The fact that Joshua was Aaron's choreographer, teacher, and employer only made the power dynamic more apparent.

But it was love, and Aaron was happy — happy enough to endure the sporadic fights. He had the best sex of his life with Joshua. It was intense, deeply emotional, and ever-changing. There was no way to predict exactly what would happen when they had sex. Joshua fancied himself a top, but Aaron managed to flip him a good percentage of the time. They loved fucking, loved the sense of connection, and it truly didn't matter to them who was fucking whom — that is, as long as the outside world still thought Joshua was the top and Aaron was the bottom. This arrangement suited both of them just fine.

They operated well as a couple, sharing an apartment downtown, cooking dinner together, entertaining friends. But when Aaron tore a ligament in his fifth season, the fabric of their relationship started to tear as well. It was clear that Aaron wouldn't be dancing professionally again — certainly not for a few years, probably not ever. This left Joshua without a lead dancer, Aaron without a job, and the two of them without their point of connection. The fact that they worked together kept them close, kept them functioning as a unit. If Aaron was going to do something else — and what? — how would their relationship change?

Aaron wanted to go back to school, to deepen his political leanings and find a way to apply his other interests. Joshua wanted him to remain with the company; if he couldn't dance, he could manage the troupe, handle publicity, take care of the finances, oversee bookings. Joshua didn't want to let him go. Aaron told him he'd made up his mind, that he needed to do something for himself, find a new direction. If he couldn't dance, he'd rather do something else altogether than watch other people dance from backstage.

Joshua felt betrayed, threatened. He told Aaron that if he left the company completely, he'd have to leave the relationship, too. He never thought Aaron would have the strength to walk away; Aaron didn't think so either. But he did. And true to his word, Joshua ended the relationship.

Aaron hadn't dated much in the two years since then. He had focused on his studies, gotten involved in politics again, studied massage so he could support himself during school. He'd grown his hair back out. He wasn't sure he could handle going through another breakup. But he still yearned for the intimacy he had shared with Joshua, the connection he'd lost.

He had a feeling that he might have found this connection again with Kevin. True, he was a bit leery after the whole hustling incident. But he figured Kevin wasn't lying because he was deceitful or malicious. He was lying because he was scared and young and didn't have any experience with relationships. But Kevin had the potential inside him for great intimacy, Aaron knew. He just had to show Kevin how to use it, the way Seth had once shown him the way.

SUMMER

eleven

Aaron and Kevin were sticky with glitter as they made their way across the Village. Some muscle boy wearing angel wings and tiny white shorts had tossed his "fairy dust" on them from his float as they stood watching the parade go down Christopher Street.

Aaron hadn't been to a Gay Pride parade in a few years — he'd sort of outgrown them, and thought they'd gotten too commercial and too cheeseball, with all those queens waving rainbow flags and hawking AT&T or Miller beer. But Kevin wanted to go, needed to go, so Aaron made an exception. And seeing the excitement in Kevin's eyes — it was still pretty powerful stuff for him — Aaron was surprised to find that he actually enjoyed himself.

They had both agreed not to wear any rainbow-striped accessories, for reasons both political and aesthetic. Kevin was shirtless. Aaron, disappointed that the Alliance had decided to keep a low profile by not marching, had worn an old Act Up T-shirt that said SILENCE = DEATH.

As they weaved through the revelers on the narrow sidewalks, sunburned throngs penned behind the police barricades, they drew closer to the thumping beat of dance music blasting from the stage on Washington Street, where the Pride Festival was set up. When they finally reached the festival, the crowd dispersed enough for them to stop and look around. There were two dykes making out against a wall, a group of teenage Latin boys with pencil-thin moustaches eating corn dogs, a pair of white men with matching T-shirts that said "I'm not gay but my boyfriend is" — one pushing a baby carriage and the other holding the leashes of their two long-haired dachshunds. The music was loud, if uninspired, and the greasy smell of fried onions and grilled sausages hung in the air. After soaking it all in for a minute, Kevin took Aaron's hand and said, "Let's go find the table." And off they went.

Past lesbians selling citrus-scented candles. Past vendors advertising something called "pride lemonade" for four dollars a cup. Past at least seven different church groups handing out leaflets.

After half a block, they spotted Moe standing in front of a small bridge table piled high with newspapers.

"Free newspaper?" Moe asked, holding in his outstretched hand a folded copy of the premiere issue of *New York Gay News*, which had rolled off the presses about twelve hours earlier.

Kevin took the paper and unfolded it to show Aaron. A photograph he had taken at the previous weekend's Pride Rally graced the cover. "My first paid gig," Kevin said.

Moe had offered him work as a freelance photographer for the paper, and Kevin leaped at the chance. The money wasn't great — twenty-five dollars per published photo, plus expenses — but it was a start. It might lead to other work at other papers offering more money. He'd graduated just four weeks ago (with honors, thanks to the 'A' he got on his porn-themed final project) and he was already working as a professional photographer.

"We should go to dinner tonight to celebrate, sweetie," Aaron said. "Your treat!"

"Very funny," Kevin said. "I don't get my first check for another two weeks. So until then, honey, you're buying."

"Okay, I guess I can be your sugar daddy for two more weeks," Aaron said, winking. He leaned over and kissed Kevin on the cheek and whispered in his ear: "I'm proud of you."

Moe turned away to give them a bit more privacy. And there he spotted, coming toward the table, Melody Penn.

"I hope you've got a copy of that paper for me, Moe Pearlman," she said, smiling.

"I saved one just for you, Professor Penn," he said, holding out a copy. Moe had never seen her looking so friendly, so relaxed. Perhaps this was how she normally looked, outside class. Or maybe it was just summer break, or Pride Day in particular, having this effect. Whatever the reason, he thought, it was a nice change from the snarling nastiness she'd often shown him in class.

"Hello, Mel," Aaron said, arms still around Kevin. "How's your summer going?"

"Oh, hello, Aaron," she said. "It's going very well, thank you. I've gotten some great research done, and I'm almost finished drafting the syllabus for my new Advanced Queer Theory course this fall. You are signed up, aren't you?"

"Wouldn't miss it," he answered — even as he was wondering how the hell he'd endure it without Moe by his side. "I mean, I might show up a few minutes late, but I wouldn't miss it."

She smiled.

"Well, I just wanted to stop by and say congratulations, Moe," she said. "This is important work you're doing. And I know you're going to do a great job."

Moe couldn't believe his ears. Was this praise coming from Professor Penn's mouth? Such a thing had never happened to him.

"And," she continued, "if there's ever any reason you want to come back to Empire, the door is open. I know you've taken one year off as a leave of absence, but you're welcome any time — in six months, in a year, in two years, in five years. Just come see me. We'd be happy to have you back."

Moe mentally scanned her comments for sarcasm. Why would she be happy to have him back? She certainly wasn't too upset to see him leave; that day in April when he told her his intentions, she didn't protest or plead or do anything to delay the paperwork making it official. But today she seemed genuinely friendly. What else could he say?

"I appreciate that, Professor Penn," he said.

"Happy Pride Day," she said. She winked, and then, after a wordless good-bye nod to Aaron and Kevin, she vanished into the crowd with the *New York Gay News* tucked under her arm.

□ □ □

"I know you don't like to kiss girls," said Carolyn, "so I got you this instead. Congratulations."

She handed Moe a giant Hershey's Kiss.

"Chocolate? How did you know?"

"I see the way you stand in front of the vending machine at the office, drooling."

"Thanks, but I should be buying *you* a present," said Moe, "for all your help." Carolyn had taken hours of her time to give Moe advice on hiring staffers, creating a prototype design, getting an editorial schedule in place.

"Think nothing of it."

"You want to stick around and help me hand out papers?"

"No, I just stopped by to give you the kiss. I'm going to take off," she said. "This is a dangerous place for a straight girl to be alone. A couple of hot women were giving me the eye before. And you know I haven't had much luck with guys lately. I better leave before I decide to switch teams."

□ □ □

By the time Gene made his way to Moe's booth in the early afternoon, his pale skin had already started to redden and freckle in the sun. The real reason for Gene's sour expression, though, was Dustin, trailing several feet behind, his eyes narrowed to angry slits.

Gene gave Moe a one-armed hug and a quick kiss. "Hey there, Dustin," Moe offered, but Dustin could barely manage a phony smile in return. Moe looked at Gene and raised an eyebrow that said, "What gives?" Gene's eye-rolling in response meant, "Don't ask."

Even after months of dating, Dustin still couldn't accept that Moe was a part of Gene's life. The three of them had spent a couple of evenings together — Gene thought that might allay Dustin's fears that they were romantically involved — but those nights only reinforced the notion that Gene and Moe shared years of history and personal connection that excluded Dustin. Moe had told Gene that it might be better simply to stay out of the way and let Dustin and Gene work through things together — all the while leaving himself more time to work on his budding romance with Max.

This plan had worked on some level. Dustin and Gene were now a regular item, making dates every weekend and phone calls every day. But Dustin still felt threatened by Moe, who spoke to Gene twice as often each day and saw him twice as many times each week. Dustin couldn't pretend to like him.

So here Dustin stood silent, facing away from the booth, his back to Gene, feigning interest in the silver jewelry table across the street.

Gene picked up a copy of the paper and flipped through it cursorily. "Looks great! Mazel tov!" he said. "How do you feel?"

"I feel pretty good," Moe said. "The first issue came out well, I think, and the staff is shaping up nicely, and we've gotten a decent reception here today — with the notable exception of the brunch-and-cocktails set. I guess it's hard to read when you're on the Stairmaster."

"Or shaving your chest," Gene added.

"You don't look like you're having such a good day."

"Oh, he'll get over it," Gene said, motioning toward Dustin. "He's just being petulant for a change. He wanted this to be *his* day, and didn't want to stop by your booth. I told him that if he skipped the booth, we could skip the whole day together and I'd just tend to my own booth — which, by the way, Ben and Jay are working like total charmers two blocks back. Anyway, Dustin relented, but now he's making sure I'm punished for seeing you."

"Sorry to cause so much trouble," Moe said sarcastically.

"Don't be," Gene answered with a wry grin. "This isn't over. When we get home tonight, I'm gonna fuck him till he can't walk straight. Then we'll see who's sorry."

"Ah, the delicate maneuvers of a romantic relationship," Moe said. "I'd almost forgotten."

"Speaking of which, where's *your* boyfriend?"

"I think he'd faint if he heard you use that term," Moe answered. "But Max said he'd come meet me here this afternoon. We're getting together after my shift is over."

"Getting together?" Gene asked. "Is that a euphemism?"

"No, if you can believe it. We're having dinner."

"Just dinner?" Gene pried, one eyebrow raised. "No sex?"

Moe rolled his eyes. "We're having dinner *and* sex," he said. "I'm not an idiot."

□ □ □

Max, wearing his usual ribbed tank top and tight, faded 501s with white sneakers, walked with a determined swagger through the revelers on Washington Street. Along the way, guys — ones who didn't think they liked men in their forties, ones who never imagined they'd be attracted to men with facial hair, ones who swore they preferred smooth chests — turned and watched Max cut through the crowd, oblivious.

Moe had spent the day checking out the men at the festival. Leather daddies in chaps with their butts exposed. Bears by the bunch. Police officers — a few fetishists, but several more real live police officers. There was eye candy aplenty.

But Max was in a class by himself. He didn't need any gimmicks. He radiated sex. There was no way for Moe to resist.

Once he caught Moe's eye, Max zeroed in on the booth. He greeted Moe with a strong hug and a deep kiss. Moe imagined half of Washington Street burning with jealousy. Moe being Moe, he also imagined the other half utterly bewildered: "What the hell is that hot man doing with that fat kid?" Let them wonder, he thought — although he was asking himself the very same question.

"Are you ready to go?" Max asked, grabbing a copy of the paper.

"I'll be ready in a minute," Moe replied. "I'm just waiting for the advertising guy to show up to take the next shift. He's due at three o'clock, and it's two fifty-seven now, so he should be here any time."

"I didn't eat lunch. I'm going to go grab an Italian sausage," said Max — who, unlike Moe, could say this without a hint of double entendre. "Come meet me over at the bandstand when you're ready to go."

"Will do. Won't be long."

Donald, the advertising manager, showed up at three o'clock on the nose. Moe handed over the booth quickly and headed to the bandstand. There was Max, sausage hero in one hand, *New York Gay News* in the other, ignoring the drag queen prattling away on stage. He saw Moe coming, and looked up.

"First issue looks good," he said. "You must be happy."

Moe looked Max in the eyes and exhaled. "I couldn't be happier."

□ □ □

They decided to have sex first and dinner later. Partly, this was because it was only mid-afternoon, and Moe had already eaten a pound of chocolate. Mostly, it was because sex was the first thing on their minds whenever they got together.

161

The sex hadn't changed much now that they were "dating." Moe was still doing all the work. Max still came three times. They still played porn while they were doing it.

But a few things were different. They kissed a lot now — something Max said he rarely did with anyone, although from Moe's point of view, he was remarkably skilled and strong-lipped. There was a deeper connection now, too: Max still liked his X-rated videos (the old-fashioned, "pre-condom" movies) but he also spent a fair amount of time looking Moe in the eyes, saying Moe's name aloud, and touching Moe — stroking his cheek, rubbing his neck, tousling his hair — while he was getting serviced. Moe felt more present, more appreciated, more desired from these little attentions. And once Max had his three orgasms, he would hold Moe as long as he wanted, whispering in his ear, "That's it, sweet baby, shoot that load for me," while Moe jerked off, the scent of Max's crotch still in his beard.

Max had never sucked Moe's dick, and had indicated no intention of doing so in the future. Moe thought it would have been nice if Max reciprocated once or twice — as a token gesture that he'd be willing to exert himself for the sake of Moe's pleasure. But the current setup was good enough. More or less.

After they were both spent, they decided to order dinner in, figuring it'd be near impossible to find a free table in the Village on Pride Day. While they waited for their food to arrive, Moe slipped back into his boxers and a T-shirt; Max stayed naked, stretched out on the bed. As Moe studied Max's body, he wondered if he'd ever get tired of looking at so beautiful a man.

Dinner arrived. A bacon cheeseburger for each, and two orders of fries. Funny, Moe thought, that we eat the same things and have such different bodies. Funny. Or maybe pathetic.

"How come you're all dressed?" Max asked. "You don't have to be a stickler for formality just because I'm here."

"I wouldn't eat dinner naked even if I was alone," replied Moe.

"Why not? It's your house. I walk around my house naked all the time."

"If I had a body like yours, I'd walk around the *streets* naked."

It was the first time Moe had ever said anything about Max's body to him. He'd always thought it too obvious, or feared that he'd appear too fawning. And, just a little bit, he worried that Max didn't truly appreciate how incredible his physique was, and that once Moe mentioned it, Max would realize that he was much too hot to waste his time on an out-of-shape loser like Moe Pearlman.

"You've got nothing to be ashamed of, Moe. You're a very sexy guy."

"You think so?"

"Why else would I be over here today?"

Moe was stumped. "Would you be surprised if I'd been asking myself the same question? I mean, you obviously put a lot of time and effort into how you look. So why would you be interested in someone who doesn't?"

"Do you really think I'm that shallow?"

Moe didn't answer. Maybe he had thought Max was that shallow. Maybe Moe was that shallow himself.

"I like the way my body looks, and I've worked hard to stay in shape," Max explained. "But that's not the only thing that makes a guy sexy. Is my body the only thing you find attractive about me?"

It *was* at the top of Moe's list, but it was not the only thing, so he answered, "No."

"Then why would you doubt that I think you're a hot man? I keep coming back for more, don't I?"

"Well, in your profile online, you said you didn't give a shit what a cocksucker looked like. So I figured the fact that you were letting me suck your cock didn't necessarily mean you thought I was attractive."

"Good grief, Moe, that's just a profile. It's not a complete picture of me. Sure, if I'm horny enough I'll let most anyone suck my cock. But you've got to know I don't think of you as just someone who sucks my dick. I wouldn't date a guy if he didn't make me hard. Haven't you noticed that I'm hard almost all the time when we're together?"

"Yeah, I noticed. I figured that's just how you are."

"No, baby, that's how I am when I'm with you. So take off your clothes and come eat your burger. It's getting cold."

□ □ □

"I won't be able to stay over tonight," Max said, talking with his mouth full. "I'm supposed to meet with a playwright about a new show for the fall."

Moe was disappointed, but careful not to show it. "What's it about?"

"AIDS, I know, but I can't tell you much more about it," Max said. "I'm meeting the writer tonight and he's going to give me the script."

"On Pride Day? This is one of the gay High Holy Days. Can't you take a day off?"

"I could, but this is why I'm doing what I'm doing."

"What do you mean?" Moe asked.

"AIDS," Max said. "That's why I'm at the Rainbow Stage. To deal with exactly this kind of show."

When Moe looked at him quizzically, Max proceeded to talk about his career, answering the questions Moe had never worked up the nerve (or found the time) to ask.

Max had directed a string of successful plays off Broadway in the 1970s, making a name for himself as a director willing to take risks and unflinchingly depict the real life of the gay community blossoming downtown. By 1980, Max's reputation had grown, and the tenor of the theater scene — always heavily gay, but also cautious and closeted — was changing. Max's work was seen as legitimate, rather than limiting, and he got a break on Broadway. A Tony nomination followed, as did other shows. He had arrived.

In 1983, Zachary — his then-lover of four and a half years — came down with pneumonia. Max took time off so he could care for Zachary. Zachary died a few months later.

AIDS was tightening its grip on New York. Old boyfriends and recent fuckbuddies were withering away, falling one after another. Max was paralyzed, unable to work or to think or to feel anything.

But in 1985, a playwright called — a man whose frothy musical revue *It's a Gay, Gay, Gay, Gay World* Max had directed in the Village a decade earlier. The playwright had a new show, a dark and brooding meditation on AIDS called *The Party's Over*. Max wanted to work on the show, to open people's eyes and make them see what they were ignoring. Producers, on the other hand, were reluctant to touch the subject. Nobody would front the money for the production.

Max went back to the off-Broadway theater where *It's a Gay, Gay, Gay, Gay World* had been mounted. But even in the heart of the Village, *The Party's Over* was too hot to handle. The show was dead on arrival.

"That's when I knew it was time to leave the mainstream theater business," Max told Moe, who had finished his fries and was stealing more from Max's plate. "The only place in New York that would even consider a show about AIDS back then was Rainbow Stage. So I decided that's where I needed to be. So that I could work on shows that matter. Not that there's anything wrong with a breezy musical or a comedy, mind you, but we were having a major health crisis — I suppose we still are, but it was different then. You can't imagine what it was like. You're too young to remember. AIDS was more important to me than anything else, and beyond visiting my own friends in the hospital, all I could do was dedicate my work to fighting the epidemic.

"I know Rainbow Stage isn't exactly Broadway," Max said. Moe didn't respond. "But," Max continued, "it's given me the space to put on work that matters."

"But Broadway isn't afraid to tackle AIDS anymore," Moe said, citing recent fare like *Falsettos* and *Angels in America*.

"I know," said Max. "But Rainbow Stage was there when I needed a place to do my work, and now I'm going to stay there to keep doing what's important. I've made a commitment there, and I'm going to keep it."

Moe wondered if he'd make the same decision, giving up Broadway for a crummy ninety-nine-seat venue. Or maybe, he thought, once you've proven you can reach your goal, you don't need to prove it again.

"Listen, I've got to run," said Max, reaching for his clothes. "I'll call you tomorrow and we can get together later this week. But I bet tomorrow's going to be a big day for you at work, now that the paper's hit the streets."

"Strange, I was so worried about getting the first issue out that today I felt like I could finally relax," Moe said. "Tomorrow I suppose I've got to start worrying about the next one."

Max was slipping on his sneakers when Moe leaned over to give him a kiss good-bye. "By the way, what's the name of this new play?"

"*Buried Alive.*"

"Sounds cheery."

Max was gone. Moe cleaned up the plates from dinner and straightened out the bed. Then, sitting down at his computer, he logged on to Men Online to see who was horny.

□ □ □

It had been a great day for Frank. He'd skipped Pride Day — as he had done for the past decade or more — to spend the weekend at his house in the Fire Island Pines. The weather had been glorious and the crowds had been manageable, thanks to the festivities back in the city.

Alone in the house, he had used the quiet time to relax and take one last look at *Buried Alive*. Not bad for a first effort, he told himself. But he'd give it to Max Milano for an expert opinion.

They had never formally met, but each knew the other's reputation and respected the other's work. So Max had been receptive when Frank called the week before to discuss the show. "It sounds like it's right up our alley," Max had told him on the phone. Frank had assured him that the play was ready, but added that he was open to suggestions from a more experienced theatrical professional. They made a plan to meet Sunday night to discuss the project.

The meeting was brief but cordial, over coffee in Chelsea, in a quiet spot far from the Pride Day crowds. Max seemed to like the narrative structure of the play, and said he'd look at it in the next few days and get back to Frank the following weekend.

Frank was proud of himself, and feeling nearly elated after his meeting with Max. He went for a stroll down Eighth Avenue, and seeing the boys walking hand in hand, with their arms draped over each other, Frank sighed.

But when he entered the lobby of the Chelsea Park Plaza, Frank was faced with a stack of newspapers, the *New York Gay News*. And the evening was ruined.

Here it was, the newspaper he'd learned about a few weeks earlier. And whose name sat atop the masthead but Moe Pearlman, the nasty little prick who'd insulted him to his face just a few months earlier.

Frank sat down and thumbed through the paper, figuring it would surely lead with an indictment of *Outrageous*, a personal attack on Frank himself, or an editorial extolling the virtues of promiscuity. But what he found instead was a calm and reasoned newspaper, lacking sensationalism or obscenity. Articles focused on pending legislation, AIDS funding, hate crimes, religion, and the arts. No mention of Frank or his newspaper. No discussion of sex at all. It was quite the sedate affair.

This only made Frank angrier.

New York Gay News wasn't going to compete directly with *Outrageous*; it was going to pretend like *Outrageous* didn't exist. As if Frank hadn't chronicled gay life in this city for the last ten years. As if he hadn't been the only one to call a spade a spade, and air even the dirtiest laundry in public. As if New York didn't already have a gay newspaper.

He called a theater publicist — someone he'd known for years — and got Moe's home email address, saying he needed it "for personal reasons." He didn't want to send this particular message to the *New York Gay News* address; his feelings were personal and he wanted to air them on a personal level.

Frank turned on his computer and began to compose a letter. He went through several revisions — some sarcastic and others menacing, some several pages long and others a mere paragraph — before settling on a compromise that communicated the bare essentials of his feelings.

Dear Mr. Pearlman:

Congratulations on the first issue of the New York Gay News.

The paper certainly seems respectable. Ironic, don't you think, that someone who aspires to be such a freewheeling radical would put out such a noncontroversial, safe newspaper? It's like a newspaper you'd let your parents read.

But I know the truth. You're a hypocrite, a liar, and a threat to the community. I know things about you that would give your parents heart attacks, and I know things about you that would make your oh-so-liberal publisher fire your irresponsible ass.

We've had our personal differences. Now you've threatened my livelihood. I've spent a decade building up my newspaper, and I'm not about to let some cocky kid take that away from me. So if it's a battle you want, it's a battle you'll get. But mark my words: You won't win.

Frank DeSoto

Frank reread the letter. There were many more things he wanted to say — about sexual irresponsibility, the ignorance of youth, the costs involved in the "sexual liberation" people like Moe were still ranting about years after it had been discredited. But he decided that, for the moment anyway, it was best to focus on a single issue. The newspaper.

He printed a copy of the letter for his files, then cut and pasted the text into an email. What Frank didn't know was that the publicist, reciting Moe's email address from memory, had given him the wrong information by mistake. So when Frank hit "send," his letter didn't go to Moe at MoePearlman@usnet. com — it went instead to MPearlman@usnet.com. Marvin Pearlman.

Moe's father.

twelve

There were two emails in Frank's mailbox on Tuesday morning. The first was from Katie, D.C.'s wife, politely declining Frank's invitation to spend July Fourth weekend at his beach house. "We appreciate the thought," Katie wrote, "but I'm afraid that Donovan and I just can't get away this weekend. But maybe we can get together once things have settled down. After Election Day."

Frank wasn't surprised, but he was disappointed nonetheless. The party he was planning for that Saturday night would be a great affair, as it was every year. He looked up to D.C. like a big brother, and was eager for his approval once he saw Frank's house and the extensive circle of friends he maintained — at least well enough to show up at a catered party once a year. But once again, D.C. had declined. He hadn't even found time to send the note himself.

Frank deleted the message.

But if Katie's note had saddened him, the next email left him thoroughly mortified.

Dear Mr. DeSoto:

I was surprised to find your letter in my mailbox last night. I imagine you intended your vitriol for my son, Moshe. But there are no accidents, so it must somehow be beshert, *fate, that your letter found its way to me.*

New York Gay News is indeed a newspaper that Moshe lets his parents read. We received the first issue this morning, and we're very proud of the work he is doing for his community. There's nothing that our son could do or say that would give

*us a heart attack, and we're confident that Abe Guttmacher
believes that Moshe is a responsible man as well. Otherwise he
never would have hired him.*

*I called Moshe to ask him what could have motivated you to
write such a note. He filled us in on the history of your newspaper
and directed us to your website to read an issue for ourselves.
After reading an issue of each newspaper side by side, we began
to understand why you feel threatened. It is not because the
New York Gay News has attacked you, or because my son has
personally waged war on you. It is, quite simply, because he is
putting out a product that is more professional, more balanced,
more intelligent, and more useful for the gay community.*

*Moshe tells us that his ambition is to build an essential
resource for his community — not to destroy your livelihood.
It is our belief that the biggest city in the country has room for
at least two gay outlets. Your competition, Mr. DeSoto, does
not come from my son's commendable efforts, but from your
own shortcomings. Do better work, make your own publication
better, and your newspaper will survive. If not, you will fail. But
your battle is with yourself.*

Marvin Pearlman

Frank mulled over a response, but realized there was none
that was appropriate. He could email Mr. Pearlman some of
the more horrifying details of his son's life in New York. He
could follow through on his threat to expose Moe's sexual
activities to Abe Guttmacher. He could pretend to be sorry —
but truly, he wasn't.

What he was, quite simply, was ashamed. Ashamed at
the fact that he'd let a personal vendetta escalate to such
embarrassing proportions. And ashamed that his own father,
had he received a similar note when he was still alive, would
never have risen to defend his son in the same way as Marvin
Pearlman.

□ □ □

Moe had copies of both Frank's email and his father's reply, which his father had forwarded to him. They had talked on the phone the previous night — about *Outrageous*, about the Alliance, and about the sex crackdowns in New York, all in terms vague enough to avoid personal disclosure about Moe's sexual activities but specific enough to outline the overarching political situation. Together they decided that Moe's father would respond and Moe would stay out of it. Not that Moe wanted to let his father fight his battles for him, but he wanted to show Frank that his threats were meaningless and that Moe had support he could depend on. The fact that it would naturally humiliate Frank was just icing on the cake for Moe; he didn't mention that to his father.

Finally, Moe was learning to keep his mouth shut. He didn't need the aggravation.

Besides, he had other things to worry about as the newspaper started its second issue. In the *New York Gay News*'s corner of the newsroom — a cluster of a half-dozen cubicles wedged between *Footlights* and the advertising department shared by all of Abe Guttmacher's publications — it was a busy day.

Rex, the guy he'd hired to oversee the arts section and the calendar, was sweet but a bit timid; he needed a lot of hand-holding, especially dealing with prickly contributors who were prima donnas. One writer, a book reviewer, had already called Tuesday morning, shouting at Rex about what a "shit head" he was for making minor edits in his review. Rex nervously came to Moe for advice. ("This is an easy one, Rex," Moe told him. "Don't hire him again." Such simple wisdom had eluded Rex.)

Billy, the editorial assistant who helped field op-ed pieces, selected wire stories, and proofread all the articles, was good at the first two parts of his job but not so good at the third; the number of typos in the first issue was embarrassing. Moe had to have a sit-down with him on Tuesday.

Most of all, Moe had his hands full with one of his two staff reporters. Liz, seasoned, forty-ish, was ready to go without much supervision; she had recently moved from Chicago, and since she had experience covering politics for a magazine there, Moe put her on the political beat. She was good as gold. His second hire — assigned to cover local gay issues — was a good-natured young woman just out of college named Jane. She was eager and she could write, but she didn't fully grasp some of the trickier issues she needed to tackle.

On Tuesday morning, she got a press release from the prevention director for MIGHT, Hector Vasquez, that made some fairly shrill pronouncements based on a new set of HIV statistics released by the city's health department. The data showed dramatic decreases in AIDS deaths over the previous year, thanks in large part to the widespread use of protease inhibitors. But MIGHT's spin on the data made it sound like doomsday was at hand.

"Epidemic deepening among men of color," the press release said. "Young men at greatest risk. Second wave of AIDS looms."

Jane planned to write about the impending second wave and the groups that would be hardest hit. She talked to Hector Vasquez and he gave her some juicy quotes about the danger signs in the new numbers.

The Moe sat down to talk to her, and tried to set her straight.

"The epidemic isn't getting worse for men of color," he said. "It's getting better for men of color, but not as much better as it is for white men. Look at the data: AIDS deaths were down fifty-eight percent for white men, and down forty-two percent for black men and forty-seven percent for Latino men. This isn't bad news for anyone. It's great news for men of color, and even greater news for white men. It shows that there are discrepancies that need to be addressed, but it's not bad news any way you slice it."

Jane folded her arms. "But these numbers show that we still have inequalities to deal with."

"But that doesn't mean it's bad news for anyone. Why do we have to keep sounding the alarms?"

"Well," said Jane, "Hector said that if people get complacent and think things are getting better, then they let their guard down. And that's exactly the kind of thinking that's going to cause a second wave of infections among young men. Even after all these years of prevention, young men are going to have higher infection rates than older men."

"Young men aren't at greatest risk," Moe countered. "The data show that seroconversion rates for men under twenty-five are actually much *lower* than those for men in their thirties and forties. What MIGHT has done is estimated young men's risks of infection over the course of their lifetimes, by extrapolating based on what happened to older men. This is a huge leap of faith. There's no data to support the idea that men who are twenty now will have the same infection rates over the next twenty years that thirty- and forty-year-olds have had over the last twenty years. It's pure speculation."

Jane considered this for a moment, and Moe took the chance to hammer his point home: "This second-wave rhetoric has been batted around for a decade already, and it's never come to pass. It's based on anecdotal evidence that has yet to show up in actual statistics. Stories that young men are out there having unsafe sex in droves, intentionally infecting themselves with HIV, behaving recklessly. Any time statistics come out showing that young men in fact still make up a tiny percentage of people with AIDS, groups like MIGHT come out to say that the second wave is lurking beneath the surface, that these men just haven't gotten tested yet or haven't gotten sick yet, and that this generation is a time bomb waiting to explode. It's bullshit science with nothing to back it up."

"But why would MIGHT put out a press release that wasn't accurate? If this data offers some good news, why wouldn't they be celebrating?"

"How does MIGHT make money, Jane? Donations. Over the last couple of years, people have stopped paying so much attention to AIDS. New medications mean that people are living longer and better. Other diseases have taken some of the spotlight. Hollywood has moved on to different colored ribbons. Then there was that big cover story in *Newsweek*, 'AIDS is Over.' Groups like MIGHT have watched their donations slide."

"But AIDS is just as important as ever," Jane said. "Even if people are living longer, they still need medical attention and legal help."

"That's right, but MIGHT doesn't think people will listen if they tell the truth. MIGHT knows that it made millions of dollars when people were in a panic over AIDS. They're betting that they can make millions more if they keep people in panic mode. They need to maintain panic to stay in business."

"That's pretty cynical," said Jane.

"Yes, it is," Moe admitted. "But it's also true."

□ □ □

MIGHT, Frank thought, has finally gotten it right.

As he sat in his office reading Hector's press release, he was relieved that this lazy, bureaucratic AIDS organization had finally told the truth. This was increasingly an epidemic that white men were buying their way out of, a disease that young men were too cavalier to avoid, and a disease whose worst days still lay ahead, thanks to the complacency of most gay men. The *New York Times* had run a front-page story that morning about the decline in AIDS deaths in the city. He was glad to see that MIGHT hadn't given in to premature declarations about the end of the epidemic.

He called Hector Vasquez to see if he was free for lunch.

□ □ □

When Gene got back from lunch, Eleanor was waiting for him again. In his office. In his chair.

"I took a look at your memo about advertising on the train ride from Washington today, and I think we need to talk," she said. "We've got different ideas about how this agency should be marketing itself."

Gene had emailed her a mock-up of an ad he had designed: an apparently naked, muscle-bound hunk holding a globe, strategically placed to hide anything too graphic. The text read: See It All with Final Frontier Travel.

"What's wrong with that ad?" Gene asked. He had spent two weeks working on the idea. "It's playful, memorable, and gets people's attention."

"It's male-centered and borderline obscene," Eleanor replied.

"So are a lot of our customers," Gene said.

"We need to present Final Frontier as a serious company, a group of professionals catering to the whole community. We've always been viewed as professional and serious in Washington, and that's gotten us far."

"New York isn't Washington," said Gene.

"What's that supposed to mean?"

"It means that what looks serious in Washington seems uptight here, and what might look dirty in Washington is perfectly acceptable here. I mean, have you ever seen what the local cable stations show at night? Strippers and naked talk shows and ads for prostitutes. That's New York."

"Gene, we don't have to sink to that level."

"We do if you want to get New Yorkers' business."

"I am not going to start down that path, using sex to sell our services," she said. "I've created a respectable image that has worked for this company for years, and I'm not going to change it now."

Gene stopped. He wasn't going to change her mind. Maybe later, but not now. "Do you have an idea for an ad that gets this respectable image across?"

Eleanor pulled a piece of paper from her bag. "In fact, I do."
With a pencil, she sketched out an idea. Four smiling people
sitting in airplane seats — two men on one side of the aisle
and two women on the other, each couple holding hands —
with the caption: Travel in Comfort. Final Frontier. New York's
Lesbian and Gay Travel Agency.

"This ad accentuates what we're all about," she explained.
"We're a comfortable place for lesbians and gay men, a place
where they can feel relaxed. Anyone can sell you an airline
ticket, but what matters is that we're lesbian and gay, so you
can feel like you're dealing with family when you walk in the
door."

"Family? That's the message you want to put out in the *New
York Gay News*?"

"No," said Eleanor. "I don't want to advertise in that paper.
I realize your friend is involved, but it's purely a business
decision. I'm not going to take a gamble on a newspaper that's
printed one issue. Who knows if the *Gay News* will even be
around in six months?"

"So you want to run this ad in *The A-List*? It'll look
completely corny."

"I don't want to advertise there, either. *The A-List* is just
a bar rag for young guys who want to get drunk and get laid.
That's not our audience."

"I think you'd be surprised," Gene said. Had she noticed
that they'd gotten a decent amount of street traffic during the
first few months even without advertising, driven largely by
men walking through Chelsea and seeing those two cuties —
Ben and Jay — sitting up front?

"Our target audience is men and women, of all ages,
particularly couples looking to make travel plans together.
Those are the people who want a comfortable place to make
their arrangements. That's who we need to reach. I think we
should stick to *Outrageous*. It's a serious newspaper with a
diverse readership, it has a long history in New York, and it
doesn't have any of those filthy ads for escorts and phone sex."

"Eleanor, *Outrageous* has a tiny circulation and a rotten reputation. It's pretty much a rag. I don't think it'll help us to be affiliated with a paper like that."

"Nonsense. Just because you don't like it doesn't mean it's not a good paper. We're a community-based business, and we need to be supporting our community-based institutions. You might not like the politics at *Outrageous*, but at least it's not all about sex, sex, sex."

"Actually, a lot of times *Outrageous is* all about sex," Gene said. "It's *opposed* to sex, but that's still a main topic of discussion."

Eleanor wasn't taking the bait. "I can see we have different opinions about this. But for now, we're going with my idea and my choice of outlets. So I want you to make a mock-up of this ad, and get it to me by the end of the day tomorrow."

"I'll get to work on it right away, Eleanor," Gene said. "As soon as you get out of my chair."

□ □ □

Irregular. Is there a more awful word?

Kevin had been humming Ace of Base when he walked into the free clinic to pick up his results in the afternoon, confident that he didn't have anything to worry about. He'd been tested every six months since he moved to New York, and was scrupulous about safe sex. He was a hustler, but he wasn't stupid.

But if he wasn't nervous when he walked in, he was certainly nervous when the nurse used that word.

"There appears to be something *irregular* about your blood sample from last week," she said.

"Irregular? What does that mean?" he asked.

"It does not mean that you have HIV," she said quickly, then adding, after a pause, "necessarily."

"I don't understand."

"It's nothing to worry about. It could be that the sample got contaminated somehow, or that the lab screwed up. All it means is that we couldn't read your test properly, and we'll have to take another vial of blood to do the test again."

She seemed calm, and Kevin tried to accept what she was saying at face value. Wishing he hadn't come alone, he tried not to panic. But as he rolled up his right sleeve, his only thought was: Thank God she doesn't want to take my blood pressure, because it'd be off the charts.

□ □ □

When Aaron arrived at the Alliance meeting at ten minutes past six, nobody had saved him a seat. He had to fetch a folding chair from the corner and sit behind someone else.

The discussion was already underway. Gabe was presiding, and about a dozen guys were there. Tonight, they were trying to set up a committee to get to work on a new pamphlet: Safety with Strangers. It would include suggestions for making anonymous encounters less risky — in terms of sexually transmitted diseases, physical violence, and police harassment.

The arguments were the same as always, in the Alliance or any group. Everyone wanted a voice in what the pamphlet would say, but nobody wanted to commit the time to putting it together. They wanted to tell someone *else* what to do.

"We need to make sure this isn't just about negative guys staying negative," said Richie, a veteran of Act Up and Queer Nation. "There needs to be something in here for us poz guys."

"So will you be on the pamphlet committee to make sure your issues are addressed?" Gabe asked.

"No, I'm too busy," Richie said. "I don't have the time."

Then there was the usual back and forth between the people who wanted to focus on HIV and the people who wanted to wanted to focus on safety more broadly, between those who wanted to promote anonymous encounters as liberating and those who wanted to discourage them as foolhardy, between those who wanted to explain what was legal and those who didn't give a shit about the law.

"The police are not our friends," said Marcos, a heavyset man wearing a baseball cap that said "Troll." "I don't see why we should advise people to play by their homophobic rules."

Ron, who still worried about things like his "good name," said, "Some of us don't want to get arrested."

"Been there, done that," said Marcos. A few other people in the circle nodded.

Aaron thought, How on earth am I going to get through this without Moe?

Moe had told Aaron that as a journalist, he'd have to give up his active involvement in any groups the newspaper might report on. He'd have to stop coming to Alliance meetings.

Without Moe, Aaron felt alone. As he sat outside the inner circle of seats, he realized that he didn't feel particularly connected to the others in the room. And the talk, talk, talk of the meeting struck him as so much rehash of other activist meetings, an endless tape loop of the same discussions he'd heard before.

When Aaron got back to his apartment, Kevin was already setting the table. "I ordered Chinese," he said without turning around. "It'll be here in a few minutes."

Aaron tossed his bag in the corner and sighed. "You remember when I said I'd keep working with the Alliance as long as it was fun? Well, it's not fun anymore now that Moe's gone."

Kevin was folding napkins and didn't look up.

"I'd rather spend my Tuesday nights with you, eating egg rolls and vegetable dumplings. Let those other queens worry about saving sex. I'd rather be here with you, *having* sex."

Aaron took Kevin by the shoulders and turned him around, intending to plant a kiss on his lips. But when he looked at Kevin, he saw that his eyes were red, as if he'd been crying.

"My God, sweetie, you're trembling! What on earth is wrong?"

□ □ □

Gene couldn't believe that Moe had let his father deal with Frank's email attack.

"I don't know how you restrained yourself," he said. "You must have been itching to write him a scathing reply."

Moe was draining pasta over the sink. "You know, actually I think this is something I learned from my mother. When I was in high school, it was my grandparents' fiftieth wedding anniversary, and my mom was having a big party for them at our house. I wanted to go out with my friends, and she said it was okay as long as I was home in time for the party. I honestly intended to get home in time, but I guess I wasn't watching the clock, and I didn't get home until the party was half over. I figured she'd lay some big guilt trip on me, scream at me about how I'd disappointed her and offended my grandparents. But she didn't say a thing. And that made me feel a thousand times worse. Sometimes, no response is the toughest response of all."

"Very clever, Mister Pearlman," said Gene. "I'm glad to see you've put Jewish guilt to good use."

"Me, too," said Moe. "After all, it never seemed to work on you."

Gene smiled. "You know us Catholic boys. Sin, repent, seek absolution, and sin again. We feel guilty after the fact, but not enough to change what we do."

Over spaghetti, Moe told Gene about everything else he'd had to deal with at work. Gene was mildly sympathetic, but in return offered his own stories of woe in the workplace.

"The business is doing okay, but it's not the instant success Eleanor hoped it would be," Gene explained. "I keep telling her that New York isn't Washington, and that she should adjust her business model if she wants to make inroads here. She sees what isn't working, but she refuses to listen to the obvious solutions. She second-guesses everything I do, in a way she never did in Washington. It's driving me up a wall." (Knowing it would only hurt Moe, he did not repeat Eleanor's comment about the *Gay News*.)

"Sounds like we could both use a little getaway," said Moe.

"Actually, I'm going to take a little getaway this weekend," Gene said. "Dustin got us a room on Fire Island."

"You're kidding. Aaron got me a cheap room in a house on Fire Island this weekend, too. No small feat on the Fourth of July. It should be fun. I've never been out there."

"Me either," said Gene.

"It'll be great, the whole bunch of us hanging around Cherry Grove."

Gene stopped. "I guess you'll have to tell me what it's like, sugar bear. Because we're not going to Cherry Grove. We're going to the Pines."

Moe put his fork down. "Oh, I should have realized that Dustin wouldn't dream of going to the Grove."

Although Moe and Gene had never been to Fire Island — Gene had spent his summer weekends in Rehoboth, near Washington, while Moe hadn't been willing to shell out two hundred dollars for a crappy room at the Grove Hotel — they both knew about the ongoing rivalry between the two gay beach towns. Cherry Grove was the more historic community, with small houses and a friendly atmosphere that was welcoming to women and men, young and old, beautiful and not-so-beautiful people. The Pines was where men with fabulous bodies lived in fabulous houses and had fabulous parties. Grove residents thought of Pines boys as shallow, vain, and elitist; Pines residents viewed the Grove as the Island of Misfit Toys — a place for people who didn't fit in anywhere else.

Moe said, "Maybe we can meet in the middle, in the Meat Rack." This was the forest connecting the two communities, legendary as an open-air cruising ground, the only place where Grove and Pines types would connect.

"I figure you'll be spending most of your time there," said Gene.

"You got that right."

"I don't think we'll be seeing you there. I doubt Dustin will be keen on me taking a trip through the enchanted forest."

"Still dealing with his jealousy issues?"

"Yes," said Gene. "In fact, he started therapy this week to deal with it."

Moe smiled. "You've finally succeeded in driving someone literally insane."

"Actually, sugar bear," said Gene, "Dustin's problem isn't me. It's you."

□ □ □

Thank God the guy I'm seeing isn't the jealous type, Moe thought as he lay in bed with Max that night. He knew I was a slut before he even met me.

Moe and Max didn't talk about having sex with other people, but each assumed the other was continuing to sleep around. For Max, this involved getting blown in the locker room at the gym some mornings. For Moe, it meant entertaining one of his old online buddies in the evenings, before Max came over; Moe's longtime fuckbuddies were disappointed that he didn't have much time for them anymore, and he didn't want to risk them finding new cocksuckers, so he found the time to keep them satisfied at least occasionally.

This arrangement suited everyone fine. And Max didn't complain when Moe spent time with Gene, either. He didn't seem possessive at all. Moe couldn't have asked for more.

But he did.

"I'm going out to Cherry Grove this weekend," he said to Max. "I'd love it if you could come with me."

Max was silent.

"I've got the room already, and it's a big enough bed for both of us. Fourth of July weekend. Should be fun."

Still silence.

"Have you ever been there? I mean, I imagine you have. It's my first time. Maybe you could show me around."

Max took a breath. "Thanks for the invitation, but I don't think it's a good idea."

"Why not?"

"I haven't been for a long, long time."

"Maybe it's time for you to go back, then, huh?" Moe was looking up at Max's face as he rested his cheek on his chest.

"No, I'm sorry, baby. Too many memories for me out there. You go and have a good time. I think I'll stay here."

Max was suddenly somber, and Moe was wishing he hadn't mentioned it. There were times when they seemed to be living in the same city, in the same neighborhood, in the same year — but then there were times like this when Max seemed to be in a parallel universe, inhabiting a ghost town filled with apparitions and phantom lovers. "I'm sorry I brought it up," Moe said.

Max leaned down and kissed him on the forehead. "Don't be sorry. I'm just not ready to go. Funny thing is, it's the second invitation to Fire Island I've gotten today."

Moe propped himself up on his elbow. "Oh? Who else invited you? The *other* man you're dating?"

Max knew the jealous routine was just a joke, so he didn't take the bait. "The playwright I've been working with, Frank DeSoto. He invited me to a party in the Pines."

"What?!" Moe asked, this time not joking at all. "You're working with Frank DeSoto?"

"Yeah, didn't I tell you that? *Buried Alive* is his play."

"You most certainly did not tell me that. I'd remember if you'd mentioned Frank DeSoto."

"Okay, so I'm telling you now. We're going to put on his play this fall at Rainbow Stage."

Moe sat up straight in bed, pulling away from Max. "I can't believe you're working with that asshole!"

"Calm down, Moe, I think you're overreacting here. Just because he works at the other gay newspaper..."

"The fact that he runs a piece of shit tabloid rag as a vanity vehicle for his burned-out, self-hating friends isn't the point. It's the fact that he's been one of the masterminds behind the sex crackdown that the mayor's been waging, the fact that he's been using his clout to help advance the mayor's anti-gay agenda by closing down gay sex spaces."

"You can't honestly believe that."

"Why not? It's true."

"Frank DeSoto is a dyed-in-the-wool AIDS activist. You don't remember because you didn't live here yet, but he made a lot of waves when he started his paper. He gave Act Up its first real platform."

"I know what he did a decade ago," said Moe. "He still thinks he's part of the Act Up generation, but underneath the self-righteous rhetoric, he sounds pretty much like Pat Buchanan or Jerry Falwell. He's one of the most vocal opponents of sexual liberation left in the city, and he's collaborated with some of the most vicious antigay politicians in New York."

"Moe, we're all fighting the same battles here, and even if some people use different tactics, we're all on the same side."

"Frank DeSoto is not on my side."

Max had never seen Moe like this, fired up and angry and stridently political. Most of his impressions of Moe were sweet and upbeat, eager to please and deferential, sometimes even insecure and needy.

"This community is too small to make enemies," Max said. "Maybe you need to think about it in terms that aren't so political."

"Not so political? How can it not be political? Everything I'm fighting for is political, and he's on the opposite side in almost every one of those battles."

"I've been around longer than you have, Moe. When I look at Frank, I see someone who's devoted his life to his community. I see someone who cares deeply about gay men — even if you disagree about his methods or his specific stances.

"But even more than that," Max continued, "I see a man who watched his lover die a terrible death when he was still too young to expect anything so awful. I know what that's like. I've been through it. You look at him and see someone who's damaged beyond repair. I look at him and I see a fellow traveler, someone who's endured the worst horrors you can imagine, yet somehow still finds the will to move forward and make his community stronger. You can disagree with his politics, but you can't discount his humanity."

Moe didn't respond. He folded his arms over his chest and threw his head down on the pillow, turning toward the wall. Max, mostly calm, lay down behind him. But he didn't reach out to soothe Moe, didn't kiss Moe good night. He rested his head on his own pillow, and within minutes drifted off to sleep.

His brow still furrowed, Moe listened to Max's measured breaths, but avoided the temptation to turn over and nuzzle against Max's chest. He stayed separate, the gap between them a seemingly unbridgeable chasm.

thirteen

Aaron told Moe to make himself scarce: "We'll meet you in the Pines at noon, sweetie. But Kevin and I need some time to ourselves this morning, if you know what I mean."

"I can guess," Moe said with a leer.

It was only nine fifty-four in the morning, so Moe had a couple of hours to kill. He headed down the boardwalk, straight to the Meat Rack.

Most people would think it would be empty on a Saturday morning, when the average Fire Islander was fighting off a hangover from the previous night at Sip and Twirl, or perhaps still sleeping. But Moe could smell sex a mile away, and even though he didn't know the overgrown sandy paths of the Meat Rack, he used his intuition to find a surprising amount of action for that hour.

He blew one man — an older, stocky type wearing just a pair of swim trunks — against a tree. He stumbled across two young guys — clearly Pines boys, judging from their perfect pecs — kissing and stroking each other in a clearing, and took the opportunity to service them both on his knees as they continued to make out. And when he saw one cockhound under a tree sitting comfortably in a plastic patio chair, sucking cocks literally left and right, he thought, Why didn't I think of that? While the seated man was pleasuring two standing gentlemen, Moe knelt before him and gave the cocksucker his best treatment; within one minute, the cocksucker blew his load, packed up his privates, and ceded the chair to Moe

— who continued to service all comers, without straining his knees, until a quarter to twelve.

At that point, Moe reluctantly left his seat, popped a piece of Big Red in his mouth, and headed toward the Pines.

His first impression of the Pines was that it looked pretty much like the Grove: wooden boardwalks, guys walking their dogs and pulling bags of groceries in little red wagons. But on second glance, he noticed the differences.

The Grove had small cottages perched right on the edge of the boardwalk, with names like "Dune Buggers" or "Homo Heaven" or their own house, "Queens Are Wild," which they'd rented from Aaron's massage client, Perry. The Pines had larger homes, often two stories tall, hidden behind wooden fences, with rainbow flags flying atop the roofs. He could hear splashing behind a couple of those walls, splashing that came from private swimming pools — something unknown in the Grove. And there were no women to be seen. The Grove, meanwhile, was at least half lesbians.

One man approached him, walking down the boardwalk toward the Meat Rack. Moe smiled. The man slid by without making eye contact.

I guess I picked the right side of the island, Moe thought, as he quickened his pace toward the harbor. It was eleven fifty-eight, and he didn't want to be late.

He didn't realize that both sides of Fire Island operated on gay time.

□ □ □

Moe couldn't find Aaron and Kevin in the crowd that had gathered in the horseshoe-shaped harbor, where hundreds or maybe thousands of shirtless men stood bicep to bicep. It shouldn't be difficult to spot them, he thought; they'd be two of perhaps a dozen non-white people there.

Someone called Moe's name. He recognized Gene's voice, and turned to see him waving from across the harbor. Moe made his way through the mass of muscled backs and stubbly chests until he reached Gene.

"I didn't think they let folks from the Grove come over without a passport," Gene said, greeting Moe with a kiss.

"No, we just need a few vaccinations, some pec implants, and a hit of Ecstasy, and we can get a six-hour visa."

"Well, your implants don't seem to be working. Maybe you should get your money back."

"Funny," Moe said. He looked behind Gene and saw Dustin boring holes into him with his glare. "Hello, Dustin, how are you?"

"Fine." Nothing else.

Moe looked back to Gene. "I don't want to interrupt your weekend. I'm just looking for Aaron and Kevin. Have you seen them?"

"Nope," said Gene.

"Well, when I find them I'll leave you two alone."

Gene winked. Then he reached behind him and took Dustin's hand in his.

□ □ □

Moe looked and looked, but he never did see his friends. At twelve twenty-two, people started to cheer and applaud as the ferry from Cherry Grove entered the harbor. Loud music blared — old chestnuts like "I'm Coming Out" by Diana Ross and "We Are Family" by Sister Sledge — and the boat rocked to the beat.

The ferry was crammed to capacity. With drag queens. It was an annual July Fourth event, the Pines Invasion, the one day of the year when the uptight Pines queens let their proverbial hair down and welcomed a bit of old-school faggotry back into their midst. Grove folk dressed up in tacky drag — mostly the faux-glamour or drunken-wreck varieties, plus a few of the fierce-diva and nasty-bitch types that reigned in Manhattan — and sailed into the Pines to mix it up with the muscleboys.

"I can't believe Aaron didn't show up," Moe said. "He's always late for everything, but he seemed pretty insistent this morning. Now he's missing it."

"Oh no he's not," said Gene, pointing to the boat. "That's him right there. And Kevin. And they are looking *good*."

On the upper deck stood Aaron, with Kevin by his side.

"Holy shit, they look like a couple of tricked-out crack whores," said Moe, quickly adding: "In a good way."

Moe ran over to the ferry landing to greet his friends.

A line of drag queens disembarked and filed past Moe, to the cheers of friends and onlookers. Most were having trouble in high heels on the boardwalk. A few had clearly stashed their flasks in their clutch purses and taken a few nips during the ferry ride, which didn't make the walking any easier. But even these trashy, stumbling, tragic drag queens passed right by Moe without so much as a nod, drawn by the sight of dozens of shirtless, muscular men who were, for once, paying attention to them.

No matter, Moe thought, there are only two queens here I need to see.

And there they were. Aaron in a yellow Lycra tube top and a pair of Daisy Dukes cutoffs, and Kevin in a leopard-print sheer blouse knotted above his midriff and a black leather miniskirt — very Tina Turner, circa "Private Dancer." Aaron had tucked his short braids under an orange do-rag, while Kevin sported a black bobbed wig. They each had on far too much makeup, even for whores. Both wore flats. Sensible for girls who clearly spent a lot of the day walking the streets.

"My God, Aaron, you look fantastic!" shouted Moe, who had heard a lot about Aaron's get-ups.

"Aaron? Who is Aaron?" he responded. "My name is Chlamydia. Chlamydia Johnson. And this is my partner, Cuntricia DeVille."

Moe looked at Kevin, who was clearly just getting the hang of the attitude that went with the outfits. "You can call us Clammy and Cunty," he said.

"Lovely to meet you, ladies," said Moe.

Aaron cracked a wad of chewing gum and feigned disinterest.

The throng continued to disembark, jostling Moe. He liked the scene — the music, the people smiling and shrieking and having a good time — but the crowd was starting to get to him.

"Perhaps you ladies would like to go somewhere and have some lunch?"

"Whatever you say, mister," said Kevin. "But if you want both of us, it's gonna cost you double."

□ □ □

"No, seriously, it's my first time in drag," Kevin repeated, as they sat eating overpriced, mediocre tuna sandwiches at the only cafe in the harbor. They had waited an hour and a half for the table, and by this point they were hungry enough not to care.

"Well, you wear that miniskirt like a natural," Moe said with a wink. "It's like you were born to be a hooker."

There was a moment of silence, and Moe wondered if he'd crossed the line.

Apparently not. Kevin chimed in: "No, I'm a rotten hooker. I've got this one special client, and I keep giving him the goods for free."

"I hope he's at least giving you crack," Moe said.

"Let's just say we're giving each other crack," Kevin answered, and all three laughed.

Moe was relieved. "Clammy, I'm glad to see you've finally accepted Cunty here for the whore that she is."

"Actually, Moe, I've sort of announced my retirement from the business, all kidding aside," said Kevin. "I canceled my ad in *The A-List* on Friday."

"But how are you going to pay your bills? You can't make rent earning twenty-five bucks a pop taking pictures for the paper."

"That's true," said Kevin. "But now that I've got a few published photos, I'm going to start contacting other newspapers about doing freelance work. And in the meantime, I took a part-time job working in a photo lab starting next week. It's not ideal, but at least it's in the right field, and the owner said I can use his darkroom after hours to develop my own stuff."

"Sounds like a good deal all around."

"The best part of it is that I'll have my evenings free," Kevin said, "so I can spend more time with Aaron."

"How sweet," Moe said earnestly.

"Yeah, he can't keep his hands off the merchandise," Aaron said, fondling the fake boobs — tangerines — he had stuffed into his tube top.

"Don't flatter yourself, sister," said Kevin, slipping back into character. "We both know that I'm the pretty one here."

"That," Moe said, turning to Kevin, "must be why they call you Cunty."

Before they left the restaurant, Aaron ducked into the men's room. After he scrubbed off the rouge, eye shadow, and lipstick he'd slathered on, he peeled off his tube top, left his two tangerine breasts on the bathroom counter, pulled the bandana from his head, and kicked off his flats.

"Be a doll and take this stuff home," he told Kevin when he met them in front of the cafe a few minutes later, handing over his top, his shoes, and his tacky plastic clip-on earrings.

Moe and Kevin headed for a water taxi — Kevin because his skirt made walking a chore, and Moe out of sheer laziness. Aaron decided to walk, so he left them in the harbor, strolling up the boardwalk barefoot and wearing only a pair of revealing jeans shorts.

☐ ☐ ☐

"This isn't easy in a skirt," said Kevin, as Moe helped him into the water taxi.

"Stop complaining," said Moe. "You're having the time of your life."

"Yeah, denial is a powerful thing," said Kevin, sitting down and crossing his legs.

"What do you mean?"

"You know," said Kevin, looking around at the other people in the boat. "I'm sure Aaron's been talking to you about it all week." "

Aaron hasn't mentioned anything to me," said Moe. "What's going on?" But Kevin only looked around at the other passengers.

The water taxi slowly pulled out of the Pines harbor. Moe scooted closer to Kevin. "Nobody can hear you. Tell me what the hell you've got to be in denial about."

Leaning in close, Kevin told him about the HIV test.

"I can't believe Aaron didn't tell me about this," Moe said, genuinely hurt.

"I can't believe it either," said Kevin. "He's been a wreck for days."

Moe was stung. He'd been Aaron's confidant for two years. "Why wouldn't he tell me?" he asked.

"I guess he thought it was something we should get through as a couple," said Kevin.

That didn't make Moe feel any better.

"Well, I'm sure you're fine, Kevin. It's probably just a lab error. You'll get the results of the second test this week, and you'll be negative just like you've always been."

"I hope so, but what if I'm not? What if I'm about to give up hustling, ready to be monogamous with this guy I love, and I find out that I'm positive?"

"That'd be ironic enough for an Alanis Morissette song."

"I'm serious, Moe. Can you be serious for one second?"

Moe stopped kidding around.

"Look, if you're positive — which you're not, I'm sure — you'd get on meds, like Gene. He's been positive for years, and he's doing fine. Look at him. Being positive isn't a death sentence. You take pills, and you can go on living your regular life."

"There's one problem, Moe. Gene has something that I don't have."

"What's that?"

"Health insurance."

□ □ □

Frank hadn't been in the Meat Rack since Scott died — on those rare occasions when he went to the Grove for dinner or to play bingo, he took a water taxi — but as he'd expected, not much had changed. Sandy paths weaved left and right, converging occasionally in vaguely circular open areas and then splitting again under low-branched trees. It was easy to get turned around, but as long as the bay was on the right, he remembered, the path was leading to the Grove.

Years ago, Frank used to love the Meat Rack. He and Scott would take afternoon breaks during their summer weekends at the beach to look for action. If they hadn't gotten lucky at the bar, they'd go there late at night, too. Scott always knew when and where to find the most men.

Today, though, Frank had chosen the time he thought the Meat Rack would be the *least* crowded. The Pines Invasion, he knew, would draw a huge crowd, leaving the Meat Rack largely empty. It was the perfect time for him to make his move without attracting too much attention.

The black canvas bag slung over his shoulder contained a hundred photocopied flyers and a staple gun. The flyer featured a large photograph of a naked man, either on the verge of death or freshly deceased, skeleton-thin and covered with lesions, lying on a hospital bed. Across the top, in large letters, it read: "AIDS: You're Asking For It."

Underneath, quick sentences elaborated: "Get out of the Meat Rack! Anonymous sex is high-risk behavior. Barebacking is suicide. Condoms aren't foolproof. Even oral sex kills. Those are the facts. If you ignore them and get sick, it's your own damn fault. Zip up your fly and go home before it's too late."

At the bottom, it said: HELPING EVERYONE AVOID DEATH. DON'T BE AN ASS. USE YOUR HEAD.

It didn't take more than a few seconds to staple each flyer to a tree along the cruising paths. Once, he heard footsteps on the trail and quickly put his posters back in his bag, pretending to be a fellow cruiser out looking for action. The other guy, as usual, didn't even make eye contact.

Frank relaxed. He unhunched his shoulders, took a deep breath of the warm air, and continued on his way, flip-flopping toward the Grove.

He had relaxed so much, in fact, that he heard nothing as he put down his bag, took out another poster and stapled it to a tree. Then:

"What the fuck do you think you're doing?" a voice behind him demanded. Frank turned to see a young black man, shirtless and barefoot, with a lean body and braids. Definitely angry. Frank had seen him before, but couldn't remember the context.

Now staring him in the eye, the man repeated, "I'm talking to you, motherfucker! What the fuck do you think you're doing?"

Frank was a bit intimidated, but he kept calm: "Community service," he answered.

"Community service, my ass, Frank DeSoto. Let me see that poster."

As the shirtless man tore the paper off the tree, Frank felt a bit off-balance: This guy knows me, but I don't know him, he thought. Who the hell is he?

Aaron didn't bother to introduce himself. He just kept talking. And he was pissed.

"This is your idea of community service? Putting up horrible photos as scare tactics?"

"That's not a scare tactic," Frank replied. "That's what AIDS really looks like. It's not a Sustiva ad, where people bike up mountains with their dogs running alongside them. It's this."

Aaron continued: "And this is your public service announcement? AIDS is your own fault?"

"Well, it is, isn't it?" Frank replied. "We all know how to get HIV and how not to get it. So if you get it, it's your own fault. It's about taking personal responsibility."

"Funny, I remember years ago, marching with Act Up, and one of the things we put on our signs was 'There are no innocent victims.' The whole point was to say that there aren't any *guilty* victims, either — there aren't some people worthy of sympathy or respect and others who should be blamed for their problems and left to die. You remember that, don't you? It wasn't so long ago that children and hemophiliacs were 'innocent victims' and gay men were 'just getting what they deserved.' I thought we were fighting *against* all that."

Frank paused. "That was a long time ago."

"So you're saying that fifteen years ago, everybody was innocent, and today, everybody is guilty?"

Frank thought of Scott. "Fifteen years ago, we didn't know any better."

"Bullshit!" Aaron yelled. "Fifteen years ago, when gay men were spending every weekend in VD clinics getting shots for the clap or syphilis, or getting checked out for herpes, or dealing with amoebas and parasites and hepatitis, they didn't know that their behavior was unhealthy? That's a load of crap. Maybe they didn't know about AIDS yet, but they sure knew they were playing serious games with their health — and their partners' health. They weren't as innocent as you think they were."

"You don't know anything about it, you self-righteous asshole — you weren't out of elementary school yet," Frank spat. "So don't you tell me about what things were like back then. Yes, people got VD back then, but there was no way we could have known that we'd be dealing with a deadly disease — or that we'd be spreading it to other people. You kids today have no excuses. No excuses at all for getting high and fucking around, barebacking and screwing in the bushes when you know exactly what the risks are. Like you, right this minute, cruising for sex in the Meat Rack with Lord knows how many men."

Aaron narrowed his eyes. He wasn't cruising — the idea of having sex in the woods wasn't particularly appealing to Aaron, who could only think of the bugs and poison ivy — but that wasn't any of Frank's business. He said, "You'd be doing the exact same thing if anyone still wanted to look at you."

"Fuck you." Frank turned and reached for his bag, but as he tossed the strap over his shoulder, it tipped over, dumping its contents onto the sandy path: the posters, the staple gun, and several plastic bags full of condoms.

He hurried to put everything back in his bag, but Aaron saw what had fallen out. "What are you doing with those condoms?" he asked.

"None of your business," Frank answered.

"Those are the bags of condoms that MIGHT hangs from the trees. Why the hell would you be taking them away? I thought you were so concerned about AIDS and the health of your fellow gay men."

"Putting condoms out here only encourages men to have sex," Frank said. "We shouldn't be encouraging men to have anonymous sex, and we shouldn't be giving them a false sense of security. Condoms fail. Yes, they're better than nothing, but they're not nearly good enough. We shouldn't be helping people indulge in unhealthy behavior. We should be making it as inconvenient, unpleasant, and unpopular as possible."

Aaron now realized that he was wasting his time talking to this guy — Frank wasn't some sad, burned out has-been; he was a dangerous and delusional lunatic. Aaron figured he'd spend the next hour going through the Meat Rack, ripping down Frank's flyers, and then he'd call MIGHT and see if they could send out more condoms to hang in the trees. But before he turned away, he took one more shot.

"Frank, there's only one way to keep men from having sex out here: You just stand right there and be yourself. Ain't a thing more unsexy in the world."

□ □ □

Frank was still a bit shaken when he got to the Firefly Cabaret in the Pines at six o'clock to see *Livin' My Vida Loca*, the one-man show by Hector Vasquez, the prevention director of MIGHT. He ordered a seltzer water and waited for Emmett Kane to show up.

Frank's lunch with Hector earlier that week had gone well. Frank had laudatory things to say about MIGHT — quite a change from the criticism *Outrageous* usually showered on the organization, calling it "namby-pamby," "timid," or "chicken-shit." At the end of their lunch, Frank had invited Hector to his July Fourth house party in the Pines, and Hector had mentioned that he'd be on Fire Island anyway to perform his new show. So Frank had decided that he'd check it out.

Emmett walked in a few minutes after six — still plenty early for the show, which was sure to start at least a half hour late. He ordered a Long Island iced tea.

"Nice to see you," he said to Frank, sipping from his drink, careful of the paper umbrella. "So how's everything going? Are you all ready for the party?"

"I think so. I mean, I hope so. I mean, yes, I'm ready."

"A bit stressed? Maybe you should be drinking something harder."

"No, I'm not stressed about the party. I've been doing that for twenty years. It's just been a stressful day."

"Why's that?" Emmett asked. "Did those queens from the Pines Invasion gang up on you?"

"I skipped the Invasion," Frank said. "I spent the afternoon in the Meat Rack."

"That doesn't sound like you at all."

Frank explained his little guerrilla action.

"Oh," Emmett said, "now it *does* sound like you."

Then Frank told him about his confrontation with the young shirtless guy.

"Of course, you know you were right and he was wrong," offered Emmett, who was drinking his Long Island iced tea like it was Nestea.

"I know that," said Frank. "But it's frustrating to see that kind of attitude among younger guys. After all we've been through, it seems like they still can't keep their dicks in their pants."

The lights flashed on and off.

"Show's about to start," said Emmett. "Let me go hit the men's room before we sit down. That drink went right through me."

Frank went to grab two seats while Emmett headed toward the back of the club. He stood outside the men's room, waiting for a moment, when the door opened and he found himself face to face with one of his therapy clients.

"Oh, hi, Emmett! I didn't expect to see you here."

"Sometimes I do leave the office," Emmett said. "And it's good to see you out and about. You're in a much better mood than the last time I saw you. What's going on?"

"You know that guy I've been telling you about? We're out here together for the weekend. I told him I wanted this to be a time just for the two of us, without his ex-lover monopolizing his time. And you know what? It's working. This afternoon,

201

he told his ex to buzz off when we ran into him. And when we were talking about tonight, he told his ex that he shouldn't come to the show, that he should give us some time alone. It's the first time he's put his foot down on the subject. So of course I'm in a good mood. I finally feel like I actually have a boyfriend."

"That's great news!" Emmett said. "I'm sure we'll have plenty to talk about at next week's session. I'll see you later, Dustin."

□ □ □

Gene felt strange seeing a show without Moe. But he was trying to prove to Dustin that he was willing to put a bit of effort into their relationship, that he wanted to spend time with him one-on-one.

Dustin, who had always been so quick to follow Gene's lead, had changed in the last few weeks, since he started therapy. His therapist had told Dustin to make more demands, stand up for himself, say what he wanted. Dustin had done so, telling Gene, "I want to feel like your top priority — I'm tired of sharing you with someone else. And if you can't make me your top priority, maybe I should go find someone who can."

Gene was pretty sure that this little speech was handed down verbatim from the therapist, since it didn't sound like anything Dustin would say himself. Nevertheless, Gene had decided to give it a shot. Dustin seemed happier now that Gene was paying more attention to him — even if he still had problems being remotely civil to Moe, which irked Gene no end — and they were having longer talks, more frequent sleepovers, and hotter sex than ever.

When Dustin returned from the men's room and took his seat, he pulled his chair so close to Gene's that their legs were touching.

□ □ □

Hector started *Livin' My Vida Loca* by reenacting scenes from *The Brady Bunch.*

"Growing up in the '70s in Southern California, I always wanted to be a normal American kid, like Bobby Brady," he said. "Except my

202

father looked more like Freddy Prinze on *Chico and the Man* than Mister Brady. And we didn't have a maid — my mom *was* a maid."

He riffed about his Mexican immigrant parents' discomfort with American culture and talked a lot about his older sister — a sweet little girl who grew into a rebellious heavy-metal fan. ("Her name was Bonita, but she insisted we call her Beth, like the Kiss song.") The audience was laughing — and singing along to Kiss — but the material got more pointed when Hector started talking about his teenage years.

"I wanted to get in touch with my Mexican roots," he said, sitting center stage on a stool. "I listened to Mexican music and studied Spanish. My parents were thrilled, especially when I started hanging out with a classmate named Jorge, who was fluent in Spanish. They were less happy when they found out that the only words Jorge ever said to me in Spanish were 'Muerde el elote.' It literally means 'Bite my corncob,' but that's not quite what he meant."

About forty-five minutes into the show, Hector was discussing his life in New York, where he'd moved after high school, about ten years ago, to come out for real. He talked about the first time he saw the Pride parade ("Some of these guys wouldn't feel so proud if they owned a mirror"), the first time he went into a gay bar (The Spike, an old leather bar that used to host Sunday brunch: "I'll have scrambled eggs cooked in Crisco and two slices of toast with K-Y Jelly"), the first time he took Ecstasy ("I fell in love with everyone — except, of course, the guy I was seeing at the time"), and his first time at a sex party ("For Latino Homeboyz and Black Banjee Boyz ONLY, the poster said, so I went, paid my ten dollarzzzz and spent the night having zzzzzex").

Gene was having a good time, laughing a lot. Dustin would squeeze his hand when he thought something was funny, and Gene would squeeze back.

The last segment of the show was more serious. Hector talked about how he had seroconverted the year before, at age twenty-seven. He made a few jokes about it ("It's strange that they call it 'HIV-positive,' because frankly, I can see a downside to it") and explained how it had changed his view of the city, his relationship with his parents, and his sex life: "Now, when I go on a date, we each have to bring separate syringes to shoot up!" He ended the show by checking his watch and announcing that it was time for him to take his medication: "It's Combivir. They call it that because it combines so nicely with Ecstasy. I'll see you all on the dance floor later tonight at Sip and Twirl. You're only as sick as you feel, right?"

□ □ □

"This is exactly what I was talking about before," Frank told Emmett as they walked out of the Firefly. "These young guys don't take any of this seriously. They think AIDS is one big joke!"

"The most unbelievable part of it all," Emmett said, "is that this guy is the prevention director for MIGHT. Prevention director! Some guy who hangs out in sex clubs and leather bars, having unsafe sex. He's supposed to help other people stay negative?"

As they walked back toward Frank's house to finish setting up for the party, Frank told Emmett about *Buried Alive*, and how it would address a lot of the issues they'd been talking about that evening: irresponsible young men, the risks of sexual misbehavior, the fatal folly of believing the worst was over.

"Sounds like it'll be a great show," Emmett said. "I can't wait to see it."

"I'm nervous, since it's my first stab at playwriting," Frank admitted. "But I can guarantee it'll be better than the piece of shit we saw tonight."

□ □ □

"Condom?" Kevin asked, holding out a Trojan in a wrapper as a man in a sweatshirt and black jeans descended the steps at the end of the boardwalk. "They're free, take one."

He did.

"I can't believe that asshole pulled that shit today," Moe said, now that the man had passed.

"Believe it, honey," said Aaron, "I saw it with my own eyes. Frank DeSoto is one crazy faggot."

They were sitting on the benches at the edge of the Grove's entrance to the Meat Rack, distributing the 120 condoms they'd been able to buy in the little grocery store near the dock. Aaron had called MIGHT but got a machine, since it was a holiday weekend. "We've got to improvise, girls," he'd said, and this was the best they could do. Aaron had already ripped down all of the posters he'd found.

"Screw the Alliance," said Aaron. "This is what sex activism is about. Not meetings and pamphlets and letters to the editor — no offense, sweetie. But this is where we make a difference."

"I don't want to make a difference out here," said Moe. "I want to make a difference in there."

"So go ahead," said Kevin. "We'll stay out here and hand out condoms. You go in and make the world safe for blowjobs."

"Now *that's* my kind of activism!" said Moe.

And with that, he handed his boxes of Trojans to Kevin and sauntered down the sandy path into the woods. Kevin took two condoms out of the box and put them in his own pocket. "These are for later," he said, winking at Aaron.

□ □ □

Dean and Greg, Frank's longtime neighbors in the Pines, now in their sixties, showed up first. They always did, stopping in to be polite but leaving before Frank's closer friends arrived. They sipped red wine and made small talk with Emmett while Frank finished setting out trays of hors d'oeuvres.

Next came Kyle, who had been Scott's gym partner once upon a time. He was never particularly close to Frank, but he came to this shindig every year because Frank always put out a good spread. (He wasn't much of a cook, but he knew how to pick caterers.)

A trickle of guests arrived: a couple of publicists who wanted to stay in Frank's good graces, one of the bartenders from his old disco Snow who was now a personal trainer. Around nine — one hour after the invitation suggested — people started showing up in larger numbers. There were several reporters who had once freelanced for *Outrageous*; Frank still owed every one of them money, and they all knew they'd never get a dime of it, but they came to his party anyway to see who else would show. A few other neighbors — some from the Pines, a couple from Chelsea — appeared. The gossip columnist from the *Voice* came solo, with a tiny notebook in his breast pocket to take down any fantastic bon mots, and to keep track of celebrity sightings.

Each year, as Frank's elbow-rubbing days at Snow receded further into the past, fewer celebrities worthy of boldface type showed up. But there were still enough to make an invitation to Frank's party a hot commodity in the Pines.

Vance Andrews had been a young soap opera heartthrob who frequented Snow's VIP room. He had since fallen out of favor, although he still popped up in made-for-TV movies on occasion. He arrived with his "personal assistant," a dashing man twenty years his junior, in tow.

Clarisse, a one-named disco singer who had performed at Snow when both were at their peak, made an appearance, too. She hadn't had a hit since 1979's "Man-o-rama," and she was no seventeen-year-old starlet anymore; she'd put on about a hundred pounds, and her weave was looking pretty sorry. But in this crowd, she was still somebody.

The biggest name to drop by was Steven Sovchenko, whose first job in New York was designing sets for the elaborate stage shows at Snow. Steven had recognized the opportunities that

Snow offered; he was looking for connections, and he'd gotten them there. Today, years after Snow was a bit of kitsch history, Steven was one of the hottest artists in the city. He had never cared for Frank, but he was a big believer in karma, so he always paid homage to the man who'd given him his first break. (If only D.C. had come, Frank thought, Katie would have been so impressed that I know Steven Sovchenko.)

Several B-list famous folks came, too — actors, singers, clothing designers and one or two small-time elected officials. The party was a strictly respectable affair; drug dealers had been among the biggest VIPs at Snow, but the ones still alive were strictly personae non gratae at Frank's parties today.

All in all, about thirty people showed up. The food was tasty — pan-Asian finger food — and the music on the CD player was old-school classy standards. Conversation was pleasant chatter with the occasional laugh or shriek, but generally low-decibel. A lot of guests talked about the "good old days," reminiscing about folks who were no longer around. Most people asked politely about *Outrageous*, and a few asked Frank cautiously about the *New York Gay News* — questions that he brushed off.

Frank was feeling too good to worry about that right now. He was in his element: popular, beloved, respected, remembered. A handsome Asian man in his thirties, who must have accompanied one of the invited guests, stood talking to Frank for a full twenty minutes without averting his eyes.

"So what do you do besides the newspaper?" asked the young man, whose name Frank had already forgotten. He was too busy taking in this boy's physique — lean but muscled — and his white teeth.

Frank thought, Is he coming on to me? It had been so long, Frank wasn't sure he remembered what that might look like.

But this guy kept asking questions about Frank's work, laughing at every clever quip, touching Frank's elbow. He is *definitely* coming on to me, Frank realized.

Frank hadn't gotten to ask any questions in return, like: Who brought you here? What do you do? Would you please spend the night with me? And the next night, too?

The boy was so attentive that it made Frank nervous. It also turned him on. He wanted to tell everyone to leave, and take this boy to the bedroom immediately. But he couldn't risk being a rude host. There were reporters there.

Besides, Frank relished the chance to tell someone about *Buried Alive*, to talk about his new creative direction. And this guy — Peter? Kai? Allen? — was rapt. Frank was just beginning to lay out the cast of characters in the first act when he felt a tap on his shoulder. He turned, and his giddy smile evaporated when he saw Hector Vasquez standing next to him.

"Hi, Frank!" said Hector, reaching out his hand. "Wow, this is a great house you've got here. How long have you had this place? It must have cost a fortune!"

Frank was frozen. He forgot to make introductions. In fact, he forgot completely about the handsome young man who'd been so solicitous a moment before. All he could remember was how duped he felt after believing just days earlier that Hector was one of the smart ones. He couldn't even muster a hello.

"I saw you in the audience tonight," Hector said. "Thanks for coming, it meant a lot to me. Did you like the show?"

Frank just stared.

"People were laughing a lot, so I guess it was good, right?" Hector asked, getting a bit nervous.

Then Frank finally found his voice again. "I'm sorry, Hector," he said. "But I'd like you to leave my house."

fourteen

POSTER BOY FOR BAD BEHAVIOR was the headline.

Frank had planned out his editorial, including the title, on the train ride home from the beach that morning.

When he got to his apartment early Monday, he went straight into the *Outrageous* office, took a moment to appreciate the view of the Empire State Building — lit up in red, white, and blue just hours earlier, now sandy-colored in the summer light — then shut the blinds and started writing:

In his one-man show, Livin' My Vida Loca, *Hector Vasquez proved he knows how to tell a joke. But there's nothing funny about what he has to say. It's infuriating that a young, seemingly intelligent man who should know better would engage in reckless behavior — drug abuse, partying, promiscuous sex. In Vasquez's case, it all led, predictably, to HIV infection. Such a person deserves no sympathy when he seroconverts; he made his own bed, and now he can lie in it. But the morons over at MIGHT didn't just extend their sympathies. They turned him into their prevention director! This man, who deliberately engaged in unsafe behavior, is supposed to tell the rest of gay New York how to stay negative? That, as Vasquez might say, is "loca." This poster boy for bad behavior must be made an example. Fire him now!*

His entire rant wasn't even six-hundred words, but it made the point strongly, he thought. He put a teaser — "MIGHT Makes Wrong" — at the top of the front page, above the

Outrageous banner. It was a perfect complement to his lead story about the dangers of drugs like Ecstasy and GHB, which had already caused three deaths that year at gay circuit parties, and which Frank said made those circuit parties' dark rooms into "hotbeds of AIDS."

On the editorial page itself, below his rant about Hector, was a picture of the poster Frank had hung in the Meat Rack. Frank didn't mention that he had put up the posters, or that the organization named on them had exactly one member; it didn't seem important. He also didn't mention that he'd stolen MIGHT's bags of condoms. That, he realized, would be too difficult to explain in fifty words or less. Instead, his caption said simply: "A new group of activists calling themselves HEAD — Helping Everyone Avoid Death — finally had the nerve to say what we all know is true. These posters were put up throughout Fire Island's Meat Rack this weekend. Maybe guys in there will finally learn to keep their dicks in their pants."

□ □ □

As Moe strode toward Abe Guttmacher's corner office, he mulled what his publisher might say about the cover story he had planned for issue three. They'd had several long talks in the weeks prior to the paper's launch, during which Abe mentioned "integrity" and "honesty" and "giving people the information to make their own decisions." Abe had been happy with the first two issues, coming to Moe's desk to congratulate him and offer generalized but still welcome praise: "You're doing a great job, Moe. Keep up the good work."

Then again, the *New York Gay News* hadn't printed anything particularly controversial yet. And Moe certainly hadn't run any articles that might hit Abe Guttmacher in the checkbook. It's entirely possible, Moe thought, that the boss's era of good feeling will end as soon as he gets a nasty call from an advertiser.

No way to know for sure without asking, Moe thought as he knocked on Abe's open door.

"Come on in and have a seat," Abe said, pointing to the modest leather chair in the corner.

Moe did, and without any chit-chat, explained his dilemma. He had commissioned an in-depth story about the effects of smoking and drinking on gay people's health. Jane had spent the weekend transcribing interviews with medical professionals and researching statistics online. She'd found out, as he expected, that alcohol and tobacco were far graver threats — to lesbians and also to gay men — than the designer drugs that drew most people's wrath. Drinking was far more likely than Ecstasy or Special K to lead to medical problems ranging from accidents to addiction to illness to death, and more likely than crystal meth or cocaine to lead to impaired judgment during sex. Tobacco killed more gay men each year than AIDS.

"You sound like my daughter," said Abe. "Carolyn's constantly clipping articles about smoking and leaving them on my desk."

"I'm sure she's just worried about you."

"Nonsense. She likes to get on my case. Of course it's rotten stuff, those cigarettes, but what else gives me so much pleasure every day?"

Moe was quiet. Abe looked at the pack of Marlboros on his desk, shook his head, and got back to business.

"Anyway, don't let my addictions influence you. You have numbers to back up everything you say?"

Moe nodded.

"Do you say anything about smoking or drinking that hasn't already been documented elsewhere?"

"Well, in terms of the overall effects of alcohol and tobacco, no," said Moe. "But I've never seen them framed broadly as gay health issues before. Alcoholism in the gay community has gotten some attention — not nearly as much as drug addiction, but some. Still, I've never read an article about the larger health issues involved in drinking, and I've never seen any reporting on smoking among gay men and lesbians."

"Then it sounds like you've got an important story on your hands." Abe sat silently and folded his arms on his desk.

"So that's it?" Moe asked. "You're not worried about your advertisers? I know we have cigarette and liquor ads."

Abe shook his head. "You're not the first person to say that alcohol and tobacco are bad for you. They put warnings in their own ads, for God's sake. You're not making any wild accusations here. If the sponsors get upset and threaten to pull their ads, it's probably just talk — they don't place ads because I run a hedonistic paper, they place ads because they want to reach gay readers. That'll still be true next week, and the week after, and as long as we keep reaching gay readers, they'll keep placing ads."

Moe hadn't thought of it that way. He nodded.

"And, in the end, if a few of them pull their ads, I'll deal with it," Abe said. "That's my job. Your job is to put out a newspaper that tells gay New Yorkers what they need to know. So you worry about that, and let me worry about the advertisers."

As Moe stood up and walked toward the door, he knew he was lucky to have a boss like this: a straight man who didn't pass judgment, a businessman who saw beyond the ledger. "Thanks, Mister Guttmacher," he said as he walked out.

"Don't mention it," came the reply. "And please, call me Abe."

□ □ □

While Aaron sat in the waiting room, Kevin saw the nurse. This time the news was much better.

"The results came in fine," she said. "You're negative."

Kevin, who'd been holding his breath since he sat down, finally exhaled. "Thank God."

"You seem surprised. Did you think you might be positive?"

"Well, it's always a possibility, isn't it?"

"Only if you're doing things that put you at risk."

Kevin didn't say anything.

"Do you have multiple sexual partners?" she asked.

Kevin looked at her and said, "I used to."

□ □ □

Gene thought Eleanor would be thrilled at the deal he'd lined up. He thought wrong.

Gene had pulled a few strings and managed to hammer out an arrangement for Final Frontier to be New York's official travel agency of the Crystal Ball, a circuit party scheduled for Thanksgiving weekend in Las Vegas. It would get Final Frontier lots of exposure and bring hundreds of new customers in the door to buy the weekend package, which included airfare, hotel, and party admission prices. Sponsoring the event wouldn't cost much, and the agency would make up a large part of the expense from the per-ticket commission the party promoters would kick back. But when he called Eleanor in Washington to give her the news, she wasn't happy.

"Those circuit parties are just an excuse for guys to get high and have sex," she told him. "I've read about them. About how people have been overdosing and dying on the dance floor, and about how much unsafe sex takes place. This isn't the kind of thing I want Final Frontier to be associated with."

"It'll provide instant name recognition," he argued. "It'll get new customers in the door, and once they've done business with us for this weekend, they'll be much more likely to call us next time they're planning personal vacations or business trips. Besides, we'd be sponsoring a gay community event. I thought you wanted to get involved in the community."

"That," she said, "is not my community."

After Gene hung up, he had to call the organizers and back out of the deal. They weren't happy, but Gene knew it wouldn't take them more than a few days to replace Final Frontier. The agency, on the other hand, had just lost a golden opportunity, and Gene had just lost a lot of credibility.

□ □ □

"I'm glad one of us is having a good day at work," said Gene.

"Empress Eleanor again?" asked Moe. "But she's not even there today."

"She's learned how to bitch long-distance."

"You can tell me about it tonight," Moe said. "I'll make dinner — and by that, of course, I mean I'll order the pizza."

"Sorry, sugar bear, I can't get together tonight," Gene replied. "I have plans with Dustin."

"I thought you'd probably need a break after a whole weekend together in the Pines."

"Actually, the weekend was pretty wonderful. We're sort of on a roll."

"Will wonders never cease. I imagine your relationship will truly flourish once Dustin gets that restraining order against me."

"Don't be a drama queen. I'm going to see you tomorrow night for that show."

"Oh yes, Chekhov. That should be a great evening of fun and frolic for us."

"Are you complaining?"

"Not at all. Although I should tell you that I had a talk with Carolyn this afternoon about reviewing shows for *Footlights*. I don't think I'm going to have much time to write for her while I'm busy trying to get the newspaper off the ground. So I've put reviewing on hold after this week's show."

"That is so selfish of you, Moe. Didn't you ever think about me? What am I supposed to do without your press seats? Pay for tickets myself?"

"It's nice to know that after all this time, the basis of our relationship is still so firmly rooted in love and companionship."

□ □ □

There wasn't any restaurant at Seventy-fourth Street and Central Park West. But Dustin had told Gene to meet him on the corner after work, so there Gene stood, waiting for his date to show up, wondering where exactly they'd be going for dinner.

Dustin arrived within a couple of minutes, wearing a natty gray suit and a devilish smirk. "I see you found it all right."

"Yes, but what did I find?"

"Follow me."

Dustin led him under a dark green awning and into a large apartment building. He said hello to the doorman: "I'm here to show Mr. Macintosh the apartment." They were given a key and dispatched to the elevator bank.

"What's going on?" Gene asked as they entered the elevator.

Without saying a word, Dustin put the key in the slot next to "Penthouse," turned it, and they took off for the top floor.

The elevator doors opened into the most glorious apartment Gene had ever seen: It took up the entire floor, with spectacular views overlooking Central Park. The furnishings were a bit much — very stylish in a sort of deliberate, consciously tasteful way — but it was hard to criticize the space overall.

"What are we doing here?" Gene asked.

"I'm showing you this property," Dustin said.

"What are you talking about? There's no way I could afford this place. It must cost two million dollars!"

"Gene, please. It costs almost three times that much."

"So I ask again: What are we doing here?"

"I thought that instead of spending the evening in your studio in Little Italy, we could spend the evening here in this luxury West Side penthouse apartment."

"But how?"

"I'm showing the property for the owners. The owners, by the way, are in France this week. So I figured that since I've got access to the place, and nobody's going to come home...we should probably make the most of it."

"Isn't that completely unethical?"

Dustin took Gene's hand: "Come, let me show you the Jacuzzi."

Gene relaxed and gave in to Dustin's plan. It was spontaneous, sweet, and just a bit risky — Gene loved the idea.

Dustin had mapped out the whole evening. A bottle of wine to share in the hot tub. Then dinner — he'd brought food from a caterer on the Upper West Side — by candlelight on the terrace overlooking the park. And then a bit of romance in the outrageous master bedroom suite, with a California king-size bed.

"This is great," said Gene. "A night of living like the other half lives."

"I thought you might like it." And then Dustin pulled from his pocket the final surprise of the evening: a strip of three condoms.

"Wow," said Gene. "You thought of everything."

□ □ □

As soon as Moe got home, before he checked his answering machine or sifted through his mail, he logged on to Men Online. He'd been away for three solid days, and had gone straight to work when he got back from Cherry Grove.

No messages.

Moe started to panic. Normally, if he went an entire weekend without logging on, half the men in New York were climbing the walls, aching for relief. He'd been unavailable since Thursday night, and not a single guy had sent him a message. Maybe, he thought, they've given up on me. Maybe they've found other cocksuckers. Maybe they don't need me anymore.

The very thought made Moe sweat.

He checked his "buddies" list and saw three guys he knew online. He checked his notes to refresh him about their specific assets and quirks. BloMeNow was a Dominican guy named Rick who lived in the neighborhood; he was in his early thirties, tall and thin and clean-shaven, but randy as hell and very verbal. OnYourKnees was a sexy guy named Walter — around forty, dark with a perennial five o'clock shadow, and hung like a mule — but Moe rarely saw him because he had a steady boyfriend and only got to play occasionally. LickMyLolly (he had told Moe his name was Joe, Jeff, and Oliver on separate occasions, according to his notes, so Moe usually just called him "stud") was a hot salt-and-pepper daddy in his fifties who lived in Brooklyn but had a car; he preferred long sessions where he'd shoot two or three times before falling asleep in Moe's bed.

Sometimes a spider weaves a web and waits. Other times, a spider goes out on the hunt. Moe didn't want to wait, so he sent messages to all three of them, promising a group scene at his apartment at seven thirty. (It was six forty-eight, so Moe figured that was enough time for all of them to make it.)

All of them were caught off guard by Moe's message, since he rarely said hello first. But all three agreed to show up at seven thirty.

This is going to be one to remember, Moe thought, hoping that this single session might revive the sparkling reputation he'd spent so many evenings cultivating in cyberspace. He didn't want to risk being dethroned by some young pretender with no gag reflex.

He didn't have much time to get ready, but Moe thought he'd stay online for a few more minutes to see if any of his other old-time regulars signed on, so he could invite them too.

Then Max logged on.

DownTheHatch: Hey, baby. Welcome back.
HotLipsNYC: Thanks!
DownTheHatch: I sure missed you. Have a good weekend?

HotLipsNYC: Yeah, I did.
DownTheHatch: I want to hear all about it. Can I come over?

Moe froze. What could he do?

He did want to see Max, that was true. But he wanted to have his little sex party, too. And it's first come, first served, right? Or is it first served, first come?

Moe's three buddies were still online; it was possible to call the whole thing off.

But he didn't want to.

HotLipsNYC: I'm sorry, I'm not around tonight.
DownTheHatch: Plans with Gene again?

At least he had an easy out.

It's not that Moe and Max pretended to be monogamous. But there was no need to rub each other's faces in it.

HotLipsNYC: Exactly.
DownTheHatch: OK, tomorrow.
HotLipsNYC: Actually, I'm seeing a show tomorrow.
DownTheHatch: With Gene?
HotLipsNYC: Yeah.
DownTheHatch: So I guess it's Wednesday then?
HotLipsNYC: That sounds great. I can't wait.
DownTheHatch: Me either. But I guess I'll have to.

Max signed off.

Moe stopped for a second, considered phoning Max to change his mind. Instead, he turned on the shower, and while he waited for the hot water, he rearranged the seating in his apartment to accommodate service for three men at once.

□ □ □

In the darkroom at Perfect Focus Photo on West Fifty-sixth Street, Kevin was developing a roll of pictures he'd taken over the weekend. The store had closed more than an hour ago, so he was working on his own time, as he had previously discussed with the owner.

Kevin wasn't the only one in the store; the manager was sitting in his office, totaling up figures. He was usually the last one to leave.

There were some great shots on Kevin's roll. A few sweet ones of Aaron on the beach. A series of close-ups of one of the deer that had poked around outside their house. One of Aaron and Kevin together, which Kevin had taken using the timer — these weren't always the best pictures, but this one came out great.

They were in drag.

"This is one for Aaron's wall," Kevin said aloud to himself. He had longed to be on that wall since the day he first set foot in Aaron's apartment.

When his cell phone rang, Kevin jumped. He dropped the photo on the counter and fumbled for his phone, answering on the third ring: "Hello?"

"Hi," came the voice at the other end, a bit unsure. "I'm, uh, calling about the ad."

"The ad?"

"Yeah, the ad. Is this Jason?"

Oh, that ad.

"Yes, this is Jason."

"Are you free tonight, Jason? You sound like just what I'm looking for."

Kevin was about to tell the man that he was retiring from the escort business. That he'd already canceled that ad. That he wasn't particularly interested in meeting a new client — with all the extra work that involved.

But then Kevin thought about the hundred and fifty dollars, and how it would cover the weekend he'd just had on Fire Island, including the leather miniskirt he'd charged. Besides, he thought, Aaron's busy tonight with a massage client; one of his regulars had strained his back on a July Fourth camping trip. ("That's what you get for sleeping on the ground instead of in a bed, the way God intended," Aaron had told him.)

Okay, Kevin thought. One last time.

"I'll hop in a cab right now," said Kevin. He didn't have a perfect outfit, but he had his gym clothes with him, and that would surely suffice.

The guy on the phone gave him the address, a luxury building in Chelsea. Kevin knew the building but had never been inside.

"You have a buzzer, or a doorman?" Kevin asked, scribbling down the information.

"Doorman," he said.

"So what should I tell him?" asked Kevin.

"Just tell him you're here to see Frank."

□ □ □

It was still early, barely eight o'clock, when Frank told the doorman at the Chelsea Park Plaza to send the young man up. He was a bit nervous.

The problem wasn't that Frank had never hired a hustler before. He had done it maybe four times. Maybe five.

But all those had been with Scott, when they were looking for just the right guy — muscular and black, hairy and Italian, skinny and young — to join them, someone who wouldn't bother them with phone calls the next day or get attached to one or the other of them.

Now Frank was paying for a hustler alone, and it seemed more desperate than playful.

It wasn't like Frank had other sexual outlets anymore. He hadn't had sex in over a year. Hadn't had a regular sex partner since Scott's death. For the most part, he was up there in his cloister on the sixteenth floor, alone.

The night before, at his party in the Pines, Frank had the feeling that this celibate phase might end. The guy who had been chatting him up — so flirtatious, touching Frank's arm, laughing with twinkling eyes — had awakened a feeling that Frank had long forgotten. Frank had actually been hard while they were talking.

That is, until Hector Vasquez crashed the party, making Frank lose both his focus and his erection. When Frank finally remembered his paramour (what was his name again?), he had already left, sneaking away during the less-than-pretty confrontation with Hector.

Thinking about him the next day, Frank was still turned on. But he knew it would take a lot of investigation to find out who the guest had been, and who had brought him. Frank was turned on now, and didn't have time to wait. So he'd picked up *The A-List* and flipped through the escort listings — the ones Frank refused to carry in his own paper — until he found a guy who sounded similar: small, young, Asian, and in great shape.

When the young man walked in the door, Frank knew he had judged correctly. The boy was even younger and prettier than the one at his party. He was dressed in a tank top and nylon workout shorts and sneakers, and looked spectacular.

"Here's your money," said Frank, handing over a hundred and fifty dollars. This much he remembered from his previous experiences.

"Thanks," said Kevin, pocketing the cash. Then, without a word, Kevin began to undress, slowly.

As Kevin slipped out of his shorts, Frank leaned over and kissed him on the mouth. Kevin didn't usually kiss his clients, and this guy was certainly no hot ticket — he had unkempt hair, a stained T-shirt, and ill-fitting pants. His skin was blotchy and his breath stank of coffee. And to top it off, he was a lousy kisser.

But Kevin closed his eyes, determined to make this last job a pleasant one. He kissed back, taking Frank's tongue in his mouth and moaning a bit. (Guys love to think they're turning you on, Kevin had learned long ago.) Then he unbuttoned Frank's pants, sliding them down around his calves. Kevin was already hard. (This was easy enough to achieve with just a little imagination.) So was Frank. (This was a far more difficult task, but he was feeling inspired.)

Kevin, eager to get Frank's tongue out of his mouth, pushed him away and knelt down on the hardwood floor, taking Frank's cock between his lips. Frank gasped — when was the last time he'd gotten a blowjob? Had it been more than a year? More than two? Three?

Kevin's mouth was warm, and if Kevin wasn't the greatest cocksucker in the world — "A bit slower, and watch the teeth," Frank said to himself, but not aloud — Frank was in heaven. He thought of the man from his party the previous night. The resemblance to Kevin was enough so that even with his eyes open, Frank could carry on the fantasy.

Frank could have shot his load then and there, into this young hustler's mouth. But Frank wanted to make this last — first, because he was feeling romantic, second because it had been so long since he'd gotten this kind of attention, and third, because he'd paid good money for this and didn't want to waste it. He pulled Kevin up by the arms. Even standing, Kevin was a good six inches shorter than Frank, who embraced him and held him close to his chest, breathing heavily.

"Let's go to the bedroom," said Frank. "I want to take this slow."

Kevin nodded.

The bedroom wasn't the neatest it could be, so Frank kept the lights off. He pulled up the blinds on the window, letting in a bit of glow from the city lights just starting to go on. Frank stripped off his remaining clothes and lay down on the bed, pulling Kevin on top of him. Once again, he kissed the boy. And once again, Kevin went along.

Frank caressed Kevin's body — such soft skin, such definition. Kevin kissed Frank's chest and Frank inhaled his scent — young and fresh, the smell of clean sweat and cheap deodorant.

They rolled about slowly in bed, Frank taking almost half an hour to touch and lick every part of Kevin's body. The whole time, he imagined it was the man from the night before, the man he might have had in his bed, the man who might have done all these things without asking for payment or walking out the door after sixty minutes.

Still, Frank thought, this was something.

He continued to fantasize that this was not some young hustler, but that flirtatious party guest, intrigued by Frank's wit and charm, amazed by his intelligence, in awe of his years of activism and accomplishment. Someone who read his newspaper, someone who couldn't wait to read his script. Someone who relished his kisses and hungered for more.

Without looking at Kevin, he said, "I want to fuck you."

Kevin stopped and considered it for a moment. "I've got a condom in my bag," he said. It was one of the condoms he and Aaron had been giving out in the Meat Rack. The only one left.

When Kevin went to get the rubber, Frank lay back on the bed. His head was swimming. Kevin returned with the condom, and Frank said to him, again without looking him in the eye: "Why don't you put it on for me?"

Kevin knelt between Frank's legs and unrolled the condom onto Frank's cock, which while not rock hard, was still sufficiently erect to get the job done. Frank had a bottle of lube — lube he'd used for nothing more exciting than jacking off to old videos — by the bedside. He told Kevin to put some on, and he did.

Kevin lay down on his back next to Frank, waiting for Frank to roll over on top of him.

"No, no, on your stomach," Frank said, and Kevin complied.

Frank studied the boy's back, his muscular ass. It had been years since he'd done this, but it all came back to him. The parties, the baths, the great times he'd had. Glancing up, he saw the lights on the Empire State Building come on, and he was transported in time. Suddenly, he was thirty again. He was happy again. He was sexy again. And this boy in his bed wasn't some hustler, wasn't even some party-crashing poseur trying to get laid with a few easy compliments. Frank looked down at the body ready to take him inside, willing to accept him, happy to arouse him. And it was Scott.

The light was dim, and Kevin's face was hidden in the pillow. This made it easier for Frank. He felt a warm tenderness, a deep affection, perhaps a twinge of love. He also felt a deep, intense desire, a stirring inside him that he hadn't felt for ages. Yes, it was Scott, back in their bed, alive, healthy, and ready to make love.

Sensing an awkward delay, Kevin began to grind his hips, hoping to kickstart the action. It worked. Frank positioned himself above the small boy, holding himself in push-up position with his left arm while his right hand aimed his cock at Kevin's ass below him. Slowly, gently, lovingly, Frank guided his cock inside him, tears welling up in his eyes, and then simply held it there while Kevin adjusted.

Kevin sighed and rotated his hips. Frank thrusted slowly in response. As he continued, he bent his elbow and lay on top of the boy, bearing all his weight on him, kissing the back of his head. Scott, he thought, Scott, Scott.

The condom was crumpled inside Frank's right hand.

fifteen

This is what makes Frank hard: memory.

Any time he wants to get off — which, these days, means any time he's masturbating — he takes a mental trip back in time.

Those were sexier days.

Men were more attractive, not so hung up on biceps and colored contact lenses and sculpted hair. It wasn't that men had bigger dicks or bigger brains or bigger hearts back then. It wasn't that they were more butch or less selfish. It's that somehow, they seemed to know who they were, and sold themselves on their own terms — top or bottom, masculine or feminine, skinny or chubby — instead of trying to become something they weren't. They were real.

Sex was hotter then, too, lurking in every dark bar, parading in every bathhouse. It was free, in every sense of the word, and it was raw, randy, raucous. There was nothing to worry about, nothing important anyway. Scabies and crabs and syphilis and gonorrhea and anal warts and urinary tract infections — he'd gotten most of those back in the day, but they weren't anything to get too upset about. He wasn't even sure which he'd had himself, and which were Scott's problems. They were just background noise.

Of course, Frank was sexier back then, too. His hair was thicker, his waist slimmer, his skin tighter. There was a time when his face had not yet contorted into a resigned grimace, when his aura radiated positive energy. (In fact, it was a time when people had auras, which just goes to show how long ago it was.) Frank took care of himself in those days, too, making sure he wore the right clothes, listened to the right music, and watched what he ate.

But Frank wasn't that man anymore. If other sexy men still lurked the streets, they weren't looking at him, and if sex was still loose and crazy and spontaneous, Frank didn't want any part of it. As he looked ahead to his fiftieth birthday looming in the foreseeable future, he was certain all that reverie was behind him.

That's why he had to dig into the past to find anything to turn him on.

AIDS seemed to cast a pall over any sexual thoughts in the present tense. Safe sex? A pale imitation of the real thing. It wasn't just that he hated condoms — although he did. He wasn't aroused by barebacking — in fact, quite the contrary, it enraged him. The turn-on was the memory of condomless sex before AIDS, when there weren't any rules to be flouted — back in a time when fucking raw was simply the norm, something you did out of pleasure and desire, not out of some illusory, suicidal sexual-political ideology or some thrill-seeking, fatal attraction to disease.

Sometimes all it took to go back in time was to slip in a video of an old movie that he remembered. An old Falcon title, something like "The Other Side of Aspen." Online, these days it was usually sold as a "pre-condom classic," a term that can only be seen as an anachronism, since the notion of sex with condoms was completely alien at the time. But more than the term "pre-condom," it was the term "classic" that riled Frank, who remembered when the movie first came out — remembered seeing it with Scott, in a movie theater. Those theaters had since closed down (thanks in part to Frank's efforts) and most of the actors in the film were dead. But in Frank's memory, he could still sit in those dirty, broken cinema seats, and see those actors standing before him and Scott as they jerked themselves off.

Other times, Frank conjured up his own mental movies of trysts he'd had years before.

There was an all-night orgy he had gone to in 1979 that he'd never forget. Coked up out of his mind, Frank had blindfolded Scott and laid him down on the bed in the master suite of the host's apartment. He sat on Scott's face, pinning his arms, and while Scott ate his lover's ass, Frank orchestrated a string of guests — seen by Frank but unseen by Scott — to fuck Scott. This had been a longtime fantasy that Scott had confessed to Frank a few months earlier, and the drugs and the situation conspired to give Frank the courage to make it happen. There must have been eight or nine guys who fucked Scott that night, while Frank ran the show. Scott was thrashing in ecstasy, and Frank was in his element.

There was the night a year later when Frank, with the help of a Quaalude to relax him, took Scott's fist up his ass for the first and only time. "And you thought there was no way we could be closer," Scott had said afterward, laughing.

There was their trip to the Caribbean, right when things were most tense between them. They had sold Snow, their new bar The Cellar hadn't yet taken off, and money was tight. They were fighting a lot. But outside the city, their bonds were renewed, and they fucked on the beach, on the lanai of their bungalow, in the dune buggy they rented. They fucked and they fucked, and all was forgiven.

Surely, Frank had tallied hundreds of sexual experiences that didn't involve Scott. Guys he had blown in the toilet stall at Snow. Men he'd sucked off at the baths. Fuck-buddies he maintained for years. He'd had boyfriends before Scott, and the occasional one-night stand after Scott's death. He even had boy toys on the side while he and Scott were a couple. But those other men were lost. Frank's memories were only of Scott, or of group experiences he had that also included Scott.

It's as if, when Scott died in 1987, he'd gained sole possession of Frank's erotic imagination. Anything that didn't involve Scott faded and soon vanished.

So he focused exclusively on memories of sex adventures he'd shared with his late lover. Adventures that took place in that time before the world collapsed, when nobody foresaw their imminent demise. There was no black cloud hanging over every fuck in those days, no warning label on every guy's penis. Sex was what it was. You didn't have to consider the consequences. Innocent, yes, that's what that asshole in the Meat Rack hadn't understood. People before AIDS weren't innocent — as in "not guilty." They were innocent — as in "naive." And happily so.

Would that such a feeling could be recaptured, Frank thought. Then he could be hard just living in the present.

But reality doesn't measure up to wishes, so memory had to suffice for Frank. Not that his memory was completely reliable. He had subconsciously edited out some of the uglier bits of his past: the fights he'd had with Scott about their escapades, the sex he'd had out of spite or boredom, the jealousy that some of the raunchier scenes had evoked. The intermittent impotency that came from Scott's drinking disappeared upon reflection. And Scott was always healthy and hale in his memories, never the gaunt and weak man he became in later years — when their sex life all but disappeared.

He had also added things to his memories. Scott was notoriously silent in bed, but in Frank's memory he became a verbose narrator, spewing raunchy monologues and groaning out his pleasures and desires. And sometimes, Frank had unknowingly inserted Scott into situations where he had never actually been; for instance, Scott was probably never in a dirty theater with Frank watching "The Other Side of Aspen," because Scott hated dirty theaters. Nevertheless, there he was in Frank's memory, sitting in the next chair with his fly unbuttoned.

Perfect or not, these memories were all Frank had to draw upon most of the time. He found that he didn't jerk off more than once a week anymore, and he hardly ever felt sexual tension or attraction to anyone he met either. But as sex receded from Frank's daily life, it remained ingrained in his imagination, with all the inaccuracies, revisions, and touch-ups increasingly indelible. These memories were the only thing that still piqued Frank's sexual interest, the only things that pressed his buttons.

It was one of these memories that possessed him the night he had sex with the hustler. He was taken by a mental image of Scott that he had long forgotten, in 1978 or 1982 or some other year, lying face down in their bed in the dim light of a New York evening. The skin on his back shiny with sweat, his body language welcoming and trusting.

Scott lay in that position, just as the hustler had, waiting silently for Frank. Scott had rotated his hips slowly, just as the hustler had, hoping to entice him. Frank had accepted the invitation, lying on top of Scott, just as he had done with the hustler, careful not to put too much weight on him or penetrate him too quickly. Lovingly, he had entered Scott, drawing gasps and sighs from his lover as he lowered himself onto his back. The feeling of human connection, of the bond between two men who loved each other, of complete abandonment of self, was what Frank recalled.

He hadn't used a condom with Scott; nobody used condoms in those days. The feeling of skin on skin, of two bodies melding into one, was what he remembered.

That was what he recaptured with the hustler: the long-forgotten memory of a night that might never have happened.

FALL

sixteen

Frank couldn't remember the last time he had so many handsome men staring at him.

He stood by Max's side at the edge of the stage while Max gave the actors notes before their Thursday morning run-through of *Buried Alive*. Frank didn't offer his own comments — on this front he deferred to the veteran director — but the actors knew that he was the playwright, and that he had lived most of the scenes they were playing. They stared, as if they thought there was something they could glean, a crucial affect or expression, if they just looked at him hard enough.

They were almost all young, in their twenties, playing dual roles as '80s twenty-something gay men in Act I and '90s twenty-something gay men in Act II, wearing different outfits (and, in two cases, wigs) to create different looks.

The only exception was thirty-two-year-old Jeremy Wilson, the lead actor playing Freddy, the protagonist. He needed to pass for a man in his twenties in Act I, but as his generation's sole survivor, also pass for a man pushing forty in Act II. A fake brown moustache helped set him in the '80s in the first act; a salt-and-pepper beard helped age him in the second.

In all, there were six actors on stage. They weren't the sexiest men Frank had ever seen. But they were looking at him, paying attention to him. And while Max was going over blocking for a few key scenes, Frank was imagining what each one of them looked like naked.

They were so pretty, Frank thought, it was a shame that most of them had to die in his play. Twice.

Then again, it was a shame that so many men in real life had to die even once.

Frank blinked, snapped out of his trance, and looked toward Max. This is no time to be maudlin, and no time to be thinking dirty thoughts, he said to himself. Tomorrow is opening night and we've got work to do.

□ □ □

"I never realized how emotional it'd be," Frank told Max as they left the Rainbow Stage for a lunch break.

"Most playwrights feel that way the first time they see their work on stage," replied Max.

"That's not what I meant," Frank said. "Yes, it's a bit disconcerting as a writer to see my own words being acted out by total strangers. It'll be even weirder tomorrow night watching how an audience full of strangers responds to those strangers on stage. With the newspaper, I don't get to watch people's reactions when they read it. But what I meant was that it's very emotional to watch the show as a member of the audience."

"Why's that?" asked Max.

"Putting the words down on paper was cathartic — like taking these ideas I had and getting them off my chest. It made me feel lighter," Frank explained. "But now that I'm hearing these words come back at me from someone else's mouth, it's stirring up a whole new batch of memories and emotions inside me. And it makes me feel heavier."

Max stopped on the sidewalk. "Frank, this play is supposed to make you feel heavier. *Buried Alive* is a heavy play."

Frank realized he might have insulted Max by commenting on the tone he'd given the show. "Of course, Max, it's very serious stuff. And you've brought out the feeling I had intended the play to have. I just hadn't expected it to bring out those feelings in me, after all these years."

Max looked at Frank. "I think I know what you mean."

"My whole motivation for writing it was to speak to young gay men — it was all about Act II, where Freddy tries to warn the younger men about what they're doing. Freddy's despair and anger as an older guy who's been through it before, that's what I thought would be the main message. But watching it on stage, I kept focusing on Act I, and Freddy's own life before AIDS. It's a much harder act to watch for me, because so much of it came from my own experiences," Frank said. "The scene in Act I where Freddy finds his best friend dead in his bed — that really happened to me. And the part at the end of Act I where Freddy is standing alone, wondering if his friends are in heaven or in hell — that really happened to me, too."

"Those things happened to a lot of us," Max said. "We just don't talk about it so much anymore."

Frank closed his eyes. "No, I guess we don't."

Over lunch, before Frank went home to work on the latest issue of *Outrageous* and Max returned to the theater to prepare for that evening's dress rehearsal, the two forty-something men sat over burritos and reminisced about the old days, with all their horrible glory and glorious horror.

□ □ □

It's hopeless, Moe thought, absolutely hopeless.

His favorite 501s hadn't fit him the night before, and Moe knew they'd never fit him again. He was going to have to concede defeat and buy a bigger size. It shouldn't have been a big deal, but as he sat at his desk, editing, on Thursday afternoon, he was depressed.

He'd switched from a thirty-two-inch waist to a thirty-three a year earlier, and that wasn't a traumatic transition. Bumping up to a thirty-four in the spring wasn't the end of the world either — Moe still considered that within the range of normal girth. But now he was facing a thirty-five-inch waist. Morbidly obese, he thought.

"You remember that girl in *Willy Wonka* who eats a piece of blueberry gum and turns into a giant blueberry? That's how I feel," Moe told Gene on the phone.

"Sugar bear, if all you were eating was blueberry gum, we wouldn't be having this discussion."

"So you're saying I brought this on myself? Talk about blaming the victim!" Moe said, mostly — but not entirely — teasing.

"Moe, you did bring this on yourself. You eat too much and you never exercise anymore. But there's no victim here. You've got two choices: Either get your ass back to the gym and stop eating ice cream for dinner, or get over your personal issues and learn to accept yourself the way you are. It's simple."

"Maybe for you. You've never had to watch your weight."

That was true enough.

"Look, Moe, I can't bring myself to feel sorry for you. You should be on top of the world. You've got your dream job. You've got your dream man. You've got a great apartment, a decent salary, close friends, good health, and all the cock you can handle. What else could you possibly want?"

"Just one thing: a thirty-two-inch waist."

"Wishing won't make it so."

"You're a jagged little pill today, even more than usual. What's going on?"

"Empress Eleanor again. She's on her weekly rampage."

Their latest feud, Gene explained, was about salaries. Eleanor had, without consulting Gene, hired a new assistant manager to start in the office the following week. Gene told her that rather than hiring a new staffer, she should increase how much she was paying the people who were already working there. He had told her before that Ben and Jay weren't making enough money to live in New York; Jay had recently moved in with his sister to save on rent, and Ben was sharing a two-bedroom apartment in Jersey City with three other people. Eleanor had argued that Ben and Jay were making as much as their counterparts in Washington. Gene tried explaining that

New York is a more expensive city than Washington, and that it takes more money to live there, but Eleanor wouldn't budge. "It wouldn't be fair," she'd said that morning.

"So that's it? Argument over?" Moe asked.

"No, it's not over," Gene said. "But I won't win. Remember who's the boss."

"*Who's the Boss*. Starring Tony Danza and Judith Light."

Gene snorted. "Good Lord, Eleanor is no Judith Light."

"I don't know how to say this, but you're no Tony Danza, either."

"You're feeling insecure about your body today, so I won't make any cruel remarks about your physique."

"That's very Christian of you."

"Thanks, I guess. But seriously, I never win arguments with Eleanor. Sometimes it feels like it's not worth my breath anymore."

"You got her to switch your ad from *Outrageous* to my newspaper this summer," said Moe.

That had indeed been one battle that Gene had won. Gene had told her that the *New York Gay News* was a better place to reach potential customers. In the end, though, Eleanor had made the move because she saw how many other advertisers had switched, and how many more readers the upstart newspaper had than *Outrageous*. (She still refused to consider *The A-List*, however, despite the fact that its readership was larger than either of the newspapers.)

"True, but that was an easier battle — lots of people dropped their ads in *Outrageous* this summer. I don't think I'm going to win this time," Gene said. "There's only so long I can bang my head against a wall."

"And exactly how long is that?"

"I'll let you know."

□ □ □

Melody Penn's Advanced Queer Theory class seemed to last forever. Aaron was fidgety. He wasn't following Mel closely — at least not by the time the third hour of the afternoon seminar rolled around. Aaron asked himself, Who ever thought of a three-hour class? There are only a few people Aaron enjoyed spending three hours straight with, and Melody Penn and the group of eight brown-nosing grad students who sat around the table were not among them.

On the board, Mel had written a few terms, but Aaron wasn't paying enough attention to remember what they signified: "panopticon," "matrix of power," "intraclass." And the name *Judith Butler*.

God, he was bored. When Moe took classes with him, they used to be more bearable. But there was nobody else in the room Aaron particularly liked, nobody else who made him laugh.

Thank goodness, he thought, it's my last year of coursework.

Before the summer, Aaron's self-image had been tied up in the things he did: graduate school, activism, massage. Aaron had always invested a lot in what he did, whether it was dancing or protesting, writing papers or doing drag. But lately, that had begun to change. The people in his life were his main focus now — most of all, Moe and Kevin. These were the two people on his mind as he sat through Mel's droning lecture: Moe, who he wished was sitting with him during class, and Kevin, who he was anticipating seeing after class was over.

It was hard to concentrate. He was daydreaming, trying to think of what he'd cook for dinner, which movie he'd see this weekend, when he'd do the laundry. He had completely tuned out his surroundings — something risky in a class this small — when he got busted.

"Mister Chiles?" Mel said brusquely. "Aaron?"

Aaron snapped back to reality to find Mel looking at him, sternly, awaiting the answer to a question he hadn't heard. The others around the table were facing him as well, somewhat smugly.

"Aaron Chiles, are you going to answer me or not?"

"I'm sorry, Mel," Aaron said sheepishly. "Could you repeat the question?"

□ □ □

"I think it's cute that at your age, you've still got attention deficit disorder," Kevin joked, when he phoned from the photo shop later the same afternoon.

"Keep talking that way, sweetie, and you won't live to be my age," Aaron joked back.

"Sorry, honey. You can spank me later."

"I just might do that."

"Stop, I'm hard already."

"Keep it in your pants until you get home. And when will that be, by the way?"

"I'm off work at six, so I can be at your place by six-thirty."

"That sounds fine. I've got a massage client at five, but he'll be gone before then. Bring some groceries and we'll make dinner."

"What do you want?"

"Surprise me."

Aaron didn't ask Kevin if he'd be spending the night. By this point, it was pretty much assumed. Kevin would stop by his place in Washington Heights a couple of nights a week to check his mail and water his plants, but otherwise he had, for all intents and purposes, moved into Aaron's apartment in the East Village. He kept a toothbrush there, and Aaron had cleared two drawers and hanger space for some of Kevin's clothes.

It had happened gradually, without any particular discussion. Kevin's occasional sleepovers turned into a regular weekend thing over the summer when Aaron had a lot more free time, and then slowly spread across the other days of the week as fall approached. Aaron had, a few times, tried staying at Kevin's, but the commute was interminable. The trip at night took over an hour, and in the morning, Aaron had to turn right around and ride back downtown to Empire — which was walking distance from his own Avenue C apartment. Besides, Kevin's apartment had always been more a place to sleep than a real home; they both preferred Aaron's, even if it was a bit small for two people.

Aaron set up for his client, unfolding the massage table, lighting a scented candle, dimming the lights, and cueing a New Age CD. He went into the bathroom to make sure it was clean enough, and found Kevin's dirty gym shorts hanging over the towel rack.

Without a thought, Aaron threw them into the hamper, on top of his own dirty clothes.

□ □ □

"I've got good news, Gene," said Dr. Chang, smiling slightly, which for the normally poker-faced Richard Chang was the equivalent of anyone else doing jumping jacks.

"Wait, let me guess," said Gene, scooting anxiously to the edge of the examining table. "My medical records got mixed up with someone else's and I've never had HIV?"

Dr. Chang's smile started to fade.

"No, I guess that only happens on daytime soaps," said Gene.

"I wouldn't know, I don't watch them," said Dr. Chang, back to his old humorless self. "But you're not so far off. Your latest blood work shows that your new combination of pills is working extremely well, and your viral load is now undetectable."

It took a while for this to sink in. First, Gene tried to remember exactly which combination of pills he was currently taking; there had been so many over the previous three years. He'd taken the one protease inhibitor that gave him horrifying, vivid nightmares. He'd taken two other pills that, while each tolerable on its own, worked in combination to give him fits of vomiting and dry heaves. One medication had helped his T-cell count but left him unable to function, with insomnia and constipation. One drug cocktail led to numbness in his feet, while yet another gave him diarrhea. But this one — a regimen he had started in Washington before his move, which Dr. Chang had tweaked slightly when Gene started seeing him in the spring — was the golden ticket. Gene wasn't suffering from any noticeable side effects, and more importantly, it was actually working.

"Undetectable?" Gene asked. "Completely undetectable? As in zero?"

"It doesn't mean there's no HIV in your system," the doctor clarified, "but it means that the level is so low that it doesn't show up on our tests."

"Does that mean I can stop taking the pills?"

"No, quite the opposite. It means the pills are working, so you need to keep taking them to keep your viral load down."

"Oh," said Gene, disappointed. "Then it's good news in the long term, but in the short term it doesn't change much."

"It might in the future," said Dr. Chang. "There are some studies being done now about giving people 'vacations' from their drugs if their viral loads stay undetectable for quite some time. But the jury's still out on whether that's wise. And anyway, your viral load has been undetectable for only about a week so far, since we took your blood."

"So it's a bit too soon to be planning a vacation?"

"Yes."

"Okay, then I won't flush the pills down the toilet quite yet."

Dr. Chang was definitely not smiling.

"Kidding!" said Gene. "Anyway, yes, this is good news. And thanks for adjusting my meds this spring. I guess your instincts were right."

"I prefer to think my medical opinions are based on more than instinct, Mister Macintosh," said the doctor. "But you're welcome."

For the next ten minutes, Dr. Chang talked about the latest HIV research, and what the next round of drugs might offer, while he gave Gene a quick examination. And then Gene was free, for another month.

"You can get dressed now," Dr. Chang said. "I'm sure you want to call your boyfriend and tell him the good news."

Gene hadn't even thought of that. As he was putting on his socks, he flipped open his cell phone and dialed Moe's number.

□ □ □

The dress rehearsal ran late; the digital clock on the VCR was blinking 11:11 when Max arrived at Moe's apartment. The lights were off and Moe was already in bed.

"Climb on in," Moe said. "I've been waiting for you." His tone was sweet, not scornful.

"I think I will," said Max, stripping off his shirt and kicking off his sneakers. "I'm exhausted."

Moe didn't ask how the rehearsal went, and Max didn't volunteer; *Buried Alive* was a subject they had agreed not to discuss. Moe accepted that Max could make his own professional decisions, but he still didn't want to hear about it. Max accepted that Moe had a visceral hatred of Frank DeSoto, but didn't let that affect his work. As for the lunch Max had with Frank — that would only have caused an argument if Max mentioned it. So he didn't.

Max climbed over Moe — wearing a T-shirt and boxers — and got under the covers. Moe, taking his cue, wriggled down beneath the blanket and took Max's cock in his mouth.

After thirty seconds, Max stopped him.

"Baby, I'm sorry, I'm just not up for it tonight," he said. Max had spent the whole day working, thinking about death, coaching actors and worrying about opening night. He was stressed out, overtired, and a bit morose. But he couldn't explain any of that to Moe without discussing Frank and his play, so he simply pulled Moe up to his chest and said, "Let's get some sleep."

Moe was more tired than horny himself; he had to close another issue of the paper the next day and needed the rest. And the idea of curling up with Max's arm around him was something akin to paradise. Moe found that after all these months, he still loved having sex with Max, but what he loved more than anything else was sleeping with him, nestled against him. There was nowhere that Moe felt more desired and cared for, nowhere he felt more peaceful when he slept.

Yet somehow, the idea of "just getting some sleep" tonight threw Moe for a loop. He had already noticed that Max was typically having two orgasms, instead of his usual three, when they were together recently. There were even nights when Max only came once — although this would be the first time that they wouldn't have sex at all. In Moe's mind, it pointed to a trend of declining sexual interest on Max's part.

And no wonder, Moe thought: The more weight I put on, the less sex he wants.

No matter how many times Max had assured Moe that he found him attractive, there was no squelching Moe's neurosis. He was sure he was fat, sure he was unsexy, sure he was quickly becoming a fat, hairy blueberry who was in no way worthy of worshipping a man like Max Milano. He didn't blame Max; if anything, he was shocked that Max had lasted this long.

Moe, utterly deflated by Max's request, nonetheless acceded, scooting up from under the covers and laying his head on Max's chest, his hand on Max's flat stomach. Max put an arm around his shoulders and pulled him closer, kissing the top of his head. "Good night, baby," Max said. Then he lay his head back on the pillow to go to sleep.

This is it, Moe thought, this is the end. This is the part where he finds someone as hot as he is. The part where he dumps me. Or at least, where that whole process gets set in motion.

Max's breathing slowed, and Moe panicked. He decided to give it one last try, one more effort to turn Max on.

Moving his face a few inches to get into the proper position, he opened his mouth slowly and took Max's nipple between his lips. As he began to suck softly, he moved his hand from Max's stomach down between his legs, caressing Max's balls gently.

Max let out a faint, tired purr.

Barely moving a muscle, Moe continued to nurse on Max's nipple and stroke his balls. Softly, slowly. He never ratcheted up his advance to a more aggressive level, and never touched Max's cock. But Moe knew which buttons to push.

Max moaned, pulling Moe in tighter.

Too tired, my ass, Moe thought. He moved his hand from Max's balls to his cock — hard, as Moe had expected. He gave it a squeeze. And then he stopped.

Moe rolled over, away from Max, and pretended he was going to sleep.

Max, by now more horny than sleepy, wasn't ready to stop. He rolled over behind Moe and whispered in his ear: "Baby, go on, suck my dick."

Eyes closed, Moe whispered hoarsely, "I'm sorry, I'm really tired."

Max knew it was bullshit, but he was willing to play along if that's what it took to get back inside Moe's velvet mouth. He told Moe, "I know you're tired, but you don't even have to move. Just open your mouth."

Max got up, rolled Moe onto his back, and straddled his face, sitting on Moe's chest. He poked his hard cock into Moe's mouth and sat back while Moe — even half-asleep, even without exerting any energy — gave him a blowjob that made him forget his whole day's worries. Moe's tongue, Moe's lips, Moe's throat all conspired to drive Max wild, to make him almost painfully hard.

Moe opened his eyes and saw Max in the moonlight, his face crunched up on the brink of orgasm. Here he was, aching for Moe, needing Moe, unable to sleep without Moe's expert service. Max looked him deep in the eye and with a guttural shout of release, shot his load deep into Moe's mouth.

Max's energy level collapsed almost instantly. He lay down in bed again, pulled Moe back onto his chest, and without a word, went to sleep.

While Max's chest had seemed like a punishment only minutes before, it now seemed like a reward to Moe. True, Max had only shot one load, and true, Moe hadn't gotten himself off; he hadn't even gotten his *shirt* off. But none of that mattered to Moe. Reassured, with the taste of Max's semen still on his tongue, Moe nestled into Max's slightly sweaty chest and drifted into the sweetest and saltiest of dreams.

□ □ □

"Give me some more," said Gene. And Dustin, with Gene's hand on the back of his head, obliged.

Now *this* is celebrating, Gene thought, as Dustin's lips wrapped around his cock again.

Moe was the first one he'd called after his appointment with Dr. Chang. Moe was excited to hear the news; he'd listened to Gene's health reports for years, and was thrilled to hear something truly good for a change. But Moe had to work late on deadline and wasn't free to get together, so Gene called Dustin next.

Dustin was excited, too, even if he didn't have as emotional a reaction as Moe. He told Gene he'd take him out to celebrate. It was a great evening: dinner at Trattoria Due Amici near Gene's apartment, then drinks at Boardwalk, the trendy Chelsea bar — Dustin even let Gene cruise the passing boys without making any nasty comments, although he did maintain a tight grip on Gene's hand. And now, dessert back at Gene's place, where Dustin was already having seconds.

"Take it slow," Gene commanded. Dustin happily obeyed.

For a full half hour, Dustin stayed between Gene's legs, keeping him hard with total devotion. Gene lay still and enjoyed it, rubbing Dustin's head and moaning from time to time, until he could take it no more.

"I'm ready," Gene said.

Dustin knew what that meant. He put his hands under Gene's legs and pushed his knees toward his chest, and ran his tongue from Gene's cock down his balls to his ass. Gene groaned loudly and grabbed his cock. He pumped his cock while Dustin licked his butt, and within thirty seconds, it was all over. He shouted out loud and his body went tense, as he shot his second load across his belly in four or five strong spurts.

Gene lowered his legs onto the bed and caught his breath, while Dustin fetched the washcloth they had used an hour earlier from the nightstand. He cleaned Gene off, then climbed in bed beside him.

"That was incredible," said Gene. "*You* are incredible."

Dustin smiled. "I'm just happy to be here with you, celebrating."

"If this is how you celebrate, I can hardly wait for my birthday."

"I don't want to spoil it, but what I've got planned is pretty much the same idea as tonight. Except you get a piece of cake at the end."

Gene pulled Dustin to him for a kiss. "I'll try to look surprised."

seventeen

"This is a joke, right?"

"No, Moe, I'm serious," said Kevin. "They want you."

"Yeah, sure," Moe replied, dubious. "*Woof* magazine wants me. Nude."

Moe had picked up *Woof* a few times — it was one of the only porn magazines that had photos he found remotely interesting: hairy guys, guys with bellies, daddies, men with beards. He didn't have much use for dirty magazines; he preferred to see naked men in the flesh, where he could actually touch them. Still, as far as that stuff went, Moe thought *Woof* was above par.

But now Kevin was standing at Moe's desk on a Friday morning, trying to get him to believe that *Woof* wanted to run photos of him. Moe wasn't buying it. He couldn't imagine who'd pay money to see him naked. He wasn't all that keen on looking at himself in the mirror these days.

"It's true, Moe," Kevin continued. "After my professor told me how much she loved the shots of you that I took for my senior project, I sent in a few of them to the editor at *Woof*. I didn't mention it because I knew you'd say no. But he emailed me yesterday and said he wants to run them in an issue this winter. You'd be December's Cub of the Month."

Moe was silent. Kevin, he realized, was completely serious.

"Wow, I guess there's one place where I'm still considered a young, skinny thing!" Moe finally said with a laugh. "Although if they saw me now, they might want me to be the Big Fat Hog of the Year."

Kevin chuckled. "I told the editor that I'd talk to you about it. He needs to make a decision in the next week. He can't publish them without written permission from the model, so it's up to you."

Moe was thinking.

"There's not much money in it. Two hundred bucks — half for me, half for you," Kevin continued. "But you'd have final approval over which pictures he uses, and it's up to you if you want to use your real name or a fake name."

Moe mulled over names: Lazy Larry Lardass. Franklin Furball. Tevye the Tubby Teddy Bear. Or simply: Moshe the Big Fat Jew.

It was a lot to think about on a deadline day.

Kevin's cell phone rang, and he answered while Moe leaned forward in his chair, smiling to himself.

"It's my mother," Kevin said ominously, covering the receiver — his mother never called without a reason. "I'll come back later."

As Kevin walked away, talking to his mother in hushed tones, Moe picked up his phone and called Gene at work to tell him about the magazine. It hardly seemed necessary; Moe could have guessed Gene's reaction perfectly:

"I don't know what there is to think about, sugar bear," Gene said. "It's a terrible idea and you'd be a fool to publish those pictures. End of story."

"That's not exactly the end of the story, because I haven't made up my mind yet."

"Look, what do you stand to gain from publishing those photos? Money? It's a hundred bucks. Hardly worth your time. Sex? I can't imagine you're doing this to get laid — you get laid enough already. Exposure? With a fake name, nobody even knows it's you so you don't gain any exposure, and with a real name, you risk a lot of negative exposure: your boss finding out, your parents finding out, *Outrageous* finding that you've got a lot to lose, but I don't see what you really have to gain."

"My parents don't read *Woof* magazine."

"Not that you know about anyway."

"Very funny. But seriously, so what if Abe or my parents see it? It's not like I'm actually doing anything in the pictures — I'm not having sex or sticking anything up my ass. And, as I recall, the photos themselves are pretty tame, just me without my clothes on. It's not like I'm bent over, spreading my cheeks to the world, or covered in hot wax, or drinking a glass of recycled beer."

"Right," said Gene. "I guess *those* photos will have to wait for the spring supplement."

□ □ □

"So, will I get to meet them, or not?" Aaron asked.

"That's what we need to figure out," said Kevin.

"No, sweetie, that's what *you* need to figure out."

It wasn't an easy decision for Kevin, and Aaron wasn't making it any easier. Kevin's mother had called that morning to say that she and Kevin's father would be coming to the city on Sunday afternoon — driving through on their way from Rochester to a three-day optics convention on Long Island. In the two years Kevin had been living in New York, they had never come to visit, something he'd taken as a statement of their ongoing disapproval of the fact that he'd moved to the city, a place his parents still viewed as debauched and dangerous. Now they'd announced a visit — albeit a brief one, just for lunch on Sunday — and he didn't know what to do.

Ever since Kevin moved to the city, his relationship with his parents, once close and warm, had been distant and mostly superficial. There were things they knew about but didn't want to talk about (art school), and things they wouldn't have had the words to talk about even if they did know (his career as a "featured dancer" and "escort"). They knew Kevin was gay

— his mother had found his stash of porno magazines when he was a high school senior — but after a total of two tearful conversations on the subject, they had agreed implicitly to avoid discussing it. Thus, they knew he had a friend named Aaron, but didn't know he was *that* kind of friend. They knew he had been working for a local newspaper, but didn't know it was *that* kind of newspaper.

Kevin had to figure out if he wanted to tell them these things — and if they truly wanted to hear. He also had to figure out how Aaron would feel. Aaron wasn't eager to sit through an awkward, potentially traumatic lunch with Kevin's family; it was hard enough dealing with his own parents. But Aaron also didn't want to be swept under the rug.

"I suppose I could have them meet me by my place in Washington Heights, and the three of us could eat up there," Kevin suggested. "Then you could avoid seeing them altogether."

"My goal is not to avoid your parents, sweetie."

"You might feel differently if you knew them."

"I'll let you know afterward."

"Well, we could all meet somewhere in Midtown. You know, neutral ground. In a restaurant. And then I could show them the photo lab."

"That sounds like an emotional parent-child reunion. Lunch in a diner on Ninth Avenue followed by a tour of the light tables. I can hardly wait."

"Do you have a better idea?"

Aaron thought for a second, and then came up with a solution: "Bring them here."

"Here? To your apartment?"

"Why not?"

"Somehow I think if they came here, they'd have a hard time imagining that we were just friends. I don't think most guys entertain their friends' parents over brunch in their houses."

"Really? Most guys I know would do just that."

"I'm being serious."

"So am I. Sit down and I'll explain."

Kevin sat and buttoned his lip while Aaron kept talking.

"First, let's think about you. Where will you feel most comfortable? In the apartment you're never really in? In a Midtown diner? Or in this apartment?"

"Here."

"And as for your parents, they want to make sure you're doing okay on your own in the city. They'll be happy to see that you have friends, that you can do grown-up things like entertain and cook. A nice homey meal will set their mind at ease much more than some cheap lunch in a restaurant or eating off mismatched plates in your apartment."

"But what if they ask about you, about us?"

"Honey, I don't know your parents, but they're not going to ask anything. They will, however, figure it out without having to ask, and you can tell them about your life without saying a word."

Kevin had to admit it was an inspired plan.

"Okay, we'll do it here," Kevin said. "Now what are we going to serve?"

□ □ □

The tension was palpable before the show even began.

Moe was sitting alone, in a third-row seat, as Max's personal guest. Moe didn't really want to see *Buried Alive*, but he knew he couldn't criticize it intelligently until he saw how awful it actually was. That's not how he put it when he accepted Max's offer; he told Max, "Of course I want to see your work on stage!" But in truth, Moe was there to gather more reasons to hate Frank DeSoto. His pulse was racing and he was shifting in his chair before the lights went down.

Gene and Dustin were sitting four rows back, in the press seats Moe had given them the previous week since he wouldn't be needing them. Gene gave a cursory wave, but didn't come over to say hello for fear of pissing off Dustin, who was pretending to read the program.

Max, meanwhile, was taking care of a few last-minute changes with the lighting designer, while Frank paced nervously in the back of the theater, watching the crowd shuffle in.

It wasn't a big crowd, but it was enough to sell out the tiny Rainbow Stage for opening night. Ninety-nine seats. D.C. and Katie showed up ("We can't wait," Katie told him in the lobby, although D.C. seemed less enthusiastic) so Frank figured he had at least two audience members on his side. But he was really keeping his eyes open for critics. He knew that a mere blurb in the *Times* or the *Voice* could cement a success. He also realized that even *The A-List* could bring in patrons with a kind word. He saw Moe Pearlman in the audience, and knew the *New York Gay News* would savage him, but he held out hope for the others. But as eight o'clock approached, he didn't see any critics he recognized. And Frank was nervous in a way he hadn't been for years.

□ □ □

Despite a couple of flubbed lines and one missed lighting cue, Act I came off well, Frank thought. The first scenes were almost frothy, comic and light-hearted and a bit sexy. The way Max had directed them, the characters were sweet and cute enough that the audience could get attached to them; because of that, it had more impact when they started dying a half hour into the show. Freddy the protagonist's speech about heaven and hell ended the act, and when Frank stood in the lobby during intermission, pretending to study the posters on the wall, he overheard more than one person sniffling.

But it was Act II that packed the emotional wallop of the evening. As a new crew of young men started to drop like flies, the audience watched Freddy — who had gone from giddy to bereaved in the first half of the play — go from revitalized to infuriated in the second half.

252

Freddy's new, young lover, Dino, gets caught up in the club scene in Act II, snorting crystal meth, staying out all night at discos, meeting men over the Internet for casual, frequently unsafe sex. When the first of Dino's friends finds out he's infected with HIV, Freddy warns Dino that this is a warning sign, and that if he doesn't change his lifestyle, he'll suffer the same fate that Freddy did a decade earlier when he saw all of his friends — all of them — die.

Dino doesn't want to hear any of it. "This is my body and my life, and you don't have any right to tell me what to do. You say you love me, but if you can't let me live my life the way I see fit, that's not love."

Freddy lets loose with a long speech:

"Loving someone isn't about letting them do whatever they want. It's about helping them make the right decisions. I love you, and because I love you, I want you to stay around. I want you to be with me for a long, long time. I want you to make smart decisions, take care of yourself, and avoid making horrible mistakes. My friends didn't know any better until it was too late. For you and your friends, that's not the case. You know what to do and what not to do. Yes, you're free to make your own decisions, regardless of what any politician or preacher or boyfriend might say. But if I didn't warn you, if I watched you walk over a cliff, if I saw your entire generation standing on the edge of the abyss and didn't try to stop you, that wouldn't be love. That would be negligence."

"Times have changed, Freddy," Dino tells him. "We're not standing on the edge of any abyss. AIDS today isn't what it was when you were my age. We've got medications. We've got job protections. It's not a death sentence anymore."

"A lot of things about AIDS have changed, Dino, it's true, but in the end it's still the same," says Freddy. "AIDS is still a death sentence. You just have a longer time on death row."

☐ ☐ ☐

In the final scene, Freddy stands beside Dino's hospital bed, first crying at yet another loss, but soon pounding his fists against the wall as he rails against the attitudes of young, naive men who thought they were invincible.

"Is this what it takes to get through to you?!" Freddy screams at Dino, lying near death in his bed. "We used to think education was the solution, but your generation had the information and still got the answers wrong. We thought love and community, the sense that we were all in this together, would bring this to an end. But you didn't give a shit about anyone but yourselves. Is this what you wanted from me instead? Rage? Fury? Is this what might have saved you? Would you have listened if I'd screamed louder instead of pleading softly? If I'd punched you in the face instead of kissing you? Tell me, damn you, because somewhere in this city there's a kid, some teenage kid just coming out, and I want to know what I need to do to keep him from being buried alive."

□ □ □

"Great show, Frankie," said D.C. in the lobby afterward, with the phony, upbeat enthusiasm of someone who worked in politics.

Katie had clearly been crying; her mascara was smeared, and she was holding her fashionably Euro-styled rectangular glasses in her hand. "Yes, Frank, you really captured something up there."

"Thank you guys so much for coming."

"We wouldn't have missed it for the world," said Katie.

D.C. patted him on the back, the way that straight guys do. "Friends come through when you need them, Frankie."

Frank looked at Katie, who was rolling her eyes. But it was too late for subtlety; D.C. was already in his oily, get-out-the-vote mode.

"Speaking of which, Frankie, now that the Democratic primary is over and the real campaign is under way, things are bound to get ugly. You know how these things go: They'll run ads and try to smear the mayor as some sort of conservative, a bigot, a homophobe. But that's not the mayor we've all known for the last four years, is it?"

"I know what you're getting at, D.C.," said Frank. "And don't worry. I'll be endorsing the mayor for reelection in the next issue." Even though the mayor had backed off his sex crackdown in the spring after getting some bad publicity, he had shown enough good faith in closing dozens of places over the past year to earn Frank's support.

D.C. gave him another hearty pat on the back. "Glad to hear it, Frankie. You know the mayor has done a lot for the gay community. It's nice to know he can count on your support."

Katie couldn't take any more. She slid her glasses back onto her nose and tapped her Movado. "We've got to run," she said.

"I understand," said Frank. "But let's get together soon."

"You got it, Frankie. Good luck with the show."

"Tell the mayor I'll get him front-row seats," Frank called after them. Without looking back, D.C. chuckled aloud.

□ □ □

"Great work," said Moe. "You really kept the tension building."

While he'd been waiting outside the theater, Moe had tried to think of something nice to say about the show. And it was true: Max's direction was solid, and the pacing did build nicely.

"Thanks, baby," said Max, leaning in for a kiss.

Moe hoped that was the end of the discussion about the show: "Want to go home and celebrate?"

"I can't," said Max, as they started to walk down the sidewalk. "They're having a cast party tonight and I should stop by. You can come with me, though."

The idea of walking in as Max's date appealed to Moe on one level; he pictured Frank DeSoto fainting dead of shock.

But he couldn't stomach the idea of spending a night toasting that shit head.

"No, I don't think so. You go ahead without me."

"Are you still hung up about Frank? I'd have thought you'd get over that once you saw the show and realized that you were getting all worked up over nothing."

"*Nothing*?" Moe tried to restrain himself.

"I mean, you said yourself that it was a good show."

"No, I said your direction was good. The show, on the other hand, was a load of horseshit! It's the most offensive, self-involved piece of crap I've ever heard. The only person who should have been buried alive is Frank DeSoto."

"I thought part of being a journalist was being able to see both sides of an issue," said Max, intending to wound Moe. It worked.

"Oh please, this play isn't about showing another side of an issue. It's about how Frank DeSoto was smarter than everyone else in his generation, and even more so my generation. He's some Christ-like figure sent down from the heavens to get gay men to repent for their sins — and the sins of their ancestors. If it were really his story, you'd see all those young guys in Act II *wanting* to get AIDS and die if only to escape from his self-righteous moralizing!"

"That's not funny," said Max, stopping on the sidewalk.

Moe stopped, too, and raised his voice: "Frank DeSoto thinks he can save gay men from themselves. 'If only they'd listen to me, this whole epidemic would end!' Give me a break. For someone who made his fortune off gay men's lust for dancing and fucking and snorting coke, he's got a lot of nerve playing the messiah."

"That was a long time ago," said Max, leaping to Frank's defense. "Frank has been a leader in the gay community as an AIDS activist for years."

"AIDS activist? Is that what you call it? Encouraging the government to regulate sex again? Silencing any discussion of gay men's sexual desires and behavior by branding people who still have sex as murderers and lunatics? That's activism? When the government does it, or religious leaders do it, we call them homophobes. Why is this asshole any different?"

"He's different because he's been through it himself."

"Then he, of all people, should know better."

"I happen to think Frank is right about a lot of things."

"Really? Like what?"

"A lot of young guys don't take AIDS seriously enough. They don't know what it was like to watch friends and lovers die. They don't understand what's at stake. They don't want to hear about it because they don't want anything to ruin their fun. They're spoiled brats who think they've got a *right* to party and screw all they want."

"We do have that right. Not because we're young, but because we're human beings."

"But you have to accept the consequences of your actions."

"Maybe we do accept them," said Moe. "We're not all idiots. We're not all irresponsible. We're not all suicidal. We *do* understand what's at stake, and we do listen to people who've been through it. But in the end, it is our decision to make about what we do with our own bodies."

"Is that why you think I spent all those years at Act Up meetings? So that you could suck as much cock as you want?"

"No, Max," said Moe. "That's why *I* spent all those years at Act Up meetings. I was in Act Up, too, when I was in college. I wanted to make sure people knew what was risky and what was safe, to make sure their rights were protected and their medical options were expanded. I wanted gay men to keep every option available to them to have sex safely and knowledgeably, and every treatment available to them if they got sick. I don't know what *you* were doing at those meetings — assuaging your guilt and exorcising your personal demons while you were cruising, probably — but I know you weren't just looking out for the next generation."

"There was more to it than that and you know it."

"Yes, you'll excuse me for being glib, but what do you expect from a spoiled brat like me? I'm sure you had some ideas about helping other gay men. You wanted us to know how to protect ourselves, to know how to stand up for ourselves, to stand up to doctors and politicians and preachers and homophobes. You wanted to educate the next generation of gay men. And for the most part, you succeeded. But now that you've educated us, you can't tell us what to do with that information and you can't blame us for the decisions we make."

"So that's what activism is about for you? Sex? That's it? It's not about community, public health, social change, caring for one another?"

"It's about all those things, sure. But when it comes right down to it, it's about sucking cock."

"Well I can tell you one thing," said Max. "I know one cock you're not going to be sucking tonight."

And with that, Max turned on his heels and walked away, leaving Moe standing alone on the dark sidewalk.

□ □ □

"Max Milano! There you are!" As soon as the actors noticed that Max had arrived at the opening night party, they swarmed around the director. He didn't have a chance to say hello to Frank before he was surrounded by his cast, showering him with accolades. Max looked over to Frank and gave him a wink, then turned back to the crowd of young performers, beaming and talking excitedly.

There were perhaps two dozen people at the party: the actors, Rainbow Stage staffers, and their guests. Frank didn't know anybody except for Max, so he spent most of the party on the edge of the room near the food.

While most of the people were introducing each other to their friends and lovers, and congratulating each other on their performances, Jeremy Wilson — the lead actor as well as the host of the party — came over to Frank.

"You were great tonight," Frank told him. "A real leading man."

"Thanks, Mister DeSoto," he replied, shaking Frank's hand.

"Call me Frank."

"Okay. Thanks, Frank. Can I ask you something?"

"Sure."

"How much of what you wrote is true? It's a pretty horrible story, with everyone around Freddy dropping dead. Is this fiction, or did this really happen to you?"

There were some details that Frank had pulled directly from his own life; others — indeed, the vast majority of the second act — were fabrications. But Frank didn't bother to explain in detail.

"By and large," he said, "it's true."

Jeremy paused for a moment. "It's hard enough for me to pretend those things are happening to me when I'm on stage. I don't know how you lived through those things happening to you in real life."

Frank said, "I don't know how I lived through it, either."

□ □ □

Sitting in a booth in the back of Ebony and Ivory, a piano bar down the block from the Rainbow Stage, Gene was a bit distracted; people around the piano up front were singing "What I Did for Love" from *A Chorus Line*. Dustin had Gene's hand in his, but he didn't really have his full attention.

"So what did you think of the play?" Dustin asked, trying to get Gene to focus.

"A bit melodramatic, don't you agree?"

"Well, yeah." That was pretty much beyond dispute.

"I'm also not crazy about the messages it was trying to get across."

"Like what?" Dustin asked, happy that Gene was now blocking out the distracting music, but wondering if he'd missed the messages that Gene had picked up.

"Let's see: First, the only guy who isn't really having any fun is the only guy who survives, so that message is 'Don't have any fun.' Then, all the younger guys turn out to be irresponsible morons who inevitably end up dying, so the message is 'You'll pay for breaking the rules.'"

"Well that's not necessarily a bad message in terms of HIV prevention, right?"

"It's a completely bogus message," said Gene, letting go of Dustin's hand. "Do you think only reckless guys get HIV — or that only guys with HIV are reckless? Sometimes people are careless as hell yet somehow they stay healthy. Sometimes, people take a lot of precautions but end up positive despite their best efforts. And sometimes, unlike in that play, people who have HIV stay alive for more than a few minutes after they're diagnosed."

Dustin wasn't sure what to say. They had never really spoken at length about AIDS. Dustin didn't know any of the details about Gene's history — when he seroconverted, how it happened, what kind of medications he'd been on before, whether he'd ever been seriously ill. He knew that right now, Gene appeared to be in good health, and his medications were apparently working well enough to eliminate HIV from his bloodstream. He hadn't pried into the past, and Gene hadn't volunteered anything.

But tonight, spurred on by the play, Dustin asked questions and Gene answered them. As the pianist played the score from *Gypsy*, the light from the candle on the table flickered in Dustin's eyes, and Gene told his story.

eighteen

Gay men would call it "Sunday brunch." To Mr. and Mrs. Salazar, however, it was just lunch, the same as it would be on any other day.

Otherwise, it was most certainly not an everyday meal for Kevin's parents, sitting on an uncomfortable futon trying to make small talk. Mrs. Salazar — a petite woman with fine features, whom Kevin closely resembled — was perched on the edge of the cushion, because her feet wouldn't reach the floor otherwise. Mr. Salazar looked similarly awkward, squinting to scan the unfamiliar room while propped up on two red throw pillows.

They had already run through the bare essentials of polite chit-chat with their son's friend; they knew he was a graduate student at Empire, that he was from Ohio, and that he used to be a dancer. They also knew that he and Kevin had met "at a party." They did not ask what kind of party.

Aaron asked them a few questions about Rochester and the conference they'd be attending. Although Mrs. Salazar usually did most of the talking, at this point her husband — a husky, broad-faced man with a quiet but imposing presence — gave a brief spiel about his work in a laboratory doing optics research. Aaron couldn't help notice that for someone with a deep knowledge of optics, his eyeglasses were hopelessly out of date.

Mrs. Salazar was chiefly interested in her son, so as soon as Aaron excused himself to start setting out the food, she began asking Kevin questions. She didn't ask anything about school — Kevin's parents had skipped graduation that May, as a not-so-subtle reproach to his chosen institution of higher education — but instead focused on his current situation and how he was supporting himself.

"Perfect Focus is paying me ten bucks an hour, and the owner lets me use his darkroom for free," Kevin said. "I stay after hours a couple of nights a week and work on my own photography."

"What for?" she asked. "Shouldn't you be doing work that helps pay your rent?"

"Creating a portfolio does help pay my rent," he answered. "It'll help me get a decent gig as a photographer some day."

"Some day?"

"I'm already doing freelance work for one newspaper. And I've got an interview at another one tomorrow." He was happy to have this tidbit — he had saved it up so he could reveal it at just the right moment — so he could prove to her that he had chosen a realistic career path.

"Really? Which newspaper?" she queried.

Aaron, who was listening in on the conversation from the kitchen area, where he stood slicing bagels, stopped to hear Kevin's reply.

"It's a daily newspaper called the *Queens Reader*. They liked my work and asked me to come in to talk to the editor."

She seemed satisfied with that half-answer, and didn't ask the name of the paper Kevin was *already* working for. For one tense moment, Kevin waited for that question, but when it didn't come, he stood up to help Aaron bring the food to the table.

Aaron carried a tray with four kinds of bagels, three kinds of cream cheese, tomatoes, and onions. It was all supposed to be very New York. The kind of thing that would impress people from Rochester.

There were two small pitchers, one with orange juice and the other with iced tea, on the counter. Kevin went to bring them to the table, but as he turned around, he bumped into Aaron and spilled the drinks on the floor and on himself.

"Oh, sweetie, I'm sorry!" Aaron cried.

Kevin froze. Surely his parents must have heard that.

If Mr. Salazar heard it, he didn't betray any emotion; he was scanning the photographs on Aaron's wall with a blank expression. Mrs. Salazar, on the other hand, clearly heard it — her eyes were open wide. But she didn't say anything either.

Aaron broke the silence. "I'll clean this up, Kevin," he said — although it felt awkward to call Kevin by his first name. "Why don't you go put on a clean shirt?"

Kevin, embarrassed, grabbed a shirt out of the closet and ducked into the bathroom to change while Aaron mopped up the spill with paper towels. Mrs. Salazar helped. Kevin emerged a minute later, tucking the tails of a clean oxford into his pants.

"That's lucky, dear, that Aaron has a shirt that fits you so nicely," she said.

"This is my shirt, Mom," Kevin said.

"Oh," she said slowly. Kevin could almost hear the gears turning in her head. The big question she had been thinking but had not asked — Why are we meeting in Aaron's apartment? — was suddenly answered without a word. Only her husband didn't get it.

"Come and sit down," she called to him. "Kevin and his... *friend* have put lunch on the table."

"I'll be right there," he said. "Kevin, can you come here for a second?"

"Sure, Dad, what is it?" Kevin asked, walking over to him.

"This picture, on the beach, who are these girls?"

It was the photo from Fire Island, from July Fourth weekend. Mr. Salazar had taken the photograph off the wall and was looking at it intently, scrutinizing it.

Kevin thought, *Oh shit, I can't believe I forgot to take down the incriminating evidence!* But he managed to remain calm.

"Those are just a couple of friends of ours that we met this summer."

"Really? They look familiar."

Sweet Jesus, Aaron thought as he brought over another pitcher of juice, *that man really does need a new pair of glasses.*

□ □ □

Frank watched the Sunday matinee from backstage; Max had invited him. It was a whole different perspective on the performance. As he sat on a stool in the wings, he could see the actors getting ready for their entrances and hear the techies calling cues.

Frank spent intermission talking to Jeremy Wilson in the dressing room. He didn't venture into the audience until the show was over.

Max told him the house was sold out, but even a sold-out house at Rainbow Stage was a small crowd, so it didn't take him long to notice Angie and Lou Zacarias, Scott's parents, leaving the theater.

"Oh my God, what on earth are you two doing here?"

"We're surprising you, sweetheart," said Angie.

"You're darn right you are! I had no idea!"

"We tried to come up for the big opening night," said Lou. "But we couldn't get a flight out of Louisville until today."

"Why didn't you call to tell me you were coming?"

"It wouldn't have been much of a surprise then, would it?" said Lou with a wink.

"We made sure you'd be here," said Angie. "We called the theater to see if anyone knew if you'd be coming, and they passed us along to the director, Mister Milano, and he said that he'd make sure you were here."

That explained the backstage invitation. Frank hadn't thought anything odd about it. He'd appreciated the gesture, and now that he knew what Max had helped to arrange, he appreciated Max all the more.

"We brought this for you," said Lou, holding out a bottle of champagne.

"You shouldn't have," said Frank, accepting the gift.

Angie hooked her arm through Frank's elbow. "There's more, dear," she said. "Lou and I are going to take you to dinner tonight to celebrate your theatrical debut."

"That's really not necessary," said Frank.

"Shush, Frank," said Angie. "Lou's paying."

She smiled and Frank relented. "I guess I can't argue, then."

"That's my boy," she said.

They exited the theater arm in arm, with Lou trailing a few steps behind. On the way to the restaurant, Frank told Angie how she had inspired him to write the show in the first place.

□ □ □

Gene couldn't move and he couldn't see. His hands were tied and he was blindfolded. He couldn't talk either, because there was something in his mouth.

Dustin's cock. Everything was going according to plan.

Gene had a very specific idea of how he wanted to spend his Sunday afternoon, and he had spelled it all out to Dustin in detail. Gene wanted to be handcuffed in the leather restraints he'd bought that morning on Christopher Street, and blindfolded with the leather mask (fur-lined, to balance the kinky with the comfortable) he'd found at the same store. Dustin was then going to force Gene to service him: suck his cock, lick his balls, eat his ass, sniff his armpits, and anything else that came to mind.

That afternoon, after brunch, they had started playing in Gene's bed. It started off a bit awkward — Gene was resisting the restraints, and Dustin didn't immediately realize that the struggling was only pretend — but it heated up quickly. Once

Gene was immobilized, Dustin had unbuttoned Gene's shirt and removed his pants and underwear. Then Dustin stripped himself — quickly and without any sense of teasing, since Gene couldn't see him anyway.

He had skipped the kissing, since Gene had told him that it shouldn't be part of the scene, and got right to the blowjob. He put his knees on either side of Gene's face and sat down on his chest, pinning his arms. He forced the head of his cock in Gene's mouth, then grabbed Gene's head and pulled it toward him, stuffing his dick into Gene's mouth. He wasn't fully hard yet, but it didn't take long. Gene kept trying to cry out — fake protests — but his words were muffled; his hot breath and the vibrations from his mumbling only served to make Dustin harder, and thus make it more difficult for Gene to be understood. And so it went.

Gene was pulling against the restraints, but not too hard. Despite his feeble thrashing and verbalizing, Gene was happy right where he was.

Although the scene was new to him, Dustin grew more confident and started to enjoy himself. He spent a great deal of time forcing Gene's head down on his cock. When he thought he was getting close, he pushed Gene's head onto the bed and made him lick his balls. He pushed both his balls inside Gene's mouth and told him to use his tongue on them. He put one hand on Gene's forehead, pushing him down and keeping him still, while he used the other hand to tweak Gene's nipples behind him.

He even started talking dirty to Gene, telling him he was going to make him do whatever he wanted. Dustin didn't usually have this kind of raunchy talk in his repertoire, but he found it a bit easier without Gene looking at him. He felt like he could take the lead for once.

So he did. He turned around and sat on Gene's face in the other direction. "Now eat my ass," he commanded, and Gene — who was usually on the receiving end of a rim job — complied without complaint. And he must have been enjoying it; his erection was pointing straight up.

A sight like that wasn't easy for Dustin to resist. He bent over slightly and took Gene's cock in his hands, stroking it. Gene moaned and crooked his neck forward so he could keep eating Dustin's butt. As Dustin's grip grew firmer, Gene got harder and his cock leaked precum. Dustin leaned further down and put his mouth on Gene's cock, then readjusted himself, putting his own cock back into Gene's mouth.

Sixty-nine wasn't Gene's favorite position — he liked to concentrate on one thing at a time — but again, he complied. At least at first.

"Stop it, you're getting me too close," Gene said — or tried to say. His words were muffled by Dustin's crotch. Dustin kept sucking, bringing Gene closer to the edge. Closer.

By now, Gene was finished pretending to be powerless. He bit down on Dustin, who quickly withdrew from his mouth.

"What the hell?" Dustin asked, looking back.

"I'm telling you to stop, you're getting me too close. You're going to make me come."

"Oh yeah?"

"Yeah. So stop it." ·

Dustin was still in the scene. "I don't think there's much of anything you can do about it. You're all tied up."

Gene pulled his right hand toward his face — there was plenty of slack, since the cuffs were connected under the mattress by a strap wide enough to fit a queen-size bed and Gene only had a double — and, with his outstretched fingers, pushed the blindfold up onto his forehead. Under the pressure of Gene's direct gaze, Dustin's resolve withered almost immediately.

"This isn't what we talked about," Gene said.

"What do you mean?" Dustin asked, suddenly unsure of himself again. "I thought I was supposed to tie you up and, you know, have my way with you."

"Weren't you listening to me? You were supposed to tie me up and make me *service* you."

"Isn't that the same thing?"

"No, it's not the same thing at all."

It took Dustin a second, but he got it. Sort of. "So you want to focus on my dick, not on yours?"

Not exactly, Gene thought, *but close enough.* "Yes," he said, "that's what I want."

"I understand now. I'm sorry."

"That's okay. Do you think you can do what I want?"

"I think so. I mean, focusing on my dick isn't such a difficult thing to do."

"That's my boy," said Gene. "Now put this blindfold back on me and let's get down to business."

□ □ □

Moe was making up for lost time.

He hadn't been online much for the last several weeks, since he and Max had been spending more nights together, and he'd been working long hours at the newspaper, even sometimes on weekends. Some of his cyberbuddies were feeling neglected; they were sending notes asking things like "Did you get married?" or "Have you moved?" or "What's going on, got your jaw wired shut?"

He hated to disappoint. And he was terrified at the prospect of being dropped from their lists of preferred cocksuckers. So he decided to arrange a little Sunday afternoon suckfest for a group of his buddies from Men Online. Eleven of them were currently online; he checked his notes to see which ones might play well as a group. Moe was expert at figuring out who would mesh. It took about six minutes to arrange the event.

Tony (whose online handle was ItalHunk4u) was the first to show up, at four fifty-two. He was olive-skinned, lightly hairy, with a naturally solid build; he had a quiet demeanor and a persistent hard-on — both of which were assets in such a scene — but his most memorable quality was his scent. Moe didn't know what it was, but there was something in Tony's chemistry that was like catnip, making Moe drool mindlessly as he sniffed his armpits and nuzzled his crotch. He was one of Moe's favorites; they had played for nearly two years. Moe told him to come a few minutes early so he could have a bit of special attention one-on-one before the others arrived.

Tony came in and stripped immediately, giving his host a wink and a lascivious grin, then strode over to the couch. Moe, wearing boxers and a flannel sleeveless shirt — unbuttoned halfway, to encourage people to play with his nipples but still covering up his gut — knelt before Tony on a cushion he'd placed on the floor, and went right to work. It wasn't long before he had Tony's scent rubbed into his own beard, and a glazed look in his half-closed eyes. He kept things slow, savoring Tony's cock, careful not to induce a climax before the others arrived.

Tim (SukMyStik) rang the buzzer at four fifty-eight. Punctual as always. Moe got up and excused himself for a moment to buzz him in. Tim was huskier and hairier than Tony, and a bit older — in his late fifties. He was also much more verbal, and liked to talk shit while he got serviced. Moe didn't mind, as long as he wasn't expected to answer.

Sitting naked side by side on Moe's love seat with their matching goatees, the two of them were a good pair. Tony made sure to pay attention to Moe, playing with his nipples even when he was blowing someone else. Tim kept the scene going with his raunchy monologue, even when Moe's attention was elsewhere: "Yeah, suck your buddy's big cock! Yeah, buddy! That boy's mouth feels good, doesn't it? He's gonna suck this daddy dick in a minute. He's gonna take care of both of us. Two big cocks for this cocksucker to play with today!"

Moe always was adept at creating good combinations. His boxers were wet with precum.

When Randy (LikeAHorse) came at three past five, Moe moved the action to the bed, where they could all be more comfortable — or as comfortable as possible with Moe trying to get Randy's ridiculously large cock down his throat. In his thirties, bearded but mostly smooth and unremarkable-looking in a sort of nerdy way, Randy wasn't Moe's top choice for a solo fuckbuddy. But he knew that in a group, Randy's sizeable endowment made for a great show; other guys loved to see it get fully hard, and were always amazed to watch Moe take the whole thing in his mouth. Tim, on this particular afternoon, had plenty to talk about. "Holy shit! That monster cock is gonna make that boy choke! Oh shit! He's taking that whole thing! Look at that! Look at that hungry cocksucker take that big fat cock to the root! Fuck, that's hot!"

Randy was on all fours, fucking Moe's face on the bed and grunting, while Tim lay next to Moe, his face up close to Moe's face, giving his running commentary directly into Moe's ear as he jerked himself. Tony squatted over Moe's legs, further down the bed, silently rubbing their cocks together as he watched Randy thrusting from behind. Nobody was watching the porn on the TV.

Moe wondered what was keeping Pete (CreamyCenter), until the buzzer rang at twelve past five. "You got another cock coming up here? This ain't enough for you?" asked Tim, but he knew the answer already and smiled. Moe, currently trying to cram both Tim and Randy's cocks into his mouth at the same time, was too busy to get up. So Tony hopped off the bed and walked over to the intercom to let in the last guest.

Tony came back to the bed and stood on top of the mattress, balancing himself against the wall. Tim and Randy backed off and Moe got on his knees. Tony took him by the ears and pushed his cock into Moe's mouth, so deep that Moe could smell that irresistible scent in Tony's pubic hair. Randy knelt behind Moe on the bed, reaching around to play with his nipples, rubbing his beard on Moe's neck, kissing his ears, pressing his swollen cock against Moe's back. Tim stood next to the bed, narrating the scene.

Then the door opened.

"Goddamn, another hot man!" said Tim. "Our little cocksucker is kinda busy right now, man, but get naked and he'll take care of you too. He's a hungry boy today! Just look at him taking care of this guy. He's been blowing all of us, and I know he's gonna love blowing you too!"

Moe waited for Pete to come to the bed. Pete wasn't usually shy; if he wasn't as verbal as Tim, he still had plenty of nasty things to say to keep things interesting. He liked to slap his cock on Moe's face and make him beg for it — again, something that didn't particularly turn Moe on, but that made good theater for a group scene. He was also a nice looking guy, around forty, blond, clean-shaven, barrel-chested, and hairy front and back — although Moe couldn't help thinking that Tim was going a bit overboard in his adulation, calling him "superstud" and "musclepig."

"Come on, superstud, take off that shirt and those pants," Tim was saying. "Let's see that cock of yours. Let's see what this boy is getting!"

Pete still didn't come to the bed. Maybe something's wrong, Moe thought. Maybe he knows one of these guys and doesn't like him. Maybe he's not into the group. Maybe he's waiting for me to go to him and get him involved. Maybe he just needs personal attention.

Moe released Tony's cock and removed himself from Randy's embrace. He stepped off the bed and turned toward the doorway to see what was wrong with Pete. And that's when he saw Max: arms folded, with all his clothes still on. He had a cold stare on his face, and a bunch of white lilies clutched in his left hand.

Time froze as Moe searched for something to say. The three guys on the bed kept stroking their cocks in slow motion, watching Moe and this new addition, unsure what was going on. Even Tim was at a loss for words.

Max, without a smile, broke the silence. "Were you expecting someone else?"

Moe opened his mouth, but before a sound came out, the buzzer rang again. And Max's question was answered.

There were many things Moe wanted to say. That he had planned to see Max later that night to apologize for Friday night's argument. That he had missed seeing him on Saturday. That he didn't want to lose him. He wanted to tell Max that he'd throw these other guys out of his apartment. But he didn't say anything; it was Max's move.

Max put the flowers down on the counter and pushed the intercom buzzer, letting Pete in the front door.

"Get back to your buddies," Max said. "I'm going to watch."

□ □ □

Moe had never felt so self-conscious, sucking his four buddies while Max sat in a chair next to the bed and watched. No matter how much Tim urged him to, Max wouldn't take off his jeans, wouldn't join in the scene, wouldn't even touch himself despite being visibly hard beneath his denim. He was strictly a voyeur, his eyes solely on Moe.

The four guys used Moe in every imaginable position: stretched out on his back, lying on his stomach, kneeling on the floor, head hanging over the edge of the bed, sitting in a chair. He had cocks in his hands, in his mouth, rubbing his chest, against his back, jerking over his face. His nipples were swollen, his cock was dripping precum, his breathing was fast — his body responding the way it always did when he was put through the paces. But he couldn't stop thinking about Max quietly sitting there.

Moe was on his stomach, face down in Pete's lap, a cock in each hand, when Tim turned to Max and said, "Come on buddy, you gotta get a taste of this boy's mouth. It's unreal."

Max shook his head.

"Just come over to the bed and take a look at him, going to town on his buddy's cock."

Max shook his head again.

272

"He's hungry for it. You should really give him what he wants."

Max stood up and started taking off his clothes.

"Yeah, that's it!" said Tim. "Let's see how many cocks he can take."

Max pulled his briefs down and left them on the floor. Tim reached out to take his cock in his hand, but Max pushed it away. Max joined the four other guys around Moe, but he wasn't going to be part of the group. They could all look at Max — and they did, eagerly — but nobody could touch him.

He spit into his palm and stroked his cock, kneeling over Moe's backside. As Moe blew his other guests, Max rubbed his cock against the crack in Moe's butt. Moe tried to look over his shoulder to catch Max's eye, but Max's eyes were closed, shutting the rest of the room out entirely.

Moe closed his eyes, too. He could tell Randy from Tim from Pete from Tony by their smells, by the size of their cocks, by their tastes. The four of them took turns sitting at the head of the bed, with Moe's face pushed down on their dicks. When one guy got close to the edge, he'd let another take a turn while he cooled down a bit. This way, they could keep the scene going for hours.

Max kept rubbing his cock against Moe's ass. He knew Moe was getting worked up, with all those men taking turns at his mouth, Tony making sure to reach under him to tweak his nipples and rub his chest. Moe was giving himself over to the physical sensations of the moment. He even started grinding into the mattress, arching his back and moving his ass as Max straddled him.

One by one, the men came in Moe's mouth. First Tony. Then Pete. Then Randy. Then, with a loud scream, Tim. With each load, Moe's gyrations got more intense.

When they were finished, the four men sat on the bed, spent, waiting for the grand finale. Moe remained stretched on his stomach, sweaty, eyes closed, with Max on top of him, grinding against his butt.

"That mouth is all yours, man," said Tim. "You've got it all to yourself."

Max didn't reply.

"He wants you to shoot in his mouth, man. That's what he wants."

Moe turned around and opened his eyes, nodding at Max.

Max opened his eyes and looked at Moe. "No, he wants me to fuck him."

"Buddy, he's a cocksucker. He doesn't like to get fucked," said Tim. But Max just kept grinding into Moe, who was still catching his breath.

"We'll see," Max said, grinding slower and harder. He leaned forward, putting his full weight on Moe's back. He lay his whole body on top of Moe, reached his arms around him, hugging him tightly and rubbing his hard nipples. He continued humping Moe as he breathed hot breath into Moe's ear, driving Moe crazy.

Moe bucked off the mattress, meeting Max's thrusts as Max played with his chest.

"You want me to fuck you, don't you?" Max whispered into his ear. "You want it, I know it. You want me inside you. You want me to fuck your ass."

Moe didn't say anything. What the hell was going on? Was this a scene that Max was playing? Did he really want to fuck Moe? Was he trying to punish Moe for Friday's fight by making him do something he didn't want to do? Was he trying to make Moe demonstrate that his connection to Max was so deep that he'd do something he didn't like? Was he trying to set himself apart from these other buddies by proving he could make Moe desire things he never desired before? Was this a sign of love or a sign of revenge? A symbol of intimacy or a symbol of disdain?

Whatever it was, Moe realized, didn't matter. He wanted Max to understand that he cared about him. If Max wanted to fuck him, so be it. He was willing. He nodded.

"You want me to fuck you?"

Moe nodded again.

"You want me to fuck you?"

More nodding.

"Say it."

"I want you to fuck me."

"Say it louder, so all your buddies can hear."

Max pulled on Moe's nipples and bit his earlobe.

"I want you to fuck me," he said. "I want you to fuck me right here."

Max sat up and pointed his cock, unsheathed, at Moe's butt. He spit into Moe's crack and started to rub it in with a thumb.

"Spread your ass and beg me to fuck you."

Moe did as he was told. His four buddies stared in astonishment. They'd all been certain that this was something HotLipsNYC most certainly did *not* do.

"Please fuck me. I *want* you to fuck me."

Max plunged his thumb into Moe's butt, and Moe wriggled and moaned. "Please fuck me. I want you."

Max slicked up his cock with his other hand and started to jack himself while Moe writhed on the bed.

"I want you to fuck me! I want you to fuck me!" Moe cried.

And with that, Max took one final stroke on his cock and shot his load all over Moe's back.

"Moe, you don't know what you want," said Max, reaching for his briefs on the floor. He quickly dressed and walked out, leaving the flowers on the counter. Moe lay there on his bed, Max's cum drying in the small of his back, with Tony, Tim, Randy, and Pete sitting open-mouthed and stunned.

nineteen

The review of *Buried Alive* was a rave.

"Unafraid to tell the truth," it cheered. "It should be mandatory viewing for every gay man under the age of thirty."

It wasn't surprising that the review was a love letter. It was in *Outrageous*, and despite bearing the byline of a freelancer who was a personal friend, it had actually been written by Frank himself. In fact, he wrote it before the show even opened.

Frank had also devoted his entire back page to an ad for the show, which he had given the Rainbow Stage for free. This wasn't a major sacrifice of advertising space; his ad pages had been declining steadily since the debut of the *New York Gay News*. The new paper already boasted a larger press run, and it was thicker too. *Outrageous* was down to sixteen pages per issue, the smallest size the printer would handle, while *New York Gay News* was printing twenty and twenty-four pagers nearly every week.

He'd been running *Outrageous* at a loss for a few months, since advertisers who were wary of his publication now had another option. Meanwhile, he was constantly stiffing writers and photographers who worked with him. He couldn't cover the costs of printing anymore. He would fall behind in paying his distributor, then find a new distributor who would extend him credit. Frank's time was running out.

The two papers' distinct personalities were becoming increasingly apparent. The lead story in the latest issue of *Outrageous*, written by Frank, took a swipe at MIGHT for raising money through Summer Loving, its annual Labor Day circuit party on Fire Island. ("Circuit parties are where people get HIV, not where they fight it," he wrote.) The main attraction in the *New York Gay News*, in contrast, was not the lead story that their political reporter Liz Hurst had written detailing the mayor's "mediocre" record on gay issues, but rather the debut of a new so-called humor column about HIV called "Positive Spin" — written by none other than Hector Vasquez, NIGHT's erstwhile prevention director, whom Frank had successfully pushed to have fired. Moe Pearlman clearly thought that AIDS was something to kid about, Frank thought.

The *New York Gay News* did not, however, have a review of *Buried Alive* in its new issue. Frank guessed it would run the following week, but in any case, he wasn't too eager to read what Moe might have to say.

He was more concerned that *Buried Alive* hadn't been reviewed by any of the other papers at his corner newsstand. Maybe it's too soon, he figured. Then again, maybe the Rainbow Stage isn't on their radar. He decided to get a cup of coffee and call Max to see if he'd read anything.

□ □ □

Moe was distraught: Max hadn't responded to several voice mails and emails. What's more, Moe hadn't had anyone to help calm him down. Aaron had been off somewhere with Kevin Sunday night, and Gene hadn't returned his messages either; he'd turned his ringer off for some reason. So first thing Monday when he got to the office, Moe called Gene at work to tell him about the whole horrible scene with Max.

"You can spare me the details of your depraved orgy," Gene said. "I can't bear to imagine the things you do in your free time."

"God, what a sex-negative queen you've become," said Moe. "We used to do most of those things *together* in some previous life."

"I don't remember that at all."

"I'm sure."

"Tell you what," said Gene. "You go right ahead and tell me about your little sex party, and I'll tell you about what Dustin and I did this weekend."

"Let me guess. You watched him put more pins in his Moe Pearlman voodoo doll?"

"Well, there was that. But there's more. Things that made us turn off the phone. Dirty things."

"All right, you win. I don't want to hear anything that might give me a mental image of you and Dustin in the throes of ecstasy. We'll skip the sex talk."

"Good, so cut to the chase. Is it over with Max?"

"I don't really know. Maybe it is. This is the first time he's ever stopped talking to me. I don't think I've made this big a mess with anyone I've dated in years."

"Yeah, since we were together."

"You're the one who made those messes, not me."

"Ah yes, and history is rewritten once again."

"Um, we're talking about me now, remember? Try to focus."

"Of course, you fragile little flower. Go ahead."

"I suppose I'm not surprised. It was probably just a matter of time until it ended."

"Why do you say that? It sounded like things were going fine."

"We weren't really a good match."

"The age thing?"

"No. I mean we don't belong together. Look at Max, and then look at me."

"You shouldn't think of it that way," Gene said. "Your fight might be about politics or AIDS or your sex life or that stupid play or any number of things. But it is not about how you look."

"So you don't think I'm fat as a house?"

"I *do* think you're fat as a house. I just don't think that has anything to do with why Max is upset."

"Great, now I'm just a joke to you. For your information, I'm making plans to take some of this weight off."

"Going back to the gym? Exercising? Eating less?"

"Next Monday I'm going to go an entire day without eating. A health fast."

"Next Monday is Yom Kippur. That hardly counts as a weight-loss program, sugar bear."

"Give me some credit for trying," said Moe. "It's funny, now that I think about it, that you always call me sugar bear. You've given me the nickname of a mascot for a children's sugar cereal. How was I supposed to stand a chance at winning the battle of the bulge? It's no wonder I've gotten so fat that no sane man could want me. You drove me to this subconsciously. I'll wind up overweight, diabetic and alone before I'm thirty, thanks to you."

"Elton John," said Gene.

"What about him?"

"That's where your nickname comes from, you idiot. It's an Elton John lyric, from 'Someone Saved My Life Tonight.' It's not a reference to a children's cereal. So don't blame me for driving you to obesity."

"I blame you for everything else."

"True, but I won't be saddled with this guilt. Besides, you look more like the Sugar Smacks frog."

"You really know how to cheer a guy up."

"Is that what I'm supposed to be doing? I thought I was supposed to be your reality check. I'm sorry, can we start this conversation over again? I'll try to get my character down."

□ □ □

Eleanor called around eleven to say she'd be coming into the office as usual the next day, but with someone in tow: Mandy Majors. Gene's new "assistant."

Mandy was a friend of Eleanor's; they had met on one of Eleanor's weekly visits to New York. Mandy — although

280

currently "between jobs" — had some experience managing a small card store a few years back, and she had given Eleanor some unsolicited advice on how to run a business in New York. Eleanor, who never took any such advice from Gene, ate up whatever the ever-so-slightly flirtatious Mandy had to offer. And soon enough, as if the idea had come out of thin air, Eleanor was offering Mandy a job.

Imagine that.

He wasn't sure what to think. He told Ben and Jay that Mandy would be coming in on Tuesday morning.

"Will Mandy be our new mommy?" Ben asked in a baby voice.

"We like Papa Gene the best," said Jay. Then they looked at each other and giggled.

I guess they're not worried, Gene thought.

So he called Dustin to see if he was free for lunch, to talk about his concerns.

Dustin, trying to gauge whether he was supposed to be upset at Eleanor or unconcerned about the whole situation, asked, "What does everyone else think about this?" He meant Moe, of course, but didn't want to say the name out loud.

"I don't know," said Gene. "I called you first."

Dustin quickly named an Indian restaurant in Chelsea where they could meet, and then he nearly floated away.

□ □ □

Dustin was so happy after lunch, so elated that he had apparently moved up to the top slot on Gene's list, he hardly had anything to talk about when he walked into his weekly afternoon therapy session in Emmett Kane's office.

In just over three months of therapy, Dustin had begun to take charge of his life, particularly when it came to Gene. He no longer did whatever Gene felt like doing, whenever Gene felt like doing it; now Dustin made his own desires known, speaking up for himself when he disagreed with Gene.

He had been worried at first that Gene might leave him, that perhaps Gene was only dating him because he was so pliant, so agreeable. Instead, by being more assertive, Dustin had succeeded in bringing the two of them closer. They spent every weekend together, and plenty of weeknights, too. They talked every day. They did things that Gene wanted to do — like visiting piano bars, which Dustin had never cared for — but they also did things that Dustin liked. Cooking together, for instance, or shopping for antiques. And Dustin's carefully measured assertiveness seemed to be paying off: Gene called him *first*.

Dustin was feeling more secure about himself and his relationship than he ever thought possible, and he owed much of this feeling to Emmett's advice.

"I'm glad you're feeling better about yourself," Emmett told him, "but the credit is all yours. Therapy is just a way to help you tap into your own strengths and insights. I didn't give you any powers you didn't have already."

"I feel like we've passed a turning point," Dustin said. "I hardly ever hear about Moe anymore. We hardly ever fight. The sex is great — really great. And Gene's health is better than ever. He found out this week that his viral load is undetectable. I wouldn't be surprised if, come spring, I was looking for a new apartment for us to share."

The very thought made Dustin smile.

Emmett furrowed his brow.

"Dustin, is there something you've forgotten to tell me?" Emmett asked.

"You mean about moving in together? There's nothing to tell, really, that's just an idea — "

"That's not what I'm talking about."

"Then what are you talking about?"

"Is Gene HIV-positive?"

"Yes, he is. I thought I told you that at the very beginning."

"You most certainly did not."

"I swear I thought I did. I remember we talked about HIV the very first session."

"That's right, we did. You told me that you were HIV-negative. But you never bothered to mention that Gene was HIV-positive."

"I suppose you're right. But yes, he's positive. Does that make a difference?" It hadn't made a difference to Dustin — well, a small difference, but not enough to keep him away from Gene.

"It most certainly does," Emmett said loudly. His voice was tougher than before. "You're putting your health at risk — putting your own life on the line — for the sake of this man? You must have less self-respect than you thought."

This was quite a blow coming from Emmett. But he responded. "I'd put everything I have on the line for Gene. I love him."

"And Gene — the man who's so willing to put your health in danger — does he love you?"

"Yes, he does."

"Really?" said Emmett. "Has he ever said so?"

Dustin sat for a second. Gene had shown his love in many ways, but no, he had never said the words aloud.

For the remainder of the fifty minutes, Emmett sternly lectured Dustin on the risks of serodiscordant pairings — relationships between men with different HIV status. Most of these couples failed, Emmett insisted, because the men's perspectives on life, the views they had of the future, were so different. In many more cases, he said, the negative partner ended up infected, only to have the lover leave him, his emotional and physical health shattered. Even in the best of cases, Emmett said, where the love endured and the negative man managed to avoid infection, the positive lover would eventually become sick and die, leaving the survivor scarred and prematurely alone.

"There simply isn't any possible happy ending for a couple like yours," Emmett said. "Better to end it sooner than later."

"You don't know what you're talking about," Dustin said. "Gene and I aren't like that. We're good together, and we're going to stay together. He'd never do anything to hurt me or put me in danger."

Emmett didn't respond. He merely sat in his brown leather chair, impassive, staring at Dustin like a disappointed father.

Dustin, who had come into Emmett's office full of happiness, walked out with sweaty palms.

□ □ □

"They want me," said Kevin.

"And who wouldn't?" said Aaron.

"Mazel tov," said Moe, raising his glass of Sprite.

As the three of them waited for the pizza, they sat sipping sodas while Kevin told them about his successful interview that morning at the *Queens Reader*.

"They loved the shots I took for the *Gay News* — especially the shots of the raid last month at Club Lux, those pictures of the two drag queens smoking in the back of the police car. They said it told several stories at once, without being obvious. They also liked some of the posed photos I took of Aaron at the beach because they said it showed that I could do both journalistic photography for their news section and more creative portrait shots for their arts section."

Aaron was grinning broadly, happy to have contributed in some way to Kevin's good fortune.

"So what are the terms?" asked Moe, getting down to business.

"They're offering me a hundred dollars a photo, as a freelancer, so I won't have to spend all day in their office, even though I'll need to be out in Queens a lot. It shouldn't interfere with my work for the *Gay News*, although I'll have to cut back on my hours at Perfect Focus. I'm going to talk to the manager tomorrow to see if I can work out some kind of deal where I work a few evenings a week in exchange for access to their developing equipment. I think he'll go for it."

Moe was relieved that he wouldn't be losing Kevin altogether; he had spared Kevin for the day for his interview, but couldn't imagine running the paper without Kevin popping in occasionally with new photos. Aaron was worried about Kevin working too many hours, but he was excited about his new gig. Kevin was thrilled at the prospect of earning enough money to support himself — something he'd struggled with since Slick closed and he stopped hustling.

"Only part I'm not looking forward to is the commute," said Kevin. "Queens is fucking huge! Getting to Long Island City is one thing, but getting out to Forest Hills is like going cross-country. Or so I hear — I've never actually been there."

"It probably doesn't take any longer than it takes to get from Aaron's apartment to yours," said Moe.

"Exactly," said Kevin. "How often do I make that trek?"

"I guess I wouldn't know," said Moe, winking.

"Not often, trust me," said Aaron. "He's pretty much a fixture at my place."

Kevin looked at him. "Do you mind?" Like he had to ask.

"Not at all, sweetie," said Aaron. "Not one bit."

□ □ □

After Kevin's big news, the pizza arrived, and they went around the table as they ate. Moe told the boys about his situation with Max. (They assured him that relationships have endured rougher seas — as they knew firsthand.) And Aaron talked about meeting his in-laws.

"I'm like one of the family now," Aaron said, noting that Mrs. Salazar had given him a kiss on the cheek when she left — as much affection as she ever showed her own son.

"My goal wasn't to get you into the family," said Kevin. "I don't even like being part of that family myself."

"I know you don't mean that, sweetie, and besides, it can't be any worse than my family."

"I guess everybody hates his own family," said Kevin.

"Not Moe," said Aaron. "He loves his parents. And they love him."

Moe nodded, chewing silently. It was true. He had a ridiculously nondysfunctional relationship with his parents. He actually enjoyed their company.

"That," said Kevin, "is the weirdest thing about you, Moe."

The bill came. Moe, being the expert number-cruncher, tallied up the tip and divided the total by three (even though Moe had eaten more than either of them). Aaron took the money to the cashier on his way to the men's room.

Now that they were alone, Kevin said to Moe, "I don't want to bug you, but you still haven't told me what to do about *Woof*. I promised the editor I'd let him know this week."

"I'm still thinking about it. On the one hand, I look like a blimp in those photos. On the other hand, I'm only getting fatter, so those might be my last chance to fit on a single page of a magazine."

"You look good in those pictures, Moe."

"Thanks. I'm just not feeling so good about my body lately. But I am considering it. I'll let you know."

They got up to put on their coats. Moe looked down at the crusts on Kevin's plate and asked, "Are you going to eat those?"

□ □ □

Moe was halfway home when he heard someone barking at him on the sidewalk.

"Woof!"

He ignored it, kept walking.

"Woof!"

286

Moe stopped and turned around. There was Gabe, from the Alliance. Moe hadn't seen him in months. And Gabe had certainly never woofed at him before.

"Hi, Gabe. How've you been?"

"Not as good as you, Moe. Looks like the paper's doing well. And looks like you're doing well, too."

Gabe reached out and patted Moe's belly. Then, with a big grin, he growled.

Moe didn't know what the hell was going on. He had flirted with Gabe shamelessly at meetings, at bars, and at sex clubs before, and Gabe had never shown any interest.

"Um, thanks," said Moe.

"You're...beefier than I remember."

That's one way to put it, Moe thought. "I guess so."

"It looks good on you. The beard, the belly, the whole package. You've become quite the hot little bear."

So that's his issue, Moe thought: *He's a bear chaser. Now it makes sense. I used to be too* thin *for him.* "Thanks," he said. "That wasn't really my intention, but..."

"Well, it should be. Woof!"

Gabe rubbed Moe's stomach through his jacket. Although he was grateful for the attention, particularly from a guy as hot as Gabe, Moe was a bit uncomfortable having someone rub his belly like he was some erotic Buddha.

"How's the Alliance doing?" Moe asked. "I haven't gotten any calls since the summer."

Gabe stopped rubbing and looked Moe in the face, his head cocked. "Not too well. You know how it is. Different people have different agendas. They have other things to do. There are five or six of us who still have meetings every other week, but there's not a whole lot we can do other than react to things as they happen. When Club Lux got busted — you know, you ran the story about it — we tried to organize a protest outside the police precinct, but it rained and only three people showed up. That was pretty much the end of the big plans. Now we're focusing on writing letters as individuals and distributing condoms to the kids on the piers. Pretty sad, I suppose."

Very sad, thought Moe, *but not surprising.*

"Listen, I've got to get going, but it was nice to see you, Gabe."

"You too, stud," said Gabe. He reached in his pocket and pulled out a card. "We should get together some time."

"Sure."

Gabe put his hand on Moe's stomach one last time and leaned in to kiss him. And right there on the street, Moe felt tongue.

□ □ □

As they were walking back to the East Village after dinner, Kevin and Aaron talked about apartments.

"It's silly to keep paying rent on my place in Washington Heights when I'm hardly ever there," said Kevin. "And if I'm going to be commuting to Queens, I'll be up there even less."

"What are you suggesting?"

"I've been thinking that maybe I should give up my apartment and move in with you. You know, officially."

Aaron stopped. "I've been thinking the same thing."

"You have?"

"Yes, sweetie, I have. I didn't want to bring it up because I thought it might scare you. The idea of giving up your space."

"That doesn't scare me, as long as I'm somewhere with you."

Aaron's heart swelled. "There's only one problem. My apartment isn't any more convenient to Queens than yours is. I'm on the wrong subway lines."

"That's true."

"Unless..."

"Unless what?"

"Unless we both give up our places and move," said Aaron. "My lease expires in a couple of months. We could get a new place together, a bigger place."

In a matter of minutes, the idea became official. As they walked through the East Village, they began discussing neighborhoods, timing, what amenities each wanted in a new apartment.

Opening the door to Aaron's, Kevin flicked on the lights.

"It'll be hard to leave this place. It was really the first apartment of my own," said Aaron, who had moved in when he broke up with Joshua. "But I'm ready."

The light on the answering machine was blinking. Aaron pressed "play."

"Hey Aaron, it's Moe. I'm assuming Kevin is there with you? I know I just saw you a half hour ago, but I wanted to tell him that I made up my mind on my walk home. Publish the photos."

□ □ □

Dustin needed to take the edge off after his appointment with Emmett. He went to the gym, but that didn't help. He thought a late dinner with Gene would do the trick, so they made a plan and Dustin took a cab over around nine.

Gene needed to relax, too, to take his mind off Eleanor's impending visit; she was due to arrive the next morning on the Metroliner, as she always did on Tuesdays.

Dustin brought a bottle of Chianti from a shop near Gene's house. He also had a bag with a change of clothes, since he thought after a late dinner with a few glasses of wine, he'd stay over — something he rarely did on worknights.

With wine glasses in hand, Gene and Dustin made dinner together: Dustin cooked angel hair pasta with chicken, while Gene made a mesclun salad. Working with Gene in his small kitchen, Dustin thought that Emmett had it all wrong, that he and Gene were a good pair, working well together. He tried to put Emmett's comments out of his head; he didn't want to think about them, and certainly didn't mention them to Gene.

If the first glass of wine helped them to unknot their muscles, the second and third glasses with dinner made them both frisky. In fact, when they finished dinner, they left the plates on the table — something Gene would never do ordinarily — and headed straight to bed.

There was a lot of sloppy kissing — kissing because it was something they both enjoyed, sloppy because of the wine — and clumsy shedding of clothes. Once they were both naked, making a jumble of Gene's previously neat bedclothes, they moved on to other things.

Gene and Dustin didn't have a routine when it came to sex. The menu of options was fairly standard — fucking and sucking, the occasional toys, once in a while an experiment like that weekend's adventure with handcuffs and blindfolds — but there was no set script, no typical amount of time they spent, no predictability.

Tonight, Gene was feeling nastier than usual. He bit Dustin's lower lip while they were kissing, twisted Dustin's nipple a bit too hard, pulled on his balls for a second longer than usual. He pushed Dustin down on the bed and climbed on top of him, talking raunchy talk about how Dustin was going to "suck those fucking balls" and "worship that big cock" and "lick that hot ass."

Despite the Jeff Stryker-style trash talk, Dustin complied, happily.

Gene was sitting on his face, Dustin's arms pinned beneath Gene's knees. Dustin licked Gene's ass while Gene worked his nipples. "Get that fucking tongue up there, cocksucker!" Gene commanded, and Dustin obeyed.

"Look at that, your cock is rock hard, you cocksucker," Gene scowled. "You like licking that ass, don't you?"

Dustin managed a muffled "Yes, Sir."

"That's right, boy, you keep licking that ass," Gene continued. "You keep taking care of me, and I'll take care of you."

With that, Gene bent down and took Dustin's cock in his mouth. Dustin squirmed. Gene took Dustin's balls in his hand and squeezed them. Dustin gasped. "Don't you stop licking that ass!" Gene ordered. So Dustin went back to rimming while Gene worked his cock and balls roughly. He'd get Dustin close to the edge, then stop sucking his cock and pull harder on his balls — just a bit of pain to keep his mind off ejaculating. Then he'd start up again, and stop again. All the while, Dustin kept licking his ass, going slowly but steadily insane as Gene teased him.

It took about fifteen minutes of this for Dustin to crack: "Please, Gene, let me come," he begged.

Gene grinned a drunken grin. "What'd you say?"

"Please, *Sir*, I want to come," Dustin said. "You're making me crazy."

"Well, cocksucker" — Dustin loved that name — "you can get off. But not until you get me off first."

"Yes, Sir."

"You're gonna service this cock until you make me shoot. You got it?"

"Yes, Sir."

"*After* I shoot, then you can get yourself off."

"Yes, Sir."

Still squatting over Dustin's face, Gene turned around to stick his cock in Dustin's mouth. While Gene was changing positions, Dustin raised his arms off the bed so he could work on Gene's nipples while he sucked; he knew that was a surefire way to make Gene lose it.

"No way, cocksucker," said Gene, pushing Dustin's arms back onto the bed and holding them down. "You're gonna do this using just your mouth."

This is going to take a while, Dustin thought. But there were few ways he'd rather spend an evening, as his own cock — hard, even though nobody was touching it — attested.

Gene took his time in Dustin's mouth. He'd pump his cock for a while, and then sit still and tell Dustin to work his tongue, or move his lips, or open his throat. He'd let Dustin get him close to orgasm, and then pull his cock out, leaving Dustin's mouth open, his tongue stretching for Gene's cock, just out of reach. He kept up this game for the better part of a half hour. Dustin never lost interest.

Then Gene decided he could stand no more. He shoved his cock all the way into Dustin's mouth and held it there. "Milk that fucking cock," he ordered. "Work that tongue. Make that cock feel good."

Dustin went to town on Gene's cock, which was a good seven inches when hard — and it was surprisingly hard considering how much he'd had to drink. Dustin wasn't an expert by any means, but he knew how Gene liked his cock sucked, and he had pretty good gag control. That was enough.

Climax was fast approaching, Dustin knew. But he was caught off guard when Gene shouted, "Take it, you cocksucker!" — and shot his load straight down Dustin's throat.

It caught Dustin so completely by surprise that he didn't realize exactly what was happening until the second or third spurt, at which point he pushed Gene off him and sat up with a sober start.

Gene was on the floor, on his naked ass. "What the fuck is wrong with you?"

Dustin was choking. "No, what the fuck is wrong with *you*?! Did you just shoot in my mouth? Did you just shoot your goddamn positive load in my mouth?!"

"Yes, I just shot my goddamn positive load in your mouth," Gene spat. "What's the big deal? You know I'm undetectable now. So there's nothing to worry about."

"You've never *asked* me if you could shoot your load in my mouth," Dustin said, wiping his mouth and expectorating. "We've never done that before."

"And you've never called it my *positive* load before."

Dustin's head was swimming. Was it the wine? Was he just tired? Was he making too big a deal of this? He knew oral sex wasn't a big risk, and he knew that Gene had virtually no HIV in his semen. But still, he thought, Gene shouldn't have assumed anything. He was furious.

Gene's head was swimming, too. He hadn't planned to cum in Dustin's mouth. He knew he should have asked. Maybe he just got carried away, maybe he had too much to drink. Or maybe this was something he had wanted to do for a long time, and finally felt like he could because his viral load was undetectable. He wasn't really putting anyone at risk.

Dustin, who had never made a big deal out of Gene's HIV status before, had drawn a line down the middle of their sex life: Positive Gene and Negative Dustin. Maybe Dustin hadn't meant to talk about Gene's "positive load" — but the fact that it slipped out meant that it had been in the back of Dustin's mind for a long time. Gene felt deceived.

"I think you should go home," Gene told him.

Dustin nodded, and started dressing. "I'll get a cab."

But before he left, Dustin stopped to use the bathroom. From where he lay in bed, Gene could hear Dustin gargling with Listerine.

twenty

This is what makes Gene hard: control.

When it comes to sex, he's always in the driver's seat. It's the only way he can enjoy himself.

He is not a top. That's not to imply that he's a bottom, either, but simply that choosing one side isn't the point for him. He doesn't like any label that might allow someone else to make assumptions about him. He likes to set the agenda himself, and keep his partners playing defense.

Many gay men who are heavily invested in sexual control find themselves drawn to leather. Not Gene. The leather scene, with its highly codified symbolism and rituals — black armband on the right bicep, yellow hanky in the back left pocket, nipple rings and harnesses and cigars — leaves him cold. It all seems too predetermined, too rigid, too obvious. Men in leather bars can agree who's going to do what to whom without exchanging a single word. Gene prefers to keep people guessing about what he's into, and to take charge without getting their explicit consent in advance.

Sure, he can be as sexually codependent as any other guy, doing whatever he thinks his partner wants him to do. But there always comes a point — after a few minutes, a few dates, a few months — where Gene flips things around, changes the rules unexpectedly, just to remind the other guy that he's the one in charge, even if he's got his knees in the air. He loves it when he can get a partner to do something he didn't plan to do, or maybe didn't even want to do.

This need for total control doesn't exist outside the bedroom. He's willing to compromise or share control in most areas of his life. That's why he was so willing to accommodate Dustin's requests about things like cooking, antiquing, and socializing. He was even open to Dustin's demands on his time, although it meant seeing less of Moe. Gene was flexible, willing to cut Dustin some slack and let him have his way once in a while. Their relationship was a democracy — flawed and crude, but sincere.

But Gene's sex life has always been a dictatorship, fascist all the way.

Six years earlier, when Gene first met Moe in a men's room at George Washington University in D.C., Gene already knew that this horny undergrad was an avid tearoom queen. He'd seen Moe hanging around the student center toilets many evenings before, and he guessed (correctly) that Moe wasn't the type to be satisfied with one cock. So by the time he actually got inside Moe's memorable mouth, he knew exactly what he needed to do to control him.

He got Moe to come home with him, taking him out of the place where Gene would have to compete with an endless stream of other men. He got Moe to focus on Gene's dick alone, and while he did, Gene told Moe how sexy he was, how much he wanted him, how he never wanted anyone else to suck his cock. Some of this was true (Moe was a cute little number when he was twenty) and some of it was just talk (Gene wanted thousands of other men to suck his cock, even if he had to admit that Moe was more talented than any of them).

Pretty soon, Gene had Moe coming directly to his apartment every evening, skipping the tearoom altogether. Within a few weeks, he had Moe addicted to his cock. Moe was still blowing other guys between classes while Gene was at work; Gene figured this much out without being told. But Moe was hooked, and focused in a way he had never been before on a single dick.

Then, one Friday evening, Gene turned the tables. Moe came over for his usual cock-worship session, and Gene pushed him down on the bed and blew him instead. Not a fantastic blowjob, but slow and devoted and deliberate. When it was over, Moe, out of breath, wanted to reciprocate, but Gene told him it was time for bed, and without asking Moe if he wanted to stay, Gene simply turned off the light and lay down on his futon beside Moe and drifted off.

Moe was swooning, which was all part of Gene's plan. What Gene had not planned on was falling for Moe in return. But that's what happened. Love.

Their sex life got a bit more varied; although Moe still spent most of his time sucking Gene's dick, Gene kept him on his toes by mixing things up occasionally. Perhaps a half-dozen times, Gene got Moe to fuck him — more important, he got Moe to want to fuck him, and then he let him do it. Three times, Gene fucked Moe. (He never succeeded in getting Moe to want this, but he did succeed in getting Moe to stop protesting.)

Gene gained a large measure of control over Moe sexually. After six months, Gene decided to test how far he could push his new boyfriend. One night, after nearly an hour of making out and dry humping, as Moe was on his knees before him unbuttoning his fly, Gene made a simple statement that changed everything.

"I want us to be monogamous," he told Moe.

This idea held no appeal for Moe. He loved cock, wanted it all the time, and found it pretty much whenever he wanted it. He didn't have any problem reconciling his love for Gene and his lust for other men's cocks. But now Gene wanted him to choose. Moe was confused. Gene clearly wasn't prudish — after all, they'd met in a tearoom. So why make the demand now?

"Things are different now," Gene told him.

"Why?" Moe asked, getting up off his knees and sitting on the bed.

"Because I love you." And he kissed him sweetly.

This wasn't a lie. Gene was in love. But that's not what his request for monogamy was about. Is it ever?

Moe didn't fully understand what was going on. He had never been in love before. He didn't know that he could try to work out an honest compromise. He didn't know that he could do what so many people, gay and straight, do in this situation: pledge monogamy and simply keep the infidelities a secret. For Moe, this was lying, hypocrisy, something people did when they were ashamed of their sexual desires; it didn't cross his mind to say yes but mean no.

Gene, being five years older, was more experienced in matters of the heart and the crotch. He had no intention of being faithful, even in a so-called monogamous relationship. Most men understood this double-talk. Gene had a feeling that Moe didn't — not simply because he was so young, but because he was so guileless in his sexuality. He wanted to find out for sure.

"Can't we talk about this later?" Moe asked.

Gene said no. And Moe, terrified that he'd never be able to suck Gene's dick again, was forced to make a decision while Gene sat there, fly open, still hard. He said okay.

It was difficult for Moe, but he stuck to his guns. He stopped going to tearooms, stopped visiting the video booths, stopped picking up guys on the street. Gene did the same — or so Moe thought. But Gene was still screwing around, in the same old places. In fact, he could cruise the tearoom at George Washington even more now, since he knew Moe was deliberately avoiding the building to prevent temptation.

Their relationship deepened, and their sex life got more interesting. Gene knew that Moe was used to monotony in his sexual activities — blowjob after blowjob after blowjob — and variation in his sexual partners; now he had to reverse the equation, to keep Moe interested in one cock. So they did it outside, in cars, on the roof, in the shower, in Rock Creek Park, and once on a Metrobus. They did it with blindfolds, with tit clamps, with chocolate sauce. They did it in army fatigues, police uniforms, starched shirts and ties. It wasn't perfect, but they held it together sexually, while emotionally they became quite dependent on one another.

Monogamy — real on Moe's part, alleged on Gene's part — was simply taken for granted. Gene was in control, and Moe trusted him.

Then one day, after they'd been together for almost three years, Gene went to see his doctor about a throat infection. Strep throat, it turned out, easily treated with antibiotics. But as long as Gene was already in the examining room, his doctor decided to run some blood tests. And that's when he found out he had HIV.

Gene and Moe had been tested shortly into their relationship, and they'd both been negative. Moe had been faithful, Gene could be certain. Gene had been the one sleeping around.

He told his doctor that he'd had sexual partners on the side — particularly for fucking. (Although he knew he could occasionally talk Moe into it either way, he knew that Moe didn't much like it, and the more he grew to love Moe, the less he pushed that issue.) But he always used condoms.

"Those aren't perfect," his doctor told him. "They've never done any good studies on condom breakage or leakage, but you know they've got a five- to ten-percent failure rate as birth control."

"I don't spend much time thinking about birth control."

"That's not the point," said his doctor. "The point is that condoms break frequently enough for a whole lot of women to get pregnant. So you can bet that they break frequently enough for a whole lot of men to get HIV."

Gene had the best of intentions. Well, maybe not the best of intentions — he was sneaking around behind Moe's back, making him live up to a code of conduct that he disregarded completely — but he certainly set out to keep himself and Moe safe. But now he had to tell him.

The HIV wasn't the main issue at first. (That was something they would both focus on later, after the break-up that came within weeks of the disclosure.) The "cheating" wasn't important to Moe, and the lying wasn't even the worst part — although it was somewhere on the list of wrongs. The main issue for Moe was that he had sacrificed his own sexual desires to please someone else. He'd never make that mistake again.

What did Gene learn from the whole situation, which quickly unraveled his love affair? He learned that nobody can achieve total control when it comes to sex. But that only increased his resolve to control everything within his power.

With the guys who followed the breakup, Gene controlled every move: when to disclose his HIV status, when each man would cum, what his partners would desire. He avoided dating strident men and stuck to pliant, malleable types — guys who wouldn't put up a struggle for leadership in the bedroom. Guys who would take orders — even taking orders to give orders — and like it. Guys who knew that everything was tenuous, temporary, contingent on Gene's continuing approval.

Unfortunately, not many guys like this sort of situation for anything more enduring than a quick tryst. So Gene had trouble finding an appropriate boyfriend. For three years after Moe left him, he had a series of quick affairs and one-night stands. For emotional intimacy, he continued to turn to Moe, who, after several months of not speaking to him and another several months of bitterness, had become something more than a friend, even when he moved away to start graduate school. There was still love beneath the betrayal and resentment. For Moe, Gene remained his first love. And Gene often thought that Moe would be his last. Yes, he knew, there might be others, but everything was different now that he was positive. Life was finite, relationships had expiration dates, intimacy had limits. He'd never be as open and intricately entwined with another person as he'd been with Moe.

And then he met Dustin. At first, he was the very definition of malleable. He submitted fully to Gene's control and came back for more. He was attentive, interested. The HIV didn't put him off — not that they talked about it much, but Dustin *didn't seem concerned as long as they used protection. Gene didn't bother to tell him that he'd used protection when he got infected. But he did make sure that whenever he fucked Dustin, he always pulled out before he came, even though he was wearing a condom. And he never came in Dustin's mouth — even though, as Moe had always told him, there's hardly any risk of infection that way.*

At first, Gene looked at Dustin as a plaything. A handsome plaything, true, but just a plaything. Not a romantic interest. But when Dustin started making demands — stop seeing Moe, come up to my apartment, let's go antiquing — Gene looked at him differently. Maybe, he thought, there's a chance that this could develop into something. If Dustin cares enough to make his desires known, he must care enough not to simply walk away. Besides, once Moe got involved with Max, Gene realized he couldn't rely on him forever. So Gene bent, acceded to Dustin's requests — even the difficult one about seeing less of Moe. And as Gene saw less of Moe, he confided more in Dustin, and they grew closer still.

Dustin was the first man in three years he called his "boyfriend." He wasn't sure he loved him — probably not, or not yet anyway, or at least not in the same way he had loved Moe, or perhaps still did love Moe. But he cared for Dustin.

However, there was one place where Gene could not relinquish absolute power. He would not let Dustin dictate their sex life.

It hadn't been an issue until the week Gene found out his viral load was undetectable. For him, that changed everything. Now he could do more — come in Dustin's mouth, maybe even come inside him if he was wearing a condom — without worrying about endangering his health. But he and Dustin had struck a delicate balance in bed, and the smallest shift sent it crashing down. As long as Gene had been extra-careful to avoid exposing Dustin to any danger, Dustin hadn't had to think about the HIV divide in their coupling. But as soon as Gene pushed the boundaries of what he thought was acceptable — coming

*in Dustin's mouth — Dustin pushed right back, and made it
crystal clear that even though he had never explicitly talked
about them as a serodiscordant couple, he was cognizant of the
medical distance between them. Dustin thought of Gene as a
positive guy — an increasingly reckless positive guy, perhaps.*

*If the boundaries of their sexual behavior were going to shift,
Dustin, as the negative man, would need to give his approval
and define the new boundaries. Even if Dustin wasn't the
one explicitly setting the sexual agenda, it was now suddenly
apparent that he maintained veto power over Gene's decisions.*

*Gene felt fenced, feared, watched, doubted. He'd been
forced to acknowledge that there was another person in bed
whose feelings and health and desires needed to be explicitly
considered. For Gene, this was total emasculation. He was
the poz, the eunuch, the risk, forever impotent. No matter how
deeply he looked into Dustin's eyes, he knew he'd never be hard
again.*

WINTER

twenty-one

Ben and Jay were giggling like twelve-year-old girls when they strolled in to the Final Frontier office on Monday morning.

"What's so funny?" asked Gene, who had arrived first.

More giggling.

"What? What is it?"

They couldn't stop.

Ben pulled off his gloves, put his backpack on his chair and unzipped it, pulling out a brown paper bag. He slid out a magazine and flipped to the center spread.

Woof. Moe. Naked.

The giggling got louder. Gene rolled his eyes. In the back of his head, he knew that the December issue was due on newsstands any day now, but he hadn't thought to check on the way to work. He took a quick glance at the photo, just long enough to feel embarrassed — for Moe and for himself. He looked away, without checking out the rest of Moe's photos.

"Isn't that your boyfriend?" Jay asked, trying to control himself.

"No," Gene answered.

They stopped laughing. They looked confused.

"Isn't that Moe?" asked Ben.

"Yeah, that's him. But he's not my boyfriend."

"Seems like you go out with him all the time," said Jay.

"Yeah, you made Thanksgiving dinner together last week," Ben added. "And you went to Montreal together last month."

That was all true. Ever since Max had abruptly ended things with Moe, and Gene had pushed Dustin away that fall, they'd been spending almost all their time together, including a weekend away to forget about their respective failed relationships.

"Sure seems like you love each other," said Ben.

"We do," Gene admitted. "But he is not my boyfriend."

"Then what is he?" Jay asked.

Gene couldn't think of an answer. His friend? His ex? His buddy?

"Gene's naked love slave!" Ben teased.

"Gene's hairy little sex cub!" Jay added.

Gene wanted to put an end to this right away.

"He is not my love slave or my sex cub," Gene said. "For your information, we do not have sex."

That shut them up — for a few seconds.

"You love each other and spend all your time together but you don't have sex?" Ben asked quizzically.

Gene nodded.

"Sounds like a boyfriend to me," said Jay.

□ □ □

"Hey there, centerfold! Look who's famous!"

Kevin was standing at Moe's desk with *Woof* in his outstretched hand. Moe gasped and grabbed the magazine.

"Page twenty-three," said Kevin. "Cub of the Month: Moe."

Moe had opted to use his real name, figuring that anyone who knew him already would realize it was him. It seemed more honest, anyway.

He had seen Kevin's contact sheets, but not the layout, so he was curious to see how it all looked. Moe examined it closely.

There was the lead page, with two pictures of him still mostly dressed — unbuttoned flannel shirt, unbuttoned jeans, but still PG-13 at the most. Then came the centerfold, one big color shot spread across two pages: Moe wearing just an open shirt with cutoff sleeves and a pair of workboots, sitting on a bale of hay — one of the pictures they'd taken at his friend's farm upstate. His belly looked a bit big, his cock a bit small, and he had on a phony class-picture smile, but it could have been worse. It could have been one of the pictures from the last two pages, a collection of black and white naked shots taken in his apartment: spread-eagled and face down on the bed (looking like a bottom), getting out of the shower (looking fat), sitting up holding a teddy bear (looking silly).

This was a mistake, Moe thought, *there's nothing sexy about these pictures.*

"It's pretty hot, right?" Kevin asked.

Moe didn't want to hurt his feelings. It was Kevin's idea in the first place, and the photographer was not the problem as Moe saw it.

"These look great, Kevin," he said.

Kevin smiled.

"And now you can submit them to the *Queens Reader.*"

Kevin laughed. His new gig in Queens was going well — several assignments every week. But it was mundane stuff: library closings, water main breaks, traffic accidents, school plays — the antithesis of porn. His editors there would definitely not approve if they knew he had taken X-rated pictures. Fortunately, he figured, they'd never have to know. As much as he hated the commute out to Queens, the Queens residents at the paper rarely made the trip into Manhattan; if they never came into the city, they'd never stumble across Kevin's spread in *Woof.*

As Kevin stood over his shoulder, Moe flipped back and forth through his pages, focusing on the flaws in his appearance. Shouldn't have made this expression. Shouldn't have sat like that. Should have sucked in my gut. He didn't hear Carolyn sneak up behind him.

"What're you looking at, guys?" she asked.

Moe's first instinct was to close the magazine and hide it, but it was too late.

"Oh, my God!" she said. "Is that *you?*"

Moe nodded.

"What magazine is that?"

"*Woof.*"

"Why is it called *Woof?*"

"It's a magazine for bears — that's what gay men call big, hairy guys."

"I don't get it," said Carolyn. "Bears growl. They don't say 'woof.' "

"Gay bears do."

"Can I see?" she asked. And Moe handed it over.

She stared at the first page. "I can't believe it!" she said.

"Maybe you shouldn't look at the rest," Kevin said, reaching for the magazine.

"No, no, it's okay," she said, giggling uncomfortably. "It's just not what I was expecting to see when I came to work this morning. My coworker. In a porno magazine."

She turned the page to the centerfold and Moe did something he rarely did: He blushed. There was no joke he could crack to change the fact that Carolyn — his colleague, his boss's daughter, a straight girl — was checking out his merchandise. He knew there was a certain type of gay man who bought *Woof* because he liked paunchy, hairy guys. But what kind of straight women liked looking at guys like that? Were there any? Moe didn't know, and he was not about to ask Carolyn about the heterosexual bear community. He held his breath and waited for her to say something.

"Well, well, you certainly didn't leave much to the imagination, did you?" she said, closing the cover. "I've seen more of you than I ever thought I would!"

"More than I ever thought you'd see, either," said Moe.

"Well, the...um...*hay* is really slimming," said Carolyn, who had regained her composure. She smiled, and Moe relaxed.

"Kevin took the pictures," he told her.

"I see, a team effort."

"It was before the paper launched," Kevin piped in.

"Yeah, so we didn't mean for it to get connected to the company," Moe added.

"I wouldn't worry about it," said Carolyn. "It doesn't say your last name, or where you live or work or anything. The only people who'd know it's you are people who already know you."

"Yeah, and those people already know Moe's a slut!" Kevin said, joking.

Carolyn froze and Kevin quickly got embarrassed. There was a brief silence, then he excused himself.

"I guess I should put this away before your father sees it," said Moe. "You handled it pretty well, but your father would probably faint."

"I think he's got bigger things on his mind today," Carolyn said.

"Like what?"

"He's in a meeting right now with Alan, the business manager, and the accountant. They're crunching the numbers as the year gets close to the end, so they can plan a budget for next year. And it doesn't look too good, from what he tells me. He won't give me details, but I can tell by the way he's been acting."

"I don't want to hear that," said Moe, putting *Woof* in his desk drawer and closing it. "Let me know if you find out anything more concrete."

"Of course I will," said Carolyn.

Moe's phone rang. "You should get that," said Carolyn. "And, um, congratulations on the magazine."

Moe answered the phone. It was Gene.

"Woof," was all he said, in a deadpan voice.

□ □ □

The light on Frank's answering machine was blinking when he got home from the drugstore. But he walked right by the machine and into the bathroom, where he opened the bottle of

Tylenol he'd bought. When was the last time I had a hangover? he wondered.

But then, how many times did he have reason to celebrate?

The previous night had been the strike party for *Buried Alive*. Its initial six-week run at the Rainbow Stage had been extended due to popular demand for another four weeks; the Sunday matinee the previous day was its closing performance. Frank had hoped that the show might be extended again, but the theater had another play ready to open the following week, and couldn't bend any more.

Still, it was a good run, he thought — no thanks to the press. He got a dismissive review in *The A-List*, an expectedly abusive blurb in the *New York Gay News*, and nothing at all from the *Times* or the *Voice*. The only positive review came from the *City Star*, a right-wing mainstream daily, which lauded the show for "giving homosexuals the overdue scolding they deserve." The review noted: "More than a decade ago, 'The Normal Heart' sounded a similar alarm, but 'Buried Alive' proves that these promiscuous scoundrels still need to be awakened from their suicidal dreams." Not exactly what he was looking for. But word of mouth must have been good, because tickets sold well.

The party itself was something of a blur. He remembered that Max didn't stick around for long. He remembered meeting a bunch of theater people, from the Rainbow Stage and elsewhere, but didn't recall their names. Other details were even more sketchy: three or four or six glasses of whiskey, a chat with the star Jeremy Wilson that may or may not have been inappropriately sexual, a high-speed cab ride home that made his head spin. Falling asleep on the couch with one shoe on.

Frank took two pills and swallowed them with a glass of water. Then he stepped into his bedroom, closed the shades to block out the morning light, and collapsed on the bed.

The answering machine, he remembered. He got out of bed, walked back into the hallway, and pressed the button.

"Mister DeSoto, this is Jennifer Sloane from Deluxe Printing. We still have not received payment on your account, which is now sixty days overdue. I'm afraid you've left us no choice but to terminate our contract with you effective immediately —"

Frank hit the "delete" button. He had fallen behind in paying his printer over the summer, and as advertising at *Outrageous* declined in the fall and the late fees rose, he had found himself in a hole he couldn't dig out of. He'd have to get another printer. But not today. Not with this headache.

He played the next message, hoping it'd be better news. It was.

"Frank DeSoto, this is Constance Price from the Royalton Playhouse. We met at last night's party?"

Frank was drawing a blank.

"I was the woman with the blond hair and red glasses."

A vague picture emerged in his mind. Sally Jessy Raphael?

"And a tattoo on the back of my neck."

Not Sally Jessy. It was coming back to him. A tattoo in the shape of two women's symbols intertwined. Small and tastefully concealable for business situations, but still daring in its way. She had shown him at the party. A lesbian, an avowed fan of *Outrageous*. ("I went to a couple of demos with Act Up once upon a time," she had told him, presenting her credentials.) And, it was coming back to him, she was the artistic director of the Royalton, an off Broadway theater.

"I spoke with our business manager after I got home from the party," her message continued, "and he loved the show as much as I did."

Frank's headache started to subside.

"We have a slot open next summer," Constance said, "and we'd like to talk to you about transferring *Buried Alive* some time around June, just in time for Gay Pride. We'd probably end up recasting it, but we'd definitely be interested in keeping

Max Milano on board. Anyway, please give me a call today and we can talk about the specifics."

Frank fumbled to find the "rewind" button, to listen to the message again. Could he have heard her correctly? They wanted to pick up his play? A transfer to off Broadway? He had never really entertained such a hope.

Before he called Max to talk about the next move, he dragged the phone over to his bed. Now he really did need to lie down.

□ □ □

"It's time, Perry," said Aaron in a soft voice.

Perry turned over slowly and sat up on the massage table. Aaron excused himself to wash his hands, giving Perry a chance to put on his underwear in private.

When Aaron came back from the bathroom, Perry was sitting on the edge of the massage table in his briefs.

"I mentioned that it was a possibility, but now I can tell you that it's actually happening," said Aaron. "I'm moving."

It was the first time Aaron had said it aloud. He had been afraid of jinxing everything before it was official. But he had to tell his clients, so now it was out in the atmosphere. No taking it back.

Perry looked sad. "All the way to Queens, right?"

"Yeah, Astoria. We're signing the lease tonight and moving over the weekend."

"Astoria," Perry said, drawing out the syllables, rolling it over in his mouth like it was some mythic medieval paradise. Or a disease.

"It's not so far, just a few stops on the N train. You can get there in no time."

Perry stood up and reached for his oxford.

"But I know some people won't want to travel that far," said Aaron. "So I'll be getting a portable massage table that I could bring to your apartment." Aaron didn't want to do outcalls, lugging a massage table on the subway, but he couldn't afford to lose his steady customers.

"I'll make the trip, don't worry about it," said Perry. "That's proof that you're a great masseur, Aaron. Because I used to think nothing could make me leave Manhattan."

"I used to feel the same way."

□ □ □

Riding the subway out of the city alone at rush hour was a new experience for Aaron — and not particularly a pleasant one at first. The station was littered with crumpled newspapers and paper cups, and the train was crowded with commuters and smelly strangers who jostled him constantly. He wondered how people put up with this every day.

But when the N train went above ground in Queens, giving people a place to direct their gaze other than at each other, his mood lightened. Arriving in Astoria on the elevated tracks, Aaron descended to street level to find the neighborhood — his neighborhood — busy but not hurried, alive but not harried.

Walking the three blocks to his new apartment, he took in the flavor of the place: the old-fashioned bakeries with wedding cakes in the windows, the hardware store selling sponge mops and aluminum wastebaskets, the diners advertising moussaka and spanokopitas, and the stucco-covered funeral home, "Established 1928." It wasn't like anywhere he'd lived before — not like the raucous frenzy of the East Village, or his faux-urban college campus in Columbus, or the suburban development near Dayton where he grew up. There was something appealing about Astoria, an echo of a small town with its central boulevard and its quiet side streets lined with houses, but with the same subway that ran through Midtown close at hand.

He started to think that maybe leaving Manhattan wasn't such a big deal after all. He'd been there for years and had plenty of memories. And he'd still spend a lot of time there. But his home would be here, across the river, in a different area code, in a multi-family house with a flower garden. With Kevin. Together in the place they'd share.

He turned onto his block and saw Kevin already standing by the front gate. Dustin was with him. They waved.

Dustin had been invaluable in their search for a new place to live. He was the one who suggested Astoria. "It's close to Manhattan, convenient to the subway, affordable, and there are even a few gay people around," he'd told them. Plus, it was roughly midway between Aaron's classes at Empire and Kevin's office at the *Queens Reader*. Dustin had shown them five places before taking them to this one on Sunday, a house divided into four apartments with the owner, a little old Greek lady, living in the basement unit. They liked it right away.

And the little old Greek lady had liked them, said they were "handsome young men." Did she realize they'd be sharing a bed? Was it worth mentioning? They decided it wasn't. It was already pushing it to mention that Aaron might have massage clients coming to the house during the day; after a moment of hesitation, she took that in stride. She told them they could move in right away; they said they'd need a week. They agreed on the price, and she told them to come back the next night to sign a lease. And here they were.

It was moving quite quickly, but what were Aaron and Kevin giving up? A cramped studio in Alphabet City? A place in Washington Heights that they never used?

They went inside to the landlady's basement unit. She served them tea and set out a box of cookies from one of the bakeries Aaron had passed. They sat for a moment, made pleasant small talk, relaxed into each other.

Then, without any further delays or formalities, they signed the papers, said their good-byes, and headed out together. Kevin, as usual, had a camera in his bag, which he pulled out and handed to Dustin. "Take a picture of us in front of our new home," he said. Dustin obliged, and then the three of them walked to the subway and took the N train back into the city. Leaving Manhattan had taken all of fifteen minutes.

□ □ □

Moe was working late with Jane, his reporter, poring over the papers he received around five o'clock. MIGHT's proposed budget for the next year was due to be announced that Friday, but Moe had wrangled a copy a few days early. He had an inside connection: the new prevention director — the man who had replaced Hector Vasquez.

The rest of the world knew the new director as Brandon Dexter, a buttoned-down forty-something who always wore a striped tie. Moe knew him as GagOnThis, a raunchy leatherman who, according to Moe's database, had an eight-inch cock and could shoot four times in a single session without ever going soft. He was an old buddy from Men Online. Moe had often helped him out in a pinch, in the way that only Moe could, so Brandon decided he'd let Moe get a jump on analyzing MIGHT's budget.

Programs were being cut almost ten percent across the board. Salaries were frozen, and staffing was going to be reduced. Something was awry, but there wasn't a quick explanation in the paperwork. There was talk of "reduced resources" and "declining income," but no explicit rationale. Individual donations were off a bit, but corporate donations were up a bit — that couldn't explain the financial problems. Overhead had risen, but not ten percent.

Moe had also gotten a copy of the previous year's budget, which Jane was going over for the sake of comparison. She'd become quite a decent reporter in her six months on the job; she had learned not to trust what community leaders had to say, and to question every explanation no matter how logical it appeared at first glance.

Sure enough, it was Jane who figured out the missing piece of the puzzle. Comparing the two budgets line by line, she realized that the big shortfall was not due to any particular item increasing in cost or decreasing in revenue. The problem was that there was one item in the previous year's budget that was missing completely: the Summer Loving circuit party on Fire Island over Labor Day weekend.

Summer Loving had apparently suffered the same one-two punch that had felled Hector Vasquez: Frank DeSoto railed against the annual fundraiser in *Outrageous* that fall, and a week later, Emmett Kane pressured the board of MIGHT by writing an indignant opinion article for the *City Star*.

"How ironic that an AIDS organization would make money off a circuit party where men get high and then have sex in the dunes. Fighting AIDS by spreading it doesn't make sense to people with brains. Either this party — more of a group suicide, actually — should go, or the idiots at MIGHT should close their doors, because they have clearly lost their way," wrote Frank. Emmett echoed him: "By encouraging men to attend a depraved circuit party like Summer Loving, MIGHT promotes the very behavior it claims to be combating. Perhaps MIGHT is simply trying to ensure it will have thousands of clients for decades to come? This party must be stopped."

It worked. Hot on the heels of the Hector Vasquez fiasco, MIGHT wasn't eager to look even worse in the mainstream press. Sure, the party brought in nearly three million dollars every year, but a bad reputation could cost MIGHT much more in corporate gifts. The board opted to spike the party, but they hadn't yet made an official announcement to that effect. Here it was for the first time, in black and white, squeezing MIGHT's bottom line, leaving the organization millions of dollars short, forced to make cutbacks.

"Another triumph for the HIV police," Moe said sarcastically. "They have managed to destroy MIGHT's single largest source of cash every year, leaving them less able to fight AIDS."

"I guess they'd say it was worth it to shut down that party," said Jane. "I mean there were those two guys who overdosed last summer, and I've heard there's a lot of unsafe sex in the woods."

"Jane, there's a lot of unsafe sex in the woods every day on Fire Island," said Moe. "And a couple of guys overdose on drugs every weekend in New York, at a disco or a bar or in their houses. That's not unique to this party. So that's a lot of bullshit. But you know the greatest irony?"

"What?"

"They did this to shut down the party, but all they accomplished was to shut down the fundraiser," said Moe. "Next Labor Day, there will be a big party on Fire Island. Some promoter will make sure of that: It's part of the regular circuit, and people plan to go every year. There's still going to be a DJ on the beach, drugs everywhere, sex in the woods, and thousands of guys paying fifty dollars to get in, just like every year. The only difference is that this time, there won't be any condoms handed out, there won't be any drug information handed out at all, and not a penny of the cover charges will go to charity. The queens who go to these parties don't give a shit if it's for a worthy cause or not. They just want to have a good time. And they'll keep having their good time. MIGHT just won't reap the profits."

Jane looked at the budget. Ten percent cutbacks. "That's depressing," she said.

"No, it's fucking ridiculous," said Moe.

Moe would have started on one of his rampages against Frank DeSoto — Jane was quite familiar with them by now — but he heard someone shouting his name. A woman's voice, down the hall. He turned and saw Carolyn in her father's doorway.

"Moe! Come quick! Something's wrong with my father! I think he's had a heart attack!"

He dropped the budget and ran toward his publisher's office, Jane close behind him.

Carolyn was at her father's desk, kneeling, tears in her eyes. Moe couldn't make out what she was doing until he walked around the desk and saw Abe Guttmacher sprawled on the floor next to his chair. Carolyn was frantically trying to lift him and prop him up against the wall but he was too heavy.

"I was supposed to have dinner with my parents tonight. He said he'd be ready to leave around seven," Carolyn explained, sobbing. "It's not like him to be late, so when it got to be seven fifteen, I came to see what was keeping him. And I found him here."

Moe told Jane to call 911 while he went to help Carolyn, who was slapping her father's cheeks, pleading, "Daddy, Daddy, wake up." But Abe's face was pale, his eyes half-closed, his body limp.

twenty-two

As Moe stood next to Jane at Abe Guttmacher's funeral on Wednesday morning, in the chill of the Mount Sinai Jewish cemetery in Forest Hills, there were two thoughts in his head. One was that he needed to buy new clothes, because he couldn't button his old black sport coat anymore and the black Gap khakis he had on — the only black pants he owned that were within an inch of his current waist measurement — were about to bust open.

His other thought was this: *Abe Guttmacher was a mensch, a good man.*

He wasn't quite a father figure — Marvin Pearlman filled that bill well enough — but he was something more than an employer.

Whatever he was, Moe knew that Abe had given him an opportunity nobody else would have given him. Beyond that initial job offer, he put his trust in Moe to shape stories, supervise staff, and create an entirely new forum for the gay community — even though it was a community Abe himself wasn't part of. He hadn't balked at articles critical of the mayor, or stories that talked explicitly about anonymous sex and illicit drug use in terms that were not exclusively condemnatory. He had trusted Moe's judgment when he suggested hiring Hector Vasquez. And Abe had backed Moe when he wrote stories that pissed off major advertisers. He believed in Moe, in a way no other mentor — Melody Penn? — ever had. Even Moe hadn't been sure that he was up to the task of running the newspaper, but Abe knew.

As the rabbi read the eulogy, Moe watched the tears running down Carolyn's face, as she stood next to her mother, maternally stoic in her shock. A black limousine was parked at the edge of the cemetery, with at least a dozen cars behind it. More than fifty people were gathered on the dead grass, in between the uniform marble headstones capped with Jewish stars.

After the eulogy, the casket was lowered into the ground, and a line formed alongside the grave. Each mourner, starting with the immediate family, shoveled dirt onto the casket, using a small trowel to dig into the mound of loose earth next to the gravesite.

As Moe waited in line, listening to the bits of rock and dirt hitting the casket, he forgot about how his waistband was pinching his stomach, and how his shoulders were straining at the seams of his jacket.

Abe Guttmacher was a good man, he thought as he took the trowel. *I don't know what I'll do without him.*

□ □ □

Eleanor didn't know what the hell she was talking about. And Gene didn't hesitate to tell her so.

After six weeks on the job, Mandy Majors, the woman Eleanor had hired to be Gene's "assistant," had figured out how to solve Final Frontier's problems: move to Brooklyn.

Mandy hadn't bothered to mention this idea to Gene; she was usually civil to him but didn't really treat Gene like her supervisor. She knew she could always go over his head, directly to Eleanor. And that's exactly what she had done the previous night: Eleanor came to New York, as usual, and Mandy told her that she needed to talk to her alone. That's when she made her pitch to move the travel agency to Brooklyn. Without Gene there to offer the obvious rebuttals, Mandy had convinced Eleanor that her plan was a good one. It would save on rent and overhead, and bring the company in closer contact with the lesbian community, which was concentrated more in Park Slope, Brooklyn, than in Chelsea.

"Pretty convenient, isn't it? Park Slope is where Mandy just *happens* to live," Gene told Eleanor on Wednesday morning, when he caught whiff of the scheme for the first time. Ben and Jay were out front, out of earshot; Mandy, predictably, hadn't shown up for work yet, giving Gene a chance to talk to Eleanor in private.

"That's not what it's about, Gene," Eleanor offered. "Her arguments make a lot of sense."

"No, they don't. There's an old saying in New York, Eleanor. There are only three things that matter when you're looking for a place: Location, location, location. And in gay New York, that location right now is Chelsea."

"But rent here is double what it'd be in Park Slope."

"Your business here more than compensates."

"Does it, Gene?"

"Eleanor, the majority of our business is walk-in, off the street. We could either be near Eighth Avenue in Chelsea with thousands of gay people walking by every day, or on some quiet street in Brooklyn with a few dozen. The numbers just aren't there. And the people who are there are more likely family types with kids and less disposable income."

"You mean *women*," Eleanor spat. "That's what you mean. You want to stay here where the boys are. But this is a *lesbian* and gay company, and we need to go where the lesbians are, too."

"Eleanor, this isn't about gender, it's about business," Gene countered. "There are more gay men than lesbians in New York, they live in a more concentrated area, and they spend more on travel. That's not sexism. That's the truth."

"Mandy told me you wouldn't understand."

That was it.

"Isn't that a surprise. She comes up with this brilliant idea — based on reducing her own commute, maybe, but certainly not on any market research — and decides that she shouldn't bother bouncing it off her supervisor, because he certainly wouldn't understand, being a man and all. So she waits until you're here, makes sure there's nobody to object, and sells you a line of bull that you're too stupid to reject. Eleanor, you don't know anything about New York. You never have. But I always thought you knew a thing or two about business. Now I'm wondering if I've given you too much credit. Mandy is a huckster. She flirted her way into this job, and now she's going to sweet-talk you into flushing this company down the toilet."

"I don't see where you're one to talk, Gene. It's not like this place is booming under your command."

"That may be, Eleanor. But I've been telling you all along, what we need is to be more aggressive, make a greater impression, pull out all the stops. But you always want to play it safe, not offend anyone. That might work in Washington, but it doesn't work here. You've been bucking my ideas from the very beginning, and that's why we haven't been moving forward. But now, with Mandy in the picture, you're actually looking to move backward, make things even worse."

"I happen to think that Mandy is on the right track," she said.

Gene was steamed. "Then stop this train, Eleanor, because I'm getting off."

□ □ □

After seeing two massage clients before lunch, Aaron spent the afternoon in the library at Empire, researching ideas. He needed to put together a new term-paper proposal for Melody Penn's course in Advanced Queer Theory.

Mel hadn't liked his first topic: the role of class in the evolving AIDS epidemic. Aaron had planned to write about how, in the early days of the disease, AIDS discourse centered on sexual orientation, morality, infirmity, and nationality — as gay men, drug users, prostitutes, hemophiliacs, and Haitians fell ill. Attention soon shifted to racial categories, as numbers surged in the black community, particularly among women. But now, Aaron argued, the disease was undergoing a shift into class-consciousness, where the question wasn't who got ill or why, but rather who could get treatment. Middle-class people of any race, who had contracted HIV through any means, had access to the latest medications, as long as they had health insurance — which surely was, in America today, a sign of middle-class status. The working class and the poor — anyone without insurance or access to private physicians — would remain ill, whether they were drug-using hustlers or "innocent" children infected through blood transfusions. Class, Aaron posited, was the most important divide in the epidemic today.

Mel didn't bite. "Too literal," she told him. "This isn't a course in current events. I want to see theory, methodology, cultural *critique* — not cultural *reporting*."

So it was back to the library for Aaron. He only had a few hours before he was due to meet Kevin — who was currently shooting yet another fatal traffic accident on Queens Boulevard, the second that week. But even under time pressure, Aaron was coming up blank.

He was starting to understand how Moe felt. Not that Mel saw Aaron's ideas as frivolous, the way she had discounted Moe's insistence on the significance of pop culture. But she still didn't think Aaron was getting at the heart of queer theory. He was too stuck in gay reality.

□ □ □

Aaron's number got called first, so he left Kevin in the waiting room — with its soiled chairs and fluorescent lighting — and went to room 5, where the nurse was waiting. It didn't take more than two minutes. Good news is always quick.

When he came out, Kevin was gone, so Aaron sat and waited for him, a bit nervous but mostly excited. After a few minutes, Kevin emerged from room 3 with a big grin on his face.

"Negative?" Aaron asked as Kevin approached.

"Negative," Kevin replied, putting his arms around Aaron. "You, too?"

"Me too."

They held the embrace for several seconds as relief set in. They had viewed this test as a formality, proof of what they already assumed to be true. But the final hour or so before they actually picked up their results at the free clinic — Kevin still didn't have health insurance, and Aaron's was through the medical center at Empire, which would never assure his confidentiality — made them both a little nervous. Maybe they hadn't been as certain as they'd thought. Anything Kevin might have registered in his last month or two of hustling wouldn't have showed up on his last test.

But none of that mattered now. Negative results all around. Nothing could be more positive.

Aaron took Kevin's hand and strolled out of the clinic past eight or ten people who sat chewing their cuticles and reading bilingual medical pamphlets, awaiting news of their fate, their expressions still an anxious stare.

It was barely five thirty in the afternoon, but it was already getting dark. Winter was here — and with it, this early Christmas present. They had both cleared the evening of any obligations. So Aaron and Kevin walked, hand in hand, over to the subway and headed uptown toward Washington Heights, where they spent the evening boxing up Kevin's apartment. Joyfully.

□ □ □

It is impossible to find a babka in Greenwich Village.

Moe hadn't realized this before; then again, he didn't often go babka hunting. As people might have guessed simply by looking at him, he knew all the best bakeries in his neighborhood — which ones specialized in cannoli, or black-and-white cookies, or blueberry tarts, or eclairs. But this time he needed a different kind of pastry, one for a shiva house: big enough to share, pretty enough to set out for company but not too extravagant, something that might bring the mourners a hint of sweetness without making them gasp in gastronomic ecstasy. And Jewish, definitely something Jewish. A babka.

But such a thing was impossible to find in the bakeries near his apartment. Moe decided that he'd better try his luck on the Upper West Side, closer to the Guttmachers' building. If he couldn't find a babka on the Upper West Side, there wasn't one to be had in Manhattan.

Fortunately, it didn't take long. Just off Columbus Avenue in the low eighties, he found a small storefront bakery that had just the thing, with cinnamon and slivered almonds to spruce it up but still looking somewhat humble. He had them box it and tie it with white string, and he was off to the Guttmachers' apartment on West Eighty-second Street.

He had only been there once before, the previous Passover, and it couldn't have looked more different. The dining room table, stripped of its festive tablecloth, was covered with cakes and cookies on trays. The lights were dimmed and the mirrors were covered with bed sheets — a Jewish tradition for mourners. The crowd gathered in the living room, where three squat shiva chairs sat next to the overstuffed sofa and the wingback chairs. Carolyn sat on one side, her brother on the other, and their mother, the widow, in the middle. Carolyn's sister-in-law, playing hostess, took Moe's coat and showed him in.

He recognized a few people: Carolyn's cousin from Barnard, whom he'd met at the Passover Seder. The rabbi, whom he'd met at the funeral that morning. Alan, the business manager of the publishing company. (Jane, his reporter, had been at the cemetery that morning — still a bit shaken from witnessing the whole scene on Monday night — but when she asked Moe if she should make a shiva call, he told her it wasn't necessary.

She wouldn't have known what to do with her Presbyterian self anyway.)

By seven o'clock, according to Moe's reckoning, there were twenty-six people in the apartment — far more than the ten people needed to make a minyan and conduct the nightly mourning service. Abe Guttmacher was well-liked. A crowded shiva house is proof of that, Moe knew.

Moe took a seat on the sofa across from Carolyn, sitting numbly in her shiva chair, a folding seat that rested low to the ground with a hard back. He sat on the edge of his cushion and leaned in so he could look in her eyes. He didn't know what to say, but Carolyn didn't seem to mind.

The rabbi led a quick service, no longer than ten minutes, with Hebrew prayers that he recited and English responsive readings that everyone read aloud.

Afterward, Moe walked Carolyn to the dining room table and cut her a piece of his babka.

"Are you going to do this for a full week?" Moe asked. He knew that seven days of shiva was traditional, but he also knew that the Guttmachers weren't strictly observant.

"Yes, we're doing it the old-fashioned way," Carolyn said. "Death makes everyone feel more pious, I guess. Even my mother."

Then she whispered in Moe's ear, "Come with me."

She didn't take him by the hand, but simply turned and walked out of the living room. Moe followed. She crossed the foyer, past the powder room and down a small hallway, opening the first door on the right. Moe followed her in, and she closed the door behind him.

Her childhood bedroom.

Carolyn hadn't lived here for fourteen years. When she went to Cornell as an undergraduate, she had spent the summers in Ithaca. And when she returned to the city after graduation, she found an apartment with two girlfriends. Now she was living on her own, a single thirtysomething in a junior one-bedroom near Gramercy Park. But while Carolyn's brother's room had become the guest room and computer room, her parents had kept Carolyn's room just as she'd left it when she was seventeen: canopy bed with white frills, white princess phone, a white teddy bear, a Renoir poster on one wall and a Duran Duran poster on another. She sat on the bed and Moe sat beside her.

"I just needed to get out of there for a minute," she said. "It's nice having people over, but it's a bit suffocating already. I don't know how I'm going to handle a week of this."

"Do you want me to leave you alone?"

"No, I'm talking about those relatives and business associates and the rabbi. I don't really want to see all of them right now."

"That's okay, we'll just stay in here. In nineteen eighty-four."

He pointed to a Culture Club poster. Carolyn giggled.

Then she got serious again.

"You know, Moe, I've got some bad news."

"Worse than what's already happened?"

"No.... Well, maybe...well, I don't know. You might think so. But you can't tell anyone I told you."

Moe nodded. "What is it?"

"They're going to close down your newspaper."

"Who is?"

"Alan, the business manager. He was Daddy's assistant, and he's in charge of the company as of yesterday. He's going to make an official announcement on Friday, but I had to tell you now."

"Why would he shut down the paper?"

"Money."

"But the paper's been getting bigger. Ads are picking up and so is circulation."

"Yes, but the paper is still a long way from being profitable. That's one of the things that he and Daddy were meeting about on Monday."

"So you knew this was going to happen?"

"I knew that Alan wanted to close the paper to help balance the budget for next year. But I also knew that Daddy was firmly opposed to that idea. He wanted to give the paper more time to get on its feet and turn a profit. He kept pushing Alan to come up with another plan to save money — cutting corners or trimming here and there. But he didn't. They kept fighting about it, arguing. Daddy was so upset on Monday —"

Carolyn started to cry on Moe's shoulder.

"Moe, I'm sorry."

He couldn't stand the idea of being consoled by Carolyn, who had just buried her father.

"Carolyn, put things in perspective," Moe said. "It's sad, yeah, but it's not such a big deal compared to really bad things that happen. So don't be sorry. I'm just glad we got the chance in the first place."

But inside, he, too, was bereaved.

□ □ □

Frank walked down to the Village in the cold. The brisk twenty-block journey didn't bother him a bit; his head was still in the clouds two days after offer from the Royalton Playhouse.

He saw Max waiting for him in the window booth of a diner that he'd never noticed before — nothing special, just a diner. It didn't matter. Frank didn't care about the food.

All he cared about was what Max thought of the Royalton's offer. Max had agreed to meet with the folks at the Royalton the previous day to talk about details on Frank's behalf. "I can't do it," Frank had told him on the phone. "I'm so excited, I'd say yes to anything they offered."

So Max went. He recognized one person from the old days, when he used to work off Broadway, but the rest were too young to know Max personally. They knew him strictly by reputation.

"It looks like a good plan," Max told Frank as they ate their cheeseburgers. "They've got an opening in June that lasts through mid-July — which is perfect for me because Rainbow Stage is dark over the summer. They want a new cast, but they want me to direct it. And they're willing to pay a fair sum for it."

Fair sum didn't mean anything to Frank, so Max explained: "Not enough to quit your day job, but more than Rainbow Stage paid."

That left quite a range, but it didn't matter to Frank.

"Like I said, I'd say yes to anything," he told Max. "I can't believe this is happening. When I wrote *Buried Alive*, I saw it as a political thing, something to shake people up and make them think. I never stopped to think that it might become a piece of real theater. I mean, off Broadway, how incredible is that? I haven't been this excited about a new project since I launched *Outrageous*, and that was years ago. This is like a whole new beginning for me."

"It's the same for me, Frank," said Max. "I took on *Buried Alive* because I thought it was the right show for Rainbow Stage, and I thought it had something important to say. But I never figured it'd bring me back to the same theaters I used to work in, the ones I thought I'd left behind."

"I guess it's a new beginning for both of us," said Frank.

□ □ □

Moe took the subway downtown after his shiva call. He was despondent. The paper was going to close. It hadn't even been six months.

He was so wrapped up in his thoughts that he almost missed his station. He bolted out the door only to get his sport coat caught in the door. When he tried to tug it loose, it ripped. A perfect night.

Moe climbed the stairs to street level. He hadn't gotten a single block when he saw Max sitting in the window of the diner.

He stopped. Moe hadn't spoken to Max since their big fight. He'd left eleven voice mail messages, but Max didn't return his calls. He sent seven emails, but Max never responded, and blocked him when he tried to chat online. He had seen him sitting in the diner on occasion, but Max had made eye contact exactly three times, and each time had quickly looked down at his food without any acknowledgment. Even in the winter air, Moe could feel the chill.

Max was sitting with someone, but Moe only saw him from behind, and couldn't make out who it was. Just as well, he thought. He's probably found a new boyfriend.

After perhaps thirty seconds, Moe's thoughts drifted back to the newspaper, and he turned toward home.

He peeled off his too-tight pants and called Gene to tell him the news. They hadn't talked all day.

"Sugar bear, I'm so sorry," Gene said, without the usual sarcasm. "What are you going to do?"

"I don't know," said Moe. "I've had about forty-five minutes to think about it. I need a bit more time."

"That makes two of us," said Gene.

"What's that supposed to mean?"

"Well, I tried to reach you today to tell you..."

"You left me a message this morning while I was at the funeral," said Moe. "I called you as soon as I got back to the office in the afternoon, but you weren't in the office. What's going on?"

"I don't think I'm going back to that office."

"Why not?"

"I kind of quit today."

"Kind of?"

"Okay, I quit," Gene clarified. "But I have the feeling that I could un-quit tomorrow if I really want to. All I'd have to do is apologize to Eleanor and drink Mandy's Kool-Aid."

Gene told Moe about Mandy's plan to move Final Frontier to Brooklyn.

"Brooklyn?" Moe said. "That really *is* the Final Frontier."

"No, that's Staten Island," Gene noted. "Brooklyn is more like *A Bridge Too Far.*"

"So are you really going to walk away from this job, after all the years you've put in with Eleanor?"

"I think so, sugar bear. Looks like you and I are a couple of unemployed, single girls."

"I am not technically unemployed yet," Moe said. "I've got a couple more days."

"That's nice, they decided to get another issue out of you before they closed the doors."

"That's the icing on the cake."

"Icing on the cake? That gives me an idea," said Gene. "Want to go for coffee and dessert? It'll make us both feel better."

"I'll pass on dessert, thanks."

"I can't believe what I'm hearing," said Gene. "Can you please put Moe *Pearlman* back on the phone?"

"Believe me, I'd love a piece of cake. But I've got to fit into these stupid khakis every night for a week of shiva calls," said Moe. "I can't have my cake and eat it too."

"Are you going to be okay tonight?"

"I suppose," said Moe. "I just need to get my mind off things for a while. It's been a rough week."

"What are you going to do?"

"Well, there's one thing that always gets my mind off my work."

"I see."

"And at least I don't have to wear those stupid tight pants."

"You probably don't have to wear anything."

"Please, I do have to cover up. I don't want to scare them off."

With that, Moe said good-night and dialed Men Online to see who was available. Not too busy on a Wednesday night in December. But there were a handful of old buddies on the prowl.

Tim (SukMyStik) was online. But he hadn't asked for Moe's services since he witnessed the ugly scene with Max that autumn. He must have gotten spooked by the whole situation. He didn't even say hello anymore unless Moe said it first.

Brandon Dexter (GagOnThis) — the new guy at MIGHT — was online too. He'd heard about Abe over the grapevine. He sent Moe a message: "Sorry to hear about your boss. You doing OK?" Moe wrote back: "Yeah, I'm OK." No need to tell anyone about the paper closing; they'd find out soon enough. Moe was half hoping that Brandon would offer to come over, but he didn't. He probably thought it'd be inappropriate to bring up a blowjob so soon after talking about death. Moe felt the same way, so he didn't say anything else.

There were three other men ready for service. One was a regular. One was a guy who had been a regular a long time ago but had then disappeared into boyfriendland for a year; now he was back and hornier than ever. One was a married man Moe had met only once. Moe checked his notes. The first was hot, Moe remembered, but his notes also confirmed that he was a cum-and-go kind of guy. The second was very verbal and liked Moe to talk back; Moe wasn't in the mood. The married guy had a huge cock — Moe didn't need to check his notes to remember that — but was also skittish and nervous, since he was still married and terrified of bringing some disease home to his clueless wife.

None of these guys fit the bill for Moe at that moment. Sure, he'd be up for some cocksucking. Even mourning couldn't extinguish a libido like Moe's. But what he really wanted was some companionship. Someone who'd stick around for a while, without asking too many questions or requiring too much play-acting.

He turned down all of his suitors and shut off the computer.

Then he called Gene and asked if he'd come over and spend the night.

Gene didn't make any jokes.

"I'm hopping in a cab right now, sugar bear," he said. "I'll see you in fifteen minutes with a pint of ice cream."

twenty-three

It was a rotten end to a rotten week.

Alan, the business manager, called the staff of the *New York Gay News* into a meeting at ten on Friday morning. His speech was short and not particularly sweet.

He spoke in vague terms about "this week's tragedy" and "ongoing financial difficulties" and "an uncertain advertising climate."

But there was nothing vague about the bottom line: The shutdown was to take place immediately. They'd send this last issue to press in the afternoon, and that was it. Those employees who also worked at the company's other newspapers — the advertising manager, the production department, the classified ad guy — would stay. The others — the reporters, the arts editor, the editorial assistant — weren't so lucky. They'd each get two weeks severance. Alan didn't take any questions, but nobody had any questions to ask.

The staffers weren't actually surprised, because Moe had told them the previous day, despite Carolyn's admonition not to say anything. She wasn't in the office all week anyway, so she'd never know that he broke his promise.

Moe was devastated, but he tried to put on a good face for his staff. Jane didn't feel the need to hold back. It was a brutal one-two punch for her — the horror of seeing Abe die and the sudden loss of her job, a job she was only now feeling confident in. She was crying, out of anger and frustration. Moe told her he'd write her a recommendation by the end of the day. What else could he do? She picked up her backpack. "I need to take a walk," she said, although Moe wasn't sure she'd come back to finish revising her story about MIGHT's budget woes.

The other few employees — Liz, Rex, Billy — returned to their desks, took things down from their walls, and emptied their drawers. After just six months, a lot had accumulated around these desks. Most of it would end up in the trash.

Moe went through the archives to collect a copy of every issue he'd put out. There were only twenty-four. He didn't need a box to take them home; the whole stack fit in his knapsack. This only depressed him more.

He sat at his computer and wrote a brief editor's farewell note to run at the bottom of the front page:

Abe Guttmacher, the publisher of this newspaper, died of a heart attack on Monday. He was fifty-eight years old.

First and foremost, his death is a tragedy for his family — his wife and two children. It is also a devastating loss for all who knew him. I am unfortunate and fortunate enough to count myself among this group.

Abe was the moving force behind the New York Gay News. *He was an open-minded, involved publisher who helped steer his newspaper away from both prudery and titillation, simple-minded advocacy and sensationalistic exploitation, in an effort to create what this community had never seen: an outlet where all opinions were welcome, but facts — spelled out with candor but treated with a keen sense of proportion — ruled the day. It is a testament to Abe and to gay New Yorkers that this newspaper found an audience that continued to grow.*

But with Abe's passing, so too this paper will cease. Without Abe's support, in every sense of the word, the newspaper cannot continue. This marks the final issue of the New York Gay News. *And for that, Abe's death is truly a loss for us all.*

□ □ □

Moe was writing headlines and photo captions when Alan came over to his desk. "Can I speak to you, Moe?"

"Sure," Moe said flatly, without looking away from his screen.

"In private?"

Moe turned, saw that he was serious, and got up to follow Alan into his office. He took a seat.

"I wanted to speak to you alone, Moe, because I need to discuss something that doesn't concern the rest of the staff."

Moe was listening, silent but curious.

"I think you know that Abe and I had different opinions about the viability of the *New York Gay News*."

Moe nodded.

"Yes, well, I want you to know that our differing opinions were not a reflection on the quality of the newspaper, or your skills in putting it together. I never questioned whether the newspaper was a good newspaper. My only concern was that it wasn't making money."

No reaction from Moe.

Alan continued. "I spoke with Mrs. Guttmacher yesterday, and with Carolyn also. Now, they don't have any official say at this point about whether the paper goes forward, but they were quite insistent about one thing in particular, and out of deference to Abe's judgment and his legacy at this company, I conceded. Even though the paper is closing, you can continue working here if you'd like."

"I don't understand," said Moe.

"Mrs. Guttmacher told me how much you'd given up to take a chance on this newspaper, that you'd dropped out of a doctoral program."

"Yes, I did," said Moe. It wasn't worth mentioning that he'd been looking for the exit at Empire anyway.

"And Carolyn told me that you were a great editor, very knowledgeable, and we'd be fools to let you go."

Moe smiled.

"So we've created a position for you, as associate editor at *Footlights*. It's a new job, and you'd need to work out the details, but you'd be helping Carolyn. She's been overworked lately, and she'll be needing a lot of assistance to get through the next few months. She tells me that you're quite the theater fanatic, and we can all see that you know how to write and edit and stick to deadline."

That was Carolyn talking, Moe knew, since Alan didn't concern himself with such things. "I appreciate that," he said.

"So if you're interested..."

Moe was caught completely off guard, and didn't know how to react. He had been stewing about Alan for the past two days, angry that one man could sink his entire newspaper without any obvious remorse. Did he honestly want to keep working for him?

Then again, he relished the chance to get back to writing about theater, and he knew he'd enjoy collaborating with Carolyn; they'd always gotten along, and always had similar opinions, but they'd grown much closer over the previous six months. Besides, there was no other prospect on the horizon. What else was Moe going to do?

Moe stood up. "Thanks for the offer," he said. "I'll think about it."

□ □ □

Moe wasn't the only one getting offers. Sitting alone in his apartment in Little Italy, Gene was fielding a few of his own. The day before, he had put out feelers via email to a few former colleagues in Washington and some people he'd met in New York who might have leads. On Friday, he started getting nibbles.

One was from a small travel agency in the Village. It was a kind offer, but it was for an entry-level slot, and the pay was too low.

Another call came from the guy who set up the Gay Travel Expo every spring at the convention center on the west side. *This wouldn't be a bad gig,* Gene thought, and the pay was fair. But it was, at best, a temporary solution.

Then, late in the afternoon, he heard from Karen Baker, who had given Gene his first job ten years earlier, at her small travel agency in downtown Washington. Gene worked for her for three years, and they got along quite well, but she was always having financial problems. When Eleanor opened Final Frontier, she lured Gene away with a small raise and a promise of increased job satisfaction that would come from working for his community. He and Karen parted on mostly amicable terms.

Within a year, though, Karen's small business was bought by Capital Travel, which was gobbling up independent agencies around the District, creating a chain with outlets in shopping centers, office buildings, and malls.

Capital Travel now boasted thirty-one locations and Karen was a vice president. Her old branch had lost its manager the previous month, and then she got the email from Gene. It was kismet, she was sure.

"Gene, it'd be just like old times. You'd be back in the old office again," she said. "Except this time you'd be running the place."

Gene was intrigued. The pay was about the same as he'd been making with Eleanor, but the health coverage was better. (Karen didn't understand how important this was to him.) And since Capital Travel was a large chain, there was room for advancement.

"I mentioned you to the company president this morning, and he was very excited at the idea of bringing you on board," she said.

"Does he know I've been working at a gay agency?"

"Gene, that's what he's most excited about," she said. "When Capital started buying up little firms, they thought they could use one overall approach that appealed to everyone. But now they're realizing that they need to target their customers, depending on the neighborhood they're in. With your ties to the gay community, and the clients who already know and trust you, you're a natural to help Capital expand its downtown office."

Gene hadn't thought of that.

"If you're interested, you should come down this week and talk to him about the job," she said. "Are you interested?"

He looked around his apartment. Nothing bulky, nothing bolted to the ground. Nothing that couldn't be moved.

"Yes."

□ □ □

Frank wrapped up his latest issue on Friday afternoon and sent it off to his new printer. He decided to go for a walk on Eighth Avenue to check out a few stores and maybe get a haircut. With a spring in his step, he started down the sidewalk, and in the first block he ran into Katie. She was dressed all in black — from her long wool coat to her Italian leather boots.

"How've you been? How's D.C.? I called him right after the mayor won reelection, but I never heard back."

Katie looked at him, then away. "Things were really crazy right up through Election Day. Then, once that was all over, we decided we needed a break — Donovan hadn't taken a day off in almost a year. So we headed to Bermuda for a week."

"But D.C. is back at work now?"

"Yes he is, Frank, I'm sure he'll call you soon."

"Oh, no big deal," said Frank. But in truth, he took it personally.

An awkward pause hung for a second, then Katie broke it: "So how's the play going?"

"Actually, it closed last weekend. But I just found out that it's going to transfer to an off Broadway theater next summer."

"That's incredible, Frank! You should be so proud."

Frank briefly told her some of the details, about Max and the Royalton and the scheduling. She seemed truly impressed.

"Frank," she said, "did you get an invitation to our Christmas party from Donovan?"

He had not.

"Well, it must have gotten lost in the mail, then. But I guess I can just tell you now. It's next Saturday night at our house, from eight o'clock on. You can pretty much guess who's going to be there — a bunch of gallery people I know, and people from the administration who work with Donovan. The mayor. You should definitely come."

Frank had never been invited to their Christmas party before — even though he extended them an invitation to his July Fourth party on Fire Island every year.

"I'm sure the mayor would love to meet you," said Katie, "after you wrote that editorial endorsing him."

"I'll be there."

"Great, I'll tell Donovan," she said. "I'm sure he'll be thrilled."

They kissed good-bye and Frank, elated, continued walking downtown, but after a dozen paces, Katie turned around and called to him.

"Frank!" she yelled. "Bring a guest!"

And just like that, Frank deflated. He didn't have anyone to bring.

□ □ □

"What the hell are we supposed to buy — apple juice?" Gene asked. It's hard to figure out what to bring to a party when the hosts don't drink.

"Why don't we just stop by that bakery on Ninth Street and pick up some chocolate chip cookies? They both like those," said Moe.

"You mean *you* like them. Jesus, I knew I should have had a beer before we left."

"Oh, it won't be that bad. It's just a little farewell party. It won't last long, and we can go out afterward so you can liquor up."

"Promise?"

"Promise."

The walk over to Aaron's soon-to-be-former apartment on Avenue C was brisk, in the cool December air. Moe and Gene were flushed when they arrived.

"Sweetie, chocolate chip cookies! You know those are my favorite," Aaron exclaimed, kissing Moe hello.

"Better check to make sure none are missing," said Gene. "I let Moe carry the box."

"She's my sister," Aaron said to Gene. "She can take as many as she wants."

Moe and Gene hung their coats on hangers over the curtain rod in the shower and came back to Aaron, who handed them cups of cold Diet Coke. There were only a dozen or so people there, but that was more than enough to make the studio feel crowded — especially since there were several boxes piled in one corner, items from Kevin's place in Washington Heights. They hadn't yet begun packing up Aaron's place; that was the next day's chore. Hence the party on Friday night, which Aaron had arranged only the day before.

"I can't believe you're leaving," Moe said. "I'm going to miss you."

"Honey, I'm moving to Queens, not the moon," Aaron said. "There's a big difference."

"That's true. I've always dreamed of visiting the moon," said Moe.

Aaron smiled. "You will be getting your ass on that subway and coming out to Astoria, missy, and there's no two ways about it. You can't live your whole life in Greenwich Village."

"No?" asked Moe. "Why not?"

Aaron turned to Gene. "Is he always like this?"

"Only when he's in a good mood," Gene answered.

"Which reminds me, you shouldn't be in such a good mood," Aaron said. "Kevin told me about the paper. Honey, I'm so sorry. What are you going to do?"

"I'm not sure."

"That's not like you," said Aaron. "Ain't you gonna tell your sister the details?"

"Later, yes," said Moe. "But not now. I don't want to spoil your party. You've got to be the hostess with the mostest tonight. Tomorrow when you're packing, I'll call you and distract you with the details."

"All right, honey, but you better give me all the dish. I'm worried about you."

"No need to worry," said Moe. "Now go offer your guests some refreshments. They're looking parched."

Glancing around the studio, Moe recognized a couple of other faces, people from Empire. "We haven't seen you in so long," they told him. (True, six months isn't such a long time, but it was long enough for Moe to forget their names.) "How's the newspaper doing?" Moe wasn't in the mood to talk about the newspaper. Besides, everyone would know soon enough, when the last issue hit the streets on Monday. So he said, "It's going fine," and then excused himself to get another cookie.

Gene recognized one guy, a neighbor of Aaron's who'd been a customer at Final Frontier. "Bob Greco," he said. "You helped me book that gay Caribbean cruise, remember? God, I had the best time. Mostly a bunch of old queens in couples, but still enough cute young guys to make it worth my while. How're things over at the travel agency?" Gene, too, didn't feel like talking about it, particularly with a stranger he only vaguely recalled working with. "Things over there are fine," said Gene, figuring it was probably the truth.

There were several people neither of them recognized. A few artistic types who'd gone to school with Kevin, a woman who lived upstairs from Aaron, one of his massage clients. ("Ah, the elusive Perry," Moe said when Aaron pointed him out. "He does look like he's well put together. But I'd have to see him naked and oiled up to really make a judgment." Aaron replied, "Yes, honey, that's how I prefer to see him, too.")

Moe hated making small talk with strangers unless he planned to have sex with them, and there wasn't anyone at this party who floated Moe's boat. That's why he had brought Gene along, so he'd have someone to chat with while his hosts were otherwise occupied. So the two of them spent most of their time together. Today of all days, they both had plenty to talk about.

While they were deeply enmeshed in conversation, Kevin joined them.

"Hey, Kevin," Gene said. "Nice job on Moe's photo spread in *Woof*."

"Thanks," said Kevin.

"The guys in my office really liked them," said Gene. "Or, I guess I should call them the guys in my *old* office."

"Yeah, Moe told me that you quit your job. Guess the two of you will be sharing a cab to the unemployment office next week, huh?"

"Actually, no," Gene said. "I've already gotten a lead on a new job."

"That's terrific, congratulations," Kevin said. "Then it'll just be Moe sitting at home, eating bon-bons and watching Oprah."

"Bon-bons sound good, but I don't care for Oprah," Moe said. "Besides, I got an offer today, too."

Moe told Kevin about the potential job at *Footlights*.

"That's great news," Kevin said. "When do you start? Right away? I suppose you won't even have to clean out your desk."

Moe clarified: "I haven't decided if I'm going to take the job yet."

"What's the other option?" Kevin asked.

"I was thinking about hustling," Moe said, winking. "With that spread in *Woof*, I should be able to attract paying customers. What do you think? If I recall, you have some expertise in that field."

Kevin smiled. "I think it's a great idea," he said. "New York's premier bear hustler."

"Here, dear," said Gene, grabbing the box from the bakery off the counter. "Have another cookie."

Moe shot Gene a look of cool disdain, then quickly cracked a grin. Gene put the box back on the counter before Moe could actually take a cookie. But as he turned to put the box down, he spotted another guest he recognized walking in the door: Dustin.

"What the hell is he doing here?" Gene asked Kevin.

"Oh, shit, I didn't even think about it," Kevin answered. "Dustin was the real estate agent who found us our new place in Queens. He was so nice to us, I invited him to the party. I didn't stop to think..."

"Too late," said Gene. Dustin had caught his eye, and was coming over before he even greeted Aaron or unzipped his jacket.

"Gene, so nice to see you," he said in a voice dripping with sarcasm, extending his hand for a handshake. "And look, you've brought a date. Moe Pearlman, I believe? What a *surprise*! You two always did make such a nice couple."

"Dustin, just drop it," Gene said.

Kevin butted in. "Dustin, please let's not have a scene," he said. "There's plenty of room in this apartment for you to stay out of each other's way."

"I don't know about that, Kevin," said Dustin, gesturing toward Moe. "This one takes up a lot of space."

Without opening his mouth, Moe poured his cup of Diet Coke over Dustin's head, which drenched his coiffed hair before dripping down his face onto his suede jacket.

"I can't believe you did that!" Dustin barked, running his hand through his wet hair.

"That's funny," Moe replied. "I can't believe I waited this long."

□ □ □

The party ended soon after that. Dustin left immediately, and Moe and Gene followed a moment later, with apologies to Kevin and Aaron — who were understanding, if not particularly amused at the stunt.

"Call me tomorrow," Aaron said. "I still want to hear about this job thing."

"Will do," said Moe, kissing him goodnight.

Moe and Gene ducked into an East Village bar for a beer. There was nobody there to stick up for Dustin, so they had a good laugh at his expense, telling nasty stories about him — something they had never done before.

Then they got serious. Gene hadn't signed any contracts yet, but he was going to head down to Washington the following week to talk to the president of Capital Travel; barring any unforeseen problems, he would move before the holidays.

"I don't want you to leave New York," said Moe.

"I know, sugar bear. That's the only thing I'm sad about. But we've done the long-distance thing before."

"Yeah, I'm still paying off my phone bills."

They left after one drink, before they got too sentimental. Moe kissed Gene goodbye and put him in a cab home. Then he started walking across town to the West Village.

And there he was, in the window booth at the diner: Max, hot as ever, still wearing a tank top in December. He didn't look up.

Moe stood outside for a moment, then steeled himself and went inside. He walked over to Max's table. "Mind if I join you?"

"Go right ahead," said Max, munching casually on his burger and fries as if everything was perfectly comfortable between them.

"I haven't heard from you in a long time," said Moe. "You never answered any of my messages or emails."

"I've been busy," said Max, eyes on his food.

"I figured as much. I just wanted to see how you were doing."

Max looked at Moe and saw that he was sincere. He softened.

"Actually, now that you mention it, I've been doing great," Max said.

Moe figured he'd met a new lover, some hot muscle guy. Probably the man he'd seen Max eating with earlier that week.

"New boyfriend?" he asked.

"No, nothing like that," said Max. "I've got a show opening at the Royalton next summer. My first off Broadway show in more than a decade."

"Max, that's wonderful!" said Moe, relieved that it wasn't a new boyfriend. "What's the show?"

"*Buried Alive.*"

Moe's smile curled downward. "Oh."

Max didn't want to get into this again, so he changed the subject: "And how have you been?"

"Well, I'm a porn star now," he said, figuring that was the most unexpected thing he could throw on the table.

"Huh?"

Moe told him about *Woof*, which Max hadn't seen.

"That's, um, great news, I guess," said Max. "You must be feeling better about yourself, then."

"I'm feeling kind of shitty, actually," said Moe, and he went on to explain about Abe's death, the paper's closure, Aaron moving away, Gene leaving town. It was a lot to handle at once. Alone. "It's amazing how quickly things can change," he said. "Six months ago, I had a great new job, a great new boyfriend, and great friends I saw all the time. Now all of that is gone."

"Moe, I'm sorry," said Max.

Moe had been hearing that a lot lately.

"I'm sorry, too," said Moe.

"About what?"

"About us."

"Why are you sorry about us?"

"I fucked it up. I didn't know what to do with you," said Moe. "I wasn't sure how to get past our arguments, or how to bridge our differences, or what it was that was keeping us together."

"Keeping us together?"

"Yeah, I never really understood what you saw in me, why someone like you would bother with someone like me."

"Moe, you're a smart, sexy, funny guy," said Max. "That's why I would bother with someone like you. I told you that many times, but you never wanted to hear it."

That was true enough.

"Why did *you* want to bother with *me*?" Max asked, turning the tables. "You've already got a sort of a husband in Gene — and don't tell me again that you don't have sex, because that's not what I'm talking about and you know it. You've already got a best friend in Aaron. You've already got fuckbuddies with half of New York City. Why did you want me?"

"Well, it's pretty much the same as what you said. You're a smart, sexy, funny guy."

"That's not you talking, Moe," said Max. "What was it really?"

Moe looked down at Max's plate and stole his last french fry. Then his gaze panned over Max's chest, up the tank top hugging his torso, to the cross still dangling on a gold chain, adrift in his chest hair. Finally, Moe's eyes rose to Max's face, and he looked directly at him.

"I've spent my whole life looking at beautiful men," Moe said. "And you were the most beautiful man who ever looked back."

twenty-four

There weren't any curtains covering the windows yet, so Aaron and Kevin rose with the sun. It was their first morning in Astoria.

Motionless, they lay together for a few minutes soaking in the warmth in their new apartment, in their new bedroom (imagine, Aaron thought, a whole separate room just for the bed!), on their new queen-size mattress. A real live bed, one that never folded into a couch or served any other purpose. Aaron's futon, permanently in its upright position, now graced their living room. (They had left Kevin's old single mattress propped against a Dumpster in Washington Heights.)

Kevin still had a couple of hours before he needed to head over to the *Queens Reader* — now only a twenty-minute commute — and Aaron didn't have his first class until noon on Mondays. So they pulled themselves out of bed, put on their sweats, and picked up where they had left off the night before, unpacking the boxes they'd moved on Sunday afternoon.

Aaron worked on the kitchen while Kevin took the living room. While most of the things they'd decided to keep were Aaron's — he had been on his own far longer, and generally had nicer things — there was some commingling in the new apartment: Aaron's plates but Kevin's glasses, Aaron's silverware but Kevin's tea kettle, Aaron's pots and pans except for Kevin's cookie sheet. As Aaron mixed and matched their belongings in the white metal cabinets, he noted how different this was from when he'd moved in with Joshua many years earlier. That time, Aaron left his few possessions behind, and learned to live as part of Joshua's existing house, like a fussy plant or comfortable chair. This time, he and Kevin were building a home together.

The toaster was missing, though, and Aaron was sure he'd packed it. He figured he must have mislabeled the box; it was probably in the bathroom or the bedroom or somewhere else in the apartment. He turned and left the kitchen, entering the living room, and that's where he saw Kevin hanging photographs. The poster from the Joshua Browne Dance Company hung over the fireplace, but the smaller pictures were spread across the wall next to the futon. On one side were the pictures that Aaron had on his wall in the East Village: protests, old friends, memorable performances. On the other side were pictures of Kevin: family snapshots, his high school graduation picture, and one fairly racy shot a photographer from *The A-List* had taken at Slick that showed a sweaty Kevin dancing on a box, wearing just a black jock strap. In the middle there were photographs of the Aaron and Kevin together: in drag on Fire Island, sharing a piece of cake at Kevin's twenty-first birthday party that August, and the photo that Dustin had taken of them standing outside their new home in Queens.

"Like it?" Kevin asked, as Aaron stood admiring the arrangement.

Too choked up to speak, Aaron turned and kissed Kevin on the lips.

"Let's go back to bed," he said, leading Kevin into the bedroom.

They had been so tired from the move the night before that they'd gone straight to sleep. So this morning romp marked the first time Aaron and Kevin had sex in their new apartment, in their new bedroom, in their new bed.

Everything was new here. It was the first time Aaron sucked Kevin's cock in a room without curtains. It was the first time Kevin bit Aaron's neck in an outer borough. It was the first time Aaron called out Kevin's name in a building that had a yard, and a gate, and an old Greek landlady.

348

And it was the first time each one — Kevin first, then Aaron — fucked the other without condoms. They hadn't even bothered to put them in a box. They'd left them behind in Manhattan.

□ □ □

Gene stopped by Final Frontier before it opened on Monday morning. He figured he'd be alone — Eleanor was in Washington, and Ben and Jay wouldn't be at the office yet. Gene wasn't looking for drama. He just wanted to clean out his desk.

As he tossed his knapsack on the floor and booted up his computer, he noticed that someone had already taken over his space. Mandy's mug sat next to his monitor, a framed photo of Mandy's cat Martina on the other side. Didn't take her long, Gene thought, the chair barely had time to cool. Not that he was surprised. Besides, this only made it easier for him to leave.

He opened his email and deleted all of his messages. Then he went through his drawers looking for anything of value. Mostly it was junk, paperwork and such that ended up in the garbage. He put his Rolodex, the spare tie he kept in his drawer, and his copy of *Woof* magazine in his backpack. In one drawer, under a box of staples, he found the picture Ben had taken on Pride Day, of Gene in front of the Final Frontier booth, standing next to Dustin. Gene used to keep this on his desk but had removed it in the fall.

He took one last look into Dustin's eyes, and ripped the photo in half. He chucked Dustin into the trash, and flipped over his half and wrote on the back: "Sorry to leave you, boys. Papa still loves you. Thanks for everything." He left the torn photo on the front desk for Ben and Jay to find. Then he walked out the door and locked it behind him.

□ □ □

Frank walked down to his corner newsstand to pick up the *Times* and a cup of coffee. As he waited on line by the cashier, two men in front of him were checking out a porno magazine. Jesus, it's nine in the morning, Frank thought — don't you ever think about anything else?

One man was talking in semi-hushed tones to the other: "This is that guy I told you about, the one I met online. Best fucking blowjob I've ever gotten. No shit."

"That guy?" said the other, pointing to the open magazine. "He doesn't look that hot to me. A bit fat. Hasn't he ever heard of a gym?"

"I know, dude, but I'm serious. He might need to lose some weight, but this guy has got the sweetest mouth in New York. He lives in the Village. I'll give you his email address if you want. I guarantee, you won't be thinking about his fat ass once you get inside that mouth."

Frank was growing impatient — with the slow checkout girl and these two horny queens in front of him. But as he glowered at the guys behind their back, he caught a glimpse of the person they were talking about: Moe Pearlman, naked, baring his butt in some porno mag.

"What magazine is that?" Frank asked one of the men, tapping him on the shoulder.

The man, realizing he'd been overheard, was a bit embarrassed, but he managed to mumble the title and point to the magazine rack in the rear of the newsstand. Frank added *Woof* to his morning purchase and paid the clerk.

This is it, Frank thought as he walked home. *That kid has finally gone too far, and I'm going to bring it all crashing down.*

Frank began composing a letter in his head, a letter to Moe explaining that he'd just ruined his career and sullied the name of his newspaper. He'd take him on, one-on-one.

But no, he thought, *maybe Marvin Pearlman would like to know what his son's been up to in the big city.* Frank still had his email address. He could see just how much Moe Pearlman could count on his daddy to defend him.

Or better still, he decided, stick with simplicity: send the magazine directly to the publisher of the *New York Gay News*, and show him what his dear little editor does in his free time.

Yes, that was definitely the best plan. He wouldn't even have to put a return address on the envelope — he'd be completely untainted by the scandal as Moe lost his job and was publicly disgraced.

He stopped in his lobby to pick up the new issue of the *New York Gay News*, to find the proper mailing address. As he opened the paper in the elevator, he saw Moe's editor's note announcing Abe Guttmacher's death and the publication's demise.

The *New York Gay News* was no more. It was right there in black and white.

He had often dreamed of his competitor's demise. In his fantasy, of course, the *New York Gay News* had withered on the vine, rejected by readers and advertisers alike, in favor of the wiser, more daring, longer-standing *Outrageous*. In reality, the *New York Gay News* had been beating *Outrageous* in terms of revenue, advertisers and circulation, and *Outrageous* probably couldn't have withstood another six months of declining fortunes. But fate intervenes, Frank thought, and Abe Guttmacher's death came as a blessing in disguise — a chance occurrence, to be sure, but even though he was an agnostic, Frank wasn't about to balk at divine intervention.

Advertisers were sure to come crawling back to *Outrageous*. And readers who wanted gay news would only have one place to turn. *Outrageous* would be the exclusive voice of gay New York once more.

Coming so soon after he heard about *Buried Alive*, this bit of news was almost too much for Frank to handle. So much to celebrate! As soon as Frank opened the door to his apartment, he flung the *Times* and the *Gay News* and *Woof* on the sofa, went to the refrigerator to get the bottle of champagne Angie and Lou Zacarias had given him, and popped the cork.

He couldn't remember the last time he'd had a drink in the morning. Then again, he couldn't remember the last time he'd had such a good reason. He had won — even without playing his newfound trump card.

There's one problem with champagne, though. It's not meant to be drunk alone. Champagne is meant to be shared by people in love — or at least somewhere close to it. It's romantic, intimate, sensual.

The closest thing to romance Frank could remember was the boy he'd fucked last summer. What was his name? Jonathan? Jackson? Jason? It was Jason, the sexy little Asian boy he'd found in *The A-List*. Just thinking about that night gave Frank a hard-on.

Frank didn't usually pick up *The A-List*, since he didn't spend much time going to bars and clubs. The most recent copy he had was a couple of months out of date, but he thought that might suffice. He flipped to the back, to the escort ads, hoping to find Jason's number.

Nothing.

Dejected, he went back to his kitchen table to reread the farewell note in the *New York Gay News*, as he sipped champagne from a juice glass alone. His erection waned.

Then the phone rang.

"Mister DeSoto? It's Jeremy Wilson. From the Rainbow Stage?"

The actor from *Buried Alive*. "Yes, I remember, Jeremy, and please call me Frank."

"Frank, right, Frank, I'm sorry. Well, Frank, I, um, ran into Max Milano over the weekend and he told me that *Buried Alive* is going to transfer to the Royalton."

"That's correct."

"And I was wondering if you'd given any thought to casting," said Jeremy. "Because I had a really great time playing that part this fall, and I'd love to play it again off Broadway."

Frank was unsure if Jeremy was eager for the part because he so admired the play, or because he wanted to perform at the Royalton — a place that would look impressive in his bio. It didn't matter. Jeremy was eager. As Frank recalled how sexy Jeremy had looked during dress rehearsal, letting loose on stage, talking him up at the cast party, his erection returned.

"We haven't started thinking about casting yet, Jeremy."

"Oh." (Disappointment.)

"But I'd be happy to discuss it with you, in person."

"Great!" (Relief.) "When would you like to get together?"

Frank looked over at the open bottle of champagne, and down at the bulge in his pants.

"I'm free right now," said Frank. "Come meet me in my apartment and we'll talk about the part."

"I'll take a cab and be there in twenty minutes," said Jeremy.

This must be my lucky day, thought Frank. *Let the celebration begin.*

□ □ □

What's there to do on a Monday morning? It had been so long since Moe had free time on a weekday, he'd forgotten. Television talk shows seemed more inane than ever, and morning radio was simply unlistenable.

So after sleeping until nine fifty, he did what he usually did when he was bored: He logged on to Men Online. There weren't many people online, it being a workday, so Moe took the opportunity to update his "Buddies" list, removing the guys he hadn't seen in a while and the ones he didn't care to see anymore. He boiled the list down to a core group of seventy-seven regulars.

Someone whose screen name looked only vaguely familiar sent him a note:

TastyTubeSteak: Long time no see.

HotLipsNYC: Guess so.
TastyTubeSteak: You looking?

Moe scrambled to find a photo of this guy in his computer. When he opened it, the face didn't ring a bell — sort of nondescript, clean-shaven, glasses — and the picture was blurry. He needed to check his notes.

"Nice enough, but can't get it up," his notes said. That was all he needed to know.

HotLipsNYC: No, not today.
TastyTubeSteak: OK, maybe another time.
HotLipsNYC: Maybe.

I've got to get out of this apartment, Moe said to himself, *or I'm going to sit here all day.* Strange thing was, he wasn't even horny. Just depressed and a little restless.

He pulled on a pair of torn sweatpants and a dirty flannel shirt, and completed the ensemble with a baseball cap and old sneakers — the kind of outfit people wear to the laundromat. Moe wasn't feeling up to anything more elaborate.

With his winter jacket open (he couldn't zip it anymore), he walked to the diner. There was a stack of the *New York Gay News* inside the door; he grabbed a copy and sat down alone. He ordered one of those ridiculously large diner breakfasts — a stack of pancakes *and* eggs *and* bacon *and* sausage *and* home fries *and* toast, with a thimbleful of orange juice — and stared at the newspaper. His last issue.

And it was good. The story about MIGHT's budget woes in the wake of the campaign to close the circuit party was a great front-pager. The arts section was lively and well written, the calendar listings expertly laid out. This was a worthwhile paper, especially for something produced by such a small staff on a limited budget.

Did anyone else care that something this good would be lost? Some thirty thousand people allegedly read this newspaper every week. Would they be upset? Would they start reading *Outrageous*, or would they simply buy one less publication every week, leaving them more time to mull the cartoons in *The New Yorker* or the blind items in Michael Musto's *Village Voice* column? He'd never know.

Moe was blue because he was unemployed, but even more, he was sad as a gay New Yorker to lose the *New York Gay News*. He had tried to create something useful for his community, and he was sure he had succeeded more often than not. In the end, none of that mattered. It was one man's decision to start it, and another man's decision to end it. And Moe wasn't either of those men.

The pancakes were undercooked, mushy in the center, so Moe was sticking to the crispy edges, drenching them in syrup. His head was down, studying the paper, rereading each article.

Then he heard it: "Woof!"

Again with the woofing, he thought, looking up and expecting to see Gabe. But instead he saw a sexy little man two booths away, also eating alone, staring at him. He appeared to be around forty, with a shaved head and long black goatee, thick eyebrows arched over deep green eyes. His grin was pure mischief.

"Woof!" he said again, right at Moe, who never felt less woof-worthy. "Can I come join you?"

Moe looked back down. Nothing but bad news in his booth — mushy pancakes and the newspaper. "I'll come to you," he said.

Moe moved to the other man's booth, sitting opposite him and extending his hand. "I'm Moe," he said.

"Yeah, I know," said the other man.

"You do? I'm sorry, have we met?"

"No, I recognized you."

"From where?" Moe scanned his mental file, category by category: Empire, the newspaper, Men Online. Nothing.

"I saw you in *Woof*." And there was that grin again.

☐ ☐ ☐

355

"So who's this guy exactly?" Gene asked, tossing his duffel bag on Moe's floor. "Your message just said you 'met someone' this morning. I don't know what that means coming from you."

Moe was putting lunch on the table. Thai food, delivered.

"Well, I met him over breakfast at the diner," said Moe, taking the lid off his pad thai. "His name is Cubby."

"Cubby?" said Gene, removing his coat. "What is this, the fucking Mickey Mouse Club?"

"It's a nickname."

"What's his real name?"

"Julian."

"Hmm, I understand. Cubby is better."

"Anyway, he's a sexy little guy, barely comes up to my chin. And he called me over to his table and we started talking. Turns out he'd seen my picture in *Woof*."

Gene sat down at the table. "Wow, your life as a porn star is paying off already."

"Don't joke. It might be," said Moe. "We got to talking, and he asked me what I do. So I told him that I just lost my job at the newspaper, and I'm not sure what's next. And he says that he's launching a website called Man2Man next month, aimed at gay men. It's got financial backing from the guys who used to run the baths in Midtown — they've been looking for a new venture since the baths closed down. There are already a few people on board, one guy who used to work at *The A-List*, a guy who wrote a freelance piece for me at the newspaper, and a couple of other people I don't know."

"What's the site about?" Gene asked.

"Well, it's going to have a big section of personal ads and online profiles for cruising."

"You know a thing or two about that."

"Yes, and there's more. There'll be a main section with gay news from around the country, and other features like an advice column, a sexual health column, bar listings, restaurant reviews, travel stories — all sorts of stuff updated regularly."

"And what, pray tell, would you do there?"

"I don't know. Maybe work on the news. Maybe start some kind of gay 'Sex and the City' column about being single in New York. Maybe check out the escorts to see if they're telling the truth about their measurements. We haven't discussed it yet. But he wants to talk to me about a job."

"A *job* job, or a blowjob?"

"Either way," said Moe, winking. "He's coming over this afternoon."

"He's coming to your apartment for a job interview?"

"For whatever. A date, a trick, a job, all three. It doesn't matter. I'm ready for anything."

"And if you have to suck him off...?"

"I'll do what I have to do," said Moe. "Not that it's such a chore. I mean, he's pretty hot."

Gene fell silent and dug into his basil chicken.

"What're you thinking?" Moe asked.

"That you should forget all this nonsense and come to Washington with me."

"Right now? I can't. I have this guy coming over, and you're leaving in like half an hour."

"No, I don't mean right now. I'm just going down for an interview today, I'll be back tomorrow. I mean, you should *move* to Washington with me, assuming I get this position."

Now Moe was silent.

"Move with you?"

"I'm serious," said Gene.

"Why?"

"Look, sugar bear, I've gotten used to having you around every day, talking to you on the phone every hour, seeing you every night, going away together, eating together, seeing shows together. I don't want to go back to the way it was before I came to New York, where we saw each other every couple of months and had to worry about our phone bills."

Moe resisted his urge to crack a joke. After all, he felt the same way.

"Besides," Gene continued, "you really don't have anything left to keep you in New York. You don't have classes or a job. Your fling with Max is over, your best friend has moved to Queens, the Alliance is defunct, the sex clubs are closed, and now I'm leaving, too. New York is always easy come, easy go. And right now, all the good stuff you've been clinging to for a year has come and gone. There's nothing keeping you here anymore."

Moe didn't agree.

"What's keeping me here is opportunity," Moe said. "This is the place where all those things were possible. And it's true, they've all fallen apart, but there are new opportunities following right behind them. Just look at what happened this morning. I went out for pancakes and met Cubby. Whatever he's looking for — a blowjob, an employee — it doesn't make a difference. It's an opportunity."

"People get jobs and have sex in other cities too, you know."

"Yes, I know," said Moe. "But where else could I have seen Donna McKechnie in the revival of *Follies* and had sex with a city councilman on the same night? Where else could I set up an orgy with five hot guys and still find a place that'll deliver pizza when it's all over at three in the morning? Where else could I go to an all-gay Yom Kippur service and sit next to a man I saw stripping on public access cable the night before? Where else could I talk about porn over pancakes with a stranger and end up with a job interview?"

Gene stopped him, lest he continue all day. "You sound like a brochure for the New York Tourism Board."

"Look," said Moe, "I know New York isn't the only place where good things happen. But I don't think there's anywhere else where so many good things can happen at once, so unexpectedly, in such bizarre combinations. And here, these things happen all the time. You never know what a day will bring when you walk out the door. Could be a crazy homeless person throwing dog shit at you on the subway, or some gorgeous man who wants to have sex with you. Could be a bakery handing out free samples, or salmonella from a hot dog in the park. Could be all of the above. I have no idea what I'll be doing a week from today: I could be working at *Footlights*, I could be working on this new website, or I might be begging Melody Penn to take me back at Empire. It was only a joke, but there's no reason I couldn't try being a bear hustler for a while. Or maybe I'll be sitting here watching TV and playing the lottery, or maybe I'll find some sugar daddy to pay my bills so I don't have to worry. Could be anything. It's about possibilities. I've never seen another place where so many possibilities present themselves, so many new things to experience. And no, they're not all great, and they're not all enduring, and they're not all healthy. But they keep coming. And that, to me, is the thrill of New York."

Gene could see that he wasn't going to get Moe to budge. So he stopped trying.

They finished their Thai food, making small talk about Gene's interview and the last issue of the newspaper. Then Gene put his coat back on, flung his duffel bag over his shoulder, and turned to leave.

Moe kissed him on the lips and gave him a strong hug. "Good luck," he said. "I hope you get the job. Even though I don't want you to leave."

"Thanks, sugar bear," said Gene. "I'll call you tonight and tell you how the interview went."

Moe watched as Gene walked out and stepped into the elevator. Then he closed the door and started getting ready for Cubby. He turned on the shower, and while he waited for the hot water, he pulled the issues of *New York Gay News* from his backpack, so that Cubby could see his writing samples. Then, before he got in the shower, he put a porn video in his VCR and cued it up to the best scene. Just in case.

acknowledgments

None of this would have been possible without Don Weise, who understood from the beginning what this project was truly about. Edmund White and Michael Carroll have my undying gratitude for helping me find Don. And thanks to Ron Suresha at Bear Bones Books and Steve Berman of Lethe Press for giving this book a second life.

I also owe a debt to Alana Newhouse, Jim Arnold, and Jim Baxter for their feedback; Jameson Currier, Stanley Ely, and Sharon Carmack for their advice; Larry Flick, Michael Paoletta, and Bert Hansen for their moral support; Mike Leeds and Brent-Alan Huffman for their inspiration; John Orcutt and Patrick Boucher for their hospitality, and Patrick Merla for his sharp eyes. And special thanks to Ephen Colter, who has helped open my mind in more ways than he knows.

My parents, Martin and Susan Hoffman, have stood behind me in every endeavor — even those that would make most parents blanch — and I thank them for offering more than anyone could reasonably expect from his mother and father.

And finally, I thank my husband Mark Sullivan for challenging me, encouraging me, loving me and generally putting up with me for all these years.

about the author

Wayne Hoffman is the author of the novel *Hard,* and its sequel, *An Older Man.* His novel, *Sweet Like Sugar,* won a Stonewall Book Award. His stories and essays have appeared in such collections as *Best Gay Stories 2010, Mama's Boy, Men Seeking Men,* and *Fresh Men 2.* As a journalist, his work has appeared in the *Washington Post, Village Voice, The Nation, The Forward,* and *A Bear's Life;* he is currently executive editor of *Tablet* magazine. He lives in New York City and the Catskills.

BEAR BONES BOOKS
An imprint of Lethe Press

Novels

BearCity: The Novel, novelization by Lawrence Ferber,
based on the screenplay by Doug Langway & Lawrence Ferber
Bear Like Me, a novel by Jonathan Cohen
Cub, a novel by Jeff Mann
Fog, a novel by Jeff Mann
The House of Wolves, a novel by Robert B. McDiarmid
The Limits of Pleasure, a novel by Daniel M. Jaffe
An Older Man, a novella by Wayne Hoffman
Purgatory, a novel by Jeff Mann
Salvation, a novel by Jeff Mann
Stealing Arthur, a novel by Joel Perry

Story collections

A History of Barbed Wire, by Jeff Mann
Desire & Devour, by Jeff Mann
Night Duty, and Other Stories, written and illustrated by Nicolas Mann
Spring of the Stag God, by J.C. Herneson, illustrated by Kupopo
Summer of the Stag God, by J.C. Herneson, illustrated
by Kiyoshi Nohara and Fedini
Waking Up Bear, and Other Stories, by Jay Neal

Fiction & poetry anthologies

Bear Lust: Hot & Hairy Fiction, edited by R. Jackson
Bearotica: Hot & Hairy Fiction, edited by R. Jackson
Bears in the Wild: Hot & Hairy Fiction, edited by R. Jackson
The Bears of Winter: Hot & Hairy Fiction, edited by Jerry L. Wheeler
Hibernation, and Other Poems by Bear Bards, edited by Ron J. Suresha
Tales from the Den: Wild & Weird Stories for Bears, edited by R. Jackson

Nonfiction

Bears on Bears: Interviews & Discussions, revised edition, by Ron J. Suresha
Binding the God: Ursine Essays from the Mountain South, by Jeff Mann
Edge: Travels of an Appalachian Leather Bear, by Jeff Mann

WWW.BEARBONESBOOKS.COM
WWW.LETHEPRESSBOOKS.COM